Published by
Strident Publishing Ltd
22 Strathwhillan Drive
The Orchard
Hairmyres
East Kilbride
G75 8GT

Tel: +44 (0)1355 220588
info@stridentpublishing.co.uk
www.stridentpublishing.co.uk

Published by Strident Publishing, 2015
Text ©Theresa Talbot, 2015
Cover art & design by Ida Henrich

A catalogue record for this book is available from the British Library.

ISBN 978-1-910829-02-8

Typeset in Plantin by Andrew Forteath | Printed by CPI Antony Rowe

The publisher acknowledges support from Creative Scotland towards the publication of this title.

C46004415 –

PROLOGUE

Glasgow, 1958

The body had been wrapped in a piece of torn sheet, then stuffed into the box.

Sally came in from the cold, stopping at the back door to stamp her feet and shake off the wet earth caking her boots. They were miles too big and tied around the ankle with string. Her skinny wee legs were mottled blue with the cold. She caught Irene Connolly watching her from a third floor window, her face and hands pressed hard against the glass. Sally gestured for her to 'beat it', hoping to God she'd go back to bed before there was trouble.

Sally's footsteps sent the rats scurrying for cover as she opened the door. Tiny claws scraped and clicked on the stone floor, tails slithering like big, fat worms.

There were two bundles stored overnight in the pantry. Sally carried them through and laid them on the table beside the third. Each held a similar bundle. Tightly bound. Carefully wrapped. Like tiny Egyptian mummies, so small they could easily fit into one box.

She pushed a strand of hair from her eyes, wiping the sweat from her brow at the same time. Despite the cold, beads of perspiration clustered on her forehead; her thin shirt had become damp and clung to her back from the sheer effort of digging the hardened earth out in the yard. Sally's small wiry frame concealed a surprising physical stamina. The mental stamina came from knowing no other way of life.

Some said she was simple – 'There's a waant wi that yin,' they'd say. Sally let them think what they liked.

The lid balanced precariously on top of the third bundle, which was still warm. It took all her weight to hold it down. A tiny bone cracked under the pressure, but she carried on regardless. She took a nail from between her teeth and hammered it into the wood. She did this with all six nails before being fully satisfied the lid was secure.

As she wiped the sweat and mucus from her top lip, she stopped dead in her tracks. She pushed her ear against the makeshift coffin and froze.

There was no mistaking the tiny cries from within.

CHAPTER 1

Glasgow, 2000

'Take this, all of you, and drink from it.' Father Tom Findlay held the chalice above his head. 'This my blood...'

The meagre congregation mouthed the words along with him. He looked out at his flock and could have wept. A dozen at best. Mostly old, mostly women, mostly with nowhere else to go. All huddled around the pews closest to the radiators. Still, at least he had a job.

He took just one sip. Meticulously he wiped the rim of the chalice clean with a linen cloth and handed it back to the old priest by his side, before walking down the stairs of the altar.

He wanted to believe he carried the sacred body of Jesus Christ in his hands. He wanted to but couldn't.

A handful of people shuffled sideways out of the pews to get their daily bread. He was desperate to give them more, but he really had nothing left to give.

The first supplicant was too frail to shuffle the few feet to the altar; he went to her first. Walking over to her pew, he smiled, pretending not to notice the faint smell of piss masked by the thick musky perfume.

'Body of Christ.' He tried not to gag as he placed the communion wafer in her slack mouth, and looked away when her ulcerated tongue licked the crumbs from her parched lips.

'Amen,' she replied, then wound her shaky arthritic fingers round his, and bent to kiss his hand. 'Thank you, Father. Thank you, Father.'

Tom felt like a complete fraud as he prised his hand away and left her rocking back and forth, her milky eyes spilling with gratitude that the priest had gone to all that trouble.

As he turned to go back to the altar there was a collective

sharp intake of breath from the congregation. He turned as his elderly colleague, Father Kennedy, stumbled towards him and fell to the floor. The weak autumn sunshine streaming through the stained glass windows gave his ashen face an undeserved healthy pink glow. His catatonic stare was fixed on the crucifix. Tom rushed to his side and felt for a pulse. But there was none.

Father Kennedy's frail body lay prostrate on the altar: the ultimate offering, gold chalice by his side. The puddle of wine became a blood-red snake that trickled its way along the marble floor, reaching out for him, pausing briefly to lick its lips before creeping into his white cassock.

★

Oonagh O'Neil popped a couple of aspirins in her mouth and with masochistic delight pushed the Dyson along the Persian rug – the only carpet of her West End home. It was becoming a daily ritual; she had a cat and asthma. But once or twice a week she'd get someone else to come and push it for her.

Oonagh had good days and bad days. Today was a bad day. Time was meant to be the great healer. But not for her. All it did was close over the gaping wound, sealing it at the edges but somehow trapping the grief inside.

She missed her dad.

Looking out of the window she presented her own forecast: 'Dull and damp with a warm front coming in from the west, but feeling cool in the northerly wind.' One of her first jobs had been as a weather girl for a low-budget satellite television station. The gig had been easy enough, the hardest part had been finding ways to make 'wet and windy' sound interesting. *Squally showers* had been a particular favourite. She had come a long way since then. Maybe too far, she mused.

The shrill of the phone made her jump. The answering machine kicked in after three rings and Gerry's voice screeched through the house. 'Oonagh, are you in? If you're there, pick up. Jeez-oh.'

She raced into the hall and grabbed the receiver. 'Hiya. What's wrong?'

'*What's wrong? Where the hell are you? No, don't tell me, in your house – on the phone.*' Gerry was well used to Oonagh's sarcasm. '*You're meant to be here to record the trail for tonight's programme. We've only got the studio until…*'

'Oh shit. Sorry, Gerry…completely forgot. Look, get me a cab and I'll be there in ten minutes.'

'*That fat bastard Ross is kicking up a stink. You know what he's like. Trouble-making little…*'

'Darling – we're wasting time. Order the taxi now, I'll throw a bit of slap on my face and by the time it gets here I'll be ready to shoot the crow.'

Without waiting for a reply she hung up and took the stairs two at a time to the spare bedroom that served as a massive walk-in-wardrobe. A row of navy jackets – identical to the untrained eye – hung on one rail. She chose the Chanel, perfect over the plain white silk shirt and cream trousers she was wearing.

It didn't take her long to put on her 'telly face.' She had it down to a fine art. By the time the taxi was blaring its horn she was blotting her lipstick with a tissue.

Oonagh perched on the back seat, and jotted down her script. As soon as it was finished she called Gerry from her mobile and dictated it to him; that way he could get it on auto-cue before she arrived. Twenty seconds was all that was needed, but she wanted to be ready to record as soon as she was inside the studio. Tonight's programme – an exposé of a Glasgow sun-bed salon fronting a money laundering racket – would be the first in brand-new six-part series *The Other Side*. It was Oonagh's baby; a hard-hitting look at Scotland's seedier underbelly. The first five programmes were already in the can. The last one just needed a few finishing touches. And she could do without any more bother from The Fat Bastard. He'd been hell-bent on trying to scupper her plans from the word go.

When she'd first presented the idea to Ross Mitchell, Oonagh had made it clear she intended to present, write *and* help produce the entire series. She'd been their main anchor-woman for over three years, presenting the weekday news each evening, but she was sick of the talking-head routine and missed researching and developing her own ideas. Ross had dismissed the whole thing. Told her it wouldn't work. Nothing wrong with the idea per se, he'd said, it was just that the public wouldn't take to her being aggressive, hard-hitting. If she wanted to branch out...why not try 'day time'?

Oonagh had known he was talking a pile of crap, and had gone above his head, taking her idea to Alan Gardner, head of news and factual programmes. Within a month she'd had a full production team, and the budget for a pilot run of six programmes. That had been eight months ago, and Ross still had the hump. Petty bastard. Petty *Fat* Bastard.

As the taxi neared the door of the studios, Gerry was out in the street, smoking a roll-up and pacing like an expectant father. Despite the obvious rush, he still had time for an over-the-top air kiss. He flapped his arms about his head.

'It's all right, I've covered for you.'

He was wearing a black tee-shirt with a picture of Charles Manson on the front and *He's not the Messiah – he's a very naughty boy* printed underneath. Despite being in his mid-fifties, his hair was carefully teased into short orange and blond tufts.

'I don't know what I'd do without you, Gerry.'

And she meant it. A good PA was vital in the business. One you could trust, not just some ambitious wannabe who saw it as the first rung on the television ladder, a stepping stone to 'better things'. It was the battle of the fittest in this game. The 'fans' who slavishly sent her mail, begged for a signed photograph, then perhaps a guided tour round the studio, were the same ones who the very next week would write to the studio bosses offering to work for nothing. It would only be a matter of time before her age and experience would be used against her, and the next bright young thing would be stepping into her Jimmy Choo's.

She walked quickly down the corridor, straight through both sets of double doors into the studio, and sat on the plush blue chair in front of the camera, crossing her legs at the ankle. She blew Ross a kiss, knowing he'd be watching from the gallery, cursing her, *not* for being late but because she was on time, leaving him little to moan about. The floor manager gave her a five second cue, Oonagh smoothed down her already immaculate chin-length bob. The red light came on above camera B.

'*Three…two…one…*'

★

As expected, she did it in one take. Oonagh O'Neil *never* made mistakes. Not on air anyway.

Gerry gave her the thumbs up. 'Brilliant.' That was his word of the month. As usual he did the mother-hen routine, unclipping her mike, teasing her hair, wiping away imaginary specks of dust from her shoulders. 'Now, Alan Gardner wants you to pop your head in before you run off.'

Alan's door was open and he was perched on his desk looking at the running order for the evening's news on his PC. 'Hi, Oonagh.' He gestured to the chair for her to sit down. 'Be with you in a tick.' He fiddled about with the order of the stories, changed the sequence, then changed them back to their original format.

'There, that's better.'

Oonagh said nothing. Just grinned. She was used to Alan.

'Oonagh, do you know if there's any footage of Father Kennedy kicking about?'

'Yeah, there must be loads in the library, there was a whole lot taken last year when he was doing those pro-life rallies. And the debate I did with him'll still be in archives. Why, what's the old git done this time?'

'Nothing,' Alan said, without looking up. 'He's dead.'

Oonagh gripped the arms of the chair. 'Dead? Bloody hell. How? What happened?'

'Died on the altar.'

'You're joking.'

'Hardly. The diocese is just off the phone. Collapsed during eleven o'clock mass no less. A trooper right to the end. Never missed a trick, did he. We'll give him forty-five seconds in the second half. Just put a still picture up, but we'd best have a bit of footage on standby in case any of the other items get…'

Oonagh didn't wait for him to finish. 'But I was meant to meet him later. I had an interview booked. He called me last night and arranged it.'

'Looks like you've got the afternoon off then, doesn't it? What did he want to speak to you about anyway?'

Oonagh felt a tiny prick of excitement. 'I don't know. But he said it was important.'

'Ach, you know what he was like. Probably nothing.'

'Nothing? Alan, I'd been badgering Kennedy for an interview for the Magdalene programme for months. Then out of the blue *he* called *me*.'

'Well, whatever it was, he's taken it with him to the grave.'

Oonagh's eyes widened, she opened her mouth to speak, Alan held up his hand.

'Oonagh, I'm teasing. Not everything's a bloody story. He must have been at least a hundred and twenty. He was going bloody ga-ga for fuck's sake. He was always on the blower to me spouting some nonsense or other…'

Oonagh stood to leave, her mind racing. 'Right, I need to

crack on, my taxi's on wait and return, so…'

But Alan was only half listening, his attention already diverted by yet another crisis.

CHAPTER 2

Glasgow, 2000

The pair drove from Govan Police Station in silence. Alec Davies felt like shit. He was tired. Tired and fed up. His eyes stung from ten days of back-to-back late-shifts, and a tension headache was beginning somewhere around the base of his skull. Despite the toothpaste and mouthwash, the taste of stale Glenmorangie lingered in his mouth. Last night had been heavier than usual. He was getting too old for this. He licked his front teeth, forcing his tongue up under his top lip.

They headed south towards the old Crossmyloof Ice Rink – a supermarket for many years now – and left into Darnley Road.

'The good houses, eh?' said the clown sitting next to him on the passenger seat. The silence had been too good to last.

They had been thrown together three months ago and it was supposed to be a six-month attachment. He didn't know if he would last without thumping him. Bloody police graduate entrance scheme. What a load of old shite.

'See this part of The Shields,' McVeigh continued, pointing out the window, warming up for a full-blown session.

Davies missed McAndrew. He hadn't really believed him when he'd said he was retiring.

'Do you know how much the flats are going for around here?' McVeigh continued.

Old men retired. Not forty-eight-year-old guys. Christ, he wasn't far off that himself, but had joined the force later than McAndrew. It would be ten years before he could access his pension, and right now that seemed like a lifetime.

McVeigh let out a low, slow whistle through the gap between his front teeth. 'Big money, that's what.' He nodded his head and widened his eyes.

It was all right for McAndrew, he could lie in bed all day if he wanted.

Davies turned the radio up. Surely McVeigh knew he was getting on his tits. He had to. No one could be that bloody stupid. Although looking at that hair and that jacket…maybe McVeigh was the exception to the rule. Davies drummed his fingers on the steering wheel; he was bored with the conversation, bored with McVeigh and bored with life in general. He couldn't be arsed. He needed his bed.

He flicked on the window wipers with his pinkie as the first drops of rain spat onto the windscreen, then gripped the wheel tight enough to turn his knuckles white. McVeigh opened his mouth to speak, but took one look at Davies' face and shut up.

As usual there were road works on the Kingston Bridge. Down to one lane northbound. The fumes from the lorry in front wormed through the car's ventilation system and caught the back of his throat, and the rain smeared the muddy city atmosphere across his windscreen.

'Where we going anyway?' McVeigh asked.

Davies double-checked the text message, a wee smile played on his lips. He hadn't exactly been a rookie cop when he'd first crossed paths with her, but nor had he been the embittered old sod he was now. She'd been different too…well had looked different anyway. The sparkle, the shine had always been there but none of the polish. Not in the early days.

He glanced at his phone again. He knew where he was supposed to meet her, but it gave him something to do with his fingers, helping him resist the strong temptation to poke them in McVeigh's eyes.

Despite the weather, once they were off the bridge it didn't take long to ease through the morning traffic into the West End. The rain was now falling in bucket loads. It created rivers along the blocked drains in the gutters, and battered off the car roof so fiercely that McVeigh raised his voice an octave in case Davies couldn't hear him. 'Oh, Maryhill.' He pointed to the road sign. 'That's my old patch!'

At least he hadn't said, 'You can see my house from here,' and for that Davies was truly grateful. He swung off the main road and into the side street just as Oonagh O'Neil was locking her car. He pulled over and grinned, watching her dodge the puddles as she ran towards the pub, out of the rain. She waved when she reached the door, letting him know she'd get the drinks in.

McVeigh's jaw hung open when he saw her. 'Bloody hell! Punching a bit above your weight there, are you no'?'

'Ach, just shut up, eh.' Davies slammed the door and walked away, leaving McVeigh to baby-sit the car.

CHAPTER 3

Glasgow, 2000

> *Father Patrick Joseph Kennedy left his home in Galway in the fifties to cross the water to Glasgow. He was a grumpy old sod, whose face was aye tripping him. Sadly his ambition outweighed his achievements and he was stuck being a crappy old Parish Priest for the whole of his sorry wee life. He was a miserable, twisted, self-promoting, sanctimonious old bastard, who rammed his beliefs down the throats of people too close to meeting their maker and thus too petrified of eternal damnation to question them. But no one could deny he was a tireless fundraiser for the Church. Each week he'd rub his hands in glee as his poverty-stricken congregation dug deep into their pensions to fill the collection plate, in order that he might live rent-free in a Victorian villa and stuff his fat face with the best of scran…*

Father Tom Findlay guessed he'd need to tweak a few of the details before the obituary would be ready to email to the Catholic press office. He'd been working on it all morning and still that was the best he could come up with. He pushed back in his chair and flicked through the top few pages of the pile of admin on the desk beside him. It was all the usual crap. The diocese was raising funds and desperately needed cash to send a terminally ill father of four to Lourdes. The budget for his drop-in centre was being slashed, and a notice from Glasgow City Council warned that unless he got a special catering licence he'd be fined by the Health and Safety Executive for serving hot food to down-and-outs. He stuffed the whole lot in a drawer and went back to the obituary. It was getting to be a bitch of a week.

Everything was a struggle these days. The obituary should have been a doddle. Father Kennedy was a news editor's dream. Despite his age he had been well on the way to becoming a media darling. A moral crusader, popping up at every pro-life rally, every anti-abortion demonstration, every let's-get-my-face-in-the-papers photo opportunity. He had never missed a trick. No point in doing good if no one knew about it. But to die on the altar, to drop dead in front of his congregation... Well, he had to hand it to the old bugger, it was the ecumenical equivalent of being killed in action.

Tom's thought of the last few months before Father Kennedy died and grabbed the collar from his neck, throwing it onto the desk. It was starting to choke him, like a noose round his neck.

'Two gentlemen to see you, Father.' Mrs Brady was at his back, and Tom slammed both hands down on the keyboard, deleting the incriminating evidence and almost rebooting his computer at the same time.

'Eh, would you be able to knock first in future please?'

Mrs Brady ignored him and shuffled out of the room, glancing over her shoulder at the computer screen, then shifting her eyes to Tom before closing the door.

'DI Davies' – the older of the two men held out his identity card – 'and this is DS McVeigh, Govan police,' he added without looking at his partner. Tom noticed Davies was wearing casuals, though the Doc Martens, buffed to a high polish, would have given him away. McVeigh had a shock of ginger hair, which frizzed at the temples. His jacket hung limply from his shoulders. Too many late nights walking home in the rain?

'Police? What's wrong, what is it?' There was nothing Tom could do to stop the nerves that had risen from his bowels, turning his stomach into a knot. He clasped his hands firmly behind his back to stop them trembling.

Shiny Shoes took charge. 'Right, Father Findlay.'

'What? Oh please, call me Thomas...Tom.' He ushered the pair to sit. Davies remained standing, and drew a look at McVeigh, who by this time was crouched on a footstool, his elbows resting on his knees. Tom supported himself on the oak desk and nodded at Davies to continue.

'Nothing to worry about, Father. Just routine. We always do a follow-up in the event of a sudden death.'

'You're here about Father Kennedy?'

'Aye. Know him a long time?'

'Right. Let me see.' Tom crossed his arms over his chest and tried to look bloke-ish. 'I've been assigned here for the past four years, so I suppose I know...knew him reasonably well. Why?'

McVeigh was picking at a loose thread on the fabric of the footstool. Davies leaned against the mantelpiece. 'Anything about his behaviour over the past few weeks that seemed, well, odd in any way?'

'No, no. I don't think so, I mean, what do you mean 'odd'?'

'Did he did he have a lot on his mind for instance? Anything troubling him?'

'I'm not really sure. No. No, he didn't. Look why are you asking questions about Father Kennedy? This doesn't sound very routine to me.'

'Know anyone who didn't like him?'

Tom stole a sideways glance at his now benign computer and rubbed the palm of his hand over his mouth. 'No, no, he was... he was really quite well liked actually.'

'No enemies that you knew about?'

'*Enemies?*' A flutter stirred in Tom's chest. 'Enemies. Jesus Christ, he was a Catholic Priest.'

'Nonetheless,' Davies continued, 'he was a bit... Well, let's face it, he made few friends on the *outside* with his extreme views.'

Tom used the back of his hand to wipe the beads of sweat

that were forming on his top lip. He felt duty-bound to defend his dead colleague and his own need to wear the collar. 'They may seem extreme to you, but they are the views of the Church.'

'You all right there, Father?' said Davies.

Tom wasn't touched by his mock concern. 'I'm just a bit y'know…surprised at all this.' He gave up on the bloke-ish stance and sank back into his chair. 'What's going on here?'

'Nothing. Honestly. Look, are you sure you're all right? You're looking a wee bit pale.'

Tom nodded his head and bit the inside of his mouth.

'Right you are then.' Davies gestured for McVeigh to stand up.

Tom was glad to see the back of them.

The obituary lost its importance after that. He tried to start again, promising himself wee treats and rewards if he finished, but the words just swam on the screen in front of him. He felt panic swell in his throat. And he felt sick.

He cooled his head on the window just in time to see Oonagh O'Neil get out of her car. He'd forgotten all about their meeting. She waved as she jogged up the steps. She looked as Irish as her name suggested. Small, slim, with chestnut hair and deep blue eyes. He was sure if he went to Dublin, the streets would be lined with thousands of Oonagh O'Neils, and all just as pretty. He ran into the hall and opened the door before she had a chance to ring the bell.

'Hi, Oonagh, good to see you, come in, come in.' He tried to sound light-hearted, and hoped she couldn't see him shaking. He was fooling no one. She walked under the arch of his arm and flashed him a smile. He breathed in her scent.

She winked at him. 'Old Spice,' she said, reading his thoughts. His face turned scarlet, and he rubbed the burning colour from his cheeks. He always looked forward to seeing her. She flirted with him outrageously, despite the fact he couldn't be interested in her, *wouldn't* be interested in her. But in her he felt he had the closest thing to a friend. His biggest sacrifice when he'd joined the priesthood hadn't been giving up sex; in fact in Tom's case that had been relatively easy. No, giving up on friendship had been the biggest single hardship, and there were times when the loneliness crushed him. But fortune had looked down upon him the day it had sent Oonagh O'Neil. And all because he'd been assigned by the press office to work as an advisor on a documentary she was making on the Magdalene Institutions.

'Tom, I'm really sorry about Father Kennedy. It must have been a huge shock to you...'

He was about to answer when she interrupted him.

'Good God, you look terrible, has it really affected you that much?'

So she had noticed too. He knew his blushing had long since subsided and that a yellow, waxy pallor had taken over.

'Christ, Oonagh...' He faltered, dropping his head into his hands. A wave of despair washed over him. Sometimes he forgot she was a journalist, and that he needed to be careful of how much he told her. Sometimes he forgot he was a priest.

'Look, we don't have to go through this lot just now,' she said, waving her hands over her research notes. 'Have you eaten?'

He shook his head. She took charge.

'Good. Get your coat, Sunshine. We're going out.'

★

The restaurant was fashionable and expensive. The waiter recognised Oonagh immediately, and nearly fell over himself to reach them.

Once they were seated, Oonagh reached across, held his hand and looked directly at him.

'Tom, if you'd rather not talk about it, that's...'

'I'm fine.' He eyed the name written in gold on the window and smiled. 'You know who St Jude is, don't you?'

'Patron Saint of Lost Causes.' Her grin beamed from ear to ear.

'Is that why you brought me here?'

He took refuge behind the ridiculously large menu and swallowed hard as he clocked the prices. He gave a weak smile and tried not to let her see how out of place he felt.

Pride, Envy and Avarice had already reared their ugly heads, now Gluttony crooked a finger and beckoned him to take the plunge. Tom knew when he was beaten and gave in gracefully. He looked at her and smiled.

'Right, lets order' she said, 'I'm ravishing.'

'You mean *ravenous*,' he replied.

'No, I don't,' she grinned, without looking up.

At least they'd escaped Wrath and Sloth. With Oonagh, Lust always appeared to be waiting in the wings.

Oonagh topped up his glass as they started to eat. Already he could feel the wine relaxing him.

'Tom.' She waited until the waiter was out of earshot, 'can I tell you something?'

'Go on.' he said, easing back in his chair, finally feeling comfortable.

'It's about Father Kennedy.'

'Yes?' Tom paused before placing his glass on the table. 'What about him?'

She gave him an awkward grin. 'Look, promise you won't laugh.'

'Go on,' he said.

'Well' – he watched her bite her bottom lip – 'it's just that I think...well, I think there's something...something not quite right about his death.'

Tom did as she asked. He didn't laugh.

CHAPTER 4

Glasgow, 2000

Oonagh walked barefoot down the aisle of a derelict church to find Father Kennedy's parched corpse waiting to give her communion. When he placed the host in her mouth, his fingers crumpled and turned to dust. He tried to open his mouth to speak. But his lips had been sewn together with rough black thread.

She woke up terrified, remembering the ghost story her father had told her, about a priest dying on the altar and coming back to finish mass. And after that she drifted in and out of a fitful sleep until it was time to get up. Then it was a struggle even to open her eyes.

At least the morning brought some degree of normality: the traffic building up outside on Hyndland Drive, and the cat driving her mental scratching at the kitchen door to get out. She slid out of bed and pulled on a shirt before heading downstairs. By this time the cat was headbutting the back door, obviously desperate for a pee. He'd belonged to her Dad. She'd thought it would be nice to have a wee cat around, but all he did was eat, sleep, shit and make her face itchy and blotchy if he got too close.

She carried her mug of coffee into the front room and fished the colour-coded inhalers from her bag. The brown once a day. The blue four times a day if she was feeling breathless. She had a green one too but just kept it shoved in the back of a drawer and kept her fingers crossed her asthma would never get that bad. She took two puffs of the brown and waited a few minutes before lighting her first cigarette of the day.

Ordinarily she'd switch on the television. Catch the early news, watch the events of the day unfold. But not today.

She took a last long draw on her cigarette, squashed the butt flat into the ashtray, then switched on the video to take another look at the previous night's airing of *The Other Side*. Although she'd seen the finished version before it had gone on air, she'd been too nervous to watch the transmission. Seeing it again now, she had to admit it was good. Bloody good. She looked forward to today's production meeting. Usually they were a waste of time – a group of navel-gazers eating trays of deli sandwiches and getting off on showing off. But today's would be different.

The doorbell rang and she pressed *Pause*. The screen froze on the sunburnt face of a startled woman coming out of a tanning salon to find a film crew peering at her.

Jack stood on the step, jangling his car keys against the side of his leg. He was pale and looked like he'd lost weight. 'Can I come in?'

She opened the door a little wider, and nodded her head. He hesitated before skimming a kiss on her cheek as he walked past. The cheeky bastard gave her bare legs the once over. A mixture of anger and emptiness flooded through her.

'What do you want, Jack?'

'Can I sit down?'

'Look, can we just get this over with. I assume you didn't come for a chair.'

'Straight-talking as usual.' He gave a reluctant, half-hearted grin. The hint of a nervous laugh at the end of his sentence. She said nothing.

'I don't want you thinking...'

'Jack, you have no idea what I think.'

They had first met when he was a guest on a debate programme she'd hosted. He'd been charming but had made little impact on her; she was used to being chatted up. And by bigger more powerful men than him. It had been months before she saw him again, at a charity ball to raise money for some good cause or other – cash for kids forced to wear last year's trainers, or something. It had been eight months since her dad had died, nine months since she'd had sex, and he'd been wearing a tuxedo. Inevitable really. A lame excuse for sleeping with another woman's husband, but the only one she'd ever been able to come up with.

Cat came through and snaked its way round her legs. She reached down to stroke it. 'Funny animals cats.' She tickled the soft fur under his belly. 'They start off fluffy and kittenish. After a few months they play less and start clawing at the door, demanding freedom. That's their hunting instinct kicking in – they always prefer the chase to the catch.'

Jack was looking out the window to his car parked on the double yellow. She could have throttled him.

'Jack, I think it's obvious what's going on here. There's no need to give this whole bloody thing a post mortem and drag it out any longer than necessary.'

'Oonagh, please.'

'Don't 'Oonagh, please' me. I haven't heard a word from you for three weeks. Three weeks! You haven't even had the decency to call me, or even email. Jesus Christ, Jack.' He kept trying to cut in, but she'd rehearsed this speech for a fortnight. 'You could have been man enough to face up to me. Don't treat me like a bit on the side.' In the dry runs she was calm and sophisticated. But now she was yelling and when she stood up she remembered she wasn't wearing any knickers. She tugged her shirt down over her thighs. 'And then you turn up at *my* home. Unannounced. I'm not allowed anywhere near *your* home, yet you think it's all right to just march through my life whenever you can be bothered.'

Jack just sat with his head in his hands, staring at the floor. Oonagh wandered through to the kitchen and pulled a pair of sweat pants from the tumble dryer, before topping up her coffee. 'Want one?'

He glanced up, taking this as some sort of truce, and nodded.

She gave him two sugars instead of one and topped his mug up with boiling water from the kettle, hoping he'd scald his tongue. She knew she'd lost the war, but there were a few battles she could win.

In the first few months she had dug her heels in, refusing to be bowled over by him. It was just a bit of fun after all. Kept him at arm's length. But inch-by-inch, he'd pulled her just that bit closer. They'd traded all the usual crap. The pasts and backgrounds. The hopes and dreams. And just when she'd dipped her toe in the water, just when she'd allowed herself to be seduced by the cosiness of it all, he'd snatched it away. What had she expected, a sodding engagement ring? She handed him the mug.

'Jack, have you ever heard the song *The Snake*?' He shook his head as he blew on the coffee. She sat down and tucked her legs underneath her. 'Well, it's an old Northern Soul song. It's about a woman who finds a half-dead snake by a riverbank. The snake begs her to help him. She's scared at first, but takes it home anyway, warms it up, feeds it and cares for it until it's well again. She even allows it to sleep on her pillow. Then one day it turns round and bites her. And as she's dying she asks him why he turned on her after all her kindness. And do you know what it says?' Jack shrugged his shoulders, sucking in the cold air trying to cool his scalded tongue. 'It turns round and says to her, *I'm a snake you stupid woman – what did you expect me to do*!'

Jack opened his mouth to speak, but nothing came out. She stood up and let rip. 'It was you who started all the crazy chat about having a future together. I knew the score, Jack. I never once asked for anything from you. But you! You were always talking about...'

He butted in, '...Having ten *scabby* weans climbing over my S Type.'

She didn't laugh at his pathetic attempt at slang in his posh

Kelvinside accent. He reached out his hand, but she didn't take it. Just glowered at it, chewing on her bottom lip.

'Fool me once, Jack, shame on you. Fool me a second time, and you're a total bastard!'

She lit another cigarette, sat down on the settee opposite him, and crossed her legs. He'd given up on the coffee and the mug sat on the table between them. 'I just don't understand,' she said. 'Is this all a game? For months you were all over me like a rash, then suddenly you're avoiding me like the plague. Are you that shallow? Once you've made your conquest it's no fun anymore?'

'It was just all getting a bit…' He hesitated while he chose the right word.

She chose it for him. '…Heavy?'

'I didn't say that, Oonagh. That was your word.'

She got up and walked over to the window, wondering where the hell all the traffic wardens were when you needed them. 'You've changed. I just feel I don't know you anymore.'

'Everything's so fucking black and white with you, Oonagh. I don't need this just now. I've got enough crap in my life. I can do without you acting the drama queen because you're not getting enough attention. Fuck's sake!' He stood up to leave.

This time she reached for him, struggling over her wounded pride. 'Jack, has something happened? Are you in some kind of trouble? Are you taking drugs or something?' She sounded like her mother.

He let out a snort. 'Apart from the odd joint you roll me, no, no drugs. I know doctors get all the best shit, but you can rest assured, Oonagh, it's nothing like that. He looked at his wrist, using his watch as a prop. 'Look, I really have to go. I'll call you.'

She watched him walk away. *Don't fucking bother* she thought and slammed the door behind him.

CHAPTER 5

Glasgow, 2000

It wasn't even mid-day and she was shattered. Her row with Jack had left her drained. Too much shit was going through her head.

She drove through the West End to the studio. As usual the traffic was thick on Byres Road, but for once she was glad. It gave her a few extra minutes to get her act together. She put on the Joni Mitchell CD, stopping at the second track, which told the story of thousands of poor unfortunates over the years. It would make a good backing track for the Magdalene programme when it was finally ready. The research was proving painstakingly slow. Oonagh had spent months at the national archives sifting through census reports, workhouse records and court documents going back centuries.

Some of the information was online but a fair proportion was still only accessible in hard copy. She rather enjoyed holding the original documents in her hands; especially the records from Lochbridge House. The few grainy photographs she had found showed a huge Victorian tower that grew out of the ground, with uniform rows of bleak windows. The red sandstone bricks had been blackened by generations of soot and misery. To Oonagh it looked independently evil, a malevolent entity casting its shadow across the city, corrupting everything it touched. But the building had been razed in the sixties. All trace of its existence obliterated. And getting accurate information on the home was an arduous task.

Oonagh had phoned the Catholic Press Team every day, and had even turned up in person once a week. But they'd refused to play ball, initially denying any involvement with Glasgow's Magdalene Institute. After months of painstaking leg-work Oonagh had feared they might have been telling the truth. She'd been surprised to discover that many of the homes outside Ireland – including the very first, in London – had not been run by nuns at all, but by other Christian denominations, often with significant state involvement…or *complicity* as she preferred to think of it. Dumping grounds across the world for women shunned by society. She knew she'd have to shoehorn that integral detail into the finished programme.

She'd been about to throw in the towel when she'd discovered the vital piece of evidence. It had been with a mixture of nerves and excitement that she'd made the final phone call to the diocese.

'Hi Denis, it's me again. Now, I know you're *not aware* that the Church had any dealings with the Magdalene Institute in Glasgow, but I've discovered the strangest thing.'

'*Really?*' The voice at the other end was dry with a hint of sarcasm.

'Listen to this…'

'*Oh, I'm all ears, Oonagh.*'

'The bill for demolishing Lochbridge House was actually paid for by the Diocese. Now, does that not seem strange to you, that the Church would pay to bulldoze a property it didn't own?'

'*I'm assuming you can back this up?*'

She said nothing.

'*Well, it was a very long time ago, Oonagh… Perhaps, well, perhaps the Church paid for the work…as an act of charity…*'

Oonagh's smile could be heard down the phone. She launched into her final assault. 'And then what do you think? Yes, you've guessed it; the Diocese actually *sold* the plot on to private developers. Now why on earth would they do that with a piece of land they didn't own? Would that be strictly legal, Denis?'

'*Aye, all right, Oonagh, you've made your point.*'

She'd been to university with Denis Flattely. Or Denis Flattery as she called him. For a time they'd worked together as reporters at Radio Riverside, just outside Glasgow, where the managing director had bullied the staff into wearing paper hats on a Friday to prove how much they enjoyed their jobs. Their paths had crossed fairly regularly over the years. With his gift for the gab, and his aversion to hard work, it had been inevitable that Denis would end up in PR. He eventually gave in and 'offered her' Father Thomas Findlay, to help her with her research…and to ensure that he could act as a technical advisor on the programme.

Oonagh knew it was more a PR exercise than any gesture of goodwill. An attempt at damage limitation. Denis was no fool. Each new day seemed to find the Church at the centre of a fresh scandal, a new ecumenical skeleton in the closet. Give him his due, Oonagh thought, he knew how to play the media at its own game.

A white van beeped its horn behind her. She stuck the car into first and crawled for three yards before being stopped again. The rooftops of the new flats built on the Lochbridge House grounds could be seen across the skyline of the Hillhead tenements. Oonagh tried not to let herself be haunted by the ghosts incarcerated in those huge living tombs. How many poor creatures had lived and died there because no one had cared enough to take them home?

Oonagh pulled into her reserved parking bay. She was last to arrive.

It took her twice as long as normal to reach the office with people stopping to congratulate her on the previous night's programme. But she liked to make an entrance. By the time she reached the meeting room her ego was well massaged, and the ghosts of Lochbridge House stuffed to the back of her mind.

Alan Gardner stood up as she entered, grinning from ear

to ear. On the desk a bottle of champagne stuck out from an ice bucket. Bottles of wine and beer rattled on the drinks trolley behind him. A dent had already been made in the tray of deli sandwiches. Ross Mitchell stayed in his seat, licking the mayonnaise from his fingers. The rest of the team gave her a mock round of applause, and Oonagh affected a theatrical bow. Alan stepped forward and gave her a hug. 'Oh it was great, Oonagh. Well done. And guess what?'

Oonagh was in no mood for guessing games, but didn't want to appear churlish. 'What? What?' She shook Alan gently by the shoulders. 'Tell, what is it?'

'Well,' he said, dragging it out, 'we don't have all the facts and figures yet, but initial results from the audience focus group are VERY positive. They love it! And…' – he stretched out the word, looking round to make sure the whole team was paying attention, nodding his head he continued – '…and the good news is…the head of factual programmes for the *network* was on the blower this morning.' He gave the word *network* imaginary inverted comas with his fingers. Oonagh wished he'd just get on with it. 'He saw the VT and he wants it. *The Other Side* is going national, Oonagh.'

The whole team let out a whoop and jumped around the room giving each other hugs and high fives. Even Ross made a half-hearted attempt at joining in, making sure he didn't miss out on the chance to bask in the reflected glory.

Oonagh waited until her glass was empty then made an excuse to slip outside, needing just a few minutes alone. She punched the air outside the bathroom – 'Yes!' – then ran in and threw up.

CHAPTER 6

Glasgow, 2000

The circus had begun.

Tom had been summoned to the archdiocesan office in the centre of the city. He took his car as far as the suspension bridge, then walked the rest of the way in the cold sunshine. His legs were heavy as he dragged his feet along Clyde Street. He was already exhausted. The morning's confession had been mental. Normally they were lucky to get two or three penitents, but Father Kennedy's sudden death had acted like a magnet for all the local loonies. The church had been crammed. Not everyone had felt the need to confess though. A few had just loitered, staring at the altar, miffed at missing the action.

The office was tucked away behind St Andrew's Cathedral, which always reminded Tom of the Louvre in Paris: an historical building with a modern glass structure trying to steal the limelight. In the cathedral's case the offending edifice was St Enoch's Shopping Centre.

It was a long time since he'd been to Paris. He wished he were back there now. Melting into the crowds. Just a guy. Not some holy man who was supposed to know the answers.

The roads were dead. It was the first day of a petrol strike, and already the country was acting like it was in the grip of a fuel crisis. The relative peace and quiet did nothing to calm him. Only gave him space to think, and right now that wasn't such a good thing. He stood on the edge of the pavement for a few moments and considered his options. He could go for a drink before facing the ringmaster. There was plenty of time. But he quickly decided against it. Not because he'd be an unusual sight in a Glasgow bar, but because today he needed a clear head.

He could just not turn up. Or he could have the decision

taken for him. He closed his eyes, waited a few moments, then ran blindly across the road. The deafening blare of a horn told him in no uncertain terms to get out of the way and he ran terrified to the other side with his eyes and mouth wide open.

His whole body was shaking, he was truly losing it. He steadied himself against the lamppost.

He was still trembling when Charlie Antonio emerged from the building and blocked his path.

'Sordid business about Father Kennedy, eh Thomas?'

'What?'

'Not every day a priest is bumped off in Glasgow.'

Tom squared up to him, careful not to raise his voice. 'But that's rubbish. Who told you that? Anyway what would you know?'

'Oh c'mon tae grips. I'm a journalist, Tommy Boy, I've got contacts. Antonio pulled on a pair of sunglasses. Tom wanted to lamp him, but was too scared.

'You're behind this, aren't you? It was *you* who got the police to come sniffing round? How bloody stupid am I?'

'Ach, stop being such a tit.'

And that's exactly how Tom felt, like a right tit. His right leg trembled uncontrollably as he struggled to keep his voice calm and steady. 'Okay, Charlie, so now what?' He tipped his chin towards the building. 'Who did you speak to up there? And what did you say?'

'Oh you know me, height of discretion and all that. Don't worry, Father, the Men In Black are keeping shtoom. I only got as far as the receptionist – torn-faced old cow. But let's face it, Thomas, it's only a matter of time. They'll need tae speak tae the press sooner or later. I mean tae say, it'll look a wee bit sus' when there's a dead priest and no bloody funeral.'

'No funeral?'

He looked straight at Tom. 'Cryin' out loud, d'you need me

tae draw a diagram, Tommy? The polis'll no let him be buried until they work out what the hell happened tae him. Do me a favour, Tommy, never leave the Church, you wouldnae last five minutes in the big bad world.' He shook his head and let out a snort as he turned his back and walked away. Gallus as fuck.

'Help the homeless, Father?' The *Big Issue* seller appeared from nowhere.

Tom had no change. He muttered something pathetic and patted his pockets as proof, before walking towards the entrance.

'Thanks a lot, Father...THANKS A FUCKING LOT!'

Tom made his way to the office on the third floor. A grey nun wearing a grey habit and a grey knee length skirt sat behind a desk in the corridor, staring at a computer screen.

'I'm here to see Father Watson. I have an appointment. I'm Father...'

'Yes of course,' she interrupted, pressing her index finger on the intercom, announcing his name. 'They'll be with you shortly.'

'*They?*'

A thin smile spread momentarily across her lips as she went back to her computer.

Tom watched the clock on the wall behind her head. It was a full five minutes before the light on the intercom flashed, and she ushered him into the room. The office was modern and impressive, with a clear view over the Clyde and the south of the city beyond. On the wall hung an antique crucifix, inlaid with mother-of-pearl. A collection of rare, leather-bound religious manuscripts were displayed in a book case in the corner. Tom thought of the *Big Issue* seller outside.

Father Watson stepped forward and offered a nicotine-stained hand. A smouldering cigarette perched precariously on the dangerously overflowing ashtray on the desk. Tom's heart sank when he saw Davies and McVeigh.

Davies was standing by the window. Tom noticed he was nibbling his pen the way ex-smokers do, and staring at the cigarette with apparent longing. McVeigh loitered by his side, his hands thrust deep into his pockets, his red hair with a life of its own.

'Nice to see you, Thomas.' Father Watson's vigorous handshake was almost strong enough to crush the fragile bones in Tom's knuckles.

'What's with...?' Tom glanced at the two policemen. Father Watson kept shaking just a second longer than necessary and looked Tom straight in the eye, squeezing his shoulder in mock concern. 'Don't look so worried, son, you've nothing to be afraid of,' he said in a way that made Tom feel he had every reason to feel afraid. 'We just need to clear this business up.'

'What business?' said Tom, wriggling from under his grip. 'What's going on?' He was speaking to Father Watson but looking at the two cops.

'Oh for God's sake calm down, Tom.' Father Watson sounded mildly irritated.

DI Davies put his chewed-up pen in his top pocket. 'Did you know Father Kennedy was allergic to penicillin?'

'Eh? Yes, of course I did, why?'

'Well the post-mortem examination revealed quantities of the drug in his body. Any idea how it got there?'

'No of course not,' yelled Tom. 'Don't you think I would have mentioned it if I did? Jesus Christ.' He didn't like Davies.

'Did you know Father Kennedy was trying to get you transferred to another parish?'

'Oh hang on a minute...'

'What did you two argue about the day before he died?'

Tom looked at Father Watson. 'Thanks!'

'Well?' asked Davies.

The room was stifling and the stench from the overflowing

ashtray was making Tom's stomach heave. He slumped into a chair. 'Tell me you don't think I actually gave him penicillin.'

Davies bit the inside of his cheek and sort of shrugged. McVeigh picked at a loose thread on his cuff, but was obviously taking in every word.

'Deliberately?' Tom said.

Father Watson filled a paper cup with water from the machine in the corner and handed it to him. 'Here.' The edge of the cup reeked of cigarettes but Tom ignored the stench and drank it anyway.

Davies licked his lips. 'You still haven't answered my question. What were you arguing about?'

'I can't remember. Something or nothing.'

Davies let out an exaggerated sigh and walked over to the window.

'Listen,' Tom said eventually, 'we just didn't see eye to eye, that's all. It happens. We worked together and lived together. Things were apt to get a bit...well a bit stressful. But for God's sake, I'd never...' Tom wiped the sweat from his forehead and felt a sting of betrayal at Father Watson's lack of support.

'Right. So you can't remember what you argued about and you've no idea why he wanted you shifted? Is that about the size of it?'

'That's about the size of it, yes.'

'You're not being a whole lot of help here, Father.'

'I'm sorry.' His apology escaped like a teenage whine. Tom's thought back to the night before Father Kennedy's death – to the screaming match between the pair of them. Either Father Kennedy had called the diocese straight away or that interfering old bat Mrs Brady had volunteered the information. But just how much did Davies know – or think he knew? Tom looked at Father Watson for a sign.

Nothing.

Father Watson put his hand across the advancing Davies and gently pushed him back. 'Come on now, Thomas, calm down, the police have a job to do, that's all.'

'But, this penicillin,' said Tom, 'where would he have got it?' He looked at Davies. 'I mean isn't this the sort of thing you can trace?'

Davies didn't seem to like being usurped as interrogator. 'Look Father, we'll talk further...'

Tom stood up and interrupted before he had a chance to finish. 'I think I'd like to speak to a lawyer.'

'Might not be a bad idea.'

Tom thought Davies was just trying to put the wind up him with his poker face and refused to let him see how bothered he was. He turned to Father Watson. 'Can I see you tomorrow? Just the two of us, I need to...talk.' He glanced back at Davies and McVeigh

'Of course, Tom, the back of ten?' Father Watson followed him out into the corridor and closed the door behind him. 'Oh and just one thing. Until this business is over I've taken you off that Magdalene project.'

'What?'

'I don't want you speaking to that lassie, that Miss...Miss...'

'O'Neil,' Tom finished for him. 'Oonagh O'Neil.'

'Yes, Miss O'Neil. I don't want you talking to any journalists. You know what they're like and we don't want this thing getting out of hand. So, tomorrow at ten. Bye, Thomas, take it easy. God Bless.'

Tom drove back towards the south-side. He was only a few minutes from the chapel house when he did a U-turn on the dual carriageway and rehearsed what he'd say to Oonagh.

CHAPTER 7

Galway, 1956

When Irene Connolly was made to pray in her bed each night for those less fortunate than herself, she often wondered who there was left to pray for. She was fourteen when she realised all was not as it should be in the world. Well, not in her world anyway.

'Don't forget to say your prayers. Night night, Darling,' and as the light went out that's when the praying began. In earnest.

He'd climb in under the cover of darkness, demanding her gratitude. What kind of daughter wouldn't want to show her daddy just how much she loved him. After all he'd done for her. Her sister, on the other hand, was a disobliging bitch he said. Damn near broke her mother's heart walking out like that. But not Irene. She'd never do anything to make her mother cry. As if he'd do anything to harm his own flesh and blood. It was only natural for a father to love his daughter. So Irene would lie there, perfectly still. Biting down hard on the sheet to stop from crying out, petrified of waking her mother. Singing songs inside her head to make it all go away. She hoped and prayed her dad wouldn't love her so much – Irene didn't understand why love had to be so sore. Eventually she stopped praying; there didn't seem to be any point when clearly no-one was listening.

But one day it seemed that her prayers had indeed been answered. In a way.

'You stupid little… How could you do this to me?' She heard the crack before she felt her head whip back from the full force of the back of his hand across her face.

He was a big man, the blow strong enough to knock her over. He towered above her, his face purple with rage. Spit flew from his mouth as he screamed at her. He shook her like a rag doll, banging her head against the wall. When she couldn't stand up any longer, he held her up by the hair.

For the first time in ages she prayed. Begged God to let him kill her. To just get it over with. But the relentless pounding continued. Her mum's screams faded into the background as each thud caused her ears to ring. But God must have been busy with more important things that night because she didn't die, she just passed out.

She woke with a taste of blood in her mouth. Her face bruised and sore, her lips thick and swollen. Her left eye completely closed over.

'Oh Irene. Pregnant. How could you?' Her mother sobbed as she dabbed her wounds with a damp cloth. Her dad sat nearby. He wrung his hands, head hung low, staring at the floor. The room was dwarfed by his huge frame. He avoided her one open eye, looked down at his feet instead.

'How could you?' her mother repeated over and over again.

How could I not? thought Irene.

'What will people say?' That seemed to spark off the madness in her dad once again. He stood up, but her mum shoved his jacket into his arms and ushered him out the front door. 'Please, Frank, leave it. Leave it just now.'

'That's me ruined,' she heard him say as he walked to the door. 'Finished,' he said as he slammed it behind him. Irene hoped her mother thought he meant his reputation in the community. She couldn't bear the idea that her mother knew the truth – that she was a silent partner in it all; a not-so-innocent bystander.

He left her pretty much alone after that. Perhaps God did work in mysterious ways.

She wasn't allowed to go to school. Wasn't allowed to go anywhere. Kept indoors, in the house. Safe from harm's way.

Her son was born before the summer was over. Kicking and

screaming his way into the world four weeks early; born upstairs in the bed he'd been conceived in. Despite her initial repulsion, her dad delivered him and did a good job. There was nothing wrong with his skills as a doctor. He'd delivered hundreds of babies in his time.

Isaac was wrapped in a towel before he was whisked away. Arrangements had already been made. Her father had connections, after all. Good connections. A young couple in New York were waiting to welcome Baby Isaac into their family. Irene managed to pull the cloth from his head as they took her son from her. Took just one peek at his tiny little face. The image of his father. 'I'll never forget you, darling boy,' she whispered. Then he was gone forever.

After that it didn't take long before it started up again. Not as often as before. And this time nothing was said. There was no need for the loving daughter routine. It was enough that she didn't scream, and kept her mouth shut afterwards. She just lay there with his enormous body heaving and grunting on top of her.

Didn't take too long. A few minutes. Then he'd pull out and leak his hot sticky mess onto her belly. Then he'd be gone. Without a word.

Then the unthinkable happened. The unspeakable. The impossible.

This time her mother sobbed and cried and begged for answers. 'Oh God, Irene, no, not again. Why're you doing this to us? What's wrong with you?'

'But Mum, I haven't been outside of this house since Isaac was born. I haven't been over that door in eighteen months. You haven't even let me go to school. And there's only one man who ever gets near my bed. One man, Mum, just one man.'

Her mother's hysteria rang through the house. 'You're a liar, do you hear me?' her mother screamed. 'You lying little bitch.'

'Oh please help me, Mum. Please.'

'This is not true, Irene. Do you hear? This is not true. You're not well, Irene. You're sick.'

'Wake up, Mum, for pity's sake,' Irene said under her breath as she ran out of the house, leaving the door wide open behind her.

★

As Irene sat down in front of the priest she struggled through her shame to find the words to describe what had happened. She couldn't think of anyone else to tell. And she figured God owed her one anyway.

★

Her dad didn't hit her when he came home that night. Well he couldn't, not in front of the priest.

Irene was sent upstairs while Father Kennedy spoke to her parents. When she was called downstairs her father was stony-faced.

'Irene we've had a chat about what's best for all of us. Now it seems you may need more care than your mum and I can give...' Father Kennedy laid his hand on Frank Connolly's arm as he spoke.

Irene looked at her mother. Weak, empty, distraught.

'What? What's going on? Mum, what's happening here?'

Her mum was wringing a hanky between her hands. 'Where have we gone wrong, Frank?'

Father Kennedy stood by the door. 'I'll leave you to it. You know where I am when you need me.'

I need you now, you bastard.

Before Father Kennedy left he turned to Irene. 'You're a very heavy cross for your mother and father to bear, Irene Connolly. No better than your sister. I'll pray for you all at mass on Sunday.' He closed the door quietly behind him. He was a considerate man.

'Thank you, Father.'

Then, and only then, did her dad's fist make contact with her face.

CHAPTER 8

Glasgow, 2000

Oonagh was rolling a joint when the doorbell rang. She wasn't expecting anyone and stuffed the fat spliff into a wooden box on the coffee table. Tom was standing on the step, looking sheepish.

'Oh. Tom. Come in, come in.'

Her Irish upbringing had left her with the overwhelming need to invite in anyone who happened to turn up at her door. Whether she wanted them in her house or not.

She glanced back down the stairs, as though the reason for his visit might be trailing behind him. It wasn't. The only thing on the step was a postcard from her PA, Gerry, telling her he was having a whale of a time on Ibiza. No surprise there.

Oonagh led Tom through to the living room, sensing something was wrong, and shooed the cat from the settee before he sat down.

'I'm glad I caught you in,' he said. 'I wasn't sure if you were working or not.'

She offered him a glass of wine as Tom mumbled some pleasantries. It wasn't yet three in the afternoon. But Oonagh, used to drinking from about lunchtime – sometimes breakfast if she'd run out of coffee – thought nothing of it. She poured two large glasses and took a large gulp of her own, then decided to take the bull by the horns.

'Is this about Father Kennedy?' she said.

'Well, yes, but…'

Her mind was working overtime and she hardly gave him a chance to answer. 'What's happened?'

'The Police, they…'

Oonagh interrupted. 'Do they think he was…?' She paused, and chose her words carefully. '…that his death may be suspicious?'

She refilled her glass, and topped up Tom's, before forcing the cork back into the bottle.

'Oh for God's sake, is this common knowledge among journalists?'

Oonagh nodded and Tom looked crestfallen that she was one step ahead. She was hardly surprised the story was spreading like wildfire. It was her who'd asked Alec Davies to check it out in the first place. Despite rumour to the contrary, the police worked very closely with all the news organisations in and around Glasgow, including her own, and passed on titbits of information to those reporters they could trust. In turn, most journalists, herself included, respected 'off the record' information, sitting on it until the top brass said otherwise. Anyway, she had her own theories to consider.

'You must admit, if it's true it's a great story. It'd make a great book.'

'Just what the world needs, another Scottish crime writer.'

'Anyway,' she said, already planning the first few chapters in her head, 'd'you still not know what he wanted to speak to me about? It's a bit strange he calls me the night before he dies?'

'No it's not. Will you just let that one go? Christ, journalists are all the same. I bumped into Charlie Antonio on Clyde Street... He's...'

'Oh that little shit.'

'Speaking from experience?' Tom asked.

'Too right.' She swigged back the wine.

'Care to elaborate?'

'Not really but...' Oonagh hesitated for just a few seconds. She knew she could trust Tom. 'D'you remember that sleazebag Mark Pattison?'

'What, that guy from the telly who was found dead in the hotel room with an orange in his mouth! Eh yes, I do remember as a matter of fact. Priests are allowed to read the papers, you know.'

'I know.' Oonagh let out a rather unenthusiastic laugh. 'Well you know there was a list of complaints against that creep as long as your arm. But he just seemed to wriggle out of every single accusation.'

'Friends in high places?' said Tom.

Oonagh raised one eyebrow. 'Absolutely. Apparently he had enough dirt on those friends to guarantee him a get out of jail free card for life.'

'So it's not just the Church who harbour weirdoes then?'

Oonagh let out a laugh. 'Tom!'

'So what's this got to do with you and Antonio?'

Oonagh swirled the wine around in her glass and chewed on the inside of her lip.

'Right, but this goes no further than these four walls,' she said.

Tom held up one hand. 'The sanctity of the confessional, Miss O'Neil.'

Well d'you remember one story mentioned a young production assistant who accused him of attempted rape.'

'Who, Charlie Antonio?'

'No! Flipping Mark Pattison. Keep up, Tom.' She tutted. 'Well the girl apparently settled out of court and got a pretty big payoff, but it was rumoured she was now a household name and the press went mental trying to identify her.'

'Did you know her?'

Oonagh let out a sigh.

'Oh my God. Was it you?'

Oonagh looked at her watch. 'That must be a world record for the length of time it's taken a penny to drop! Anyway, Charlie Antonio – or the Wee Shite as he'll be referred to from now on – found out and decided to run with the story that I was paid to put up and shut up after a serious sexual assault.'

'But you were the innocent party here.'

'Tom, not only did I get a wad of cash, but I got a really decent job out of it too.' Oonagh knew at the time the case would never have got within spitting distance of a court room. She'd have been branded a troublemaker and barred from every newsroom in the county. 'It would have looked as though I was profiteering'.

'I don't remember reading that you had anything to do with it.'

'Ah! Well that's just it. Someone tipped me the wink what the Wee Shite was planning. So I got in there first. He'd obviously stolen the legal document naming me, so I threatened to sue the 'paper for breach of confidentiality. The upshot was Charlie got the bullet from his cosy wee staff job at *the Chronicle*.'

'And?'

She felt herself blush. 'And I got an even bigger payout…and an even better help up the ladder.'

She tipped her head back and let the glass drain into her mouth.

Tom's chin hung limp in disbelief, before he broke into a half smile. 'Oonagh, you don't do anything by halves do you?'

Oonagh's own brush with Antonio seemed to give Tom a sense of reassurance. Coupled with the wine, he appeared more relaxed. He looked around the room. 'You've done well for yourself, Oonagh. Far cry from the chapel house, or my old council semi in Milton, come to that.'

Oonagh shrugged. 'I just got lucky I suppose.'

Tom sniggered at her cheek.

Books were stacked in piles on the floor, a group of framed pictures leaned against one wall. The whole thing had a just-moved-in look.

'How long have you lived here then?'

'Two years,' she said, without batting an eyelid.

Tom walked to where the books were stacked. Crouching down, he examined the spines and picked out a Charlie Chaplin biography; hard back. He leafed through the pages as Oonagh went through to the kitchen.

'Hey, guess what?' he yelled, looking up from the book. 'Charlie Chaplin's wife was called Oonagh O'Neil. Well what do you know. Quite a famous name.'

'That's nothing,' she replied. 'You should speak to my brother Eugene.'

'Your brother's called Euge…' His voice trailed off to nothing when he saw her face.

'God you're easy so wind up…I don't even have a brother. Right are you going to stop this small talk and tell me why you're here?'

He told her he was being taken off the Magdalene Project.

'Can't you get them to change their minds? I mean what's this got to do with Father Kennedy's death?'

Tom's contribution to the programme was hardly vital, and she really was at the closing stages anyway, but still, it was handy having someone on the inside, even if he was still working for the enemy. And she enjoyed his company. It was nice to have an excuse to see him.

'Oh come on, Oonagh, don't be so bloody naïve,' he shouted.

She was slightly taken aback. 'I think you've had enough wine, buster!' she said, trying to lighten the mood.

'Look, I'm sorry,' he continued. 'But if it turns out there was something suspect about his death, well, the Church will be swarming with police and reporters over the next few weeks. They seem to think you'll try to get *other* information out of me.'

'What other information?' She smiled and tried not to sound too nosey as she moved to fill his glass once more. Tom put his hand over it in an impotent protest. Oonagh ignored him and poured anyway. He pulled his hand away just in time.

She plonked herself down on the sofa opposite him and sank into the feather cushion.

'Tom, maybe it was suicide?'

'Christ knows.'

Oonagh giggled. She liked the way Tom used the Lord's name in vain at every opportunity. In a previous conversation, during happier times, he had denied it was blasphemy, claiming it was God providing choice phrases when no other words came to mind.

She'd always thought Tom an unlikely candidate for the priesthood. They shared similar Irish-Catholic backgrounds, and true enough a few boys from her school *had* gone off to seminaries, but usually they were the quiet types no one missed. Occasionally one would re-emerge months – sometimes years – later looking slightly bewildered, desperately trying to fit back in. Always trying to get back in step. Trying once more to be one of the boys. Tom was different. He was bright, smart and could be a bit of a laugh on a good day. This wasn't a good day. A waste of a good man, she'd always thought. She guessed he'd joined up as a means of escape, but from what she had no idea. She picked holes in his faith at every opportunity, and dutifully he filled them in.

'Don't the police have any leads?' she asked.

'Well, they've already questioned me. In fact I've come straight from the press office. The police were there.'

'Don't worry about it, they've spoken to me too.'

'Have they?'

Oonagh thought Tom looked relieved. She didn't have the heart to tell him it was her who had badgered Alec Davies into probing Father Kennedy's death, convincing him that he'd had enough enemies to at least warrant a post mortem examination if nothing else. She'd come head to head with Father Kennedy herself a few months back when chairing a televised debate on abortion. She'd torn him to shreds. There had certainly been no love lost between them.

'He was nothing more than a twisted old glory seeker. Tom's rebellious streak was on overdrive.

'I know!' Oonagh agreed. 'He was never off the telly.'

'Ha! You're one to talk.'

She slapped his arm and affected a thick Dublin accent. 'You're not just a wee bit jealous there are you now, Father Thomas?'

Tom gave her a petulant grin, as if to say that he could never stoop so low.

Oonagh lit a cigarette and walked through to the kitchen to fetch another bottle of wine. Tom was just finishing his second glass.

'Jee-sus, you can fairly put it away,' he said.

'Well spotted, milk monitor.' Oonagh drew heavily on her cigarette and sat back down on the settee. 'Will the police want to speak to you again?'

He shrugged his shoulders. 'Probably.'

She thought Tom had the look of a man whose battle was coming to an end. Like he wanted to run away, but had nowhere to go.

'They know I had a fight with him the night before he died.'

'Look, just because they know you had a barny doesn't mean the police believe you killed him. People fight every day. It usually means nothing.' She tried to read his expression. 'Em… you *didn't* kill him, Tom – did you?'

He just tutted. 'Christ, Oonagh, shut up. That's the least of my worries just now. There's more to it… It's not easy being a priest.'

'I don't doubt that for a moment.' Although in truth Oonagh thought it would be quite a cushy wee number.

'I feel as though everyone wants a wee piece of me. They think I can help them and I can't. I just can't. It's too much.'

'Yeah,' she said, taking his glass, unconvinced that it was as high-powered as Tom was making out. 'Here, have another drink. You've just had a bad day.'

'I'm leaving.'

'Oh. You haven't finished your drink.'

'No. The Church. I'm leaving the Church.' He let out a nervous snigger and relaxed into the sofa cushion. 'There, that's the first time I've actually said it out loud.'

'You know, I don't know why you ever enlisted in the first place. I mean you're an intelligent man, and let's face it, the whole thing's such a big bag of crap, and…'

'Oh Christ, just drop it eh?'

'What…?'

Tom looked at her. 'The "let's run down the Catholic Church" routine. It's wearing a bit thin. You know, Oonagh, for every rotten priest there are a thousand decent ones. I spend my life trying to help people who've got nowhere else to turn.' He swirled his wine round in its glass. 'Fat lot of good it does, eh?'

Oonagh leaned over and touched Tom's hand. 'Hey, come on, you do a lot of good. But you don't need to be a priest to do social work. There are loads of projects and initiatives that would be glad to have you on board. You're well qualified, you're experienced, you're great with kids… Crikey, you'd get snapped up.'

He pulled his hand away gently. 'You know, I went to college with a guy who's stuck out in San Salvador. No, not stuck. Chooses to be there. Every day he breaks the law, just by being a priest. Risks his life. Every day. He works underground, hiding people – freedom fighters – from the police. He heads a network that helps women whose husbands, sons, whole families have been dragged in for questioning, never to be seen again.'

Oonagh felt she should be making encouraging noises, but the point of the story was lost on her.

Tom shook his head. 'Being a priest isn't what I do, it's who I am.' He put his glass down on the coffee table. Oonagh slid a coaster underneath it. 'I mean, I'm a Christian, Oonagh.' He dropped his eyes and slapped his hand off his chest. 'Jesus is still the most important person in my life.'

A smile pulled at the corners of Oonagh's lips and she waited for him to laugh, but he didn't.

'So we're not all bad, you know.' Tom sniffed hard, stifling a sob in the back of his throat. 'Just as not every journalist is a money-grabbing, amoral, ambulance-chasing, dirt-raker. So just leave it will you…?' He let out a little hiccup as his voice choked.

'Okay…okay…' She held up her hands, palms outward.

Tom's eyes had glazed over and he was swaying slightly, taking on that drunk melancholic look that Oonagh knew so well. She guessed the wine had gone straight to his head, bypassing his brain, loosening his tongue on the way.

'I thought it was what I wanted. But I can't do it any longer. I'm starting to hate it.'

She felt sorry for him. Sobbing his heart out just because he'd chosen the wrong job.

'Look,' she said, 'why don't I phone out and get us some food delivered. You look as though you could do with a bite to eat.' And before he could refuse she was cradling the telephone on her shoulder and sifting through a pile of menus.

'Italian okay?'

She ordered for them both, then covered the mouthpiece with her hand and said, 'Why don't you just stay here tonight? I've plenty of room, and if you're going to see Father Watson, it's easier for you to reach town from here in the morning. And anyway, you'll be way over the limit.'

Tom considered his options for just a moment before he said yes. No one knew he was there. Anyway, who would care? He could leave by the back door in the morning without being seen.

'Oonagh...' He patted the seat next to him. 'Oonagh, sit down, I need to speak to you.'

Something about the tone of his voice unnerved her. He was staring into his glass, swaying back and forth as he swirled the wine around and around.

'What is it?' The faintest hint of fear pricked her skin, and she felt the flesh round her scalp tighten. 'What's wrong?'

CHAPTER 9

Glasgow, 2000

It threatened rain as they turned off the main road. The clinic was tucked away discreetly in Glasgow's West End, just off Great Western Road.

'Don't you think we're clutching at straws?' McVeigh asked Davies. 'I mean we don't even know if it was definitely suspicious yet. He could have taken the penicillin himself, although I can't see why he would. It's just that there's no' really much point in killing a priest, is there? My money's on it being an accident.'

The post mortem examination on Father Kennedy's body had revealed more than large quantities of penicillin; he'd also been riddled with cancer. The suicide theory was gaining ground amongst their colleagues.

Davies gave McVeigh a look. 'Just because the old guy killed himself doesn't mean there wasn't something funny going on. Priests just don't kill themselves for no reason. It's against... y'know... They're not allowed! Anyhoo, I want to know if someone was getting at him. Threatening him. Maybe he was pushed over the edge.'

They pulled up outside the ornate iron gates. A small brass plaque identified it by name only: *Kendall Hall*. A converted town house, there was nothing to make it stand out from the neighbouring buildings, which were equally impressive.

As Davies lowered the electric window and pressed the intercom to announce their arrival, a small surveillance camera whirred overhead. Security was tight, but they were expected. Once inside, he drove up the tree-flanked gravel drive and ignored a sign pointing to the rear car park, stopping instead outside the front door.

'I mean not everyone is a suspect, surely?' McVeigh persisted.

Davies just ignored his colleague, but knew from experience that it would do little to shut him up. He leaned on the door frame with his right hand, while his hand gripped the waistband of his jeans. He drummed his fingers on the wood as he waited to be let in.

A receptionist in her mid fifties, with perfectly manicured nails and a bleached blond bob greying at the roots, opened the door and led them through the main hallway into a private office with wood-panelled walls. The dark blue carpet cushioned their every step. Her smile didn't reach her eyes as she told them to make themselves comfortable. No tea or coffee was offered.

McVeigh looked round and let out a long, slow, soft whistle. 'There must be some money in this...' He looked at the ornate ceiling and then towards the leather settee. Two Howison originals hung on the wall. The place boasted the luxury and style of a five star hotel. Very swanky. The only thing missing was an eighteen-hole course round the back.

'For Christ's sake, do you ever shut up? Did they no' teach you nothing at that Uni?'

Davies realised McVeigh was used to his moods by now, but he still seemed oblivious to his part in creating them.

A door opened.

'Look boys, make this quick, will you. I've got an appointment in half an hour.'

The man before them was tall – very tall. Expensively dressed, probably early forties, too well groomed to make any guess at his age more accurate. Walking towards them, carrying a bundle of anonymous case notes, he made no attempt at an introduction. Instead he nodded for them to sit back down.

'Doctor Cranworth, we've no intention of keeping you longer than is necessary, but as I told you on the phone, we do have...'

'Yes. Yes of course,' He didn't give Davies a chance to finish. 'But I really don't know what you expect me to know about the death of that priest.' He picked an imaginary speck of dust from his shoulder with his thumb and forefinger and viewed it with distaste before flicking it onto the immaculate carpet.

Davies leaned forward, resting his elbows on his knees. 'Father Kennedy didn't exactly approve of your work here, did he?'

'No, I don't imagine he did.' The first sign of a mock smile played on Cranworth's lips.

'Didn't you threaten to sue the Church, claiming he was intimidating your patients? He probably lost you a bit of business, eh?'

'Oh for goodness sake, I own and run an abortion clinic. Do you honestly think I plan to kill every priest who speaks out against me?'

Davies felt his self-satisfied look coming on, the one he saved for when he thought he had scored a point against an opponent. 'I didn't mention he'd been killed,' he said. 'What makes you think it was murder?'

'My mistake. Well what is it then?' His voice took on a mocking sing song tone. 'I take it you're not collecting for a wreath.' He laced his fingers together and raised his eyebrows, expecting an answer.

Davies wasn't used to people being sarcastic to him, and didn't like being made a fool of, especially not in front of McVeigh. This would be all round the bloody station by tea time.

'Look here, Doctor, understand that we've got a job to do. You threaten a priest and three months later he's dead. You've got to admit it's a bit suspicious. I mean' – he nodded his head upwards – 'this place can't come cheap.' He looked around the room. 'Your *clients* can't be short of a few bob. I imagine any lost business would cost you dear.'

'Don't be so ridiculous.' He shook his head and let out an

audible sigh. 'His protests wouldn't...wouldn't even make a dent. Besides,' he added, 'it's not quite my style. Now, is there anything else?'

Davies nodded but wasn't about to be fobbed off. 'I'll call back in a few days when you're less busy. You can answer my questions then.'

'As you like.' Cranworth buzzed his receptionist. 'Show the...the *lads* out,' he said, immediately turning his attention to his papers.

They were back outside within seconds. Davies got into the car and slammed the door hard behind him. He opened the glove compartment and fished around until he found a battered packet of cigarettes stuffed in the back.

'I thought you'd given up,' said McVeigh.

'Fuck off!' said Davies.

CHAPTER 10

Glasgow, 2000

The club was dark. There was little chance of being recognised. Even those people he saw day in day out often walked past him in the cinema or the supermarket without giving him a second glance if he was wearing civvies. So the chances of anyone picking him out here, in this blackness, were negligible.

He had no great plan of what he wanted to do once inside. Dance? Maybe a drink? Pick someone up? He didn't even know if they still called it that. Talking would be nice. He'd simply decided that he wanted to be out in the big bad world for once. Call it preparation.

He enjoyed blending in. He was leaning against a wall and was genuinely shocked when someone stood next to him and strained to speak above the music. Shit, he was being chatted up? What now? Go with it? Go home?

He went with it, a few minutes passing in a daze. No harm done. He could still walk away.

The obvious questions of a first meeting unfolded… Do you come here often? Are you here alone? What do you do?

'Lawyer,' he lied.

Oh Christ, why didn't he say brickie, or bus driver, or unemployed? Was he really that much of a snob? He didn't bother bouncing back the question. He couldn't care less who this other person was, or what they did for a living.

'I've got my car outside, do you fancy moving on somewhere else?'

Jee-sus, fast worker, he thought. Was he genuinely out of touch? Was that just how things were these days? Or was it only in gay clubs that people moved in quick for the kill?

He allowed himself to be led outside, where it was just as

dark as it had been in the club, then into the passenger seat of a Volkswagen. They drove in silence away from the quiet cul-de-sac in the Merchant City, through town towards the West End. The streetlights had a hypnotic effect, keeping him in a trance. An '80s-style power ballad blasted through the stereo, providing a soundtrack that made the whole experience seem like watching the events unfold on screen. The song lasted the entire journey – precisely eight minutes according to the digital display.

It wasn't until they pulled up on Kelvin Way that the driver switched off the engine, and with it the music. The car was facing Argyle Street with trees flanking either side. A throng of mums and kids had been taking a short cut through the park the last time he'd been, while miserable-looking students had rushed to uni.

'You married or what?'

'Eh, no. No, of course not.' It was the first time they'd spoken since leaving the sanctuary of the nightclub and it gave him a kick in the guts, jolting him back to reality. He suddenly felt sick. 'Look, perhaps this isn't such a good idea, I'll maybe just get out and get a taxi or something...' He heard his wee weedy voice trail off into a pathetic whine as he grappled with the door handle.

''S'is yer first time?' the driver said, as though this was going to be a weekly occurrence. Tiny flakes of dandruff that had settled on his shoulder spilled off onto his thigh as he wriggled his trousers down to his knees.

'Shite. What're you doing?' The sickness was getting worse. He wanted to throw up. Whatever the hell he'd thought he was looking for, this wasn't it.

The guy reached across and stroked the palm of his hand against the back of his neck. 'Hey, just relax okay?'

He nodded and felt like a complete arse for being there in the first place. 'I'm sorry. I just…' There wasn't really much point in finishing his sentence.

'Hey, don't worry. No big deal.'

The driver's hand was still caressing the back of his neck, generating an involuntary shiver.

It was all the encouragement the guy needed.

He didn't move. Didn't struggle. Didn't try to get away. He just closed his eyes and lay slumped across the seat, trying not to gag as the guy's sticky groin heaved up and down beneath him.

★

His eyes were still closed when the beam of a torch shone through the window and pierced the darkness. A hand rattled on the window, and Tom sat bolt upright, wiping slabbers from his chin.

The driver made to open the door.

'Christ's sake. Don't. Just drive away. Get out of here'

'Don't be so bloody stupid, they'll have the registration number. I don't want them turning up and getting my wife involved.'

'You're *wife?* What the hell… Are you married? Oh Jee-sus.' His insides turned to water and he dissolved into the seat.

The driver opened the window. Calm as you like.

'Got a problem there have we, sir?' The policeman shone the torch into the car.

'No, no problem. We stopped because the brakes were making a funny noise. But they seem fine now, nothing to worry about.'

'So d'you want to tell me why you've got yer knob out, and why that yin's drooling away like a dog on heat.'

'I'm not drooling, I'm just…' But the driver elbowed him in the ribs.

'Just shut it? The games a bogey.'

'Right,' said the policeman, 'get yer kecks back on and show me your licence.'

The driver handed it over, while the other policeman stood at the passenger door, making sure Tom didn't do a runner.

'Look, this is ma first time... Ma wife'll kill me if she finds out.'

'Well Mr...' He took the pink slip from its plastic sheath and held it beneath the glow of the torch. 'Mr Antonio... You should have thought of that before, shouldn't you...mm? Right you two lovebirds...yer chariot awaits.' He opened the door and gestured to the waiting patrol car where his colleague was now holding open the door.

He was in no state to do a runner. Instead, he hugged a tree a few yards away as he threw up.

★

Down at the station they were made to empty their pockets.

As a plain-clothed policeman walked past he recognised Antonio. 'Charlie, what've you done now?'

'Fuck...don't ask.'

'Who's yer pal?'

Charlie Antonio gave a non-committal shrug and shook his head.

The desk sergeant sifted through a few of the belongings on the desk and picked up a driving licence. 'So, you were his passenger, yes? And is this you?' He tipped his chin.

It was impossible to look up. His shoes became the focus of his attention. He said nothing. The taste from the fat man lingered in the back of his throat and made him gag again.

The sergeant asked again. 'Can you confirm your identity please? Father Tom Findlay? Is that you?'

Charlie Antonio was almost dumbfounded. Almost, but not quite.

'A *priest*? Is that right? Aw fur cryin' out... Jesus Christ. Trust me... A piggin' priest!'

'Give them a warning and let them go,' said the plain-clothed officer to the desk sergeant.

'For God's sake, you gettin' saft in yer auld age?'

'Come on. Give the guys a break. Just send them home… Drop it okay.'

Tom wasn't listening. He was in a corner, retching away what was left of his life.

★

That had been almost four months ago. A lifetime now.

CHAPTER 11

Glasgow, 2000

He should have guessed it was all too neat – the police letting him off – but nothing had prepared him for Charlie Antonio turning up at the chapel house the very next day.

'Blackmail's a dirty word, Tom.'

'Look, I swear the stress of this will kill me. I can't take it anymore, so tell who you like, I don't give a shit.'

Charlie was obviously good at profiting from tragedy.

'What do you think'll happen to you if the papers get to hear of your wee gay jaunts, eh? They'll bloody crucify you. And what about The Blessed Saint Father Kennedy? D'ye think he'll be chuffed to bits to find out his second in command is a shirt-lifter, an uphill gardener?'

'You're in as deep as I am, you can't put me in the shit without being up to your knees in it as well.'

Charlie let out a laugh. 'I'm a bloody journalist. Bending the truth to suit the story is what I get paid for… It's what I do for a living. All I have to say is that I set you up, posed as a queer to expose your sordid lifestyle. I'll be held up as a local bloody hero. Saving all those innocent wee altar boys from your grubby mitts.'

'For God's sake, I'm gay, not a paedophile. I would never even look at a child let alone… Christ, you make me sick'

Tom buried his head in his hands, feeling a hell of a lot older than his thirty-six years.

He looked at the clock. Father Kennedy would be home soon. He wanted Charlie out.

'Just go, get out.' He nodded towards the door, but made no attempt to stand up. He was too weak. He hadn't been able to eat since his mouthful the night before.

Charlie stood up. 'For cryin' out loud, Tommy, pull yourself together. It's not as though I'm asking for a fortune. Just a wee bung now and then, to get me by.' He walked into the hall and stood by the front door. He looked back at Tom, who was staring at the floor.

'How the hell am I going to raise that kind of money?' he pleaded.

'You can hold a fucking tombola for all I care.'

With that he had gone, and the whole sordid affair had begun to fester in Tom's mind like an open, pus-filled sore.

★

He'd paid out almost a thousand pounds…and Father Kennedy was dead. But at least he'd finally told someone.

'You're going to the police with this,' Oonagh told him. 'Blackmail's the lowest of the low.'

'Don't be so bloody stupid. I can't now, can I. They'll think I killed him.'

'Em, you…told me you didn't…didn't you?'

He looked stunned. 'Oonagh is that what you think? You honestly think I could kill *anyone?* Jee-sus Christ, I wish I hadn't told you anything.'

'Calm down, Tom, I only asked.'

'Would you rather I went home after all?'

'No, I think I can handle a drunk priest with a limp wrist.' She smiled and he started to laugh, more through drink than anything else. Oonagh linked his arm, and pulled him towards her on the settee. 'Is that why you were so bloody scared when Alec Davies turned up to speak to you?'

Tom nodded his head and looked pathetic. 'I nearly shit myself when they arrived.'

Oonagh kept a straight face when she told him cops like Davies didn't really do that kind of donkey work.

'How was I to know that?' Tom was whinging. He seemed

pissed off at not realising how such things operated.

Oonagh got him back on track. 'So what happened the night before Kennedy died?'

'President or Father?'

'Look, I'm the sarcastic one here, no competition please. Just the facts.'

'Well, he came into the room while I was on the phone to Charlie. The conversation was getting more and more heated. He heard me shouting at him, and you know what I'm like, I told him to go fuck himself, before slamming the phone down.'

Oonagh stifled a giggle and put her hand over her mouth. 'My God, Tom, Father Kennedy must have been in a state of apoplexy hearing language like that. No wonder he keeled over the next day!'

They both laughed, again more through drink and nerves than anything else.

'It wasn't funny, Oonagh, I thought he was going to take a heart attack there and then. Obviously he wanted to know exactly what was going on. He'd actually come in to speak to me about some cash that had gone missing. It was more…well, *misappropriation* of funds actually. And yes, before you ask, I took it.'

Oonagh opened her mouth, but he cut in before she could say a word. 'Don't look at me like that. I was desperate. Shit, I was being blackmailed for Christ's sake. Anyway, I'd already decided I'd stooped low enough, and told Charlie Shitfeatures he was getting no more, it was finished.'

'So what did you tell Father Kennedy then?'

'Said I needed it to pay off a gambling debt. Claimed it was a dodgy bookie on the phone. Not that unusual for a priest, you know. And it was only a grand after all. I mean in the great scheme of things…' He sounded desperate and Oonagh stroked his arm, leading him gently back to the point of the story.

'Anyhows, that was all he needed. He nearly bust a gut getting on the blower to 'head office' telling them he wanted rid of me.'

'So I wonder if that's why he called me? I mean he never really liked me talking to you anyway, and always refused to co-operate with the programme. So he never really knew what was going on?'

'Hell, no!'

'So you'd no *real* reason to kill him then?'

'*Oonagh!* For fu... Stop it! I told you, I had nothing to do with it. You don't believe me, do you? Anyway, I'm going to see Father Watson in the morning. To tell him I'm leaving the Church.'

'He won't let you go without a fight. Priests are pretty thin on the ground in this neck of the woods. There's a crisis of vocation, apparently – we covered it in the news only last week.'

'Oh I don't know. When everything comes out he'll probably be glad to see the back of me.' He tilted back his head to tip the rest of his wine into his mouth.

Oonagh wasn't convinced.

★

Tom rose early the next morning and left the house quietly, careful not to waken Oonagh. He wanted to get back to the chapel house to shower and change before heading into town to see Father Watson. His head was heavy from the previous night's wine, but he felt lighter than he had done in months after offloading to Oonagh. Confession really did cleanse the soul.

But happiness is a fragile thing.

CHAPTER 12

Glasgow, 2000

'Things were different in those days. I suppose you're sick of hearing lines like that, but it's true. You could leave school at thirteen then. I remember it so well. Not as though it was yesterday mind, because you know, I can't remember much of what happened yesterday, but I remember then. I worked in a big house a few miles out of the village. Just cleaning and taking care of the laundry and the likes, you know, domestic. Oh it was funny, we used to walk there every morning. Me and Mary Donaghy. She worked in a bakery just half a mile further on, so we used to meet and share a cigarette. She'd stolen it from her brother of course. Mother-of-God, there would have been hell to pay if ever he'd found out, but we didn't care, or rather she didn't care.

'God she was a laugh… Oh can you wait just a minute, dear, there's the phone…'

Oonagh pressed the pause button on her hand-held recorder as the woman took the call. She had found Maureen O'Hara through the internet. The website had been set up by a support group trying to reunite mothers and children separated by adoption. Hundreds of people from across the world used the site. Luckily Maureen lived in Bearsden, just a few miles from Oonagh's house. And fortunately, or unfortunately, Maureen had been a Magdalene girl. Oonagh knew to tread carefully when she spoke to the former Maggies. Coaxing them to share their horror-stories took tact and diplomacy.

'Sorry 'bout that. Where was I? Tea? No? Right then. What was I saying? Oh yes, Mary Donaghy. She was a girl if ever there was. Oh God, when I think of her…'

'And what about the institute, Maureen?' Oonagh cut in.

'When did you first go to the Magdalene?' She felt a bit rotten, but didn't want to lose the thread of the story, and gently steered Maureen back onto the road again.

'Oh right, love...' Maureen's eyes darkened and Oonagh felt like a heartless shit. 'Well, as I said, we lived about twenty miles outside Galway; it could have been twenty thousand miles for all the difference it made. You know, I was fifteen and I'd never even kissed a boy, let alone...Mother-of-God, I was twelve before I knew that babies didn't come out of your belly button!'

Oonagh let out a laugh; Maureen, despite looking so serious, blushed and a smile played on her lips.

'As I said, we lived in a small town, probably more of a village really, where everyone knew everyone else. So when I saw him for the first time, God I nearly died.' She slapped her hand against her chest, breathless at the memory. 'He'd been to school in Dublin. That was like Hollywood to us. Honest to God, if he'd been a film star I couldn't have been more smitten. He was Mr and Mrs Spencer's son. Did I tell you they owned the big house? Home from school for the holidays he was. He was a bit older than me, you know, eighteen I think, so perhaps he was at University, but to tell you the truth I didn't really know the difference, and to be honest I didn't care. I'd be in the kitchen scrubbing vegetables, or black-leading the grate. Everything had to be done by hand in them days, you know. Not like today. Anyway. He used to pop into the kitchen and give me a smile, or wink at me and tell me how pretty I was looking. And the first day he leaned over and kissed me, well... Oh I thought I would just burst.

'He used to wait for me some nights when I'd finished work, and take me for a walk. He'd tell me all sorts of nonsense about how beautiful I was, and of course I believed him, every word. Daft eh? I was no beauty. One evening he took me for a drive. I couldn't believe it. I mean *me*, wee Maureen O'Hara from

Duggan, in a motor car. I remember that night more than any other. He was kissing me, and I was too stupid to know what in Heaven's name he was doing.

'When he shoved his hand up my skirt, I remember crying. I *think* I asked him to stop. I can't remember. But I remember crying. Sure, he just kind of laughed and got on top of me. I didn't realise what he was doing, but then I felt such a sharp pain I honestly thought he was trying to kill me. I'd never felt pain like it. And he was so heavy on top of me, I could hardly breathe. He held me down, and…anyway, he got off me and when I looked down and saw the blood between my legs I started screaming. It was all over the top of my thighs and trickling down my legs. I thought I was dying. "Don't tell me you're a virgin," he said. A virgin? I didn't even know what that meant. The only virgin I'd ever heard of was the Virgin Mary. I knew he couldn't mean that. Anyway he just started up the car and drove me home.'

Maureen looked down at her skirt, twisting the material between her hands. Her voice dropped to a whisper.

'Well it wasn't quite home, to be honest, he just stopped the car about half a mile away from my house and leaned over and opened the door. I'll never forget what he said as I was getting out. "Don't worry, Maureen, I won't tell anyone about this, I'm a decent kind a' fella."' She took off her glasses and rubbed her eyes with her thumb and index finger.

'Never saw him again, of course. He never came back to the kitchen to tell me how pretty I was. And there were no more walks in the evenings. Anyway, two months later I found out I was pregnant. My Mam hit the roof, and it was the first time I'd seen Da cry. That's something that stayed with me. The sight of Da crying. The next few weeks I wasn't to leave the house. The priest came round to speak to me. He told me I had broken Mam's heart. But worse, he said, worse than that was that I had shamed the Virgin Mary. So much so she would cry tears of blood for the sin I had committed. They decided it would be best if the Sisters of Mercy took me in. I would work in the Magdalene laundry in Galway until I had the baby. A couple of days later I kissed my Mam goodbye. Da went into the back yard and refused to look at me as I left. I never saw either of them again. Father Kennedy took charge after that. He came with me on the train to Galway. Said nothing for the entire journey... never uttered one word...'

'Father Kennedy?' Oonagh interrupted. 'Not Father Kennedy from here, here in St Patrick's?'

'Yes, dear, that's right. I heard he died last week. And on the altar too.' She blessed herself, making the sign of the cross. 'You know, there's a legend in Ireland that if a priest dies on the altar he has to come back from the dead to finish mass. You'll probably think that a bit ridiculous, eh?'

'No, not really,' said Oonagh.

'Where was I? I'm always doing that, losing the gist of things.'

'Father Kennedy, The Magdalene Laundry,' Oonagh prompted. By this time her mind was working overtime. She had no idea Father Kennedy had any connection to the Institutes. No wonder he was so against the idea of Tom helping her. It would have destroyed his reputation as the champion of good causes if it had got out that he had been instrumental in incarcerating young girls into a life of slavery.

'That's right,' continued Maureen, 'I'll tell you, I wasn't sorry he died, and there's many like me who'll be glad to have seen him go.' She blessed herself again.

'He would come and say mass every morning before we started work. He knew how bad things were in that bloody laundry. But we were told we were lucky. We were getting a chance to 'wash away our sins'. We did that all right. Every day we would scrub tons of soiled sheets from the local hospital. In the summer the heat became unbearable. But we weren't allowed to strip off any clothes. And the stench! Oh God, it was unbelievable. There was always someone coming down with some illness or other. But we weren't allowed any time off if we took sick. The winter was worse, mind you. It was so cold our hands would crack and blister. Frozen wet we were. And our legs would go numb and blue from standing on the stone floor all day. Anyway, I did that until I was too far gone, then I was allowed to tend to the older nuns in the nursing home until the baby was born.'

'What happened after that, Maureen? What about the baby?'

'Oh she was gorgeous. I know all babies are beautiful, but my Lord she really was something special. Alice I called her, though she was never baptised of course. I was back working within a couple of days. I got to see her every day though, she'd be in the nursery with the others. I got to help with her feed and things. But they didn't like you playing with the babies, getting too attached or stuff like that.'

'*They?*'

'The Nuns. The mammies were never allowed to hug or kiss the children, or show any kind of affection. Nuns can be very cruel you know, cold-hearted like. But every day when I saw Alice, I would whisper in her ear and tell her little stories, and tell her how much I loved her and things. And how one day I'd get a big house and we'd both live there. Fourteen months we had together. I just lived for those precious moments. I waited and waited for my Ma and Da to come and take me home. But they never did. So I was just stuck there. To be honest I wasn't even sure if I was allowed to leave, nobody told me. Anyway, one day when I went to the nursery I couldn't find her, couldn't find my Alice. I remember looking round searching for her, in her bed, in the yard, I thought she might have taken sick. I was frantic. God, I was absolutely terrified something terrible had happened. Especially with her not being baptised. I asked one of the nuns where Alice was. That's when they told me she was gone. America, they said. Adopted. Just like that. Never gave me a second thought, never gave me a second glance... I should be grateful she was given the chance to live in America, they told me, instead of bleating and crying... '

Maureen's voice trailed off as the tears fell down her cheek. Oonagh switched her machine off. She wasn't prepared for this.

'Oh God, Maureen, I don't know what to say. Couldn't you tell someone? I mean they couldn't just give your child away without your say so, without your permission.'

'Give her away? No, she wasn't just given, pet. I reckon thousands of wee babies were shunted across the Atlantic to couples who had enough money not to have to bother with all the paraphernalia of adoption agencies. But I was told I was lucky she went to such a good home. That it was a better life than I could give her...'

Oonagh felt the hairs rise on the back of her neck. She was almost too scared to voice the question. 'Maureen, are you saying your baby was sold?'

'Aye, pet, that's right. But it was common enough.'

'Oh my God, that's dreadful! I really don't know what to say.' Compassion quelled Oonagh's journalistic instincts. 'I know this is hard for you...would you like to take a break for a bit?'

'No, pet. I want people to know the truth about that place. D'you know, for years I felt so ashamed at what I was. At what I'd done. Ashamed because I was such a bad, bad girl. But I'll tell you, no matter how wicked or evil I was, I would never take a baby away from its Mam. Never. Never.' She shook her head, and for the first time lines of bitterness formed round her mouth.

'Have you managed to find any trace of her?'

Maureen shook her head. 'There were no proper records kept. And none of the babies kept their real names. Anyway, what good would it do even if I did trace her now? I'll not mean anything to her. But I just want her to know that I wasn't a bad Mam. Just need to tell her that I didn't abandon her. That I loved her very much…and still do.'

'I'm sure she knows that, Maureen. I'm sure she knows.'

★

By the time Oonagh was back in the car the tears that had welled up had spilled down her cheeks. Great fat wet blobs stung her skin before falling onto her jacket. Her sobs escaped in rhythmic gulps.

She drove towards the West End, desperate to be home. Trying to make sense of it all.

A few blocks from her house she stopped the car and put the hazards on as she ran into a pharmacy. She returned to the car a few minutes later, clutching a home pregnancy kit stuffed into a white paper bag.

CHAPTER 13

Glasgow, 2000

She looked in the mirror. Everything was as it had been before, yet she was changed.

Her fear had a shape, it had a colour: a thin blue strip on a piece of white plastic. The phone rang and made her jump. It was Jack, anxious.

'It's me,' he said.

'Hi.' Her voice was flat.

'Oh Oonagh, I'm sorry about the other day. Things are…difficult just now.'

Oonagh chewed on a ragged piece of skin on the side of her thumb. 'Look, what is it you want?'

'Eh?'

'I said, what…'

He interrupted her. *'Yes, I heard what you said. Oonagh, I just want to speak to you.'*

'Really? I thought we got everything cleared up the other day.'

'Oonagh, please stop this. Can't we talk about something else?'

'Okay.' She waited a few seconds, then filled the silence with, 'I'm pregnant'.

He didn't say anything.

'Great news, eh?'

'Christ, there's no way you can keep it, can you?'

'Good God no, that would be far too inconvenient, we can't let it…interfere with *our* lives… Or *your* life, or even *your wife's* life come to that.'

Her sarcasm sounded hollow and misplaced. She wanted to tell him to piss off. That she didn't need him. But she suddenly felt scared of being alone. She didn't want to lose him. Not right now. Right now someone else's husband was better than no husband at all.

She traced her finger round her reflection in the mirror and felt like an idiot. She'd told Tom about her fears during their 'confession-thon' the previous evening. He'd been shocked and perhaps a little horrified, but he'd had the decency to spare her a lecture.

Jack cleared his throat. *'Oonagh, darling, listen, don't worry, I'll take care of everything. You know money's not a problem, and…'* His voice on the other end of the phone brought her back to the present.

'Money.' She sniffed and rolled her head back. Her voice trembled as the words caught the back of her throat. 'Don't be so ridiculous. I earn more than I could ever spend. Why would money be a problem?' She ran her fingers through her hair, scraping her fringe back from her forehead. A tiny sob escaped from her chest. 'Christ,' she cried, 'is that the best you can do? You'll be telling me next you're a *decent sort of fella.*' She knew the last sentence would be lost on him.

'Oonagh. Calm down, Oonagh.' He sucked an exaggerated breath between his teeth. *'Come on, Darling, pour yourself a glass of wine and go upstairs to bed. Try and get some sleep.'* He was on his mobile, and Oonagh could hear his car door close and the soft beep of the alarm as he flicked on the central locking with the remote control. *'You sound exhausted.'* His breath quickened as the gravel path crunched beneath his footsteps. *'You're not thinking straight.'* His voice dropped to a whisper as he fumbled with his key in the lock. *'We'll talk properly tomorrow. I promise.'* He hung up without saying goodbye, which sent a wave of sadness washing through Oonagh's entire body.

She looked down at her belly, and then back into the mirror. Her face was pale and blotchy, and her eyes still pink-rimmed from her visit that afternoon with Maureen O'Hara. God she was a mess. A big fat bloody mess. She thought of calling Tom, she wanted to tell him that her fears had been confirmed. She was also desperate to tell him about Maureen O'Hara's baby being sold, and of Father Kennedy's involvement with the Galway Magdalene.

She thought again. By now he would have told Father Watson he was leaving the Church. She could imagine a whole flock of priests descending on the Parish House this very minute trying to talk him round.

She went into the kitchen to pour herself a glass of wine to take to bed. Subconsciously her fingers strayed onto her belly as she made her way upstairs. 'Come on, Wee Thing,' she whispered, 'just you and me.' She switched off the lights, leaving only the glow from the computer in the box room downstairs that served as her office.

'...**HELLO GORGEOUS...HELLO GORGEOUS...**' The words on the screen moved effortlessly across the monitor. She went to switch it off and decided against it: it would give her some kind words to wake to.

★

The next morning she called Tom. The machine answered, and she shuddered when she heard Father Kennedy's voice asking her to leave a name and number.

'Hello, this is Oonagh O'Neil, with a message for Father Thomas.' She tried to keep her tone business-like, but thought she ended up sounding pompous. She wasn't sure who else would listen to the message; she didn't want to make things any worse for Tom. He was probably already in the shit. For no reason she could think of, she was getting panicky. 'Father Thomas,' she continued, 'can you please call me as soon as you can. It's important. I need to speak to you... It's...it's about... about the Magdalene project. As I say, it is quite urgent. Thank you.' She left her number and hung up.

CHAPTER 14

Galway, 1957

Irene Connolly was fifteen years old and five months pregnant when they strapped her down and stuck electrodes on her head. She tried to resist the rubber bar being stuffed into her mouth, but they held her nose and throat, forcing her mouth to open. They told her to bite down onto it – it would make it feel better. She didn't believe them. She squeezed her eyes tight, and there was a brief silence before something shook her so hard she bucked against the bed. Shook her until the air cracked with blue light and caused her to burn from the inside out. Her bones turned to twigs, snapping against the force.

The first session was the worst. The first time her convulsions were so severe that she ended up with fractures to her arms, ribs and ankles. But they were good to her and made sure she got something to help mend the pain of her broken bones. It didn't take long before her memory dulled and she forgot. Forgot the pain, and other stuff, until she couldn't even remember what it was she'd done wrong in the first place. She was a very good girl after that.

She went quietly to the Magdalene Institute, where the Sisters of Mercy could take good care of her. Lucky girl. If it hadn't been for her dad she would have been forced to stay in the loony bin.

Irene wasn't kept in Galway like her mum had promised. She went to Glasgow. The Sisters of Mercy did good works there too. Frank Connolly told his wife it was for the best.

By the time her daughter was born in the January of '58, Irene Connolly was barely sixteen and registered as medically insane. They held her down again, not on a bed this time, but on a chair. They forced her legs wide apart, and shoved a bucket underneath to catch the blood, catch the mess. She knew not to scream. So instead she sang the songs in her head that took her to another place and drowned out the pain.

She didn't scream even when the baby got stuck and she heard a voice say they'd have to cut its head off to get it out. Just pushed the way her dad had told her to with baby Isaac. She pushed and someone else pulled and the tiny wee thing eventually fell out of her.

When she saw the tiny malformed torso, the misshapen head, the eyes that were no more than black empty sockets and the twisted arms and legs, she prayed the baby wouldn't last until the morning.

Irene held her through the night. Refused to let her go. Cradled that little scrap of humanity in her in her arms until every last drop of life had left the baby girl's body. For once Irene's prayers were answered. Unconditionally. The wee creature died before sunrise. She named her Patricia after her sister, and thanked God for sparing her the torture of life. Only then did she let them take her from her and wrap her in a torn sheet before stuffing her in a wooden box, like a tiny Egyptian mummy.

CHAPTER 15

Glasgow, 2000

He'd arrived back at the chapel house early, just after seven thirty that morning, parking on the street rather than the gravel drive, so as not to disturb Mrs Brady. He hadn't noticed the man sitting in the car parked just behind his, its engine switched off and the window open just three inches at the top.

'Been out clubbing again…?'

'Oh for fu… Je-sus! Are you trying to give me a heart attack?' Tom clutched his chest, and raised one hand to his throat to stop his heart escaping out of his mouth. Charlie Antonio looked nonplussed.

'Get in.'

Tom hesitated, and looked around. The street was deserted. He opened the passenger door and got inside. It was a cold morning, raining lightly, and the windows were already steaming up. Tom rubbed his palms together, blew hot breath into his fingers, then wedged his hands between his knees.

'What is it you want? I thought I told you *never* to come here.' He shivered, despite the warmth of the car, and his voice came out in an unconvincing staccato.

Charlie switched on the window wipers to clear the screen, making the pair of them visible to any early-morning joggers or postmen.

'Never rains but it pours, eh?'

'Oh God, just get this over with.'

'I've got something of yours…' He took a small dark brown prescription bottle from his pocket and held it up for Tom to see.

'Where did you get that?' Tom lunged at him and tried to grab the penicillin.

Charlie stuffed it back in his pocket, and gripped Tom by

the throat, forcing his head into the side window. 'Where do you think I got it? It's got your name on it. I took it – out of your bloody bedside cabinet, next to the bloody rosary beads!'

'Je-sus Christ, what were you doing in my house?'

Charlie shrugged his shoulders. 'Just wanted a wee nosey.'

'Well, you can't blackmail me anymore, I've got nothing to give you, I've got no more money! Anyway, I've made up my mind. I'm coming clean about this whole stinking mess. I'm not going to be held to ransom by a…' – he delved into the reserve of his courage – '…a shitty wee low life like you.'

Charlie started to laugh. 'Ach, I'm a bit hurt. There was a time you quite fancied me. Remember? Let me spell it out to you, Tommy Boy, because that collar has obviously cut off your blood supply and starved your brain of oxygen. You can leave the priesthood for all I care, come out about being gay – tell the Pope why don't you, put an advert in the Jewish Chronicle!' He loosened his grip round Tom's throat, and sat back in his seat, pulling down on the cuffs of his jacket. 'No, they can't lock you up for being queer anymore, but by Christ they'll go to town on you for killing that old priest!'

Tom sat bolt upright. 'Is this meant to be some sort of sick joke? I didn't kill Father Kennedy. That bottle proves nothing, I got that prescription for a dose of tonsillitis months ago. I didn't poison anyone. I wouldn't know how!'

'No? Well why don't you just tell that to the polis then. Oh I'm sure they'll believe you. Of course by that time you won't be able to hide behind your collar. You'll just be another Catholic at the mercy of the Big Boys in Blue. No. No. Let me rephrase that. Another *bent* Catholic who's just killed an old man dying of cancer…after robbing the Church oot a' hundreds…at the mercy of the Big *Proddie* Boys in Blue. D'ye think they'll go quite easy on you then? Think maybe they'll no give you too hard a time of it? Even if you do get off with it, where'll ye go?

Everywhere you turn the papers'll be two steps in front. The press love this kind of stuff.' Charlie rubbed his hands in glee.

'It was you ya bastard, wasn't it? *You* killed him.'

'Nice try, Tom. Close, but no cigar.' Charlie let out a snort. 'Aye, everyone'll believe that. I killed an old priest for no reason whatsoever. What's my motive, Tom?'

'To get at me.'

'You? And who the fuck are you? Och, don't flatter yourself.'

'You probably stole that medicine weeks ago. Had this planned all along. How did you get it without me knowing?'

'You're really losing it, you know? I took this *after* that poor old sod died. He nodded his head towards the house. 'Not exactly Fort Knox in there. You could do with a better security system. I know somebody in the business, could get you sorted with a wee alarm at cost. Anything for a pal.'

Tom knew it was no great shakes for Charlie to get in and out of a house unnoticed and uninvited; according to Oonagh he was well known for it. It wasn't unheard of for journalists to raid people's bins in the hope of finding that tell-tale piece of salacious evidence to back up a story, and it wasn't beneath Charlie to go that one step further when he felt he had to.

Charlie straightened in his seat and switched on the engine. 'Now you listen to me. I'm not blackmailing you. I just want to know I can call in a favour when I need to. Not that an extra few quid won't come in handy now and again mind you. Now beat it, piss off, get out, I'm in a hurry.'

★

The meeting was arranged for ten. This time Tom wasn't kept waiting. He was led straight into the third floor office by the same grey nun he had seen before.

Father Watson didn't greet him with an outstretched hand. Instead he remained seated behind his desk and nodded at Tom to sit opposite.

'Right. What's going on?' He spoke through his usual haze of cigarette smoke. A big man who, despite his dog collar, looked like an ex prize fighter. He took a long final draw and swallowed hard before stubbing out the butt on the overflowing ashtray. He looked directly at Tom. 'I know you're up to your neck in something. I just don't know what. Now, I want to know exactly what's been going on…'

Tom's mouth was dry. His prepared speech evaporated. Everything was falling apart at the seams. His early euphoria on leaving Oonagh's house had long gone.

'Tom! *Father Thomas*. Are you listening to me?' Father Watson was squinting at Tom through the thin plume of smoke as he lit yet another cigarette. 'Now, whatever it is, I can help you. BUT, I *can't* help you if you don't tell me what's wrong.'

Tom held his hands to his face and rubbed his eyes. 'Christ, it's complicated. I don't know where to start.'

'You're darn tootin' it's complicated, son. One minute I've got Father Kennedy ranting and raving on the phone, telling me he wants rid of you, next day he drops down dead, his body full of poison.'

'Look, I had nothing to do with *that*. I swear it.'

'Well, if it's any consolation, I believe you. It was probably suicide. The poor old soul was demented with pain towards the end.

'We found some notes he'd written while we were going through his things. Notes about joining Jesus and God in Heaven…seeing his mother again, and, well just stuff like that really. Nothing that made any sense. He probably just, well, just couldn't take any more.' He shook his head. 'Silly old fool, he got penicillin from the dentist last year apparently. Kept it. He might have been planning this for ages. Don't even know if there was enough penicillin to kill him. But he'd taken paracetamol and stuff too. To be honest he was going a bit, well, strange towards the end. He was telling people things – daft things – all sorts of nonsense. Did you no' notice anything?'

His fellow priest had seemed his usual self. It had been quite a shock to learn of Father Kennedy's cancer. Hadn't even know he'd been ill. He felt lousy for not having spotted the signs. Suicide was looking more and more likely to be the cause of death, but that was *not* good news. Suicide was the ultimate sin. It would send shockwaves through the Church.

'What kind of things was he saying?'

'Doesn't matter. Never mind.'

The earlier rain had stopped. The weak autumn sunshine squeezed through the clouds and made a silver snowdrop on the desk between them.

Tom took a deep breath.

'I think it's best if I leave the priesthood.'

'For whom?'

'Eh?'

'Best for whom? Who would it be best for?'

'Look, I just don't *believe* anymore.'

'So? Do you think you're the only priest who feels like this?'

Father Watson stood up, walked round the desk and perched himself on the edge. He was tall enough for both feet still to touch the ground. He leaned over and touched Tom on the shoulder, his body blocking out the glare from the sun, which had been hitting Tom square in the eyes. Father Watson re-lit his cigarette, which had gone out, blew on the match and threw it into the ashtray.

'I should really give these things up. But then there's few enough things in life to enjoy, and we do without enough pleasures already, don't we?' A pause, a few more draws then: 'Is it a woman, Tom, are you in a bit of bother?' He pushed his tongue through his lips and wiped away a piece of filter tip with his fingers. He squinted his eyes as the smoke snaked its way up his face. 'You wouldn't be the first priest to…'

Tom interrupted before he got any further. 'No, nothing like that.' Not a *complete* lie. 'I just don't get it, I just don't believe in it anymore.'

'Right, listen to me. You're going nowhere.'

He pointed out the window to some far off place, his cigarette squeezed between two fingers. 'I've got one priest lying in the morgue after going sideways, and I've got another saying he's packing his bags cause he's having a crisis of faith. How d'you think this'll look? No. I'm sorry, but that's not on. Think of our reputation.'

He softened slightly. 'People look up to us, Tom. Look up to the Church. It gives *them* something to believe in. Even if it sometimes seems like…it's shite… At least it's well-meaning shite. And the Church needs *men like you*. Guys who can make a difference.'

'What difference do I make?'

Father Watson leaned towards him, blowing the smoke through the side of his mouth. 'You kidding? Look at all you do for those poor youngsters at that homeless place.'

He knew he was being buttered up. Only six weeks ago he'd been lambasted by Father Watson for telling the kids about safe sex.

'And what about all your counselling and stuff,' added Father Watson, going along with the wee game. 'You set all that up single handed. Most of those kids don't have anyone else, Tom. Times have changed you know. It's not enough for priests to pray over the sick and the dying. We need guys like you out in the community. We need to make our presence felt.'

Tom nodded, conscious of the colour rising in his cheeks. He bit his bottom lip, which was trembling.

Father Watson slid off the desk and walked to the window, arms folded. Tom sensed that his moment of glory was coming to an end.

'Besides, we've got to show a united front on this one. What do you think it'll look like if you walk away now, especially after the way you've been carrying on?'

'"Carrying on"?'

Father Watson either didn't hear him, or just ignored him.

'Now, the police have agreed to release Father Kennedy's body, so we can start the preparations for his funeral. The Mass will be at St Patrick's of course, and all the big nobs from the Church'll be there. We'll get the kids from the primary school to do some readings, sing a couple of hymns. Give him a good send off.'

Nothing seemed to be sacred to the Watson PR machine.

'There'll still need to be a fatal accident inquiry of course. That might easily allude to death by misadventure. In his confusion poor old Father Kennedy took penicillin rather than his usual medication. It was a single error, but with his age and advanced illness, it proved fatal.'

He paused for just a second. 'Now, it's been decided next Monday's best for the funeral, so that gives us a few days to handle the press, you know how these things are. Oh, and of course in your grief-stricken state you'll need some help. I'll be sending a curate round to take care of everyday business. Give you a bit of a break.'

Father Watson returned to his desk and Tom took this as his cue to exit stage right. Even when he stood up he was still dwarfed by Father Watson, who stooped over the desk pretending to sift through a pile of documents.

The older priest spoke without looking up. 'Now, you will take my career advice on board, Tom, won't you?'

He stood upright and held out his hand for Tom to shake, this time looking him straight in the eye. 'Oh and by the way, in case you're thinking of jumping ship, I know you've been helping yourself to the odd bit of overtime pay and a wee monthly bonus, but don't worry, we would never prosecute our own, Father Thomas.' He held his gaze. 'Now, I'll be seeing you before Monday. Take care and God Bless.'

CHAPTER 16

Glasgow, 2000

She turned the key in the lock, but the door jarred against the safety chain. She called out through the space, 'Mum, it's me.'

Footsteps quickened down the hallway. 'Hold on, I'm coming, I'm coming.'

Her mum's hair was damp and hung in soft waves around her face. She pulled her dressing gown tight across her body, her face flushed. Oonagh felt the tug on her heart. She leaned forward, kissed her on the cheek, 'Oh Mum, you old slapper, the middle of the day and you're still not dressed.'

'Get away.' They linked arms, and Fran O'Neil gave her daughter an affectionate squeeze and a crinkled grin with every step.

'You all right, Mum?'

'Uh uh…more than all right in fact.'

When she opened the kitchen door Oonagh felt the colour drain from her face. He sat at the table, but stood up when they entered the room.

'Oonagh, Owen; Owen, Oonagh.' Her mum beamed, arm outstretched to present her trophy, although it was hard to tell which she considered the better prize.

Oonagh shot her mum a look, taking in the situation. Owen held out his hand. 'Pleased to meet you, Oonagh. Your mum's told me a lot about you.'

'Oh really? Wish I could say the same.' Oonagh looked down at his feet and raised an eyebrow. 'Very Bohemian. They all the rage in Clarkston?'

'Oh these,' Owen laughed, 'no they're shower shoes, I'm just…'

Her mum cut in. 'Oonagh, I'm glad you came round. I've

been wanting you two to meet for…'

'Eh, Mum, excuse me, do you mind telling me what the hell's going on? Who's he?'

'Oonagh, Owen and I are….are…'

Oonagh decided she'd throw up if her mum said 'boyfriend'.

'…Owen and I are friends.' She clocked Oonagh's expression. 'Now honey, I know this is a bit of a…a…surprise…'

Well, at least she had the decency to be embarrassed.

'…but Owen and I have been seeing quite a lot of each other recently…'

'A friend who just happens to drop in for a shower. How very bloody convenient. I get the picture, very clear it is too. And how long has this being going on? I mean, where d'you pick him up? I hadn't realised your social life was quite so bloody spectacular.'

'Oonagh. Please. I thought you of all people would understand. You know how lonely…'

'Lonely. Don't bloody dare talk to me about being lonely. Dad's not even been dead five minutes, in case you've forgotten, and here you are sitting with some… some…eejit that we know nothing about.'

'Oh for goodness sake, Oonagh.' Her mum looked mortified but let out a laugh. 'Stop being so…so pompous.'

'I actually came to tell you something, to ask for some *motherly* advice. Well, don't bother, I can see I'm in the way.'

Fran looked at her and pulled out a chair. 'Och you're being ridiculous,' she tutted. 'Look, sit down, the kettle's on and…'

'Mum. Are you being serious? I'm not sharing a table with him.' She tossed her head in Owen's direction. He looked as mortified as her mum. 'How can you betray Dad like this?' She looked at the pair of them and bit down on her lip to stop her chin from trembling. 'It's…disgusting.'

'Now stop this, do you hear me? What do you expect me to do? Grieve for the rest of my life? In the name of God, Oonagh, it's been two years. I'm only fifty-seven, that's young nowadays. You're getting on with your life; what's wrong with me doing the same? Or am I not allowed a life because I'm your mother?'

'Don't make me laugh. Do you call working fourteen-hour days and anaesthetising myself with pills and booze a life?'

Owen stood up, scraping the legs of his chair along the tiled floor. 'Perhaps I should just go, Fran. This is obviously a private matter.'

'Yeah, good idea,' said Oonagh.

But Fran put her hand on his shoulder and sat him back down. 'No, no, stay where you are, Owen. You're right, it is private…between the *three* of us.'

'Well, at least I know where I stand. Thank you very bloody much.' Oonagh's voice choked, her eyes brimmed over.

'Oh grow up. You haven't been to see me for nearly two months, then when you do decide to pop in I'm read the riot act for having a boyfriend.'

The word stung Oonagh.

'Oonagh, it's your choice if you want to ruin your life wallowing in grief. It's not what I want for you, and it's sure as hell not what Dad would have wanted.'

'Don't you dare tell me what Dad would have wanted.' She pointed a perfectly manicured nail onto the table, as if somehow it might split the couple.

'Oh, you're acting like a spoiled teenager, Oonagh. You're a bright, intelligent woman with the world at your feet, but look at you, you're letting grief turn you into a shell. D'you think this is the worst thing that'll ever to happen to you? Let me tell you, Oonagh, there's a lot worse than losing your father. You need to start facing up to life instead of hiding behind this…self-pity. You should be grateful for what you've got.'

'Oh, I'll thank God, shall I? Thank God for making me feel so shitty all the time?'

'Oonagh, you can't expect me to put my life on hold just because that's what you want. You're too demanding, Oonagh. You're too needy.'

'I'm NOT needy.' She banged her fist on the table, causing the cups and Owen to tremble. 'I never ask anyone for anything.'

'No, Oonagh, you don't ask – but you expect. You expect people to work and play as hard as you do. And to grieve as hard too. But I'm just not up to it, Oonagh. I can't do it anymore.'

'Well bully for you for being able to switch off so easily.'

It was turning into a battle for which she was ill-prepared. She was losing control, losing order in her life. She wanted things back as they had been.

'Listen to me, young lady, this is my house, understand. *My* house, *my* home, and I'll have whoever I want in here. If I want Jack the Ripper doing a naked jig on the table then I'll have it. And if you can't accept that, then you shouldn't just barge round here uninvited.'

'Yes, Mother, your house – bought and paid for with *my* bloody money.' She could have cut off her tongue. 'Oh Mum.... Mum, I'm sorry. I shouldn't have said that.'

Fran slumped into the chair, the fight gone from her all at once. 'Just go, Oonagh.'

★

Oonagh slammed her fist hard against the steering wheel – 'Shit' – and drove home to the West End, fighting back the tears. She imagined the stoic Owen with his easy manner and shower shoes comforting her mum now. She felt a complete idiot – and wanted to cry.

Back home she decided to take a walk to Kelvingrove Museum. The fresh air would do her good and she needed space to think. And anyway, if she were out in public she'd be less likely to start bubbling. But the picture of her mum with her new boyfriend wouldn't leave her. She felt wretched, abandoned and…totally fucked up. She bit her lip to stop it trembling.

Picking up speed, she marched down Byres Road, turned left past the old part of the hospital and onto Argyle Street.

★

Oonagh instinctively made her way to the Egyptian sarcophagus and ran her hand over the huge stone coffin that held the body of an ancient high priest – his image carved on the outside. It was worn smooth in places by the many thousands who had stroked it over the years. Her problems were always diluted here, surrounded by things thousands of years old.

Doesn't really matter how bad things get, how dreadful the situation looks, everything ends the same way. Everything ends up dead.

She sat down and hugged her belly, and was shocked by a sudden bubble of maternal instinct. 'Hello, Wee Thing,' she whispered. 'You as scared as I am?'

She'd decided fairly early on that there was no place in her life for a child, but that had been before. Now, things were different; perhaps Wee Thing wouldn't be such a bad thing.

But what's the point if everything ends up dead?

The electronic twang of *The Yellow Rose of Texas* echoed round the gallery. Frantically she fished in her bag for her phone and rushed towards the exit as she answered.

Tom's number appeared on the screen. She'd forgotten about him.

'Hi, I was just thinking about you,' she said. 'I left a message on your machine this morning. Oh by the way, Father Kennedy's voice is still on it, you'll need to change that.' She was outside by this time, and could talk freely.

'Right, something to do while I'm having my nervous breakdown.'

'As bad as that?'

'Worse. Listen, are you free later? Can you meet me somewhere?'

From his hushed tones she guessed he wasn't alone. 'Why

not come over to mine, I'm just making my way home now. Anyway, there's something I need to tell you. And wait till you hear what it is. Hey, by the way, I thought you'd been told not to see me anymore, order of the Holy Catholic and Apostolic Church.'

'This is the rebel in me coming out. Didn't I tell you my nickname at the seminary? Mad Chicken-Hied Findlay, on account that I used to bite the heads off live chickens.'

'What was your nickname really?'

'Plook.'

★

She was only home minutes before he was at the door. He must have left the house as soon as he had hung up.

Oonagh led him through the living room, and straight into the kitchen. She took her coat off, and stretched to reach the hook on the back door, craning her neck round to see his face.

'Help ma Boab! What's happened to you? You look dreadful.' His eyes were bleary and black-rimmed, and he hadn't shaved.

He laughed. 'God, Oonagh, for a journalist you've certainly got a way with words.'

'No really, you look awful.'

He sat down at the massive pine table. Oonagh pottered around behind him, steeling glances every few seconds. He really was in a bad way. She put on the coffee and took two filled rolls from a paper bag,

'I stopped off at the deli on the way home and bought some lunch. I take it you haven't eaten?' She put cups and plates on the table and fished out two custard tarts from another bag. Only then did she sit down opposite him.

He was sitting bolt upright, elbows on the table, lips pressed tight. Oonagh made conversation but could tell he wasn't listening. He seemed to be miles away. Only when she poured the coffee from the glass pot and pushed the milk and sugar towards him did he speak.

'Thanks,' he said, trying a half-hearted grin as he slid the milk and sugar back unused.

Oonagh heaped three large spoonfuls into her own cup, followed by a huge splash of milk.

'Sweet tooth?' Tom asked.

'I like my coffee like I like my men...weak, wet & milky.

He grinned at her and shook his head. She could see he was starting to relax. Slightly.

'How did Father Watson take the news? Try to persuade you to stay? That's the usual isn't it?'

'Oh he *persuaded* me to stay all right.'

He told her about the meeting, and his earlier visit from Charlie, giving her all the gory details. Left nothing out. She, on the other hand, said nothing about the exchange with her Mum. By now she was thoroughly ashamed of it, and not only because of the cheap jibe at the end. But she shoved it to the back of her mind, along with the picture of Owen in his shower shoes and all the rest of the crap, and instead concentrated on Tom.

'Bloody hell, you're in it deep.'

'Oonagh. Christ's sake, never join the Samaritans, they'd have to employ a locum to cope with the increase in suicides.'

'Oh I'm sorry.' She genuinely was. 'I flunked out of my final year of charm school.'

'I'd still ask for a refund if I were you.'

She gave him that one.

'And before you ask, for the tenth time, no, I didn't bloody kill Father-Bloody-Kennedy. Jee-sus, I'm beginning to wish I had, it would have been less pigging stressful.'

She nodded. Her mind had stepped up a gear. 'Never mind about all that. Guess what I found out about the Magdalenes?' She didn't wait for him to answer. 'Tom, listen to this. Babies weren't just taken away from their mothers and put up for adoption, they were sold. Sold! The Church was running a bloody baby-trafficking racket.'

He just looked at her. Said nothing. Just looked.

'Did you know about this?'

He shook his head. 'Dunno, don't think so. No.'

'Well, don't you think it's something that should be exposed? I mean bloody hell, does no one care?'

He raised one shoulder. 'What good would it do dragging it all up now. I think you should just put it to bed.'

She felt chilled to the bone. As though the whole rotten world was in on the act.

'Put it to bed? No bloody way.' There was a panicky edge to her voice. 'And I'll tell you this, it won't be stuck in as part of the tail end of the Magdalene story. No way Jose. I'm going to do a special on this. Blow the whole thing wide open. This'll cost the Church dear. And I don't just mean money, Tom.' Her eyes had filled with tears and she was shaking.

'Calm down a minute, Oonagh, don't just lash out for the sake of it. People can't wait to put the boot in to the Church. But, come on, we give a lot of practical help to people who just don't have anywhere else to go. Most our funding comes from public donations and every time something like this happens our budget gets cut to nothing.' He dropped his head into his hands and rubbed his face hard. 'God knows we're trying to make amends for the past, but it's bloody hard when it keeps getting raked up.'

Oonagh breathed deeply and ran her fingers along the rim of her eyes. 'It's not about you, Tom. I'd never jeopardise any of your work. But this is something I have to do.'

'I'm just saying, the Church isn't a lot of doddery old men in black suits. It's a business, understand? They can be ruthless when it comes down to brass tacks. I just don't want you getting into something that you can't...'

'Handle?' she cut in.

'Well yeah,' he replied. 'Put it this way, you don't really know what you're dealing with here.'

She didn't like this. 'You know more than you're letting on, don't you?'

'No, I don't. But I know a helluvalot of things went on in the past that sometimes are best left there. Things were different in those days. Y'know loads of families were split through poverty, or one thing or another. For God's sake, the Government shipped thousands of kids over to Australia after the war, why're you not harping on about that?'

She gave him one of her looks, but he carried on.

'And you know yourself that most of the Magdalenes weren't run by the Catholic Church, something that seems to be conveniently overlooked these days!'

'Yes, yes.' Oonagh waved her hand in a bid to shut Tom up. 'I'll make sure I mention that at the end of the programme.'

'Oonagh,' he said, 'all I'm saying is that what seems abhorrent now maybe wasn't so dreadful at the time. Anyway, most of the people involved are either dead or on their last legs. What's the point?'

'Yeah, what's the point,' she said, 'if everything ends up dead?'

Tom put his hands. *There you go*, he seemed to be saying.

But she wouldn't let it drop. 'I bet Father Kennedy knew about all this. Oh. That's another thing. Jeezo, I nearly forgot.' She patted the table. 'He was actually involved in the Magdalenes – and not just in Glasgow, but Galway too.'

Tom looked done in. 'What difference does that make now? Don't you think I've got more things to worry me?'

'I happen to think it makes a *lot* of difference actually. I mean it's funny how he never mentioned it.'

'Look, Oonagh, lots of priests were involved. Don't read too much into it.'

'What time's the funeral on Monday?' He was getting on her wick now and she couldn't be bothered arguing the toss.

'Eleven, why?'

'I'll need to get a crew together.'

'Crew?'

Footage of Father Kennedy's funeral would be a fantastic touch for her Magdalene documentary, now that she knew how instrumental he had been in the running of the home in Galway. She already had a rough commentary planned. She'd have to mask the filming as an everyday news item about his death though, The Church would never agree to it if they knew what she intended to say about him. And she was already way over budget for the programme. She told Tom.

'No, you can't do that, just leave it will you, for God's sake the man's dead. Can't you just let it go?' He'd finished his rolls and was picking at the pastry on his custard tart. Again, Oonagh refused to let go.

'No, Tom, I won't drop it.'

'Who're you trying to get at here?' He left his pastry for a moment. 'The Church, Father Kennedy, me?'

She was gutted. She'd expected Tom to be as angry as she was. His reaction left her bitterly disappointed. 'Whose side are you on, Tom?'

'*Side*?' He swung back in his chair in a huff. 'It's not about sides, Oonagh, don't be daft.' He let his chair fall back onto all four legs and looked at her. 'Look, I know you're as mad as hell over all this.' She was about to interrupt him but he didn't stop for breath. 'And I'm not defending anybody here, but Oonagh, you're not stupid, you know it was nearly impossible for single girls to keep their babies back then. It wasn't just a problem with the Church. It was society in general.'

Oonagh tightened her lips and stared hard at the table.

'Oonagh there's not a week goes by when I don't see first-hand the mess of some screwed-up family. Pregnant teenagers shagging old men for a few bob for their next fix. Passing their weans round their pals when they're out begging, cashing in on the sympathy vote. Can't you get it into your head that maybe some of those kids who were adopted were at least given the chance of a decent life?'

She'd heard enough.

'Oh come off it, Tom. That's a cheap trick, that is. Why are you so keen to defend them?'

She stood up to get fresh coffee, but he grabbed her by the arm.

'*Them*, Oonagh?' He forced her round to look at him. '*Them*? I'm part of them, have you forgotten?'

She wriggled free, surprised at his grip for such a wee man. Her mum's words rang in her ears. "*You expect too much of people, Oonagh.*" She was sick of fighting and wanted to change the subject.

'By the way, the test was positive,' she said, rubbing the flesh on the top of her arm, trying to make Tom feel guilty. 'I'm pregnant.'

He didn't look shocked. Or guilty. But then Tom was a trained councillor, and trained councillors never looked shocked at shocking news. And rarely fell for the guilt card. Oonagh knew from experience.

'Well,' he said, 'it looks like you've got better things to worry about too. Have you told the father yet?'

'Told my father? My Dad's dead.'

'What? No, the father of the baby. Bloody hell, wake up, Oonagh.'

Her mum was right. Two years on and she was carrying her grief around like a guide book. Referring to it before getting on with her life. A word or even a smell could bring it back like a blow to the stomach. While her mother shared afternoon delights with her new lover, Oonagh paid seventy-five pounds an hour to a therapist twice a month for the privilege of talking. Suspended grief he called it. Seventy-five pounds an hour. She was in the wrong job. Either that or didn't have enough friends. Or the right sort of friends.

'Oh right, of course, yes.' She felt embarrassed now that the penny had dropped. 'I spoke to him the other night, on the phone. Last night in fact.'

'And?'

'And what?'

She couldn't bear to go into the full details of the conversation with Jack. 'I'm meeting him later,' was all she said.

God, her therapist would have a field day with this. Poor Oonagh, looking for a father-figure to replace the dead one she couldn't have anymore. And instead she'd got herself a husband. Someone else's.

'I don't know what to do, Tom. I mean I can't keep Wee Thing can I?' She rubbed her belly affectionately with both hands.

'It's got a name already? Just make sure you think long and hard before you make any major decisions, Oonagh.' He reached out his hand and squeezed her wrist. 'And make sure it's *your* decision.'

'Father Watson was right, the Church could do with more priests like you. Just a shame you're not willing to be a bit more rebellious at times.'

'For what it's worth, I'll say a prayer for you tonight.'

'Well, when you speak to God, give him a message will you? Tell him he's a right bastard.'

'Well, at least you still believe, Oonagh. At least you still believe.'

Father Watson unlocked the bottom drawer of his desk and took out a bundle of papers. The envelope was addressed to Oonagh O'Neil in Father Kennedy's spidery handwriting. He threw it in the bin. Then he unfolded another document written in the same scrawl.

> *It is a terrible thing that we have done, and for all of that we must ask God for Mercy. Mercy and forgiveness. In my own defence all I can say is that at the time I believed what we were doing was for the best. But for the lives we have destroyed, that is little comfort. And for those who say they took no part in the events, I will say this: all it takes for evil to flourish is for good men to do nothing…*

He couldn't stomach reading it anymore. Not again. He held it by the corner and set all three pages alight. An involuntary sigh of relief escaped as he watched the words curl and die in the grey ash. He dropped the burning letter in the wastepaper bin on top of the envelope addressed to Oonagh O'Neil. Then he stood and watched until Father Kennedy's last confession disappeared with the flames…

CHAPTER 17

Glasgow, 2000

Oonagh arrived at The Rogano a good ten minutes early and decided to wait for Jack at the bar. She'd just hoisted herself onto a stool, and was about to order a drink, when she caught Charlie in the mirror.

'Oonagh O'Neil. How the devil?' He gave her a wee wave.

Smug bastard. 'Well if it isn't Charlie McNae-chance.'

She cancelled her drink and walked over to the booth where he was sitting. She gave it the once-over. 'This place must be going downhill, eh.'

She bumped into him from time to time. The media was an incestuous business, especially in Glasgow, and Charlie Antonio was always on the lookout for work. Always on the make. He smoothed back his hair and wiped his hand over his mouth when she slid into the seat facing him. Normally she avoided him like the plague. They weren't exactly bosom buddies.

'I'm glad I saw you, Chaz,' she said, 'I want a wee word.'

He looked genuinely intrigued. 'Oh?'

She got straight to the point. 'You've been pestering a friend of mine, and I want to tell you to back off. No, make that, I'm warning you. Back off or else.'

'Or else what?'

At least he didn't bother with the pretence of not knowing who or what she was talking about.

'Just take this as a warning, Chuck.'

He let out a laugh, which came out as his usual snort. 'D'ye think I'm scared of you and a poofy wee priest? Do's a favour, love.' His voice dropped to a hiss as he noticed a waiter standing by the booth. They both ordered in a hurry to get rid of him. Another gin and tonic for Charlie; a glass of dry white for

Oonagh. She was about to down it in a oner when she caught his eye, and instead took just one sip.

Charlie's hair was thick with gel and curled slightly at the nape of his neck. His dark-blue double-breasted suit was out of vogue and had seen better days. The jacket had a tell-tale hump, probably from being hung on a car's coat hook. Luckily for him, the Burberry raincoat folded on the seat beside him had just crept back into fashion.

'Look Chas, why don't you just leave Tom alone? He's done nothing wrong, give the poor guy a break.'

'Nothing wrong? Are you mental? He's killed a bloody priest.'

'That was suicide. You're clutching at straws and you know it. He couldn't hurt a fly.'

'Some bloody investigative reporter you are. Fuck's sake, O'Neil. He's as guilty as sin.' Again another snort-like laugh.

'If you back off...' She was playing for time. Drummed her nails on the table. Sized him up. 'Look, I'll make it worth your while if you leave him alone. Okay?'

'Worth my while? How?' He traced his finger along the mahogany veneer on the table.

Oh Christ, did he actually think she was coming onto him? She ignored his wee fantasy.

'I know you're hardly flavour of the month right now, Chuck. So back off and I'll make sure you get a few decent jobs – well-paid jobs that could lead to other things.'

'It's your fault I'm in this state in the first place.'

Oonagh refused to take the bait.

'I go to that Sheriff fucking Court sometimes three times a week just to try and pick up a story I can sell on.'

She felt a very slight pang of sympathy. It was a tough time for freelancers.

'It's ok for staffers,' he jabbed his finger toward her face, 'they treat a day in court like a fucking holiday. Saves them having to go out in the bitter cold, chapping on doors, asking some poor sod if they're upset their wean got ……'She cut him off. She knew it was a tough gig, but that wasn't her problem right now.

'Don't push it, Chazza. It's your call.'

She sat back in her seat and let the wine slip down her throat, easing the tension through her body. She allowed herself a smile. She didn't know how long Charlie had been in the bar, but judging by the flush in his face, he'd had enough to give him a bit of Dutch courage.

As she wrapped her fingers round the stem of her glass he leaned across the table and covered her hand with his. He seemed to soften.

'You know, Oonagh, I find you very attractive at times.' He paused. 'And you owe me one. So what do you plan to do about *that*?'

'Shave my head and grow a moustache? Now piss off you shitty little creep. Deal's off.' She pulled her hand away and downed the rest of her wine in one swig. She stood up and walked out, stopping briefly to speak to the doorman.

Charlie was left to pay for the round.

★

Outside, Oonagh stopped to catch her breath before punching Jack's number into her mobile. 'Hi… No, change of plan… Meet me at Sarti's instead… Right, see you in five.'

The streets were thronging with office workers struggling to get home, and the sky was dark and heavy, with fat clouds threatening to burst. She quickened her pace as she made her way to the Italian café bar a few blocks up. The first few drops of rain fell just as she reached the front door.

Inside it was quiet. It was still early, and mid-week, the best time to get a table anywhere. Just a few people sitting downstairs next to a counter that sold an enormous selection of Italian meats and cheeses.

Jack was sitting upstairs. She spied him immediately through the wooden banister of the spiral staircase. Dark-blue mohair Italian suit, with a dark shirt to match his silk tie. His grey hair was cropped close to his head; from a distance it added a few years to him. He often joked he was going prematurely grey, and he probably had been ten years ago, but not now. His glasses – Oliver Peoples – were perched on the end of his nose as he read the menu. Even sitting down he looked outrageously tall.

She climbed the stairs slowly, keeping her breathing controlled. Her asthma was playing up a bit and she wanted to appear calm when she reached the top.

He caught sight of her as she reached the second-top step. Stood up, put his glasses on the table, and walked over to meet her. Kissing her on each cheek. Always the gentleman. When she'd first met him it was one of the things that had attracted her to him. Now she found it slightly irritating.

He guided her over to the table and held out her seat. Only when she was fully comfortable did he resume his position opposite her.

'How did you get here before me?' she said, a bit annoyed.

He patted his thighs and smiled. 'Turbo-charged.'

Her heart did a little somersault and she cursed him for being so good-looking. Bastard.

A mixture of smells rose from the kitchens downstairs. She took a deep breath, closed her eyes and flared her nostrils to savour the aroma.

'Hungry, Oonagh?'

'Mmm, I could eat for two,' she said sarcastically, patting her belly. She looked down at the menu in front of her. She'd decided what she wanted to eat on the way there; the menu was just an excuse for not to having to talk for a few minutes. She laboured over it, running her index finger up and down, stopping every so often to illustrate the point.

'Oonagh, I've been worried sick about you. The other night on the phone, well, I didn't mean... You know how I feel, it's... It's just that...' His voice trailed off without her interrupting. Normally she would fish him out of sticky situations. Throw him a lifeline. Reel him in before he had the chance to incriminate himself. It was a pattern that had developed early on in their relationship, he'd seen to that.

He changed the subject. 'How's work? I'm sorry I missed the programme the other night. Something came up.'

She looked up from the menu. 'Eh? Oh never mind, I'm sure you'll catch it next week. Lasagne I think.'

'What?'

'Lasagne, I'll have the lasagne, always a safe bet in here.'

'Oonagh, listen.'

'Oh and a bottle of Pinot Grigio.' She put her menu down, folded her arms and looked up to indicate she was *now* ready to listen. He droned on for a bit, and she settled down for the usual spiel. She was only half listening, but managed to pick out a few key phrases, carefully chosen for maximum impact. '...position...responsibilities...reputation...not the right time... perhaps in a few years...blah de blah de blah...' Tuning in and out without missing too much was easy; she'd heard it all before.

'Oonagh, I have to say, I'm really surprised at your attitude. I thought you had no qualms about termination. You always said it was a woman's right.'

'Yes, but bloody hell, I never said it should be compulsory!' she shouted. He looked round, embarrassed in case anyone had heard her wee outburst. Witnessed her faux pas. Only the waiter was upstairs with them and he didn't count, he was only a waiter after all.

'Don't worry, I can hardly keep it, can I.' It was more of a question than a statement. But he didn't pick up on that. The relief on his face was tangible. Suddenly he was ten years younger.

'Oonagh, this doesn't have to change anything. I know I've been a bastard these last few weeks. I've just had a lot on my mind. But you know how I feel. I can't live without you.'

She felt weary and was glad when the wine arrived. He was still droning on.

'Look, why don't we go away, take a holiday, somewhere warm? A break'll do us good.'

Jack *never* had trouble getting away – when he wanted to. One of the perks of being so successful; always at some conference or other. He was pouring her a second glass, celebrating getting off the hook so easily. Children were never on Jack's agenda; baby seats just didn't cut it in a Jag.

The old Jack came flooding back, grinning from ear to ear. '....anywhere you like Oonagh. What about Rome? We could tour round Italy, or...well, you choose.'

He was certainly prepared to pay through the nose for this. Not surprising really. Every day, babies were being bought and sold for thousands of pounds, including on the Internet. Apparently the going rate for a healthy blond, blue-eyed boy was upwards of ten grand. Oonagh wasn't sure of the market value for a dead one. Not so much she reckoned. A good holiday was probably top whack.

She ate silently, while he seemed unable to contain himself. The euphoria of his great escape.

The bottle of wine on the table was soon empty. He ordered another one. Try as she might, she couldn't share his enthusiasm.

'I thought you had the car with you.'

'Lighten up, Oonagh, I can handle a couple of glasses of wine for Chrissakes.'

Was this man sitting before her really the best she could do?

'You'll know the devil when you see him, Oonagh,' her Dad had told her, often when they'd sat and chatted into the wee small hours,

a bottle of brandy on the table between them. On those occasions her mum had constantly bobbed up and down, returning with batches of cheese and toast and saying things like, 'You drunkards need something to soak up the alcohol,' at the same time plying Oonagh with more booze to persuade her to stay overnight. It had usually worked.

'Tell her about the night you actually saw the devil, Con,' her mum would prompt her dad, and right on cue he'd reply, 'Oh I don't know if she's ready for that story, pet.'

'Just tell me the story, Dad, before I sober up!'

'Well, it was a dark foggy night in Dublin, and I'd missed the last tram home. I'd been out on a date with your Mammy, d'ye remember, pet?'

'Oh indeed I do, Con.'

'Bloody hell, get a move on, Dad.'

'Aye right. Anyway I noticed a man coming towards me. As I say it was dark, and there were no street lights, so I couldn't make out his face. As he got up beside me he stopped and struck a match to light his cigarette. He looked right at me, right into my eyes, and said, do you have the time, Con? I'd never seen him before in my life, so how did he know my name, eh?'

'Dad, knowing someone's name doesn't exactly earmark him as Beelzebub.'

'Shush, I haven't finished yet. Anyway, something told me not to answer him. I'd heard if you speak to the devil of your own free will then he can claim your soul as his own. I ignored him and hurried on. After just a few steps I thought I heard the faint sound of horses' hoofs. Clip clop, clip clop. I turned round to see him walk away in the other direction, but he stopped for a moment and turned to give me one last glance. He smiled at me and winked as if to say, "We'll meet again, Con," before walking on. Then that dreaded clip clop sound was there again. This time it was louder, it echoed through the entire street. As I watched him walk away I looked down, and, Oh Dear

God, it was the most frightening sight I have ever witnessed. Instead of legs he had the cloven hooves of a goat.'

'You had a lucky escape that night, Con,' her mum said in all seriousness, cutting the slices of toasted cheese in half, slicing off the crusts for Oonagh.

He looked at Oonagh in earnest. 'Listen love, the point of the story is that you'll know the devil when you see him. Try to recognise him if you can.'

'Dad, I'm a bit old for you to be telling me not to get in with the wrong crowd, but okay, I'll keep my eye out for Satan!'

Oonagh looked across at Jack, the man rejoicing at the impending death of their unborn child. His pointed tail neatly hidden by his Aquascutum jacket, his cloven hooves well disguised under his Patrick Cox shoes. Surely she deserved more than what such a sod had to offer. As an only child, she'd lost half her family when her Dad had died. She suddenly felt very protective.

'I can't do it, Jack.'

'Take a holiday? Course you can, Dah-ling.' His tongue licked the outside of his lips as he guided a piece of garlic bread back into his mouth with his pinkie.

'No, you stupid fuck-wit!' She slapped both hands on the table, 'I can't go through with the abortion.'

Jack was visibly shaken. She realised he'd probably never heard her swear before, at least not in anger.

'Oonagh, get a grip of yourself.'

Jack put his glass on the table and looked round. A few tables nearby were now occupied, but her voice had failed to carry and no one was taking any notice.

'For Christ's sake, woman, what's got into you lately?'

'Well I've seen everything now. You're completely cool about killing a child, yet the thought of poor social etiquette throws you into a state of apoplexy? You really are an arse. Are you mental?'

'Oonagh.' He reached over and held her wrist. 'Listen to me, a baby would spoil everything, you haven't really thought it through, have you?'

'Jesus Christ, Jack,' She pulled her arm away and rubbed her wrist, 'I've thought of nothing else! And I don't see how things could be any more *spoiled* than they already are. Do you honestly think we can just go on as before? Do you for one minute think I can just pick up where I left off? Get real, Jack. It's over.'

'Fine. But you're not having this baby. Do you hear me? Over my dead body.'

She'd had enough. 'You really have lost it this time. I know what's wrong. You're worried in case Jean finds out. She'd go nuts. You're worried she'll take you for everything. The house, the business, the lot. She'd screw you, absolutely screw you.'

'Well don't expect me to hang around and play happy families.'

She stood up to leave, leaning both hands on the table, putting her face as close to his as possible.

'Jack, I'd rather employ Myra Hindley as my live-in nanny than let you have anything to do with this baby.' She jabbed her index finger into his chest. 'I don't want you or your filthy money anywhere near *my* baby, okay?'

As she swung round to leave, her bag sent the half empty bottle of wine crashing to the floor. It attracted just the right amount of attention from nearby diners.

CHAPTER 18

Glasgow, 2000

Oonagh spread the grainy black and white photographs out on the floor in front of her. A teenage girl grinned back. It was 1958 and the girl's face was flushed with pride. The pride of a victory that had marked the end of a three-day riot that had closed the doors of Glasgow's Magdalene Institute for ever, ending a two-hundred-year reign of terror and abuse.

No one seemed to know exactly what had caused this violent and final outburst. But it had ended with the girls breaking out and running up Maryhill Road in a defiant lap of honour.

Laughing, screaming, hysterical with relief. Captured on camera. Immortalised.

Oonagh picked up one of the pictures for a closer look. It showed a group of women, no more than girls really, running along the middle of the road. In the background loomed Lochbridge House, empty and barren but still imposing itself. She recognised some of the nearby tenements; they stood to this day.

The front runner was a valiant teenager, her gap-toothed smile grinning into the camera. Holding her hand, and lagging slightly behind, was a tall, skinny lassie with wiry hair, and scared eyes. Oonagh had looked at the picture so often she felt she knew them. It would work well in the opening credits of the programme.

She hadn't managed to trace any of the girls. Still, the interviews she had managed to record had made her weep. Gut-wrenching stuff: mothers trying to trace children they'd last seen as babies thirty, forty or even fifty years ago. Grown men and women searching for perfect strangers, just for the chance of calling someone Mum for the first time ever.

The programme was coming together nicely, like the pieces of a jigsaw. For maximum impact she would slot in the footage of Father Kennedy's funeral near the end, after a section on the Irish institutes. There was some shocking material in that part: how one hundred and thirty-three unmarked graves had been discovered in a cemetery on convent grounds near Dublin in the early Seventies; the bodies of one hundred and thirty-three women who had lived and died in the Magdalene. The dark secret had only come to light when the Sisters of Charity had sold the land and the bulldozers had moved in. But the ensuing public outcry had ensured the nameless souls now lay in the city's Glasnevin Cemetery. It had made headline news at the time, and Oonagh planned to mix footage of the mass reburial with shots of Father Kennedy's own funeral. It was a cheap shot, and she knew it. Call it dramatic licence. There was no record of him having had any dealings with the Dublin convent, but he'd been instrumental in Glasgow and Galway, and that was good enough for her. She couldn't actually say he'd committed suicide, but with a few well-chosen words the audience would make up their own minds. It was Oonagh's version of parallel justice.

She sat down at her PC to rejig the final running order. The only thing left to film was Father Kennedy's funeral. That would be on Monday, just a few days away. She made a few quick calculations in her head. Oonagh reckoned the whole thing would be done and dusted within the next week.

It was past midnight, but she battered away at the keyboard to keep at bay thoughts of Jack.

Her eyes switched from the screen to the black and white photographs still scattered on the floor, to her belly, then back to the screen. She picked up her favoured picture again and traced her finger along the face of the girl with the scared eyes.

She wandered through to the kitchen and had to feel for the

light switch in the hall. She could see nothing in the complete blackness. Even the street lights were out.

She switched on the kettle and, as usual, Cat wanted food. He snaked around her ankles and stood on his hind legs, head-butting her lower thighs. She clapped him and he purred with satisfaction and anticipation.

'You're so bloody lucky,' she said as she poured out a mound of dried food from the Tupperware container.

The kettle reached boiling point as the phone rang.

She wasn't too fazed. She was used to getting calls at all hours.

'Hello?'

It went dead. But as soon as she put it back in its cradle it rang again.

'Hello…?' This time she was slightly irked.

Once again it went dead as soon as she spoke.

She dialled 1471 – number withheld.

It rang a third time. She grabbed the receiver, 'Listen, who is this…?'

A high-pitched child's voice squealed with delight. *'It's me, Mummy.'*

'Oh, em…' Oonagh was taken aback to hear the little girl on the other end. 'No, I'm not your mummy. Are you on your own, or do you have…?'

'Peek-a-boo, Mummy. I can see you.'

'No, I'm not your mummy – I'm…is there a grown up with you?'

'Mummy please don't kill me – I'll be good, Mummy.'

Her legs buckled and she steadied herself against the wall. 'Who the hell is this?'

The child's voice distorted into a man's low, rasping growl. *'Abortion's a sin. Didn't your priest ever tell you that, you fucking murdering whore.'*

Oonagh screamed and threw down the phone. She was trembling, breathless.

When it rang again she screamed in panic and knocked it out of its stand with the back of her hand, then grabbed it and hung up again before he had time to call back.

Shaking, she staggered back into her office and slumped down on the chair.

Adrenalin rushed through her veins. A tell-tale asthmatic wheeze rattled in her chest as she gasped for air and tried to gulp back the tears at the same time. She hugged herself and shook uncontrollably. Fear, panic, anger, confusion; they all fought for pole position. She rummaged in her bag for her inhaler, then realised she'd left it upstairs. 'Fuck!' She sat for a few seconds trying to take in what she'd just heard. She breathed deeply and tried to relax back into the chair.

As she exhaled slowly and opened her eyes, Oonagh O'Neil came to know the true meaning of fear. The screen saver had kicked in and brought with it her worst nightmare.

… I ' M … I N … T H E … H O U S E … Y O U … STUPID…BITCH…I'M…IN…THE… HOUSE…YOU…STUPID…BITCH…

Rooted to the spot, she stared straight ahead, uttering a pathetic plea for help. 'No. Oh God no. Oh dear God, please, not this…'

The tightening in her throat moved down towards her chest and fear stole her breath.

Retching with panic, a vein throbbed in her neck. Her pulse became a deafening thump inside her head. She grabbed the phone, but instead of the dialling tone, the deep rasping voice taunted her from the other end.

'Did you think I'd gone away? I told you, I'm in the house, you stupid fucking bitch.'

She held the phone in both hands, and screamed as she battered it off the desk, smashing it in a desperate, vain attempt to make it go away. Then she threw it to the ground and grabbed her mobile instead, before bolting from the room and out through the front door. In a blind, barefooted panic she stumbled down the three steps onto the street outside, tripped on the last one and was sent flying to the ground.

The pavement stung the heel of her hand and tore the skin from her knuckles. Searing pain shot through her arm as her elbow cracked on the ground, and her knee scraped along the concrete. Still she held onto her cellular lifeline, which was glued to her palm. The cold night air caught the back of her throat and tightened her chest still further. She tried to scream, but could only utter a strangulated asthmatic groan. Without her inhaler she'd be helpless in minutes.

She crawled on all fours into the middle of the road and punched 999 into the key pad. It rang, once, twice.

'Answer the phone, answer, please answer!' she cried at the mouthpiece.

At last she was connected.

'Police. Police. I need the police.' Her voice came out in a high-pitched comic squeak. She tried desperately to control her breathing. Her body performed involuntary spasms from pain, fear and cold. A thin t-shirt, cotton drawstring trousers and bare feet offered little in the way of protection from the elements. She looked up and down the length of the street; its emptiness stretched on for ever. The street lights were out and the blackness engulfed her. One house had a light in the front window, but she could barely move.

The operator stayed on the line. Tried to calm her, told her help was on its way. But still she felt so utterly alone. Alone and afraid, her asthma attack squeezing the life from her chest, piercing her lungs.

She crawled to the kerb and crumpled onto the wet pavement. All the while her eyes were fixed on her front door, which lay wide open. *If he comes out now I'm finished.*

There was no way she could make a run for it. Her lungs felt as though they were going to burst. The lack of oxygen was making her head spin, and the blood pumping through her veins was also whooshing in her ears. The sound grew louder and louder, until she realised it was the squeal of a siren. The car zoomed towards her, the headlights growing larger and larger until it screeched to a halt outside her house. She thought she saw the flashing lights of an ambulance in the distance as the sour taste of bile rose in her throat.

She dropped her head between her knees and threw up onto the kerb.

Only then did she allow herself to pass out, the faces of the Magdalene girls swimming in her head.

CHAPTER 19

Glasgow, 2000

There was no mistaking *that* smell or *that* sound. Yesterday's dinner mixed with the stench of sick lingered stale and heavy in the stifling heat. A trolley crashed down a nearby corridor, and the clang of metal against metal echoed round the building.

The last time she'd been in a hospital had been when her Dad had been ill.

'Don't worry, Dad, you'll be out of here by the weekend,' she'd promised. It had been her turn to lie.

He'd hung on for a whole month before dying. Why did they call it a stroke? To her the word conjured up a gentle caress, not a fatal blow. Every day she'd sat for hours, stroking his forehead, holding a plastic infant cup to his mouth, gently coaxing him to take just a sip. Talking to him until she was hoarse. Once or twice she'd thought he'd smiled at her, but the doctor explained it was just a reflex action in the muscles around his mouth. She prayed to God the tears that fell from his eyes and landed on the pillow were caused by the same muscle reflex.

She hadn't been with him when he'd died. She'd gone home to get some clean clothes and half-decent food for her mum. She hadn't been gone twenty minutes, but as soon as she'd stepped back into his room she'd seen the pain etched in her mum's face and had known instantly that he had gone.

*

'Hi there, feeling any better are we? You gave us all quite a fright y'know.' The nurse was Irish.

Oonagh opened her eyes and tried to focus. She was in the treatment room of A&E. A corridor with five or six bays, each separated by an orange fibreglass curtain that reminded her of the photo booth at Central Station. The main lights overhead were out, the lamp above her bed was thankfully angled away from her eyes. A mask over her nose and mouth was linked to a nebuliser feeding her oxygen, but still the smell of strong disinfectant caught the back of her throat. Her mouth was dry and she instinctively sucked on her tongue and licked her lips for moisture. She was aware of a dull ache in the back of her neck, and down her body. Her elbow throbbed from her fall and the wound on her hand had turned red and prickly.

The nurse pulled back the curtain and a young doctor took her place. Swamped by a white coat miles too big, her dark hair was scraped back into a lank ponytail. Her eyes disappeared into two black rings above round girlish cheekbones that seemed out of place with the dark hollows above. She flicked through some notes attached to a clipboard as she walked towards the bed. Oonagh noticed her nails were bitten down to the quick.

'Do you smoke, Oonagh?'

'Thanks, but I don't think I'm allowed to, what with the oxygen and…' Oonagh pointed her index finger at the oxygen mask and, with an exaggerated comic gesture, shrugged her shoulders.

It was the wrong time for jokes. The Doctor was in no mood for one-liners and wore the stony expression she probably used for Friday night drunks.

Oonagh continued on a more serious note. 'Well yes, yes actually I do, but I think this attack was caused more by stress than fumes.'

'How many a day? Ten, twenty, more, less?' she continued, ignoring Oonagh's self-diagnosis.

Oonagh lay her head back onto the pillow and let out a low moan. She removed the mask from her face, confident in her ability to breathe again. 'Look, there was some madman in my house, the attack was panic-induced, nothing to do with cigarettes.'

Her voice had regained its strength and came out louder than intended. She swallowed hard. Her throat felt coarse and raspy. The doctor raised her eyebrows, and put her notes down on the bed.

'It's okay, I'm finding it hard to give up myself, but then *I* don't have chronic asthma.'

'About ten a day, sometimes more.'

'Well you know the score, I'm sure you don't need me to tell you how dangerous it is.' She told her anyway. 'You may not be so lucky the next time.'

'I don't feel very lucky *this* time!'

'Anyway, panic's over, for now. We've stabilised your breathing, and we're monitoring your airways. Your peek flow's on the up so I don't think there's too much to worry about.'

Oonagh rubbed the back of her neck. The ache continued.

'You'll feel a bit sore for a day or two, we had to stick a tube down your throat to help you breathe, getting lugged on and off a stretcher can also cause a bit of bruising, oh, and you probably pulled something when you fell.'

Oonagh thought the last part was probably added as an afterthought, in case of any legal comeback under the Patient's Charter.

'Now, the police want a word, you up to it?'

Oonagh nodded.

'In the meantime, is there anyone you want us to call?'

There was no one. She was in a city she'd lived in all her life, and there was no one. Most of her friends would be tucked in bed with a warm man by now. A phone call from the hospital would reduce her mum to a quivering wreck; Tom had enough on his plate; her PA, Gerry, was in Ibiza; and she could hardly call Jack.

The events of the past evening came flooding back to her and she realised she wouldn't be calling Jack again. The sudden loneliness overwhelmed her and she broke down. The doctor looked down at her feet, embarrassed, and drew a circle on the floor with the toe of her white clog before shuffling out of the cubicle, the racket of her heels clattering against the lino and bouncing off the stark walls as she left.

CHAPTER 20

Glasgow, 2000

'Did you actually *see* anyone in the house, Oonagh?'

She pressed the heel of her hands against her eyes and rubbed hard. The red prickly wound streaked black from her mascara.

'No.'

Her standard-issue paper robe rustled as she clasped her hands in front of her. The faint smell of alcohol, mixed with bile, lingered on her breath.

She licked her fingertips and tried to wipe the black grime from under her eyes. Perhaps this wasn't the best time to talk to the police. They sat by the side of her bed, good cop bad cop, or the Maryhill equivalent. Good Cop, Crap Cop?

She recognised Good Cop, but couldn't remember his name. They'd met briefly about a year ago, when she'd covered a story about a serial rapist who had terrorised women in the West End. The maniac had carried out a reign of terror for the best part of a decade, raping over twenty women in and around the University campus. There had been little to go on, and few clues: he always wore gloves and a condom and made his victims comb out their pubic hair afterwards. The Police had needed as much help from the press as possible and the investigation had made up a third of a three-part programme on the Scottish Crime series.

In the end he'd been caught after his girlfriend had recognised his photo-fit, which was plastered across every television screen and newspaper for miles. However, she hadn't turned him in right away, only when one of his victims had fought back and he'd arrived home one night with what looked like a love bite on his neck. She'd thought he was two timing her. Her motive for turning him in was jealousy and revenge. Pure and simple.

'There was no evidence of any forced entry and, well to be honest it doesn't look like anything's been disturbed.'

'How would you know!'

Crap Cop sat back, looking slightly miffed.

'Look, I told you, I got this weird, threatening phone call, and then someone messed about with my computer. The message on the screen said he was in the house.'

There was a six-inch gap where the orange curtain round her bed failed to meet the wall. A teenage boy lay on his side next door, pupils so enlarged that it was impossible to tell what colour his eyes were. His rotting teeth jutted out at random angles from his gums like a row of condemned houses. Oonagh stretched over to tug the curtain closed. It budged an inch then stuck.

Good Cop decided to have a go. 'How do you know it was a man, Oonagh? Did the message say it was a man?'

'Oh for God's sake stop splitting hairs! All I know is that someone was in my house, and whoever it was made sure I knew it.'

'What did they say in the phone call – did they threaten you at all?'

'No – not really, they were just a bit weird. I can't really remember what they said exactly,' she lied, 'just that it scared the shit out of me.'

'And you didn't recognise the voice on the phone?'

'No. It was disguised. One minute it sounded like a child, the other a man – but it was both the same person.'

'Probably just weans having a carry on. Gadgets can make your voice sound like Darth Vader or Betty Boop – they're ten a penny.'

She shook her head. 'But the message on the PC?'

'Is there anyone with a grudge against you?'

Crap Cop took over. 'Maybe it was a pal playing a practical joke.'

Both Oonagh and Good Cop gave him a look and he shut up again.

'We don't know yet that the two incidents were related. It's possible it was just a break-in. They probably came in during the evening while you were out, just left that message on your computer for a laugh...'

'Oh ha bloody ha.'

He continued. 'I know. It's far from funny! But some people do strange things for kicks'.

Oonagh stared at him. 'D'you mean to say someone expertly broke into my house leaving no trace, stole nothing, called me with a perverted, disgusting message, and *then* left a message on my computer screen just frighten me? Oh come off it!'

It was Crap Cop's moment of triumph. 'D'ye ever leave a back window open when you go out, Oonagh?'

'Well, yes sometimes, but I need to leave it open for the cat.' She knew it was a feeble excuse. Good Cop became Bored Cop and shared a knowing look with Crap Cop. Oonagh read it well.

'We'll do door-to-door inquiries tomorrow, check CCTV of the street to see if that sheds some light. I know it's horrible, but these break-ins are more common than you'd think.'

'Okay, so it was easy enough for them to break in. So why didn't they take anything then?'

'D'you know for definite nothing was taken?'

'Well, no not really, but...'

'You'll probably find a couple of bits n' pieces gone when you check. They don't take anything too big nowadays. Used to be videos, tellies n' stuff. Now it's just credit cards, cash, things like that.'

They got up too leave.

'We've arranged for a car to pick you up and drive you home. Doctor said you can get out in a few hours. If you want we can get a WPC to stay with you in the house for a wee while.'

'No thanks, I'll be fine with just the ride.'

'And we can arrange for you to speak to someone from Victim Support?'

Oonagh didn't answer him.

Crap Cop stood behind Bored Cop as he pulled back the curtain of the cubicle.

'You're lucky it was just a message they left you, most people are cleaning shite off the carpet for days after a break-in. It's amazing what these wee bastards get up to.' Then, in a final gesture towards community policing, he said, 'All the same, I'd buy myself a new toothbrush if I were you!'

CHAPTER 21

Glasgow, 1958

Irene Connolly pressed her forehead against the window. Darkness had already fallen, ice had formed on the inside of the glass and her breath steamed up the pane. Outside, Sally knelt on the ground and gently lowered a box into the hole. Irene looked at the mound of earth nearby that covered Patricia's coffin from the day before.

'If you're well enough to be up you'll be well enough to go back to work very shortly.' Sister Claire pushed the metal pail along the floor with her mop. It's clattering echoed around the bare walls, water splashed out onto the newly washed floor. Irene turned to get back into bed, oblivious to the trail of blood dripping down her leg onto the floor.

'Look what you've done,' the nun tutted as she dragged the mop over the mess.

Irene crouched down and pulled the sleeves of her thin cardigan over her hands. She spat on the floor and tried to wipe away the blood stains.

'Come on, Irene, get up pet.' Sister Claire gently ushered her back to bed and helped her change her sanitary dressings. Irene took the blood-soaked rags from her knickers and replaced them with the fresh ones Sister Claire had already folded for her. Pain gripped her abdomen and she wished she was lying peacefully next to her infant daughter.

Despite the cold, beads of sweat ran down her neck and her back. The ache between her legs intensified, moving up through her groin. From her fever she guessed she had contracted some sort of infection. Wasn't surprised really, given the conditions. She pulled the sheet up around her neck and began to cry. For the first time in years she longed for her father. Wished he was there to help.

She hadn't realised she'd fallen asleep until she felt someone jab her in the back. It was Sister Agatha.

'Sister Claire tells me you're up on your feet again.' She hovered over the bed like a black crow. Her hands now clasped in front. 'You'll be fine to get back to work tomorrow.' She noticed Irene's tears, which streamed down her face. 'Don't cry for your dead infant.' She gestured out to the yard with her thumb. 'That *thing* was nothing more than an abomination. It was God punishing you for the evil sin you committed. You should be thanking The Almighty it went so quickly.'

She blessed herself as she spoke. Irene told her she didn't care. Patricia was happy now, she was in Heaven. Sister Agatha told her she was wrong. Patricia wouldn't be in Heaven. God couldn't bear to even rest his eyes on Patricia as she hadn't been baptised. She hadn't been in a state of grace when she'd died, and therefore would have to spend all eternity in Limbo. At least until enough prayers and sufferings were offered up to the Blessed Virgin Mary. Then, and only then, might God in his mercy let Patricia into Heaven.

Sister Agatha seemed to think it all quite reasonable. Trading prayers for eternal glory. But Irene couldn't stomach any more.

'Fuck God, and fuck you!'

She heard the noise before she felt the pain. The nun's hand smacked hard across her face. It stung her cheek and unleashed a demon in Irene that had been building up for years.

'FUCKING JESUS! FUCKING GOD! FUCKING MARY MOTHER OF GOD! FUCK THEM ALL!'

Irene's hysterical screams could be heard through the building as the black nun struck her over and over and over again. But she continued to scream. Sister Agatha's top lip curled back to reveal her stubby yellow teeth, clenched together in anger. Globules of white spit gathered at the corners of her mouth. She grabbed Irene's hair, which had been cut close to her head, and dragged her through the dormitory and down the stairs. Her bare legs scraped across the stone steps and her feet struggled to find the ground, her heels danced on the floor as she desperately tried to remain upright. Sister Agatha only stopped when they reached the shower rooms.

Taking hold of Irene by the arms, she threw her against the tiled walls, and switched on the taps. Irene only stopped screaming when the ice-cold water hit her. Pierced her skin like a thousand tiny needles. It caught her breath and she gasped for air. She couldn't scream then. Her legs buckled from under her and she slid down the wall into the puddle that had formed at the drain. Her soaking night-dress clung to her body.

Sister Agatha picked up a fresh brick of pink carbolic soap. 'Wash out your mouth.'

Irene held the soap in both hands. Her eyes pleaded with the Sister of Mercy to switch off the water and stop the madness. But Sister Agatha was unmoved. 'Wash out your mouth,' she repeated.

Irene edged the pink bar towards her lips, scraped a corner off with her nails and began to wash.

'Properly.'

Irene scraped off more of the soap, braced herself and stuffed four fingers deep into her mouth, down her tongue. The foam slid down the back of her throat and the smell filled her nostrils. It made her gag. She felt the sickness rise from her belly. But there was nothing in her stomach to help the rising tide of vomit. Green bile gurgled up her throat and mixed with the soap suds before escaping from her mouth. She didn't have the energy to lean her head clear. The sickness oozed from her mouth and dribbled onto her chin, then down her chest.

Sister Agatha turned her head in disgust. She waited until the freezing water rinsed off the debris then turned off the taps.

Irene struggled to get to her feet. Her bruises were now beginning to show, and the skin on her legs was raw and bloody. Her body was blue from the cold.

Grabbing Irene by the wrist, Sister Agatha held her at arm's length to protect herself from the dripping water.

Despite her exhaustion, Irene fell into step beside her.

Sister Agatha stopped at the doors of the chapel and flung the girl inside. 'Take off your night shirt and lie on the floor.'

'Oh no. No more, please.' Exhausted, Irene pulled the wet, blood-stained garment up over her head and stood dripping wet and shivering in front of the altar, her thin arms trying to cover her exposed naked body, a statue of the Blessed Virgin and Christ the Saviour on either side.

'Lie down.' Sister Agatha's voice came out in shallow panting gasps as she licked beads of sweat from her top lip. 'I said, lie on the floor.'

Irene got down on her hands and knees before curling up fetally.

'Not like that. On your belly. Stretch your arms out in the shape of the cross.'

She let out a cry of pain as she eased her bruised and battered body onto the stone floor. Arching her back upwards, hoping her arms and legs would take most of the strain, trying to protect her tender weeping breasts and distended stomach.

Sister Agatha's heel dug into the small of her back. 'All the way down.'

Irene let out a groan as her knees and elbows gave way.

'Now, you will kiss the floor and beg Jesus for forgiveness.'

The last of the bile escaped from Irene's mouth as her lips pressed against the stone floor.

Sister Agatha called out of the door and someone came running.

'Sister Bernadette, watch her; make sure she stays here all

night. She must learn humility. She must learn obedience. We must help her become clean once more.'

'Oh but Sister Agatha, she'll freeze to death in here.'

A hand was held up to silence the young nun. 'It is not for us to question the will of God, Sister Bernadette.'

Sister Agatha walked out the door; the garments of the Sisters of Mercy flapping like wings behind her.

The freezing concrete burned into Irene's body. The stone floor pressed hard against her protruding hip bones and tore into her breasts. Her salty tears stung the cuts and scratches on her face.

Sister Bernadette knelt beside her. Irene could hear quiet, sympathetic sobs as the nun prayed, and could see rosary beads entwined in fingers.

Eventually Sister Bernadette lay down and tugged the edges of her black robe over Irene's naked body, in a futile attempt to give her a wee bit of warmth and comfort. She was too terrified to do anything more.

CHAPTER 22

Glasgow, 2000

Father Kennedy's naked body lay on a marble slab as it was ceremoniously cleansed by two nuns wearing protective plastic aprons and gloves. A priest stood by, ready to lift the single white linen square that covered his withered penis to allow the pair to clean underneath. Then they packed his mouth with cotton wool to fill out his sagging, emaciated cheeks, and stitched the insides of his lips closed before dressing him in a white cassock that had been cut up the back to save them pulling it over his head.

He had been dead for almost a week. By the time they finished with him, he would look better than he had done in years.

*

Oonagh stood under the shower and let the jets of hot water scald her until every last trace of hospital was washed away. It had been almost lunchtime by the time she'd got home. Both officers had insisted on coming inside with her, just to check everything was as it should have been. She'd got the impression this was as much for their benefit as for hers: to avoid any hysterical callouts later. The back window had been securely locked by their colleagues the previous night after it had been checked for finger prints. There were none, of course; wiped clean.

Her creased T-shirt and jeans lay in a heap on the bathroom floor.

Both had been grabbed out of the tumble drier in the kitchen by some well-meaning cop, to give her some dry clothes to wear home from the hospital.

By the time she turned off the shower her whole body glowed red and looked as though it had been polished. Her face was pink and flushed, with white goggle rings around her eyes; she looked as though she'd spent too long under a sun bed.

She wrapped a huge white towel around herself and rubbed her wet hair with a hand towel. In the bedroom everything was as it ought to have been.

She picked up the picture of her and Jack from the side of her bed. It was in an antique silver frame, her in a red evening dress, him wearing his tuxedo. It had been taken the night they had first got together. The *only* photograph of them as a couple.

As she put it back on the dressing table she saw it. A book of matches from The Rogano. She picked it up. Written on the inside was *'Missing you already, C!'* with two kisses underneath. She felt sick. That bastard Antonio. She'd known it wasn't some kid chancing his luck. *She*'d been the target for this job, not her house. This wee break-in had Charlie's name written all over it. Jesus, he'd probably been parked in his car as she'd run out into the street, hysterical, in her bare feet, screaming as she'd phoned the police. It was the sort of sick joke he would play.

Anger welled up inside at the thought of him creeping through her home, picking up the picture of her and Jack. Well, *that* secret was now well and truly out in the open. But that was the least of her worries at the minute. In fact, she couldn't care less.

She rested her elbows on her knees and dropped her head into her hands, furious that she hadn't recognised Charlie's handiwork the previous night. Then she ran downstairs to the kitchen and looked in her bin – the pregnancy kit was gone. The wee shite had obviously just put two and two together and chanced his arm with that phone call, and like a fool she'd fallen straight into his trap.

She decided against telling the police. The book of matches proved nothing except that he was a twisted wee shite. If asked, he could say he'd slipped them into her bag when they'd bumped into each other the previous day. And then she'd have to go into details about meeting him and their chat about Tom, and that would open a whole can of worms she could do without right now. She could handle this one on her own.

Back upstairs she fumbled through her bag, pulled out a diary and flicked to the back page, running her fingers down a list of numbers. She picked up the phone and dialled. A woman answered.

'*5182*'

'Oh hello, can I speak to Charlie please?'

'I'm afraid he's not home at the moment. Can I take a message?'

'Yes, just tell him The Stupid Bitch called,' she screamed, before slamming down the receiver. The sound of the key in the lock made her jump.

'Zat you in, Oonagh?' The voice bellowed up the stairs and Oonagh's heart sank even further. She had completely forgotten about Susan. Wednesday was her day. Usually Oonagh kept well out of the way to let her get on with things. She'd known her half her life – she'd cleaned her mum's house since forever – and when Oonagh had moved out she'd just sort of followed her.

Oonagh leaned over the banister. She was in no mood and needed a couple of hours to herself. 'Susie, shit, sorry to muck you about, is there any chance you can come back tomorrow?'

'Naw ah bloody cannae come back the morra,' she yelled, 'ah've got an appointment wae a psychic. She wiz in the Sunday Mail last week and now there's a six-month waiting list.'

'Well, what about later this afternoon – in a couple of hours say? About three-ish? I'll pay you from just now.'

She weighed up her options. 'Aye, well I suppose,' she muttered, going back out the door.

Oonagh went downstairs to her office. She still had a few things to tidy up with her script and wanted to get it out of the way. It was the first time she'd been in the box room since the previous night and the screen saver that had scared her senseless in the dark now rolled by like a bad joke.

She scooped up the photographs that lay scattered on the floor and tidied them into a box file alongside a large bundle of press clippings of Father Kennedy. She fingered them absently. There was a particularly dull one from a free newspaper of him outside Saint Patrick's with local school kids during some fund raising event, but most of them were of him leading groups of demonstrators protesting outside abortion clinics across Scotland. They even had their own minibus for the trips. Oonagh pictured them making tea and sandwiches for their big days out.

She'd almost closed the box when something caught her eye and made her heart skip a beat.

She called Tom first, then made a further two calls before getting dressed.

CHAPTER 23

Glasgow, 1958

Dawn broke, forcing the blinding winter sunshine through the stained glass window. The colours danced on Irene Connolly's red-raw eyelids. She squeezed them shut even tighter, and a low moan escaped from her mouth.

At first she thought she was back in her own home. In her own bed. Then the pounding ache in her temples spread throughout her body, spinning its web through her muscles, her bones, through every joint. And she was cold. She tried to move but couldn't. Thick crusts sealed her eyes and she felt wet and sticky between her legs.

She was aware of footsteps running on the stone floor. They stopped at her head.

'Blessed God, Sister Agatha, I think she's dead.'

She felt someone take her pulse, fingers on the side of her neck.

'Stop being so melodramatic. Get someone to help you carry her back to bed.'

The first voice was hysterical, breathless, panting. 'But look at her…her…her y'know…between her legs, she's bleeding.'

'Just get her up to bed. And get her cleaned up. The doctor's coming today. He'll take a look at her.'

They covered her naked body in a sheet before taking her back upstairs, someone at her shoulders, another at her feet and a third in the middle.

Pain shot through her as they peeled her off the ground. Her hip bones dug into the floor, her ribs felt black and blue from the pressure.

They swung her between them through the long empty corridor and up the stairs. She was aware of letting out another long moan as they dropped her onto the bed.

★

Irene woke with someone standing over her. A dark shadow of a man. The light behind him was creating a halo around his entire body. He was silent as he pulled back the covers.

Not again. She instinctively reached to his groin, just wanting the whole thing over with quickly.

The Nun slapped Irene's hands away. 'We found her in the chapel this morning, Doctor. Naked! She'd been there all night.'

She tried to speak. 'I…'

'Quiet girl!'

Irene was aware of the nun rocking back and forth.

'Obviously suffering from some form of sexual hysteria,' she heard the Doctor say. 'I can't examine her like this. Tie her hands down please.' The doctor stood back. 'And her feet too,' he added.

She was aware of her hands and feet being bound to the four corners of the bed, but had no energy with which to resist.

The examination didn't take long, nor did it take the doctor long to reach his conclusions. Self-inflicted pneumonia from spending the night naked on the floor of the freezing chapel. Superficial wounds, again self-inflicted and apparently very common in young women with a history of mental illness and sexual deviancy.

'I'm not surprised, you know,' Sister Agatha said. 'I've seen it all before, many times.'

Then the doctor's cold, rough hands pushed her night-dress up around her waist and Irene screamed uncontrollably at the pain as he explored the cause of her bleeding.

He pressed down hard on her belly with one hand, while his fingers probed the inside of her pelvis.

'When was her baby born?'

'Three days ago, Doctor.'

'And...?'

'Defective,' Sister Agatha whispered.

'Well, there's nothing too much wrong. Not physically anyway. Keep her in bed – tied down if you have to – for the next few days, until her temperature comes down.'

Irene's head swam and the voices merged into one. She was sure her eyes were rolling in her head. The fever circled over at her like an unwelcome, engulfing physical presence.

★

She was back in her own bed, at home. Being shaken, told to wake up. But it wasn't light yet, wasn't time for school. The curtains were drawn. The room was in darkness. Her big sister, Patricia, was perched on the edge of the bed, fully dressed. Her coat was buttoned up and tied at the waist with a belt. Her thick, dark wavy hair was pushed up under a felt beret. Irene wiped the sleep from her eyes, drowsy and confused.

'Irene, I have to go now.' A package wrapped in brown paper was at Patricia's feet.

'Where? Where are you going?' Irene cried, panic creeping into her voice.

'Shh, shh, you'll wake up Mum and Dad. I'm going away, Irene. I need to go tonight.' She put her arms around her wee sister's shoulders and squeezed her tight.

Irene struggled to understand. 'Is it Dad? Is it 'cause you keep fighting?'

Patricia nodded her head, tears springing to her eyes. 'Irene, I have to go. I have to go far away from here. I'm sorry, but I can't stay here. Pray to God you'll be safe.' Patricia kissed her, pressing her warm lips into her cheek, nuzzling her neck. 'God bless, little one.'

Irene's sob hiccupped in the back of her throat. 'Will you come back, Tricia? Promise you'll come back.' She grabbed at her sister's navy gabardine overcoat.

'I'll come back and get you, Darling. I promise.'

Irene felt the backs of her knuckles being kissed, and then her sister was running from the room.

Irene lay her head back on her pillow.

When she awoke the next morning she assumed the whole thing had been a dream, but when she came down the stairs and saw the red rims round her mum's eyes – and the tightness of her father's lips – she realised something was seriously wrong.

★

Galway Times

The body of a young woman has been recovered from the River Liffey in Dublin. Gardai Officers say they are not treating her death as suspicious but are keen to trace her relatives. The woman is described as being between the ages of 14 and 17 years, 5'5" in height with long dark brown hair and wearing a navy raincoat. Following a Post Mortem examination, doctors have confirmed she was approximately 3 months pregnant.

CHAPTER 24

Glasgow, 2000

Her face was pressed hard against the wooden floorboards.

Her right arm was wedged underneath her body and her head throbbed. A blinding white light danced behind her eyes. Twisting even a fraction sent pain shooting down her right shoulder all the way to her hip. She couldn't see much.

Cat sniffed around and nuzzled her face. His presence was initially reassuring until Oonagh realised he was lapping up a sticky mess pooled on the floor beside her head. She felt sick.

'Jeesus Christ, Oonagh. What happened?' She heard Tom run toward her and felt him shoo Cat away from her head. She managed to open her eyes just a fraction. From the plugs and cables and skirting board she realised she was lying at the bottom of the stairs.

She tried to answer him, but her tongue was thick and the effort made her head spin. She wanted to gag.

'Hang on, Oonagh. I'll get help.'

Her mouth tasted of metal.

'Tom, am I dying?' she managed to whisper.

'Don't be daft.'

'Give me the Last Rites.'

'Oonagh, stop it. It's more important we get you some help.' She detected rising panic in his voice.

'Please…' She clutched at his jacket. 'It's…it's…important.' She heard her own voice crackle. Tom bent his ear to her mouth. 'It's not a bad gig,' she whispered, 'getting me back into the fold.'

She felt him make the sign of the cross on her forehead, then press a paper tissue hard against her neck.

Tom's voice came out in gulps and sobs as he began his ritual, but she couldn't hear him. All she could hear was her dad…

'Honest tae God, Oonagh, it's true.'

'Oh come on, Dad, a leprechaun. Come off it.' But this was one story he never backed down on, one he'd stuck to all his life.

He was just ten years old, and had been queuing in Phoenix Park for hours to see it, a newly-washed jam jar under his arm and his threadbare jumper tied round his waist. There was no hint of the scar on his chin from the tram accident. That was at least two years off.

The leprechaun had been captured by some fella in Dublin, who'd kept it in a box.

The word was out and it was turning into an event of biblical proportions, with a huge trail of people willing to pay for a single glimpse of the little man. People had travelled for miles to witness the star attraction.

He would stand for days if he had to. The only thing that mattered was in that tent. The dark grubby blankets – thrown over a rope supported at either end by a tall pole buried into the ground – had become for him a mystical tent from the Far East, made from colours he'd seen only in the sky after a storm.

'Don't look into his eyes, they'll burn right thro' ye for sure,' came the advice of his chum. 'I hear he's over a thousand years old, with a crock of gold worth over a hundred pounds.'

'A hundred pounds? Sure we could live like kings for the rest of our lives on that.'

The chattering was non-stop. But for the ten year old boy with the jam jar, nothing mattered except seeing the living proof of everything he held sacred and holy.

At last their time came. In they went. Two at a time: her dad and his pal.

Oonagh stood behind them unseen, excitement building in her chest. All her life she'd secretly wished she'd been with him on that day, to see what he'd seen. To know for sure whether what he said *was true.*

It was pitch black at first. Their eyes took a few seconds to adjust and take in the surroundings.

Two men were inside with them. One seated on a wooden chair, the other standing by a box on top of a table, with a curtain draped over the top.

'Gee's yer money,' said the one on the chair. Oonagh's dad handed over his jam jar in payment, while his pal placed a farthing into the man's palm. 'Right,' the seated man nodded to his partner in crime.

The curtain was pulled back. And there it was.

In the box sat a little man, over a thousand years old, his grey wrinkled skin storing a millennium of knowledge and secrets. The two boys stared in wonder, mouths gaping at the sight. It was still as dark as night in the tent, but they could see him as clear as day. The leprechaun was right there in front of them.

'Janie-mac, can yis see it, can yis?' Oongah's dad didn't answer his chum. His eyes were wide as saucers. He gulped and nodded, rendered speechless by the sight.

Oonagh looked over his shoulder. There, slumped against the back of the box, was a tiny capuchin monkey dressed in a green knitted waistcoat and trousers. On its head was a hat made from an old sock. Its grey skin shone through where its fur had been attacked by mange. Yellow matter wept from its half-shut eyes, sores all over its body. Its little five-fingered hand reached up to wipe the sticky tears from its eyes before smoothing over its head like a weary old man. Its lips were parched dry and cracked.

The story would change in detail now and again. Sometimes the admission price to see this phenomenon would be a ha'penny, sometimes a farthing, occasionally it was merely the jam jar, but her Dad never faltered in his conviction that a leprechaun had been captured in Dublin, and he'd been one of the few people in the entire world privileged to see it.

A lump grew in her throat. All these years, and it had been a monkey. A bloody monkey.

She was back across the table from her dad, the bottle of brandy between them.

'Honest tae God, Oonagh, I saw it with my own eyes.'

This time, instead of laughing, she reached across and stroked his hair.

'I know you did, Da, I know you did.'

★

The front door banged against the wall as it was flung open.

Oonagh felt Tom's grip loosen and her eyes close.

'What the hell's goin' on here?' A woman was running into the hall, then screaming. That wasn't a good sign.

'Oh God, Oonagh, what the hell's happened. What've you done, pet?'

'I just found her like this.' It was Tom. 'I've called an ambulance. It'll be here any minute.'

Oonagh felt Susan's hand on her, warmer but rougher. Something more substantial than a tissue was pressed against her neck.

'She hates wet paper,' Susan snapped at Tom. 'For Christ's sake, where's they paramedics?'

'They'll be here soon, don't worry.'

Something soft was placed beneath her head.

She could hear her own breathing.

'What happened?' Susan was asking. 'Did she fall or something?'

'I don't think so. I just came in and found her like this, I think she's been stabbed.'

'Stabbed!'

No! Stabbing happened in street-brawls…

'And from what I can see she's got a gash on the back of her head too. Maybe she banged it off the stairs as she fell,' added

Tom.

'Stay with us, Oonagh.'

Tom was rubbing her hand, stroking her hair. As long as she could feel him touching her she would be okay.

'Could you no pray or something, is that no whit your mob's good at?'

'Sorry,' asked Tom, 'are you a friend of Oonagh's?

Sirens blared outside. Comforting amid the mayhem.

More shoes. A faint green blur. She hoped to God it was the Paramedics and not just a visit from the Celtic Supporters Club.

'Right, let's see what we've got here. What's happened, what's her name?'

She tried to speak. Nothing came out.

'Oonagh. It's Oonagh,' said Tom, 'I don't know what happened, I just found her like this.'

'Don't worry, we'll take it from here.'

★

The emergency team had all the information required: female, mid thirties, stab wounds and possible head trauma. But in the ninety seconds it took for the ambulance to drive the quarter mile to the Western Infirmary, Oonagh O'Neil had a spontaneous abortion and haemorrhaged.

CHAPTER 25

Glasgow, 2000

The interview room measured no more than eight feet by eight feet. It had no windows and stank of stale coffee. Brown splashes stained the walls, next to burn marks left by countless cigarettes over the years.

Tom examined the table in front of him and tried to read some of the graffiti gouged into the dark dirty wood.

Eventually the door opened and Davies walked in with a tape recorder under his arm. Tom thought he looked shattered as well as dishevelled. As he approached, he could see his eyes were red.

Davies was followed by a uniformed policewoman carrying a cardboard tray with three steaming polystyrene cups. 'Coffee?'

'Ehm, do you have any tea?'

She rolled her eyes, tutted and let out an exaggerated sigh as she made her way back to the door.

'Sorry...' Tom muttered.

She carried on walking without turning.

'A wee word, Father.' Davies pulled out a chair, swung it round and straddled it.

'I didn't realise this was your division?' said Tom. As though it was any of his business.

'Don't tell me where I can and can't work! A friend of mine gets butchered in her own home, you're found crouching over her like a creeping Jesus, and you're telling me it's not my division!'

Tom interrupted him. 'I didn't know Oonagh was your friend.'

Like his coffee-carrying colleague, Davies ignored him.

'Folk around you are dropping like flies. First Father

Kennedy, now...' – his voice faltered – 'now Oonagh. So of course it's my bloody business.'

At that moment the policewoman walked back in with the tea, and placed the cup down on the table in front of him. 'Milk, two sugars,' she said, daring Tom to argue.

He didn't. Tom hated sweet tea, but nodded his head. And he was grateful for her interruption, however grumpy. He'd been about to cry, he knew it.

Davies knew it too. 'For crying out loud, pull yerself together.'

Tom scalded his lips trying to sip the tea. ·

'Now on top of all this, ah've just found out you were hauled intae Maryhill polis station six months ago for hawkin' yer mutton in Kelvin Way! You're in the shit, Father, right up to yer rosary beads. So how about ye dry yer eyes and tell me what the fuck's going on.'

Davies pressed down two buttons on the tape recorder and the machine whirred into action. He stated the date and time for the record, said his own name and that of the policewoman, who had remained in the room. It was only when he said 'Father Thomas Findlay' that the penny dropped.

'Hang on, am I under arrest? What's going on here?'

'Father, put yer Catholic guilt to to one side just for a few minutes. You're just helping us with inquiries, okay.'

Tom felt anything but okay. 'Should I be contacting a lawyer?'

'Do you feel you need a lawyer?' Even sitting down Davies towered above him. 'Look this is just an interview, if you feel the need to call your brief, then...'

'No, no, I'll co-operate any way I can.' He meant to sound helpful, but his voice came out in a pathetic, desperate whine.

'Right, Father, do you want to tell us why you went to Oonagh O'Neil's house this afternoon?'

Tom got the distinct impression this wasn't a question, more of an order. 'Has there been any word from the hospital yet?

How is she? Please, I need to know.'

Davies relented. 'They're still working on her – as far I know. She's in surgery, that's all they'll tell me for now. Now, why were you in her house this afternoon?'

'Well, she called me and asked me to come and see her.'

'Why?'

'She wanted to talk to me about something.'

Davies breathed in heavily through his nose, his hand rubbed over the stubble on his chin. '*What* did she want to talk about?' His voice was slow and deliberate.

'Well, it's a bit delicate actually.'

Davies stood up, leaned both palms on the table and held his face just inches away from Tom's. 'Delicate? I'll give you delicate.' A pin prick of saliva shot from Davies' mouth and landed on Tom's cheek. Tom decided not to wipe it away.

Davies was struggling not to yell. Tom was suddenly glad of the machine recording their every word.

'Wise up, Findlay, this won't go away. It's not some doddery old priest who mixed up his medicine bottles. This won't be swept under the carpet so easily. Oonagh O'Neil was attacked in her own home, in broad daylight. As soon as she's fit she'll tell us who did it. At best we're looking at an attempted murder charge. Now, I think you know more than you're letting on, so unless you want me to arrest you for obstructing the course of justice I suggest you be a bit more helpful. And don't forget, a charge sheet for indecent behaviour with your name on it could still find its way into a pile of paperwork at Maryhill police station.'

'I swear it wasn't me.'

'Why did you delay calling the ambulance?'

'It was only a few seconds. I couldn't get a signal. And, well… well she wanted the Last Rites.'

'Am I meant to keep a straight face when you're talking shite? Do you honestly expect me to believe a woman like Oonagh

O'Neil would want the Last Rites?'

'You'd be surprised what people do when they think they're dying. A lot turn to God in their final hours, you know.'

'Well, fat lot of good it does, eh?'

'You don't know that, not for sure.'

Davies refused to be drawn any further on this and sat back down.

'I didn't attack her,' Tom said. 'I never touched her, I swear to God.'

'No, you probably didn't.'

Tom looked at him, confused.

'No weapon,' Davies said.

'Eh?'

'We didn't find a weapon on you, or in the house for that matter. Anyway, from what the cleaner said, it's unlikely Oonagh would have been as calm as she was with you if you'd just plunged a bloody great big blade into her neck. Look, didn't she say anything, give you any clues as to who did this to her?'

'I told you before, she was slipping in and out of consciousness... She wasn't really making sense.'

Tom slumped back in his chair. He bit his bottom lip hard, but it wasn't enough to stem the tears from rolling down his cheeks. Not that they had any effect on Davies.

'She was pregnant,' said Tom, more to break the silence than anything else. It was bound to come out sooner or later anyway, so what the hell. 'She'd planned to have an abortion, but called me this afternoon to say she'd changed her mind.'

'You know this is easily checked?'

Tom nodded.

Davies opened the door and had a few brief words with the officer in the corridor.

'Who was the father?' he asked a moment later.

'Don't know.' Tom shrugged his shoulders.

Davies immediately lost what little patience he had. 'From the sounds of it you two were fairly cosy. Wasn't you by any chance?'

'Don't be so bloody stupid, I'm a priest.'

Davies raised his eyebrows in mock surprise and a snigger escaped from his nose.

'And gay. Obviously,' added Tom. 'All I know is his first name: Jack. That's all she told me. Oh, and he's married. Look, she went to meet him yesterday in the Rogano, I dropped her off. You can check if you don't believe me.'

'Interview terminated seventeen twenty-seven.' Davies switched off the machine and turned to his female colleague, who had remained silent throughout. 'Get someone down to the Rogano. Find out what time she arrived, who she was with, the usual, and tell McVeigh to get his butt over to my office ASAP.'

Davies returned his attention to Tom. 'Right, we'll need to speak to you later, so don't go joining any strange cults in faraway places, or taking a vow of silence or nothing. You're not off the hook yet, ye' know.'

CHAPTER 26

Glasgow, 2000

Tom grabbed a taxi on Maryhill Road. He was almost at the chapel house when he remembered his car was parked outside Oonagh's and had to ask the driver to double back to the West End. It was dark by the time they got there, but the media were out in force. Photographers, reporters, television crews. Tom suddenly realised this really was headline news.

He took his dog-collar off before getting out of the cab and opened the top two buttons on his shirt. Priests always attracted more attention than he could be bothered with right now.

The police cordon was still round her house, but his car was parked just outside the boundary. A ticket was stuck on the windscreen. He swiped it off as he opened the door and got just a faint look of interest from the uniformed officer outside, but he soon recognised Tom and nodded him permission to drive off.

He drove back to the South Side in a state of shock. He'd been warned by Davies not to go anywhere near the hospital, but hunger for news on Oonagh gnawed at his stomach. He couldn't take it all in and began to suspect Davies was right. He was involved in something, up to his neck in it. The only trouble was he didn't know what. He was too close to see what was happening, as if in the eye of a storm. Like Davies, he didn't believe in coincidences.

He stopped at the off licence on the way home and selected a bottle of dry white from the chiller cabinet. There was probably some already back at the chapel house, but he decided there would be less risk of bumping into Mrs Brady if he bypassed the kitchen and went straight to his room.

He turned into the tree-lined avenue just in time to catch Charlie Antonio walking quickly away from the house. There was no sign of his car, he must have parked it in the next street. Tom's heart sank. What did he want now?

Antonio disappeared round the corner, and once Tom felt sure he was out of sight, he drove into the driveway and parked at the rear of the house. He let himself in through the back door, ignoring the red flashing light on the answering machine. He dragged himself up stairs, staying as quiet as possible. The curate was next door, in Father Kennedy's old room; Tom couldn't be bothered with any words of comfort or kindness. And he couldn't face the following day's preparations for Father Kennedy's funeral; he'd take a back seat and let the Curate take control. The whole thing was a mess.

★

It was already evening when they arrived at Kendall Hall. Yes, the nurse confirmed, Oonagh had been booked in as a day patient on Tuesday, and no, it was no trouble to give them Dr Cranworth's home address. She didn't seem to have much loyalty to her employer, and McVeigh wondered if she'd fallen for his charms once too often and this was payback time.

They drove towards Pollokshields. The only time their police colleagues were called to Hamilton Avenue was to investigate a break-in, or to answer a call about a suspected prowler in the grounds of one of the mansions.

They parked outside the gates and walked up the driveway. Even by Kendall Hall standards this place was pretty impressive. Security lights sprang into action with every footstep up the long gravel drive. The house itself was well lit, and as they neared the door they could see Cranworth through the window. This wasn't the land of the net curtain.

The door was opened by a woman clinging onto her forties for all she was worth. Despite it being Glasgow, despite it nearing winter, despite her relaxing in her own home, she was wearing a cream wool suit, edged with navy blue trim. Cream glossy tights failed to give her stick-thin legs any shape.

She balanced on four-inch spikes that disappeared into the plush carpet. Her blonde candyfloss bob had been relentlessly teased to form a massive globe around her head, far too big for her tall-but-emaciated frame.

'We're looking to speak to Dr Cranworth,' said Davies, holding out his I.D badge.

'I'm Dr Cranworth,' she said. 'Is there a problem?' She held onto the edge of the door. Her long painted nails clawed their way round the frame.

'I think it's your husband we're looking for Mrs, er, Dr Cranworth.' He'd been tempted to pretend it was her son they were after, just to piss her off, but he'd thought better of it. Her nails looked lethal. 'Can we come in?' His foot was already on the hall carpet.

'What's this about, please?'

'If we could just have a quick word.'

They followed her until she opened a door to a room where Cranworth was sitting. He turned round with a confused look. It was hard to tell if he'd genuinely forgotten who he and McVeigh were or whether he was making an elaborate gesture in front of his wife.

'It's the police, Dah-ling, they want to speak to you.' His wife stood by the door, obviously waiting for some sort of an explanation.

'The Police? Oh right.' The penny dropped. So he *had* seen them before. He looked at his wife's puzzled expression.

'We had a bit of trouble at the clinic, nothing serious, just a break-in. Can you leave us alone for a few minutes, eh?'

She obeyed and left the room, her shocked expression unchanged. Davies realised the high arch of her brows owed more to a surgeon's knife than the surprise visit from Strathclyde's finest.

'What the hell do you mean coming to my home?' Cranworth demanded once the door was closed.

Davies sat down, unfazed, while McVeigh stood by the door. Cranworth had none of the air of control he'd displayed at their earlier meeting. His face was flushed and his short grey hair was clinging to his head. There were beads of sweat round his forehead and two dark patches under the arms of his shirt. Even from across the room Davies could smell the sour odour of whiskey from his breath.

'I don't remember inviting you to sit down.'

'You didn't!' Davies retorted.

'What do you want? What's this about?'

'Oonagh O'Neil.'

Cranworth looked genuinely shocked. He glanced at the door to make sure his wife had closed it properly. 'Eh?'

'Oonagh O'Neil. You must know her, she's booked into your clinic next Tuesday.'

'I can't discuss that with *you*. Have you never heard of patient confidentiality?'

'Look, you trumped-up little arse hole. Thirty years ago you'd be plying your trade up a back-close with a knitting needle. So don't come the high and bloody mighty with me. Answer the fucking question…or do you want me to speak to your wife?'

Cranworth, shocked by the outburst, checked the door again, as if looking at it would reveal if his wife had heard anything. He ran his fingers though his hair, then brought his hand down and ran his palm over the stubble on his chin, partially covering his mouth with his fingers. He spoke quietly to encourage Davies to follow suit.

'What have you come here for? What's going on?'

'How well do you know Oonagh O'Neil? Are you having an affair with her?'

'No I'm bloody not! What the hell are you talking about?'

Davies gestured to McVeigh, who handed over a copy of the photograph that he had found in Oonagh's bedroom. Davies threw it down in front of Cranworth.

'Not exactly standard practise to carry out an abortion on your lover is it? What kind of butcher are you to abort your own baby?'

'Is that what this is about? Has she made a complaint? Some malpractice suit?' He shook his head. 'If this picture is the only evidence you've got of an affair, then I'm afraid you'll need to do better than that.'

Davies looked down at the picture. 'It's a very good likeness. The waiter recognised you right away. Pair of you are regular customers by all accounts. Said you were together last night, arguing, going at it hammer and tongs. She threw a bottle of wine over you. Does your wife know about that?'

'So what, not exactly a police matter, eh Taggart?'

Cranworth raised his whiskey glass to his mouth, but Davies leaned across and stopped him before it reached his lips, his voice soft but deliberate. 'Oonagh O'Neil was attacked this afternoon. Someone tried to kill her. Damn near succeeded and all. Now that, *buster,* is a police matter. Right!'

Jack Cranworth slumped back in his chair, the colour draining slowly from his face.

Davies took the glass from his hand and placed it on the table. 'Now, it seems you two had quite a bust-up. What happened? Did she threaten to tell your wife about your wee set-up? I also hear she refused to go through with the abortion. Don't imagine that would go down too well with the missus either.'

The beads of sweat were now running down Cranworth's forehead. He took off his glasses and rubbed his eyes with the heel of his hand. 'This isn't what you think. That picture means nothing. She's very highly strung you know. Probably a bit infatuated with me if truth be told.' He attempted a smile. 'The

145

baby's not mine. She came to me for help, and of course I tried to do what I could, but…'

Davies felt sick. 'Jesus Christ, you really are the lowest of the low. We know it was your baby. We know you were having an affair. She told her bloody priest for God's sake.'

'Her Priest? Oonagh would never confide in a priest. She isn't even a practising Catholic.'

'You obviously know her pretty well then, eh?' He took no pleasure in catching out Cranworth. 'That poor girl is lying in hospital with more tubes coming out of her than Ibrox Park. Her poor Mother near enough lost the plot when she was told. Had to be sedated.' Davies knew this to be true because he was the one who'd had to break the news to her that someone had tried to kill her daughter.

His anger rose as he looked at Cranworth. 'Can't you do the decent thing for once in your life and just admit you were having an affair, instead of making out she was some sort of bunny boiler? At least admit it was your wean? Makes no difference now anyway – she's lost it.'

Davies thought he detected a slight look of relief flush across Cranworth's face.

'I really don't know what you're talking about,' Cranworth said. 'I mean I'm sorry and all that, of course I am, but I can't help you. I don't know anything.'

Davies wasn't convinced.

Cranworth scrambled to dig himself out of his hole. 'How is she? Which hospital is she in? Is there…'

'…anything you can do? No thanks, you've done enough. Oh, and by the way, attempting to go and see Miss O'Neil would not be one of your better ideas. Stay away, ok?'

The sweat was now clearly visible on Cranworth's top lip.

McVeigh chipped in. 'Where were you this afternoon?'

'The clinic, then I played golf.'

'I suppose you can prove that, can you?'

'Look, I refuse to carry on with this until I see my lawyer,' Cranworth blurted out.

'Well, you'd better give him a ring then, 'cause I'm like a bad smell, Cranworth: I refuse to go away. I think it's best if we carry on our wee chat down at the station.'

'The station? What…what'll I tell my wife?'

'You can go tell her to whistle Dixie for all I care, now get moving, *Crippen*!'

CHAPTER 27

Glasgow, 2000

Slowly Oonagh came to. She felt like she'd downed a full bottle of gin before being kicked up and down Sauchiehall Street. The sedation was wearing off. She felt nervy and insecure, with that jittery feeling of not quite being able to remember what had gone wrong. Her head throbbed. A thick square of bandage was taped across the wound on the left side of her neck. On her right shoulder was a black horseshoe-shaped bruise. Plastic tubes fed in and out of the back of her hands, and the clear bag by the side of her bed dripped with amber liquid from the catheter that snaked from under her sheets. She knew she'd be sick if she looked at where it was coming from.

At least she was in a room on her own, and for that she was grateful. It was white and sterile, with a massive square window looking onto the corridor. Her hands strayed down to her belly. It felt empty, but she wasn't sure. A doctor eased his way into the room.

'Hi, Oonagh, you're getting to be one of our regulars.' He looked at his notes, smiling,

'Must be drawn to the smell of cabbage.'

He sat on the bed beside her. 'Do you remember much of what happened?'

She clawed through her mind, trying to piece together what led her to this, but all she remembered was the cat licking at her neck and Tom yelling at her.

'You were attacked, Oonagh. Do remember being attacked?'

She tried to shake her head but didn't have the energy. She was lonely, miserable and wanted to be in her own bed.

'Well,' he continued. 'That's no surprise, you took quite a knock to your head. Probably banged it off the stairs as you fell. You might remember more as the days pass. We've stitched up the wound on your neck. It's a typical puncture wound, so we had to give you some internal stitches as well. But they'll dissolve. To be honest, it was a close thing. Just millimetres from the carotid artery. You were very lucky you know.'

'And?' She knew he was gearing up for the big one.

He gave her a slight nod. 'We had to do an emergency D&C.'

She stared at him until he continued speaking.

'You were haemorrhaging quite badly, Oonagh, I'm afraid you lost the baby.' He patted her thigh through the single sheet and blanket, to make it all better. It didn't.

She said thanks anyway and felt embarrassed for him.

'When can I go home?'

He seemed relieved to be changing the subject. 'Stay here today, then there's no reason why you can't go home tomorrow. As long as you've got someone there to keep an eye on you.'

'In case I get attacked again?' She affected a laugh and thought if she pretended to be happy she might even fool herself into believing she was.

'Now, there's someone here to see you. You up for it?'

She looked out and was glad to see Alec Davies in the corridor. 'Yeah,' she said.

The doctor's pager bleeped and he departed for some other poor victim who needed his attention. By the time Davies entered the room a nurse was already on her knees changing the bag from her catheter.

'The doctor said it was okay for me to come in,' Davies said. 'As long as you're not squeamish.'

The nurse paused until Oonagh nodded that it was okay for Davies to stay, then she continued with the task in hand, hooking up a clean bag to the unit, and leaving with Oonagh's pee – and dignity – tucked under her arm.

'If you tell anyone about this I'll have to kill you,' she said, groaning as she let her head rest back onto the pillow.

Alec sat down on a chair beside the bed, trying not to laugh. 'Ach, I've seen worse in the mirror. Anyway, how're you feeling?'

'Don't ask,' she said, looking down at the paraphernalia of tubes poking out at every angle. 'Fair to hellish.'

'Your mum's downstairs getting some fresh air. Shall I go fetch her?'

'Just give me a minute. I hate the thought of her seeing me like this.'

Alec nodded. 'Oonagh, we need to get to the bottom of this. Can't you remember *anything* of what happened?'

She shook her head. Again.

'I questioned Cranworth earlier.'

She stared at him, astonished. 'It wasn't him!'

Alec told her about the meeting. About what Jack had said. She stroked her belly. 'I lost the baby, Alec.'

'I know, Oonagh. I'm sorry.' She thought he seemed genuinely moved. Then his face hardened. 'Cranworth denied it was his. Suggested you were maybe a bit infatuated with him. Tried to paint you as a bunny boiler.'

'Bastard!' Her wounded pride caused an aching lump in her throat that hurt far more than the bruises and stitches. 'Still, Alec, I don't think Jack would have hurt me. I mean, not like this. We did have a row last night…' That was the only thing that was clear in her head.

'And you didn't see him after that?'

'No. I don't think so.'

'We're trying to see if there's a connection with the break-in at your place the night before. Who did you see in The Rogano before hooking up with Cranworth?'

But once again the mist came down. 'Look Alec, it's not that I don't want to help, it's just…' She rubbed her eyes and felt useless and pathetic. 'My head's all over the place just now. I don't know what the hell they've given me – but by Christ I want some to take home!'

He laughed. 'You're probably still be a bit groggy from the anaesthetic.' Then he looked serious. 'Whoever attacked you was a vicious bastard. That bruise on your shoulder, that's from his heel. He stood on top of you while he pulled the blade from your neck.'

Oonagh strained her head to look.

'Oh God, Alec, I'm scared. Why would anyone want to kill me?' She tried to stop herself from welling up once more. 'My jokes can't be that bad!' She laughed and then burst into tears.

Alec leaned across and drew her close. She buried her face in his chest. Suddenly the severity of the situation hit home and she was terrified.

'Listen, you need your sleep.' He laid her head back on the pillow. 'Try and rest and we'll talk properly tomorrow. Doctor says you can go home then.'

She sniffed and dragged her nose across the back of her hand, wincing as she tugged the needle holding the drip in place.

'Just one thing, Alec: when you speak to my Mum, don't tell her that I was pregnant. She'd go to pieces.'

'Course not.'

★

Outside in the corridor, McVeigh ran towards him and thrust a steaming cup in his direction. 'Here. I got you a wee hot chocolate. Oh,' he fished in his pocket, 'and I've got that name from the Rogano.' He handed it to Davies. 'How's she doing? Want to run that name past her, see if she remembers?'

'Naw, come on. Leave her, she's dead beat.'

★

Charlie peeped through the slit in the curtains. Davies and McVeigh stood outside on the doorstep below. Davies was well protected in a padded navy blue anorak, whereas McVeigh shivered in a flimsy pin-striped jacket. Bloody coppers. Piss off.

He stayed perfectly still. They banged the door again. Harder this time. Still nothing, he remained silent at the window. At the same time the phone rang. He let it ring.

Another couple of minutes and they'd have met him coming up the front path. Lucky break or what.

After the second knock they gave up and left. Well that confirmed it. They couldn't know too much or they wouldn't have given up so easily. Arseholes!

Despite the cold, sweat had seeped through his shirt. He took off his jacket to save it too from becoming saturated. He wasn't as fit as he used to be. He'd left his car parked a few blocks away and legged it the rest of the way home, coming in unseen through the back door. He reckoned it was only a matter of time before they'd want to see him. Oh he'd talk to them all right, but not just now.

A fly buzzed on the windowsill, tossing from side to side in the last throws of life.

A bit late for flies. He picked it up and held it carefully between his thumb and forefinger. One by one he pulled the legs off. A childish pursuit that still brought the same childish pleasure. As a boy, he had sat for hours in the summer sun doing just this very thing. Still, no harm done. It wasn't as though they felt any pain. They had no central nervous system for god's sake. They *couldn't* feel any pain. What the fuck was all the fuss about? They spent their lives landing on, and feasting off shite. Hardly in a position to complain about someone else's harmless pastime? She, on the other hand, *did* have a central nervous system. She *did* feel pain. And she *did* complain about other people's harmless pastimes. Stupid Bitch!

Charlie felt the stirrings of an erection at the memory of stealing through her house. Getting in and out the previous day had been just as easy as it had been the night before. He'd come across some stupid bitches in his time but Oonagh O'Neil really did take the biscuit. Just standing in her kitchen had given him a hard-on. The second time had been even better than the first. Much better. She had actually been *in* the house. He'd stood at the foot of the stairs and listened to her in the shower. The scent of her soap and shampoo had filled the house. He pictured her wet and naked.

Led by the bulge in his trousers, he'd dared himself. Up one then two then three steps, then back down again when he'd heard her switch off the taps. He'd nearly shat himself when the key had turned in the lock. Hiding in the cupboard under the stairs he'd thanked God for his wee jaunt the night before, which, as it turned out, had proved to be a bit of a reconnaissance mission.

He'd thought she was dead as she'd lain there, saying nothing. Even when he'd pulled out the blade. Good as gold she'd been. And bloody hell, he'd really had to give it a bit of welly.

He'd felt sick when he'd found out she was still alive. That fucked up everything, well and truly. But he'd still get paid. The extra cash would come in right handy to get the electrics fixed on his car. Not being able to get the windows up and down properly really was driving him mental.

CHAPTER 28

Glasgow, 2000

The Valium was having no effect and the crisp white sheets were hard and scratchy. The room was stifling and she couldn't sleep. Which, as it turned out, was a blessing really. Every time she closed her eyes, Freddie Kruger clawed at her neck with his razor-sharp blades. She couldn't quite clear the fug from her brain and Oonagh was glad she couldn't remember being attacked.

She flicked on the portable set at the bottom of the bed and put the subtitles on so as not to wake any patients in the next room. It was nearly midnight and she hoped it would take her mind off things. The Omen was getting another go on Channel 5. The sight of Lee Remick falling seven stories from a hospital window and crashing to her death through the roof of an ambulance did nothing to calm her nerves.

She gazed out onto the city. The rooftops took shape against the sodium glow of the streetlights. Somewhere out there was a man who wanted her dead. And she had no idea why.

*

Tom couldn't sleep. The radio was on by the side of his bed and Oonagh was top of the hour every time.

'Family, friends and colleagues of Oonagh O'Neil have been left stunned by her brutal attack. The thirty-six-year-old tele-journalist is being treated in hospital after being found seriously injured in her West End home yesterday. It's reported Miss O'Neil had been stabbed, but the police are refusing to confirm any details at this time.'

Tom switched on the television. This time a reporter was outside Oonagh's house, shivering under a huge umbrella.

He'd just heaved himself out of bed when Mrs Brady rapped gently on the door. It pissed him off that she was always so timid. Before he had a chance to tell her to go away she came in with a cup of tea. He couldn't speak to her, or even look at her. Instead he just nodded to the dressing table. Her hand trembled so much that the noise of the crockery drowned out the television. Could she not request a special papal dispensation and use a mug, just this once? His mounting irritation boiled over.

'Mrs Brady! Can you just put the tea down please! And close the door on your way out.'

The cup dropped from her grip. Tom watched as the tea made an elaborate fountain. It splashed out in perfect symmetry, leaving Mrs Brady holding just the saucer. Before Tom could say anything she was on her hands and knees picking up the pieces of smashed china. He felt a slight pang of guilt mixed with his impatience and struggled to keep the despair from his voice. 'Just leave it Mrs Brady, I'll get it, don't worry.'

It was only then that he realised she was crying. There was no sound, but tears were streaming down both her cheeks. She reminded him of a young boy at the seminary, who had sobbed silently after night-time visits from the brother in charge.

'Oh God, Mrs Brady, I'm sorry, I didn't mean to snap.' He felt bad. The past week must have been tough on her too.

She lifted her eyes and looked at the television. A press shot of Oonagh flashed on the screen before some media expert started comparing the attack on Oonagh to that on Jill Dando, spouting about the dangers of working in the public gaze. Mrs Brady was transfixed by the screen.

'Her poor mother – I know what it's like to lose a daughter...' She shook her head.

To Tom her eyes suddenly seemed to be filled not with tears but with years of memories and loss.

'Mrs Brady, I had no idea you had a family... I mean I didn't realise you'd lost a child.'

'You never asked.' She shuffled out of the room clutching the broken pieces of china in her hand.

CHAPTER 29

Glasgow, 2000

The morning was a long time coming. Oonagh woke up gasping for air and was glad to see the sun rise over the city. The night had been full of demons wanting her dead...and dead babies with white eyes crawling up through open graves.

Outside, things sprang into life as the day took hold.

The nurse had already been in to tug the catheter free from between her legs and clear her hands of the needles that wired through her veins. Now she was waiting for the doctor to do his rounds – to give her the all-important nod to go home.

The stark white hospital room that had almost given her snow blindness the day before was now filled with flowers, cards, cuddly toys and bottles of champagne. She was dying for a cigarette, some decent coffee and her own bed.

★

Davies came in around eleven, his head obscured by a ridiculously large bunch of bright yellow sunflowers. She slid out of bed, not trusting her legs, and wobbled over to greet him. He steadied her as she staggered on her final step.

'How's the invalid?'

She drew him a look. 'I'm not an invalid, Alec!' – she raised her hand to slap him – 'although *you* might be if I get any more of your lip.' She hoped the quip would prove she hadn't undergone a sense of humour bypass while having her dead baby scraped from her insides.

'Not the face, not the face,' he joked as she grabbed the flowers from his grip.

'Here, give me those before you start getting in touch with your feminine side.' Oonagh buried her nose in the bouquet and read the message on the card tucked inside. *'If you're ever in a jam – I'm your man!'*

She looked up from reading it and saw that Davies was mortified, his face scarlet. She nodded – 'Thanks, Alec' – then gave him a hug. He squeezed her so hard that it hurt her ribs.

'Christ, your popular,' he said, taking in all the gifts. 'So, it's D Day then? You can go home?'

'Yip! Mum's due soon. She's under strict instruction to bring decent gear and my war paint of course.' She paused. 'I take it you'll want to question me sometime?'

'Aye. But there's no rush.'

Oonagh knew there was every rush – that the first twenty-four hours after any crime were vital if you wanted to catch the perpetrator, and they'd already missed their deadline by a day.

'No, Alec, I'm fine. Let's get this over with, eh?'

'Okay. Well, we need to work out what the hell happened, Oonagh. Now, we know you met Charlie Antonio in the Rogano just before you hooked up with Cranworth the night you were broken into.'

'How do you know that?'

'I'm a detective,' he said, without a trace of irony. 'Anyway, we need to find out if the break-in and the attack were related. I spoke to those two bloody clowns who interviewed you in the hospital…'

She wondered if Good Cop, Crap Cop had felt the infamous wrath of Alec Davies. He did not suffer fools gladly.

'Alec, I don't think they took me overly seriously, but I didn't quite tell them everything that happened…' She related the crank phone call she'd received, what the perpetrator had said about her being a murdering whore. 'I was too ashamed to tell them at the time. But now… Well.'

He cut in, obviously fired up with this new information. 'Who knew you were pregnant, Oonagh?'

She didn't have to think for long. 'No one really. I told Tom the other day. And of course Jack.' She caught the look in Davies' eye. The skin round her scalp tightened. 'No, Alec. No! It wasn't him, okay? Jack would never...' She faltered. What would he never do? Never hurt her? A month ago she would have bet her life on it. But paranoia was setting in, and with it uncertainty. Now she wasn't so sure. She nibbled on the back of her knuckles. 'I just don't think it was him.' Oonagh stood up and unwrapped one of the bottles of champagne from its decorative cellophane wrapper.

'For medicinal purposes,' she explained, and twisted the cork, but her arms were weak from the wound on her shoulder and Davies took it from her while she fetched two plastic tumblers from the bedside cabinet. He clasped his hand over hers to steady her trembling as the liquid frothed over the side of the cup. 'I'm a bloody wreck,' she said, downing hers in one go then holding the cup out for more.

It was warm and bitter, but hit the spot quickly and gave her an instant calm.

'Want to carry on?' Davies asked.

She nodded. 'Yeah. Of course.'

'Obviously whoever called you knew you were pregnant. That leaves two people. And whoever broke in also knew you'd be out that evening. Again, that leaves just two people. Now, you left Cranworth at what time? Ten-ish?'

'Yip.'

'Did you go straight home?'

She thought back to that evening. Storming out of the restaurant. Furious with Jack, she'd decided to walk through town and had grabbed a taxi at Charing Cross. If he had been parked nearby he would have had plenty of time to drive to her house and be in and out before she was home.

'I was home within minutes, Alec', she lied. 'I got a taxi straight away. There was no way he could have got there before me.'

'Cranworth's got a key to your house hasn't he, Oonagh?' It

was one of those questions-that-were-statements that she knew he liked to use. She looked to the bottom of her cup to find a reply that would take Jack out of the frame. It wasn't there, so she said nothing, immediately aware that her silence was loud enough to let Davies know what she was thinking.

'I'm bringing the bastard back in for questioning.'

'No, just stop this, right. If you do that I'll drop all charges, okay? Just leave it.' The thought of Jack being her attacker was more than she could cope with right now. But Davies wouldn't – couldn't – leave it. He opened his mouth to speak, but a soft tap on the door stopped him in his tracks.

McVeigh loitered in the doorway. 'There's a bit of a welcoming committee outside,' he said, nodding towards the window. Oonagh and Davies looked out onto the car park three floors below and saw a dozen or so journalists and cameramen huddled by the entrance. Every time the automatic double doors swooshed open they sprang to life before settling back down when they saw it wasn't Oonagh.

'We can arrange to have you smuggled out the back way. Maybe get you an ambulance home? You know what that shower can be like.'

'No bloody way. I'm leaving here with my head held high. I'm a survivor, Alec, not a bloody victim. Anyway, don't forget, I'm normally *part* of that shower. It's a big story you know. They've been on the blower all morning.' She stopped for a moment, chewing the skin around her thumbnail. 'Apparently they're asking if it's true I was pregnant.'

Alec Davies reached out his hand and guided her back onto the bed. 'You all right?'

She shook her head. 'Not really. I feel sick, Alec. Sick and pissed off with' – she looked around trying to put into words how she felt – 'pissed off with...well, everything really.'

Davies beckoned McVeigh. 'I want you to get downstairs

and tell that bunch of vultures to get lost. And if one of them even hints at asking about Oonagh being pregnant, I want them huckled down to the station for breach of the peace and obstructing an investigation.'

McVeigh stared at Davies. 'Are you sure that's an offence? I mean journalists can actually *ask* what they like, you know. Under the Freedom of Information...'

Davies didn't wait for him to finish. 'Fuck's sake. Just go downstairs and tell them to piss off, eh? Does everything have to be a big fucking under-regulation-kiss-my-ass-I-cannae-dae-that routine with you?'

McVeigh was about to turn on his heels and go when Oonagh stopped him. 'Hang on, Jim, give us a minute eh?' As McVeigh held back she turned to Davies. 'Listen, I want to talk to them. It'll get them out of my hair if I play ball.' Davies raised an eyebrow, unconvinced. She put on a mock Deep-South accent. 'Ah's dealing wit' ma own kin-folks here, John Boy.' She dropped the accent. 'Honestly, Alec, I know how to handle the press. It's better all round. Believe me.'

She had no intention of shuffling out of the hospital, wounds patched up, wobbly and shaky, nodding to waiting reporters, trying to force a smile. Playing to the crowd was her bread and butter and she had no plans to let the audience down now. She might have been left for dead having had her throat cut in her own home, but every cloud had a silver lining. She leaned over to McVeigh. 'Tell them I've left already. But make sure you say I've not gone home or they'll be camped on my bloody doorstep. Tell them I'll be doing a press conference tomorrow, and if they phone the studio later they can get the details.'

Davies still wasn't convinced, but she cut him off as he started to speak. 'Ah ah, let me explain. If I arrange to sit down and answer their questions – to play the game – they won't print any shitty stuff about me being pregnant. And Alec, I need people to see I've not become some dithery wreck.' Her eyes filled with tears and she knew she'd won him round. Her livelihood depended on her public image. On being in control. And this way she could take the lead, put her own spin on things and come out without being the helpless victim. It would all be good column inches.

★

She called the newsroom and spoke to Alan Gardener. He thought a press conference was a great idea and told her that van loads of cards and flowers and cuddly teddies and all sorts had been arriving for her since the news broke. And everyone at the studio was rooting for her and she didn't have to hurry back. The most important thing was she got well again.

Oonagh had known Alan for years and knew his bullshit when she heard it. Oh the bit about the cuddly get well messages would be kosher. But the rest? Well, it wasn't a risk she was prepared to take. She planned to be back at her desk and in front of the camera before they had the chance to line up a replacement – before they could jump at the opportunity to find someone who could do the job half as well for a quarter of the price. She thanked Alan and ended the call.

'Jim, slight change of plan. Tell them I'll be doing a press call and photo shoot in Devonshire Gardens.' It would be the perfect setting. Five Edwardian town houses turned into a West End hotel where Gordon Ramsay once cooked for the rich and famous. It would be a nice jolly for all the journalists who turned up. Ply them with plenty of posh nosh and booze and they'd write exactly what Oonagh wanted them to write.

'Christ, Oonagh, this is all a bit quick is it no'?'

'Oh stop being such an old woman, Alec.'

McVeigh didn't move until he got the nod from Davies. 'Well, I suppose. Yeah, all right.'

She hugged his neck and kissed his cheek. Already pumped

with adrenalin, desperate to get moving.

'What time?' said McVeigh.

'Tell them to call the duty press officer at the studio later. They'll give them all the details.' She hoped this would give her an excuse to cut off the questioning.

'Right,' Davies said to McVeigh, 'what're you waiting for? Next week's wages?' He let out an exaggerated audible sigh as his partner left the room.

'You can be a right misery-guts at times,' Oonagh said.

'No wonder. The man's bloody useless,' Davies said. He shook his head. 'Right, let's get back to business. What can you remember about the attack itself? Your cleaner says she popped in around one and you told her to come back later. That right?'

No pussyfooting about, Oonagh noted. 'Yeah, I wasn't long back from the hospital and wanted a bit of time to myself. To be honest, Alec, I don't really remember much of what happened after that. It's all a bit of a blur.'

'Did you open the door to anyone? Try to think. The door was open when Tom found you and there was no sign of a break-in. Were you expecting anyone? Did you ask Cranworth to come round? Do you remember seeing anyone else?'

She just shook her head. 'Can't remember.'

'Oonagh, do you know of anyone who would try and hurt you?'

Once again Davies was interrupted by a knock on the door. 'Bloody hell, McVeigh, what is it now?'

It wasn't McVeigh who slowly opened the door, it was Tom Findlay, who avoided Davies' interrogative eye but couldn't avoid the, 'Oh, it's you,' that Davies fired in his direction.

'I just wanted to see you were all right,' Tom said to Oonagh.

'Well, she's fine,' Davies said, 'so just close the door behind you, eh?'

Oonagh pushed her hand across Alec's chest, shutting him

up. 'Come on in.'

Tom faltered before pulling up a chair. He gave a nervous cough and cleared his throat before speaking. 'I've remembered something about yesterday,' he said.

Davies jumped in before Oonagh had a chance. 'What?'

'Well' – this time he did look at Davies – 'it might not even be important, in fact it's maybe nothing, probably a waste of time, but...'

Oonagh watched Davies' face redden as a vein pulsed in his temple and a muscle twitched at the side of his jaw. He drummed his fingers against his thigh. She was glad when Tom got on with it.

'Well, it's something I saw in your kitchen yesterday, Oonagh.'

'Go on,' said Davies.

'Well, you know that woman...Susan?'

Oonagh felt a flutter in her stomach.

'What about her?'

'Well,' continued Tom, 'she put two cups in the dishwasher – they'd been lying on the table – and a couple of plates too.'

Davies looked at Oonagh, who shrugged.

'And?' Davies gestured at Tom to get to the point.

'Well, that would suggest someone must have visited you just before you were attacked. Why else would the dishes be lying out?'

'Tom, I probably left them there from the day before. Or maybe Susan ate something while she was there.'

But Tom wouldn't let up. 'No. Oonagh, listen to me. I handed her the tea cups myself. They were still warm. Someone must have been with you just before you were attacked.'

Davies jumped in. 'Doesn't mean it was her attacker though.'

Tom continued, as though Oonagh had left the building. 'I'm not saying she made this guy a cup of coffee before he stabbed her, but maybe whoever was with her saw something. Maybe they're too scared to come forward. Maybe they're…'

Davies held up his hand for Tom to stop and Oonagh was glad of the break. Her head was beginning to spin.

'Right, can you just leave the detective work to me?' Davies looked at Oonagh. 'It's a long shot, but we've nothing else. Might be able to get some prints off the cups or something.'

'Or even DNA off the saliva,' added Tom.

'So let me get this clear: you reckon I made someone a coffee, then they attacked me?'

'I've tasted your coffee, Oonagh! No, seriously,' Davies continued, a little embarrassed by his attempt at a joke, 'Is anyone in your house just now?'

Oonagh picked up the phone and dialled her own number. 'Hi Mum, it's me… No, not yet, they're just getting my discharge letter ready. Listen a couple of things. First, can you pick up a packet of sanitary towels?'

She hesitated. Davies and Tom were staring at the floor. She put her hand over the mouthpiece. 'Guys, can you give me a couple of minutes?' She waited while they shuffled out of the room, then spoke to her mum again. 'Okay, secondly, can you switch on the dishwasher… No, I don't care if it's not full, just do it please, Mum. Right away. And can you make sure you put it on the hottest cycle. Thanks. See you in a bit.' And with that she hung up.

'Sorry,' she said to Alec and Tom, who were a few yards down the corridor. They both walked towards her. 'Too late, mum's just put the dishwasher on.'

Davies put his hand on Tom's shoulder. 'Thanks for telling us anyway.'

Tom knew he was being patronised.

'Listen, Alec,' said Oonagh. 'Don't say anything to my mum about this, eh? She'll be devastated if she thinks she's washed away vital evidence.'

CHAPTER 30

Glasgow, 2000

Tom pottered about in Oonagh's kitchen. The curate was taking care of things back at the ranch, and the second day of kids' rehearsals for Father Kennedy's funeral would tick along without him. He switched on the kettle, then immediately felt guilty about picking on Mrs Brady for her tea and sympathy routine.

He switched on the mini hi-fi, which sat on the worktop with a few tapes on top. He put one on, expecting to hear Billy Holliday or some other of Oonagh's jazz favourites. Instead Oonagh's voice flooded the kitchen, soft and reassuring. *'Take your time, we can stop if you want... You know it's a brave thing talking about it after all this time...'* And all the while he could hear the quiet sobs of a woman in the background. Some poor demented victim of the Magdalene Institutes.

Looking at the rest of the tapes he realised they too were mostly of interviews Oonagh had done as part of her Magdalene research. The labels gave little away. Just the first names of the women: Megan, Anne-Marie, Maureen, Theresa.

Oonagh's voice remained calm and comforting. *'You know it's only natural to feel guilt, But don't forget you were the victim in all this. You did nothing wrong...'* And still the gentle cries of the woman continued. He switched it off, taking the tape from the machine.

The kitchen door burst open, causing him to jump. Shit! Oonagh's mum's footsteps were silent in her sheepskin slippers, and his nerves were more frayed than he'd realised. He slipped the tape into his pocket. He didn't want her to think he was snooping.

'Tea, Mrs O'Neil?'

'Oonagh's leprechaun.'

'Eh?'

'Her leprechaun – Oonagh's leprechaun. It's gone. I've looked through the whole house and it's nowhere. And please, call me Fran.'

'Sorry. Her leprechaun? What's...?'

'Oonagh had a silver letter-opener with a leprechaun on top.' Her voice began to crack. 'She treasured it. Her Dad gave it to her just before he died. It was just this thing they had between them. He always claimed he'd seen a leprechaun once. She'll go mad if it's not here.'

Tom tried to usher her into the living room to calm her down. But the sound of the key in the lock sent her racing to the front door.

★

'You okay with this, Oonagh?'

She tugged her collar up round her neck, covering the stitches that held her wound closed. There were only three steps leading up to her front door. Three steps she'd taken hundreds – thousands – of times. But today was different. She wondered if she'd ever feel safe at home again.

Her mum was already inside, having left the hospital after dropping off some clothes. Tom would be with her, which would at least keep him occupied. As Alec Davies had said, Tom had been hanging around the hospital like a 'fart in a trance'.

It had been left to Alec to drive her home, and she was glad. Because that's all it was. A drive home. No emotions. No hysterics. Just a drive home. They'd taken their time and stopped at Bloody Mary's for a cucumber-gin and tonic, so by the time Oonagh climbed the three stairs to her home, the morning champagne and afternoon G&T were having an effect. Alec steadied her, holding her arm, but the butterflies in her stomach were fluttering so fiercely that they sent a wave of nausea through her entire body.

Oonagh trembled and hesitated as she inserted the key.

★

Oonagh had to prise her mum's hands from round her neck because her fingers were digging into her stitches. Despite the anaesthetising effect of the alcohol, her scar still throbbed like mad.

'There, there, Mum. I'm home. I'm all right.'

Her mum held on, as if to make sure she really was there. Alive. In the flesh. 'Darling darling girl. My baby.'

'Some baby!' Oonagh laughed. With her heels she stood easily three inches taller than her mum.

They led each other into the living room. Davies sat down on the sofa opposite the two women.

Her mum immediately spilled the beans about the missing leprechaun.

'Was it valuable?' Davies asked.

'Very,' said Oonagh, 'but that's not the point.'

'No,' continued Davies, 'but it might have been lifted during the break-in, and if it's valuable it might make it easier to trace. Oonagh when did you see it last? '

'I...' Oonagh stammered. 'I think...I'm not sure. I don't know.'

'Can you describe it to me?'

'No need,' her mum said, taking a photograph album from the bureau in the corner and opening it at the front page. She handed it to Davies. 'Oonagh has quite a few valuable pieces. Her Dad made sure she took pictures of everything. You know, for insurance purposes.'

Oonagh let out an exaggerated cough. 'Mum! Do you mind not talking about me as though I'm not here! I can speak for myself you know.'

Davies looked at the picture. His eyes widened. The little

silver leprechaun sat cross-legged on top of a long narrow blade. 'Can I take this, Oonagh?' he asked, already peeling back the protective plastic sheeting before she had a chance to refuse.

He immediately called McVeigh and told him to swing by.

★

Back in the car, McVeigh was unusually quiet. They were almost back at the station before he spoke.

'D'ye think that's the weapon, boss?'

'Aye, son, I do.'

★

Tom had left not long after Davies, thankfully taking the hint. Her mum, however, insisted on staying. Judging from her overnight bag she planned to be around for several days. Despite insisting she'd be fine, Oonagh was glad her mum was around. She wanted her close at hand.

It was still light outside, but what Oonagh needed most was her bed. Her *own* bed. Her mum brought up tea and toasted cheese on a tray – 'I've cut the crusts off, Sweetheart' – and set about plumping the already ridiculously over-stuffed pillows.

Oonagh felt herself sink back into the softness and let herself be babied. 'Thanks.'

Her mum sat next to her, brushing the strands of hair from her forehead. 'I thought I'd lost you, sweetheart.' Her chin quivered and her bottom lip went into little spasms. 'You know you're the most important thing to me in the whole wide world.'

Oonagh knew she meant it.

'Mum, about the last time...with Owen...'

'Shush now.' Her mum patted her arm. 'Don't upset yourself. You try and get some rest. I'll be downstairs if you need me, darling.' She blew Oonagh a kiss as she backed out of the room and Oonagh snatched it from the air the way she had as a child.

She waited until she heard her mum moving dishes downstairs in the kitchen. Only then did she pick up the phone.

'Hello, can I speak to Father Watson please. Yes, it's Miss O'Neil.' She drew circles on the duvet cover with her nail while waiting to be put through.

'Father Watson? Oonagh O'Neil here. I think it's about time you and I had a little chat, don't you?'

CHAPTER 31

Glasgow, 2000

She wasn't really looking forward to the meeting, but it gave her an excuse to get out of the house in which someone had attempted to slit her throat slit only days earlier.

She stretched her leg to step over the blood stain that remained at the bottom of the stairs, despite attempts at cleaning it out. She'd told her mum she was taking a walk. A bit of fresh air that was all. She wrapped a scarf around her neck to hide her stitches, and applied more make up than normal to give her sickly pallor a bit of colour. The trace of a bruise was appearing around her left eye, apparently caused by her brain bouncing up and hitting the front of her skull when she'd fallen. She'd been bleeding heavily throughout the night and felt weak and tired. It was apparently normal after a miscarriage. Especially at her age.

Fuelled by fear and anger, she made her way to the city centre. The morning rush hour was over, but Charing Cross was thick with traffic, cars still bumper to bumper as they left the M8.

*

Charlie Antonio made his way up the three steps to the front door of St Patrick's. He stopped to catch his breath at the last one. Once again he'd left his car parked a few streets back. No point in advertising that he was there.

He slipped his index finger under his shirt collar to prise it away from his sweaty neck, and wiped his forehead with a cotton hankie. In the past few months he'd noticed a slight bulge forming just above the waistband of his trousers. That gut had to go. First thing Monday he would go for a session at the gym, before things got out of hand. He needed to be one step ahead, to stay in control. It was the only way.

Before entering, he patted his breast pocket for reassurance – there would be no point in the meeting if he wasn't in possession of the trump card. But yes, the letter-opener was still there. He'd wrapped it carefully – in tissue rather than anything cotton, less chance of tell-tale fibres – being careful not to scrape off even a sliver of the blood that caked the razor-sharp blade. His own hands were gloved, but he wanted a decent set of prints before the day was through. For a bit of added security – insurance.

He shook his head. Bloody stupid bitch, leaving a thing like that lying in her hall. Someone could have been killed!

★

Oonagh didn't wait to be ushered into the office. 'He's expecting me,' she made clear to the grey nun behind the desk, offering her the merest hint of a sardonic smile before barging through the door.

The nun ran in behind her in a state of apoplexy. 'Father, she pushed right past me!'

Father Watson stood up. Oonagh hadn't realised he was quite so big and had to steady herself against the nerves that were shaking her insides.

Oonagh tipped her chin towards the nun in a show of false bravado. 'She can stay if she wants. Depends how *public* you want this meeting to be.'

The priest contemplated his options for a few moments and lit a slim cigar, sucking a few times on the end until the light took hold.

Oonagh noticed that the nicotine stains on his fingers extended almost to his knuckles.

'Trying to give up the fags,' he said, holding the cigar in front of him. 'Apparently these things are marginally less hazardous. But I suppose we've all got to die of something.' He shrugged his shoulders. 'Might as well be something pleasurable, eh?' He turned to the nun. 'Right, Sister, that'll be all.'

The nun edged out of the room.

Oonagh tried to slam the door shut behind her and felt Father Watson's eyes laughing into the back of her head as the control hinges took charge. The door eased over slowly.

'Nice of you to pop by. Mind telling what you want, Miss O'Neil?'

'Please don't bother pretending you don't know what I'm here for.'

'Why don't you take a seat?'

Oonagh would rather have remained standing, but needed to get off her feet. She sat opposite him and hoped she looked more confident than she felt.

Father Watson walked to the windows and adjusted the vertical blinds just enough to ensure the low autumn sun squeezed through and hit Oonagh in the eyes. She took her shades from her bag and turned her seat round until the light was behind her.

'So…' he said.

She opened her bag once more, took out a letter and waved it at the priest. 'The small matter of you covering up an illegal adoption racket.'

CHAPTER 32

Glasgow, 2000

'I beg your pardon?' Father Watson sniggered.

Oonagh had a good sense of humour, but didn't enjoy being laughed at when she wasn't trying to be funny.

'Listen, *Father*, don't come the innocent with me. You know exactly what I'm talking about.' He raised his eyebrows and she knew he was goading her to tell him what she knew. 'Did you think you could hide it away forever? How much did you lot make over the years? Thousands? Hundreds of thousands? More? I suppose by today's standards you must have creamed off a small fortune.'

Father Watson leaned back in his chair until the front legs lifted off the floor. He sucked on his cigar and blew circles of smoke in the air. 'You're an ex-Catholic aren't you, Miss O'Neil?'

'What the hell's that got to do with this?'

'You're not married either. At your age. And with no kids. Your life must feel a bit empty. You must feel a bit disappointed with things.'

Oonagh mused on his question for a moment before replying, 'No, not really. I would have liked to have been taller with bigger tits, but no, on the whole, Father Watson, I'm fairly happy with the hand God has dealt me. And I note that you're also unmarried and childless, despite your even greater age.'

He ignored her retort and wouldn't let up. 'You can always tell. What happened? Read the Female Eunuch at uni and decided the Church was too patriarchal? Decided we didn't quite fit your left-wing post-feminist ideals?'

She sliced through his words, unable to stomach any more. 'How dare you. My politics and religious beliefs have nothing whatsoever to do with this. Are you mental? Do you think

I'm getting my feminist rocks off with a bit of petty Church-bashing? For fuck's sake. Your mob – and yes, that's exactly what they are, a bloody mob – your mob snatched babies from their mothers and sold them. *Sold* them. And those that weren't fit to be sold were left to rot until they died. All this under some parallel moral code that made it *okay* because you could hide your crimes behind a collar. Have you any idea of the misery you've caused? You'd better pray that God truly is forgiving, because you'll burn in hell for you've done.'

She felt the beads of sweat on her brow. Her mouth was dry and parched and she was worn out from the sheer effort of not being home in bed.

Father Watson stubbed out his cigar and the smoke caught the back of her throat. He pulled a packet of unfiltered cigarettes from the drawer. 'Let's live dangerously, shall we?' He licked his lips, sizing her up. 'If you really believe all this, why don't you go to the police?' He looked directly at her.

Oonagh didn't reply.

'Miss O'Neil, I don't know where you're getting your information from but it's not true. I assume you think you've uncovered some great miscarriage of justice during your Magdalene research with Father Thomas.'

She still said nothing, let him continue.

'But whatever it is, I can assure you you're wrong. Those poor women were treated harshly, of that I have no doubt. But Miss O'Neil – can I call you Oonagh?'

'No, it's Miss O'Neil.'

'Well then, Miss O'Neil, what we have to remember is that it was a long time ago. The world was a harsher place. *Every*one was treated harshly. Even the men.'

The priest let out a wee laugh, but to Oonagh he looked predatory.

'It's understandable that the women you've spoken to are

bitter. But stories like this pop out of the woodwork every day. The Church has become an easy target for people wanting revenge – and, in many cases, compensation. Is it any wonder they sometimes *expand* on the truth? No, I'm sorry' – he shook his head – 'I'm afraid you've been the victim of some glory-seeking, compensation-hungry confidence trickster. No doubt we'll have her lawyer's letter before the end of the week. Then they'll offer to settle out of court 'cause they've not got a shred of bloody evidence.'

'This isn't about money, it's about the difference between right and wrong. You understand that much, don't you?' She slammed her hands on his desk. The wound on her neck throbbed as her blood pressure rose. She was conscious of shouting, and tried to keep her voice at a pitch short of hysteria. 'How could you be party to this?'

'Miss O'Neil, I'm party to nothing. I was barely out of my teens at the time you're talking about. Now please, I know you've recently been the victim of a serious assault, and I've no doubt this is a very difficult time for you, but you know, I've given you enough time here. This is getting beyond a joke. I'm extremely busy. You'll have to excuse me.'

'You were party to covering it up. That's enough.' She held the folded letter up of for him to see. 'Your lot were making a bloody packet from forcing innocent girls to give up their babies. Well, Father Kennedy couldn't live with the guilt. Seems he wanted to make his peace before he went. And you don't fare too well.' She waved the document right under his nose. 'He's really landed you in it. You and a few others besides.'

Father Watson dropped the smouldering cigarette onto his lap. 'Shite!' He jumped up and brushed the burning ash from his thighs. A smell of singed wool filled the office.

'Where did you get that?' He reached to snatch it from her, but Oonagh quickly stuffed it back in her bag, securing it in a zipped compartment.

'And don't be stupid,' she said. 'I've got another copy at home.' She looked for his reaction. His face turned waxy and grey and he seemed to dissolve into his clothes. This time it was her turn to snigger. 'What's wrong? Didn't you know Father Kennedy had made a copy?' She crinkled her nose at him. 'Nice try, Buster.'

She stood and opened the door to leave, but the priest leapt from behind his desk and forced it closed. He towered over her and she could smell the stale cigar smoke and sour whisky on his breath. She held her bag tight against her chest. For a fleeting moment she thought he might even hit her, then realised how ridiculous that would be with the nun outside. Instead he pressed himself against her until she could hardly breathe.

'Miss O'Neil. Please take my advice. Don't go making a fool of yourself with what you think is a last confession of Father Kennedy. He was very old, very frail. And, let's face it, everyone knows he wasn't quite...how can I put this...he wasn't the full shilling.' He bent over until his nose touched hers. His teeth were clenched as he spoke slowly and deliberately into her face. 'Now, listen to me.'

But Oonagh had done enough listening. She lifted her leg and brought her heel down hard on his foot, then hurried from the office and into the waiting lift. Out in the car she flicked on the central locking to secure the doors.

She shook all the way home.

★

Davies was standing on her top doorstep, finger on the bell. 'Where have you been? I thought you were meant to be staying in bed. You look awful.'

'Thanks.'

She was just getting her breath back. Davies had to steady her hand as she fumbled with the key in the lock.

Inside, all was quiet. A note on the fridge door explained that her mum had gone to the shops, but there were still signs of her in the kitchen: a bottle of red wine was chilling nicely in the fridge. Her mum was teetotal and presumably thought she was doing her a favour. Looking around, Oonagh cast a despairing glance at the washing machine as her red cashmere cardigan swished from side to side in a sea of biological bubbles.

She didn't get the reply she'd hoped for when she told Alec about her meeting with Father Watson. 'Bloody hell, Oonagh. Please tell me you didn't'

'Well, thanks for the support, Alec. Whose side are you meant to be on? I've just had my throat slit in case it had escaped your notice.' She stabbed the air, pointing at the wound, giving him no chance to forget.

'Don't be so bloody stupid, Oonagh. It's not about sides. But you can't just barge into folks' offices and accuse them of all sorts. You should have come and told me. Don't go charging head-first into stuff like this, not on your own.' He gave her a pitying look, then said, 'Can I see this letter you're talking about?'

She handed him the folded pages.

His face fell as he read that as a valued customer she could get free balance transfers and interest-free purchases for up to six months if she switched credit cards.

She chewed the skin on the side of her thumb as the colour on his cheeks rose.

'What is this?' Davies clenched the paper in his fist.

'I was calling his bluff, right. So what? His reaction proves he's as guilty as sin. And, what's more, after this morning I'm convinced he got rid of Father Kennedy then attacked me – to shut me up.'

Davies held the pages up in front of her and spoke very slowly, as though she were an idiot. 'Oonagh, can I see the *actual* letter that Father Kennedy wrote you?'

She was incredulous. 'If I had the letter I would have shown it to you, not taken it round to that creep Watson.'

He slumped into a kitchen chair, heavily enough to scrape the legs along the floor. 'Have you lost your marbles? What in God's name am I meant to do with this? First you accuse a priest of murder, then you accuse him of attacking you...on the strength of what? How do you know he stole your letter from Father Kennedy? And anyway, how do you know there even *was* a flipping letter in the first place? First I've heard of it.'

'Can't tell you,' she said.

'Okay, how do you know what was *in* the letter?'

Again she shook her head. 'Listen, Alec, go with me on this one. I've only just found out myself that Father Kennedy wrote to me before he died. But the letter's now missing and I had to see Watson's face to face to gauge his reaction. It's obvious he took it. I can't reveal my sources yet, but they're kosher, okay?'

Davies rubbed his eyes. 'Bloody hell, Oon, this isn't a game. You know I'll leave no stone unturned, but I can only bend the rules so far. And I don't need to tell *you* of all people about the laws of defamation in this country. Watson could hang you out to dry if you start spouting stuff like that.' He let the point sink in for a few seconds. 'So, did he actually threaten you?'

She thought for a moment, searching above her head to find the memory. Now that she was back on home turf she didn't feel quite so scared. Had she exaggerated the whole thing?

'He didn't *actually* threaten me, but he *was* standing this close,' she said, holding her thumb and forefinger together so that only a merest hint of light could be seen between them.

'How did you leave it?'

She hesitated for a few moments. 'I...' She looked at him, swallowed hard and tried to portray a picture of innocence. 'I kicked him then ran away.'

Davies groaned and dropped his head into his hands.

Oonagh was about to speak when she heard a key in the lock and put her finger to her mouth. 'Shh. Mum's the word.' It was an order rather than a request.

Davies' mobile rang before he had a chance to respond. He answered at the same time as her mum carried in a shopping bag of eats and treats. Oonagh kept the same finger to her mouth to silence her mum while Davies answered the call.

'Staying for lunch?' her mum asked Davies as soon as he hung up. 'I've bought loads. And I've popped some red wine in the fridge.'

'Sorry, I can't,' Davies said, putting the phone back in his top pocket. 'I need to go. Someone's just thrown themself off the balcony at Saint Patrick's.'

CHAPTER 33

Glasgow, 2000

Davies screeched his car to a halt outside St Patrick's, next to the waiting ambulance that was blocking half the street. A small crowd had gathered outside the church.

He met Tom Findlay walking up the steps and grabbed his arm. 'What're you doing here?'

'It's a church.' Findlay seemed bemused. 'And I'm a priest.'

Davies shot him a look that said *later* and pushed open the double doors.

Inside, mayhem. Children huddled together in the vestibule in groups of a dozen or so, some sobbing, some staring trance-like at the floor, others shaking uncontrollably. Four teachers, who themselves looked shell-shocked, fussed round the pupils trying to calm them down. This didn't look good.

'What the hell are they still doing here?' Davies pointed his thumb toward the children. 'Get them out of here. Now!' He pushed open the double doors leading into the main body of the church.

Charlie Antonio's body lay on the back of a pew. He'd landed on his back, and was almost bent in half. His front hung over the back of the pew; his head was twisted to a forty-five-degree angle on the seat. His neck bulged, hideously stretched, and his feet reached the floor of the seat behind him. A thin trickle of blood seeped from his mouth and traced a line towards his eye. His blue trousers were black where his bowels had opened and spilled out onto his shoes below.

A man was crouching by his side, feeling for a pulse, but the paramedics were already packing up.

The curate ran over and covered the body with a white linen cloth, one normally used on the altar. Spots of blood seeped through at the head and chest. The smells of excrement and incense hung in the air.

Davies held his badge out to the paramedics and tipped his head at the body. 'What happened?'

One of them shrugged his shoulders. 'Took a tumble by all accounts.' He pointing his eyes to the balcony. 'He was long gone by the time we arrived.' He picked up his kit, ready to head to his next emergency. 'Anyway he's been declared dead by the doctor, so...'

'The doctor?'

The paramedic nodded to the figure near Antonio's body and Davies suddenly realised who it was.

'Good-God-in-Govan, what is this?' Davies' voice boomed throughout the church. 'What the hell are you doing here?'

'Nothing. I...I tried to save him but he was...'

'Shut it.' Davies pointed his finger. 'And don't move. I'll speak to you in a minute.'

As Davies turned briefly to speak to the paramedics before they left, Findlay came running down the aisle.

'Who is it?' he cried.

Davies pulled the sheet from Antonio, bringing a gasp from Findlay, who thrust his hand over his mouth.

'Ach.' Davies didn't wince, just tutted and shook his head as he looked at Charlie Antonio's swollen face. 'No a nice way to go, is it?' Blood had crusted round the dead journalist's lips and nose. His skin was already blue because of the angle of his head, and his blackened tongue protruded from his mouth. 'Anyone actually see him fall?

'I think two of the teachers saw it,' the curate answered. 'Shall I...?'

'Aye, aye, bring them in.'

Davies covered Charlie's face before the two women came back inside.

The two young women – who Davies thought looked like kids themselves – fought to remain composed, careful not to let their eyes drift towards the body.

Davies indicated the man beside him. 'Father…em…'

'Cameron, it's Father Cameron,' said the curate, taking one step forward, then stepping back again.

Davies nodded. 'Father Cameron thinks you may have seen what happened.'

Both women nodded, tiny movements. One sniffed, then spoke up.

'Well the children were still lined up, two by two at each aisle…' She swept her arm up and down, showing Davies where the kids had been at the time. He nodded quickly to spur her on. 'They'd just started singing, and I was facing them, with my back to the altar, when I saw a man standing on the balcony. He was acting a bit strange.'

'Strange?'

'Yeah, he was leaning over it.' She stood on tiptoe to demonstrate. 'I thought he might have been a photographer, but he didn't have a camera, or not that I could see anyway. So, as I say, one minute he was hanging over the banister, the next he just seemed to lose his footing and… It was awful.' Her chin quivered and her colleague wrapped a protective arm round her.

'Was anyone with him?'

The other woman took her cue. 'No, he was alone.'

'You sure about that?'

She nodded.

Davies pointed to Cranworth. 'What about this man? Did you see him?'

'Now just a minute…!' Cranworth stood up, horrified at the suggestion.

Again she nodded.

'Where was he?' Davies ignored Cranworth's protests.

She pointed to the empty pew on the last row at the side.

'The whole time?'

She nodded. 'Yeah, until the fall...then he ran over to help...
But I don't really think there was anything...'

Davies stepped in. 'That's fine for the moment. We'll maybe
need to speak to you again. Leave your name and details with
one of my colleagues out front, and then perhaps you should get
the kids home.' The hubbub from the pupils was grating on his
nerves and ruining his concentration.

The curate led the two women back outside, and Davies
followed. The event had caused a bit of excitement. The crowd on
the pavement was getting bigger and spilling into the doorway,
heads twisted and stretched as they tried for a glimpse, just one
peek inside.

On Davies' instructions, Father Cameron stood guard.
Instinctively he took on a bouncer's pose: chin up, legs apart,
hands clasped in front of his groin.

McVeigh had arrived. Davies strode back and joined him
next to Antonio's body. 'Two deaths in one chapel in a week,
boss,' Davies nodded. 'It'll take a miracle of PR engineering for
the Church to come out of this one smelling of roses.'

'No wonder he wasn't answering his door,' McVeigh replied
as Davies pulled back the cover.

'Get someone over to his house to break the news to his
wife.' He winced at the smell as he patted the sheet covering
the corpse. 'I knew your luck would run out one day, big man.'
Davies' hand stopped at a bulge in Charlie Antonio's chest. He
slipped on a pair of gloves before pulling back the sheet and
jacket. A silver blade had ripped through the lining of the dead
journalist's inside pocket and had embedded itself in Charlie's
flesh 'Fuck's sake,' Davies took a step back.

'What is it? What's wrong?' It was Cranworth, craning his
neck towards the body.

The blade was partially wrapped in tissue, but the handle was clearly visible. There was no mistaking the tiny silver leprechaun. 'Now,' Davies turned to Cranworth, 'd'you want to tell me what the hell's *really* going on? And don't bother telling me you came here for a wee pray or I'll book you for taking the fucking piss.'

★

Within minutes St Patrick's was full. A uniformed officer was on his hands and knees searching the balcony, just in case Charlie *had* been carrying a camera.

The police casualty surgeon stood over the body.

'Too early to say, Alec, I'll need to do a full post mortem examination, but I don't *think* the blade's hit any major organs. Looks superficial to me, not enough to kill him. Now, falling at that angle...' She looked up to the spot Charlie Antonio had fallen from, then back down onto the pew where his body lay. 'Well, that's a different story. That would have been enough to kill him, and most likely did.'

'Right, fine. I still want this guy to have the works. I want a full toxicology report. Let me know if anything turns up. *Anything.* Was he drugged beforehand? Did he take anything that would have affected his balance? If he's had an aspirin in the past 24 hours, I want to know. And I want blood samples taken from that letter opener, go over it with a fine tooth comb.'

'You mean you want me to do all the things I would do as a matter of course.'

Davies caught himself almost smiling at her ballsy reply. 'Yes. And some,' he said.

He turned his attention to Cranworth. 'Right, you're coming with me.'

'Good God man, I don't think...'

'Doctor Cranworth.' Davies paused to exhale a long slow sigh. 'Just get into the car, okay?' He handed him over to

McVeigh.

Tom Findlay was sitting at a pew a few rows back. Davies strode over to him and said, 'At the front door, when I arrived... Were you coming in or going out?'

'Coming in. Why?'

Davies shook his head. 'Nothing. No reason.' Then, after he'd taken a step away, he added, 'Turning into a right wee angel of death, aren't you?'

Tom Findlay said nothing, but Davies could have sworn the priest was trying his best not to smile.

CHAPTER 34

Glasgow, 1958

Irene Connolly woke with the rope cutting into the flesh on her ankles and wrists.

The blood had dried between her legs where the doctor had examined her, and had left a hard red stain on her night-dress and the sheets. A deep cough rattled in her chest. It tore through her lungs and out of her throat.

'Oh, yer awake, Irene.'

Irene twisted her neck. She was still aching from her night on the church's stone floor. Sally sat by her bed. 'Sally, get me loose. Untie me, eh? Please.'

Sally leaned across the bed and began to loosen the ropes that were tearing her skin. 'Sister Agatha told me no tae do this. Said you were tae stay tied up till you went to Leverndale. That's where they're putting you, Irene. Leverndale. Honest to God.' She stopped untying the ropes just for a second to cross her heart with her index finger.

'Leverndale?'

'Aye, Irene. I heard her talking with the doctor. Said I had to watch you. Make sure you wurnie tae get loose.' She turned her head from side to side, making sure no one could hear, but they were alone in the room. 'Hey, Irene...' Sally started to snigger through her teeth, making a farting noise and spraying saliva all over Irene. 'Is it true you tried to touch the Doctor's willie?'

'Oh God, I don't know, probably,' Irene groaned, as she twisted her hands round, now free from the rope. Sally was at her feet undoing the knots at her ankles.

'Sally, this Leverndale...what is it?'

'Fuck's sake, Irene. It's the loony bin. Everybody knows that.' She tutted and sighed at Irene's apparent stupidity. Her tongue poked out from the side of her mouth as she tried to unpick the knot in the rope. 'They're putting you in the loony bin, cause yer mental, Irene.'

Sally was her usual matter-of-fact self. By now she was tugging at the knot with her teeth.

'Oh Dear God, no.'

The horrors of the electric shock treatment came flooding back. And the sense of urgency swelled in her breast. 'Sally, hurry up, hurry up. Get the ropes off,' Irene struggled and kicked her feet, desperate to be free. She jumped out of bed as soon as the last knot was undone, but her legs immediately buckled under her and she crumpled to the floor. Crawling on her hands and knees, she dragged herself the length of the dormitory, then collapsed at the door frame, sobbing. 'Help me please, Sally. I can't go back to hospital. Please, Sally!'

Sally marched towards her...but walked straight past and ran down the stars without even catching her eye.

'Sally. Please.' Irene felt the hot sticky blood seeping from between her legs once more.

Within minutes she heard the voices, and footsteps running up the stairwell. Sally led the way, with four, maybe five others following.

'You all right, Irene? I've brought help.'

Irene grabbed Sally's cardigan, clinging the way she'd grabbed at her sister's coat all those years ago. 'Oh Sally, thank you, thank you, thank you.' She buried her head in the stale wool and began to sob.

They carried her back to bed, trying not to touch the red angry welts on her skin, or the raw open sores weeping on her ribs and hip bones. Careful not to rub the bruises that blackened her legs and arms.

'Oh God, Irene, what've they done tae ye, Hen?' Bridie Flannigan rang out the wet flannel in the washbasin by the bed and held it against her head. The others kept watch by the door, while Sally pulled blankets off the other beds to keep Irene warm.

'Quick, someone's coming,' one of the girls hissed from the doorway. The footsteps grew louder on the stairs. 'Shite, it's Sister Agatha. She'll kill us!'

Irene's eyes pleaded with Bridie. *Please don't leave me.* Bridie stretched under the bed and pulled out the metal potty, which was full of blood-stained urine and stinking faeces.

'I'll tell her I'm just here to empty this, don't worry, Irene.' She kissed her fingers and pressed them against Irene's lips.

'But she'll see I'm not tied up anymore.' Irene was panicking.

The other girls backed off as the black nun approached the doorway. Standing with their hands clasped in front of them, heads down. Ashamed they were caught helping a friend. Sister Agatha had a thick leather belt wrapped around her hand, the heavy, polished brass buckle hanging at her side. To most of the girls, the threat of the belt was enough to keep them in line. A few, including Bridie Flanagan, had been on the receiving end of at least one beating from it.

'What's going on here,' the nun demanded as Bridie walked towards her, down the narrow corridor between the beds.

'Just emptying the pot, Sister,' she explained, 'keeping the smell out of the place.'

'Who untied Irene Connolly? I thought I said she…'

Bridie interrupted. 'She's awful sick, Sister. The ropes were cutting her flesh and…'

'She's dangerous. Deranged.'

'The nun's pale blue eyes gave nothing away, but a single vein bulged on her forehead. 'Tie her up again. Immediately.'

Irene saw Bridie glance back at her before raising the potty above her head.

She threw the stinking contents straight into Sister Agatha's face. It took a few seconds for the others to grasp what had happened, as the putrid mixture clogged her stubby eyelashes, ran down her face and stained the pure white yolk of her habit. Her pale face turned purple with fury under the stinking mess. She raised her right hand high above her head, the leather belt swinging into action behind her.

But Bridie Flanagan was ready. Years on the streets of the Gorbals had taught her to be quick. She tightened her fist round the handle of the heavy-based chamber pot and, with a single blow, smashed it into Sister Agatha's face. The noise of her bones breaking could barely be heard for her cries. Her nose burst open and blood poured from the wound. It ran bright red down her chin as her stubby yellow teeth loosened in her gums. A grotesque grimace of pain tore across her mouth, and the internal bleeding seeped under her skin, across her broken cheekbones. She fell to the floor, both hands cupped round her nose and mouth.

Bridie Flanagan quickly shut the double doors, and one of the other girls rammed a mop through the handles, locking it fast from the inside.

Irene Connolly sat up on the bed, while Bridie, Sally and the three others stood in a huddle, saying nothing. Just staring, their mouths hanging open in shock at what had happened. Trembling with fear and disbelief. Bridie Flanagan clutched her chest, panting.

Irene was the first to laugh. A snigger escaped from her nose in disbelief. She hugged her arms round her bruised ribs to stop the pain as the giggling rose from her belly. The others looked on in stunned silence, believing for just a moment that she really was crazy. Then they too joined in. Tears streamed down their skinny wee faces as the screams of hysterical laughter drowned out Sister Agatha's cries on the other side of the door. On the other side of reason. The euphoria intoxicated them.

They held hands and danced round and round before flopping onto the empty beds. It was Sally who threw open one of the windows. The cold night air breezed in as she hung her body out, screaming and yelling for everyone to hear.

There were eight beds in the room. All empty, except tfor Irene's. She pulled the blankets up tight round her neck and watched as the others stripped two of the beds bare and dragged them over to the open window.

'You got any matches on you?' Bridie asked one of the younger girls, who pulled a small tin of tobacco from the leg of her knickers.

'Aye, I've a few.'

'That's enough,' said Bridie, striking them off the stone floor and holding them to the bare, soiled mattress. As the flames took hold, she got it onto its side and hurled it out the third-floor window. Fanned by the oxygen, it turned into a fireball as it hit the ground.

'Right, gi' us a hand with this.' It only needed two of them to ease the metal bed frame out of the same window.

By the time they were setting the second mattress alight they could hear the clangs of support on the pipes and radiators throughout the building as the other Magdalene girls banged shoes, keys, spoons and whatever else came to hand.

The second burning bed was soon joined by lighted paper, curtains, clothes and in some cases other mattresses, all thrown from other windows of the ancient house.

Thick black smoke filled the clear Maryhill night air. The bells of Glasgow North Fire Brigade clanging towards Lochbridge House could be heard for miles. Sally tucked her knickers into her skirt and climbed out of the window.

'What the hell are you doing?' Bridie grabbed at her ankle, pulling her back inside.

'Them firemen'll put out the fire and break down the door.

They'll get us out.'

'Aye, so?'

'They'll no' be able to catch me if I'm up on the roof.'

'Good girl, Sally,' Bridie laughed as she released her grip on Sally's skinny wee legs. She leaned her back on the windowsill and gave the others a running commentary as the wee thing scaled the drainpipe. She never faltered, never hesitated, her wiry frame as agile as a monkey's as she clawed her way up.

Within seconds Sally heaved her body up onto the tiles on the roof. Others cheered as they watched. A few were brave enough to join in solidarity, and Sally reached down her hand to help them up the last few inches to take their place beside her.

Bridie and the other three lassies in the bedroom shoved Irene's bed over to the window to let her see for herself.

'Oh God, what've we started?' she exclaimed, staring up at Bridie with a mixture of fear and admiration as the hot tears sprung to her eyes.

Bridie winked back at her. 'It's not what we've started, hen, it's what we've finished.'

★

Three days it lasted. Three days when the world sat up and took notice of the plight of the girls trapped in the Magdalene Asylum. Three days that proved to be the most exciting and happiest of Irene Connolly's miserable life.

Journalists came from miles around to hear first-hand the stories of the lassies yelling from the roof top, shouting out of the windows about their treatment. For the locals it was better than the Glasgow Fair. Every day they'd put food into the buckets that hung out of the windows and were hoisted up to feed the protesters.

By the third day it was over. By the third day Glasgow City Council decided to close the doors of the Magdalene Institute. And by the third day Irene was strong enough to join the others who ran up Maryhill Road to celebrate their victory. Lagging behind, and held up, she was helped along between her two best pals: Bridie Flanagan and Sally.

She never did find out Sally's second name. It turned out that Sally herself didn't even know it.

CHAPTER 35

Glasgow, 2000

Oonagh ignored Alec's warning and gave him a five-minute head start before following him to the South Side. She flicked through the buttons on the radio but there was nothing in the news that gave her any clue as to what had happened at St Patrick's. Too early, she guessed.

Instinct kicked in and she made a call to the newsroom at the studio to tip them off. Her mind raced, trying to figure out who it was. She called Tom. There was no reply. A sinking feeling took hold of her chest and the dark oppressive clouds overhead matched her mood as she took the Kinning Park exit off the M8 and into Pollokshields.

That was when she saw Mrs Brady in the distance, struggling up the road. Heavy plastic carrier bags with gaudy red letters on the side banging against her legs. The stretched handles digging into the flesh in her hands. A thin drizzle of rain clinging to her face. Her handbag hanging diagonally over her shoulders, an umbrella neatly rolled into a special slot designed to make life easier. But she'd need to put down all four bags to get it out. And anyway, she didn't have a spare hand to carry the umbrella.

It was difficult to tell what age Anna Brady was. Oonagh suspected no one had ever cared enough to ask her, and she didn't have anyone to tell.

Oonagh sounded the horn and pulled up alongside her. She leaned over and opened the passenger door. 'Mrs Brady…Anna, get in, I'll give you a lift home.' It seemed to take the woman a couple of seconds to register who was behind the wheel.

Oonagh was used to people tripping over themselves in a bid to charm her. 'Oh it's you,' was all Anna Brady said. Her voice was flat and lifeless. She blushed slightly.

Oonagh flicked open the boot from the inside, then got out to help load the shopping. Anna Brady struggled and fumbled as she took each bag from her. Oonagh ached with pity when she saw the deep red marks they'd left on her hands. She probably did this trip two, perhaps three times a week.

'It's all right, love, I'm fine.' She seemed annoyed at Oonagh's pitying look as she put the bags in the boot.

'How're you feeling, Mrs Brady?'

Despite Oonagh opening the passenger door she got in the back.

'Fine, dear, can't complain.'

No you can't really, can you, there's no one to listen, Oonagh was tempted to say. But didn't.

She drove to the chapel house, sacrificing the scoop she was leaving behind at the chapel in order to satisfy her curiosity.

A siren wailed in the distance. Mrs Brady said nothing else for the remainder of the journey and spent the time staring straight out the side window, clutching the cheap scuffed leather handbag on her lap. It wasn't long before they were home, a few minutes at most.

Oonagh pulled up at the back of the house and collected the bags from the boot. They shared the load and Oonagh followed Mrs Brady up the stairs and straight through to the kitchen.

'Thank you, dear,' was all she said as she put the bags on the table. She didn't move, didn't make any attempt to put the shopping away.

'Can we talk some more?' Oonagh asked. 'Not if you don't want to though. Not if you don't feel…' She let her words trail away. 'I might be able to help,' she added, though doubted that she could. What could she – or anyone for that matter – do?

They sat at the bare wooden table. Anna Brady opened a tobacco tin and rolled a thin cigarette. Oonagh pulled a packet of fags from her own bag. 'Here, have one of these.'

Anna Brady licked her lips slightly and weighed up her best option. 'Okay.' Her nails were bitten down to the quick, and she tugged her sleeve down over her wrist as she reached to accept Oonagh's offer.

'Is Father Tom here?' Oonagh asked.

Anna Brady shrugged her shoulders and looked into the middle distance. 'Dunno.'

★

Jack Cranworth was standing, and leaned across the desk as Davies walked into the interview room. 'Right, I want to speak to my lawyer. Who the hell do you think you're dealing with?'

Davies put his hand on Cranworth's shoulder and pushed him back down onto the wooden chair. 'Ach sit down and dry your eyes. I can't be arsed with your spiel just now. And, just for the record, I have every right to keep you here.' He looked at his watch, 'for six hours at least. And before you start bleating on again, no you can't see your lawyer.'

'That's fucking illegal. I know my rights.'

'Really? Well in that case you'll know I can stop you speaking to your brief if I believe it might hamper this investigation. If I decide to charge you – and there's every reason at this stage to believe I *will* charge you – *then* you can speak to your lawyer. But only then. Okay?'

'Charge me? With what?'

Davies ignored him.

'I'll have your job for this you bastard,' Cranworth said.

'*My* job? Aye, very good.'

Davies switched on the tape machine and spoke into the microphone perched on an upturned empty cassette box. He went through the usual routine – time, date, people present – before turning his attentions back to Cranworth.

'Right then, do you want to tell me what you were doing in Saint Patrick's?'

Cranworth folded his arms and looked at the wall. 'I was meeting someone.'

'Who?'

He shook his head.

'Want to tell me what your connection to Charles Antonio is?'

'Charles who?'

Davies looked at his watch. 'Are you going to play games for the remaining...let me see...five hours fifty-eight minutes, or can we just get this sorted out now?'

'I really don't know who you're talking about.' Cranworth seemed to think on. 'Oh, the fat man who fell from the balcony?' He shook his head. 'Never seen him before in my life.'

'Oh right. Just happened to be in the same place as the guy who by all accounts slashed your girlfriend and left her for dead, before *himself* meeting a mysteriously sticky end? Do us a favour, pal.'

Davies was growing weary. Tired and weary. He hadn't eaten since the previous afternoon. The burning sensation low in his chest was threatening to turn into a full-blown, crippling attack of indigestion. He rubbed his hand between his ribs and grimaced as he let out a sigh.

'Heartburn?' Cranworth watched him with mock concern. 'Better watch it. I've seen it all before. Patients think they have indigestion, turns out to be a heart attack. Can take you out like that.' He snapped two fingers.

'Really? I'm surprised you deal with cases like that. I thought you just killed helpless wee weans in your line of work.' He looked back at the tape machine. 'Shall we?'

Cranworth leaned back on the chair's wooden slats. 'Do you honestly think I followed this Charles Antony...?'

'Antonio,' Davies corrected.

'Yes, right, Antonio. Do you think I followed him to a church

196

full of children and killed him?' Cranworth raised his eyes and tutted as he shook his head. 'Honestly, if you think this was some sort of revenge killing, then don't you think I'd be just a tad more discreet? I'd hardly do it in a church, then hang around waiting for your lot to arrive.'

'Naw, your right.'

'What?'

'You're right. I don't think you killed Charlie. Poor bugger just slipped and fell. Just an unfortunate accident, that's all.'

His last remark had the intended effect. Cranworth slammed both palms onto the table. 'Then why the hell am I here?'

Davies leaned forward and spoke into the machine, recording that the interview would be stopping for a short break. He was already fishing out the cigarettes from his pocket as he made his way towards the door, leaving Cranworth alone with McVeigh.

It was only one cigarette, but it made his indigestion worse. The seed of an ulcer gnawed the inside of his gut. He felt he ought to eat something, and sent out for a roll and fried sliced sausage, which he wolfed down, feeling the instant gratification that only a roll and square sliced could bring. He marvelled at how a nation responsible for the television, the bicycle and penicillin had also invented a sausage shaped perfectly to fit neatly inside a roll. It had been his saviour on many a Sunday morning after a particularly heavy Saturday night.

He wiped the grease from his lips with the back of his hand before going back to the interview room and asking the policeman at the door to organise three coffees. Davies sat down, switched on the machine and started exactly where he'd left off.

'Why were you in the Church?'

'I told you, I was meeting someone.'

'Who?'

'I can't say. It's' – he paused – 'it's a personal matter.'

'Rubbish! You went there to meet Charlie Antonio.'

'Good God, man, I don't even know who he is… Was.'

'Isn't it true you hired him to kill Oonagh?'

Cranworth looked genuinely worried for the first time since the interview had begun. No, not worried; scared. Frown lines were etched deep into his brow. He picked at the top of the empty polystyrene coffee cup and shook his head. 'No, it's not true. It's not true.' His voice was little more than a whisper. 'I want to go to the toilet.' He stood up to leave. 'I assume I'm allowed that much?'

He grabbed his jacket from the back of the chair. Davies pulled it from him. 'Aye, once you've been searched of course.'

He went through the jacket pockets and gestured to McVeigh to frisk him.

'This is outrageous, I emptied my pockets when I came in,' he said as McVeigh ran his hands up the inside of his trouser leg.

'You're lucky it's not a full cavity body search. Could yet be.' Davies opened the door. 'Right, Mr Cranworth here wants to go to the loo. Stay with him the whole time.' The policeman outside the door nodded as Cranworth stepped outside.

'You're breaching my human rights,' he said to Davies as he passed.

'Aye? Think this is bad, wait until you slop out in Barlinnie for a few nights.'

★

Davies grew concerned when, after ten minutes, neither Cranworth nor the policeman had returned from the toilet.

'See what's keeping them,' he said to McVeigh as he looked at his watch. At which point the door opened. Cranworth walked in first, the policeman at his back, pinching his nose between his thumb and finger while fanning his face with his free hand. 'Sorry to take so long, boss, your man had a wee dose of the Tex Ritters.'

'Fucking barbaric,' Cranworth muttered as he passed the two men. He put both hands on the chair before gently lowering himself onto it.

McVeigh's bottom lip quivered and his nostrils flared as Davies told him to put the tape machine back on again.

'What's so bloody funny?' said Cranworth, staring directly at McVeigh.

'You having the skitters and smelling like a rats arse,' replied Davies, clicking the top of a pen with his thumb. 'Still, look on the bright side. Means a full body search is out of the question.' Davies made sure he remained straight-faced. 'Right, back to business. What do you know about Charlie Antonio?'

'Nothing. As I've already told you.'

'I thought you'd got rid of all your shite in the lavvy. Now once more, why were you meeting Charlie Antonio?'

'For God's sake, man, you've got to believe me. I'd never even heard of Charlie Antonio until today.'

'How much did you pay him? Charlie must have thought his luck was in this week. Just goes to show you what money can buy?'

'How many times do I have to tell you I had nothing to do with this?'

'Look, pal. You maybe didnae stick the blade in yourself, but that doesn't mean to say you're not responsible. Jesus Christ, Cranworth, you've got guilt written all over you, mate.'

Cranworth shook his head, over and over again. Davies folded his arms and said nothing. The only sound came from the clock on the wall as Cranworth stared trance-like at the table.

Fifteen minutes ticked by before Cranworth finally spoke.

'You've got it wrong. I loved her, why would I want to do anything to harm her?'

'What happened then? Was he not meant to get too heavy

with her? Just sent him there to give her a wee fright? All go wrong did it?'

Davies was conscious of Cranworth's enormous frame visibly shrinking.

'That's nonsense, it's just not true. Why don't you ask her?'

Davies ignored the question. 'Well why the hell did you arrange to meet him? Give yourself a break here, Cranworth. You're not doing yourself any favours.'

'I'm not saying another word until I see my lawyer.'

'Suit yourself.' Davies turned to McVeigh. 'Get a couple of uniforms in here. Let him stew in his own juice for the next five hours before we charge him. And if he so much as farts I want to be told.' He turned back to Cranworth. '*Then* you'll be able to speak to your lawyer. And by Christ, for your sake, you'd better hope he was trained in Philadelphia.'

★

Oonagh reached over and held Anna Brady's hand, seeing the same scared look she recognised from the eyes of the other women she'd interviewed. She held the woman's gaze for a moment, seeing only misery and torment in her yellow watery eyes.

'Look,' said Oonagh, 'if ever you need someone to talk to, or...' She wasn't sure what else she could offer, and instead just squeezed her hand. She wanted to be caring, loving even, but worried that she was coming across as patronising.

Mrs Brady pulled her hand away when she heard someone come through the back door. Tom's jaw dropped when he saw them both at the table.

'Oonagh. I take it you've heard then? Did Davies call you?'

Oonagh fell back against the chair, winded by her relief that it hadn't been Tom who'd taken the tumble at Saint Patrick's. She shook her head. 'No. What happened at the chapel?' She fished her mobile from her bag and saw that she'd missed two messages, both from Davies.

'Charlie Antonio,' said Tom. 'He fell off the balcony.'

Before the shock of this news had properly hit her, Tom was pulling an audiocassette tape from his pocket and putting it on the table between herself and Mrs Brady.

Oonagh instantly recognised it as one of her own, from a pile she had at home. All with her Magdalene interviews recorded on them.

'Where the hell did you get this?' said Oonagh, kicking her chair back hard enough to send it crashing to the floor. 'That's private material. Confidential.'

'Sorry, Oonagh. I picked it up by accident. I didn't mean any harm, I only realised I had it this morning and I was about to give it back to you when I noticed the date.' He pointed at it as though she might need reminding. 'Oonagh, it's from Wednesday the eighth. The day you were attacked.' Tom slotted it into the battered ghetto blaster on the dresser behind them. In an instant a voice they all recognised filled the kitchen. 'Losing a child…' said the voice, crackling with emotion, '…it's torture. You never forget, you know. It was torture, and it still is.'

Oonagh slammed her hand onto the off switch. But Tom seemed nonplussed.

'I've heard it, Oonagh. I listened to it in the car.' He looked weary as he took the tape from the machine and stepped over to Anna Brady. 'That's you on that tape isn't it, Mrs Brady?'

'Oh don't talk rubbish, Tom,' Oonagh butted in. Wouldn't let the older woman answer. Anna Brady dropped her eyes and rolled the red hot end of the cigarette between her fingers until it went out.

Tom wouldn't let up. 'Mrs Brady, I know it's you, it's your voice.'

Oonagh tried to grab the tape from his hand, but Tom held it just out of her reach. 'Stop this, Tom. You have no idea what you're dealing with here.' But he was defiant.

The last few days had taken their toll and Oonagh was no longer in the mood to be reasonable. She clenched her hand into a fist and punched Tom square on the face. His legs buckled and he dropped the tape as he slumped onto the chair holding his jaw. Oonagh ignored his wounded expression, snatched the tape and pulled it clear from its casing. She uncoiled yards and yards of black shiny ribbon until all of it lay in a useless heap on the floor. Her voice hiccupped with emotion and she immediately felt guilty for having lashed out at Tom. He was too easy a target on whom to vent her anger.

She needed to justify herself. 'You had no right – no bloody right to listen to that tape.' A big angry mark was forming on Tom's cheek, just below his eye. 'Shit.' She was annoyed at him for bruising so easily. She opened the freezer. 'Here.' She pressed a packet of frozen broccoli against Tom's bruise. 'Sorry. I just freaked. I'm a bag of nerves since…you know.'

Tom held onto the ice pack and moved his jaw from side to side, as if mimicking something from TV. 'Alright, does someone want to tell me what the hell's going on?'

'Nothing. Right.' Oonagh was still in a huff and busied herself scooping up the discarded tape and stuffing it into a black bin-liner.

Mrs Brady's chin seemed to dissolve into her chest, but she didn't cry.

'Oonagh, leave that just now, eh?' Tom stood up with his back to Mrs Brady, as though that would stop her hearing him.

Oonagh tied a knot in the top of the bin-bag and carried it to the back door. 'So what happened with Antonio then? How the hell did he fall off the balcony?' She didn't like the look on Tom's face. 'What is it?' she asked as she walked back to the table.

Tom made a big play of his sore face and held the frozen food against his cheek with both hands. Oonagh lit another cigarette and sat down beside Anna Brady, who seemed to be in a world of her own and was stubbing out the already dead fag in the ashtray. 'Here,' said Oonagh, and handed her a fresh one.

Tom sat opposite them, trying to catch Mrs Brady's eye, but the housekeeper wasn't really focusing on anything. 'So. If you were at Oonagh's house that day, well you should really go to the police.'

Oonagh felt pig sick and sat on her hands in case she belted him on the other side of his face. 'For the love of God will you shut the fuck up about that? What difference does it make?'

Tom folded his arms, seemingly mortified at being told off in front of his housekeeper.

Anna looked at the clock. 'I need to get on.' She squeezed the end of her cigarette and put it in her pocket for later.

She got up to leave and Oonagh tried not to make her concerned smile too patronising. 'Take care,' she said, giving her fingers a squeeze. But Anna didn't respond and her hand hung limp at her side.

Oonagh watched her shuffle away and waited until she'd closed the door before turning to Tom. 'How much did you listen to?'

'Not much.' He seemed eager to be talking about the tape again. He explained that he'd been on his way to her house to drop it off when he'd stuck it on out of idle curiosity and had recognised Anna Brady's voice immediately. 'That's not the point Oonagh. It's *when* it was recorded that's the important thing. I mean she must have left your house just minutes before you were attacked.'

Oonagh picked at the skin on the side of her thumb. 'Leave her out of it. It was tough enough to get her to talk at all without dragging her into this.'

Tom didn't know when to shut up. 'But she might have seen something, maybe noticed someone hanging around outside.

As soon as I realised I doubled back over to the chapel. I thought she'd be there this afternoon. But God, see when I got there… Jeezo. It was pandemonium.'

It was Oonagh's chance to steer the conversation away from her attack and back onto Tom's big adventure. 'So what's the deal with Antonio? Were you there when it happened?'

Tom waved his hand as though he was sorry he'd missed all the action. 'No. Got there just as the police and ambulance arrived.'

'So what's the score then? D'you think he fell or jumped or what? Did you see Davies? Did he say anything?'

The frozen broccoli was beginning to thaw and melted ice trickled down Tom's face. 'You're not going to like this,' he said.

'Like what? What is it? Tell me.'

So he told her. And he was right. She didn't like it. Not one little bit.

CHAPTER 36

Glasgow, 2000

Davies didn't believe in coincidences, and the chances of two proddies turning up at the same Catholic church at the same time were slimmer than slim. By the time they drove back to St Patrick's, Charlie's body was long gone, and a minor clean-up operation was underway. Three women and a man, all in white overalls, were scrubbing the pews and pouring disinfectant on the floor. The excrement, blood and body fluids had already been cleaned away; only the stench lingered. The decision had been made to keep the church closed to the general praying public for a day or two. And, as a mark of respect, or perhaps because the Church was afraid the odour of death would linger, the venue for Father Kennedy's funeral had been switched to Saint Luke's in the Gorbals.

Inside, Davies went straight to the seat Cranworth had occupied just before Charlie had taken his tumble. He sent McVeigh upstairs. 'Can you see me from where you are?' he shouted up.

'No, not unless I...' McVeigh leaned over the wooden railings.

'For crying out loud, get back,' Davies yelled. 'Those guys haven't finished cleaning up after the last one!'

It was obvious Charlie had been leaning over the banister to check if Cranworth had arrived. He *must* have been there for a payoff. Why else would he still have had the weapon with which Oonagh had been attacked? He'd have dumped it otherwise.

Instinctively, Davies felt under the seat. Nothing. He pushed up the padded knee rests and lay on the floor. No sign of anything stuffed down the seat in front either. The row backed onto a wall and the wooden beams of the pew were screwed firmly in place. A pile of hymn books was stacked in a corner at the end of the seat. Davies didn't exactly keep his fingers crossed as he slid along the wooden bench, but knew he'd find what he was looking for if God was in his Heaven. Tucked behind the pile of books was a bulging manila envelope.

'Gotcha.'

*

Back at the station it took just minutes to match Cranworth's prints with two big fat thumb prints on the inside of the envelope, which turned out to contain five grand. A team had already been dispatched to go over Charlie's house with a fine tooth comb. This would give extra impetus to their work.

Stepping outside, Davies stretched his arms and gently teased his aching back muscles out of the crick they'd formed. Rubbing the side of his neck, he put his face upwards, this time grateful for the splashes of rain which temporarily revived him.

Something wasn't right. Call it sixth sense, call it intuition, call it experience, but something wasn't right. Why the hell would Cranworth hire Charlie to kill Oonagh?

Cranworth was no fool. If he wanted Oonagh out of the way he'd have made sure the job was done properly – and wouldn't have hired someone who knew her. Although perhaps he had no idea that Oonagh already knew Charlie Antonio. It could have been a coincidence. And he'd always known Charlie Antonio to be an ignorant wee shite, but he'd never had him down as a killer. So how did he fit in to the case?

Davies shook his head. He also had an inkling that Oonagh wasn't telling him everything. He felt a sting of betrayal.

McVeigh was suddenly in front of him, holding two steaming cups of coffee, fresh from the machine.

'Milk, two sugars, is that right?' he said, handing one over.

'Aye, and the rest,' Davies replied, taking a hip flask from his back pocket. 'The only thing that makes this stuff bearable,' he said, pouring in a good measure. It wasn't clear – even to himself – if he meant the coffee, the job, or Oonagh. He blew on the liquid before taking a sip and tried to shift the weight he felt was bearing down on him.

'It just disnae make sense,' he said aloud.

'But surely now you've found the cash it makes perfect sense. You said so yourself. Cranworth obviously hired Antonio to kill Oonagh, but Antonio bungled it. Maybe he was disturbed before he could finish the job. Bloody hell, we found the weapon on him and Cranworth's fingerprints on the cash. What more do you want?'

Davies leaned his cup on the windowsill on the inside of the entranceway as he topped it up again with Glenmorangie from his flask. He screwed the top back on slowly as his mind ticked over. 'If you hire a plumber, he brings his own tools, right?' McVeigh looked lost, so Davies didn't wait for a reply. 'And you wouldnae expect to lend a carpenter your screwdriver, would you?'

'Eh, no…'

'Well why the hell would a hired killer turn up at a job without a weapon and instead use an antique letter-opener that the poor unfortunate victim just happened to have on her hall table? Like I said, it disnae make sense.'

But he knew that shouldn't surprise him. He'd seen a seven-stone pensioner who'd been kicked to death for a couple of quid; he'd watched a dealer walk free from court after selling a dodgy E to a fifteen-year-old kid who'd ended up on a slab; and he'd seen a father of two who'd had his throat slit for wearing the wrong colour of scarf on a Saturday afternoon. So no, it didn't make sense, but sometimes things just didn't.

'What if it was all planned,' suggested McVeigh. 'A double bluff.'

'Go on.'

'Well, if he went along and tried to make it look like another break-in…planned to use a knife or something…as though he'd been disturbed…so it wouldn't look like a professional job…'

Davies pondered the idea, nodding his head slowly. 'Aye, but using Charlie Antonio? He's no killer.'

'Not that we know of,' said McVeigh. 'But if you wanted someone to break in then he's your man. He's well known for his wee uninvited visits to people. Especially those who'd rather keep their private lives private.'

Davies stopped drinking and looked at his partner. 'Aye, and it's no' as if he had his pick of jobs. He was always scrounging. Maybe he decided to branch out, stretch his wings.' He drank the rest of the coffee in a oner. 'You might have just earned yer keep, son.'

'What?'

Davies liked that he'd stunned McVeigh. But then for once he'd spouted a theory that made sense.

'Do you honestly think that's actually what happened?' McVeigh checked.

'Well put it this way, I don't think you're too wide of the mark.' Davies scrunched up his plastic cup and threw it towards the bin beside the door, scoring. Then, turning to McVeigh, he said, 'Right, I need to speak to Oonagh again. But I'm telling you, she won't like it when she finds out we've got Cranworth in here.'

CHAPTER 37

Glasgow, 2000

It was like a game of hide and seek. Oonagh raced to Saint Patrick's, but Davies had already departed. A policeman at the door told her Davies was back at the station, but by the time she reached the station the desk sergeant told her Davies had been and gone.

'Well can you at least tell me if Dr Cranworth is being held?' But no, he wouldn't budge.

Oonagh couldn't believe it when Tom told her he'd seen Jack getting led into the back of a police car. She'd been holding the packet of frozen broccoli against his battered face to stop it swelling when he'd broken the news. She knew he hadn't told her as any act of revenge for the punch to his jaw.

There was an angry red mark forming on her knuckles and it stung like hell. She wondered if kicking Father Watson then hitting Tom in the space of a few hours counted as Church-bashing. She returned to the futile attempt to extract even a morsel of information from the desk sergeant.

'Has Dr Cranworth called his lawyer? Can you let him know I'm here?'

He eyed the space on the third finger of her left hand. 'You his wife?' he asked.

'No I'm not his fu...' She held back, realising it was a rhetorical question. The guy obviously knew who she was. He'd greeted her by name as she'd walked through the swing doors. Probably watched her on the box nearly every night. She gulped down a mouthful of air. It tasted stale. Like old training shoes and pee.

She was scared – scared and sick – and had to keep her hand over her mouth to stop from retching as she left the station.

Everything was moving too fast.

Back in the car she punched she steering wheel in frustration and was almost glad of the pain that shot through her already-tender knuckles. She was desperate to speak to Davies, but his phone was switched off. Tiredness crept through her, turning her legs to jelly. She toyed with the idea of going back to see Tom, but that notion proved no match for her exhaustion, which led her back home. She wanted her mum, with her cold red wine and shrunken cashmere.

★

Davies watched Cranworth's wife through the doorglass as she slowly made her way down the stairs. She pulled her skirt taut with both hands and smoothed her hair before opening the door. Davies and McVeigh held up their cards.

'My husband's not here,' she said, already closing the door.

'I know, we've got him down at the station. Anyway it's you we need to speak to. May we?' His foot was already inside.

She held the door just eighteen inches wide, forcing them to enter in single file. Her face held its familiar startled expression, her eyes wide beneath the high, solid arch of her thinly plucked brows.

A suitcase stood near the stairs. Rich burgundy leather, her initials embossed on the side.

'Going somewhere?' asked Davies. She ignored him and led the way into the sitting room.

'Right, get on with it.' There was no sign of the dutiful wife routine Davies had noted on his previous visit. She stood by the roaring fire, tapping a long, thin, pink cigarette against the back of her hand before lighting it with a silver lighter.

'Dr Cranworth, we're questioning your husband in connection with the attempted murder of Oonagh O'Neil.'

'So?' she scraped a piece of stray filter tip from her tongue with her finger nail.

'You don't seem very concerned.'

'And?'

'Well, if you don't mind me saying so, you don't seem very surprised either.'

She shrugged her shoulders as she perched on the arm of a cream sofa, her legs crossed, leaning over to flick her cigarette into the ashtray on the glass table.

'Does the name Charlie Antonio mean anything to you?' Davies thought she faltered, just for an instant, as she dragged the ashtray closer with a long painted talon. 'Dr Cranworth?'

'No. No, I don't think so.'

'You don't seem too sure.'

'No.' She took a long draw, held it for a moment then blew it out through the side of her lips. 'I'm sure.'

'Oonagh O'Neil. How well do you know her?'

'I don't. Oh I know she was screwing my husband if that's what you're referring to.' The grey ash crept its way along the pink cigarette. A thin plume of smoke spiralled up from the tip. She tipped her chin upwards as she exhaled, her expression unchanged. It was obvious Jean Cranworth had no intention of helping in any way. And she took great pleasure in letting Davies and McVeigh know as much.

They had very little on her, nothing more than a copper's hunch, and it was clear that she knew it.

A remote control lay on the coffee table next to the ashtray. She picked it up, and pointed it, not at the television but at the blazing fire, killing the flames with one click of a button.

'It didn't bother you that your husband was having an affair?'

'Why should it?'

'And you didn't feel jealous?'

She let out a shrill laugh. 'Of what? That media pop-tart?' She stubbed her cigarette out, grinding the tip hard into the ashtray.

Davies saw the veins bulge on the back of her tanned, leathery hand and recognised an ageing process locked onto fast forward by years of sun beds and foreign holidays. She wore a black V-necked cardigan. The tendons on her neck stuck out like over-stretched guitar strings, her dark, crepe-paper skin hanging in a fold over her chest.

'You don't have any children do you, Dr Cranworth?'

She shot him a quizzical look. 'No. Do you?'

'How old are you, Dr Cranworth?'

'Forty-...' she hesitated, 'I'm forty-two.'

He knew she was lying. Either that or she'd had a bloody hard paper-round as a kid.

'Oh I get it. You think I might have flown into a jealous rage because this O'Neil girl was pregnant.' She tossed her head back as she let out the same shrill laugh as before. 'Look around you, Sergeant,'

'Detective Inspector,' he corrected.

She held her arms aloft, palms upwards. Davies imagined she'd spent hours in front of the mirror perfecting that pose.

'I have everything I want. There is nothing this O'Neil woman has that I could possibly want or need. I even have my very own husband.' She tried to raise her eyebrows, but they were as high as they were ever going to go. Her smile was smug and self-satisfied. She stood up and walked to the door.

They were outside, nearly at the car, when Davies turned round.

'Dr Cranworth, what makes you think Oonagh O'Neil was pregnant?'

A smile struggled its way to her lips. Davies saw her face twitch – as much as it could – as her tongue licked her dry parched mouth. Her lipstick bled through a mass of tiny vertical lines onto her face.

'Isn't it common knowledge? I mean, wasn't it in the

newspapers?'

'If you say so.'

Davies spun the wheels on the drive, cutting through the gravel to leave a fine spray of mud in their wake. He watched Jean Cranworth in his rear view mirror as they departed. She didn't close the door for as long as they could still see her.

★

Oonagh gently lowered herself into the bath. The hot water lapped up past her shoulders. Every bone in her body ached. The lump on the back of her head throbbed with the effort of trying to make sense of everything. She closed her eyes and allowed herself to drift off in the warmth. Thoughts of Anna Brady and her sorry miserable life flooded through her, and the wound on her neck wept in sympathy.

CHAPTER 38

Glasgow, 2000

Davies and McVeigh got back to the station in time to witness a great comic spectacle. It was a bit of a treat for McVeigh, he'd never seen him before.

'What the hell is he all about?'

Despite the rain he walked slowly through the car park, head held high, swinging a silver-topped walking stick. It was purely for show. From the look of his jaunt, his legs were in perfect working order. He was wearing a three-piece navy tartan suit, with broad lapels and a high-buttoned waistcoat. He couldn't have been more than thirty-one, thirty-two at a push, but his hair was brushed back, and huge sideburns crept down his face, developing into a massive handle bar moustache. There was no beard, his chin was conspicuously bald. It accentuated his pixie-like features. The whole ensemble was made complete by a pair of black and white spats.

'Wearing an outfit like that in Govan is the equivalent of wearing a sign with *Please Kick Me* round your neck,' Davies pointed out.

'Do you think he's a nutter?' asked McVeigh.

'That, son,' said Davies, 'is Cranworth's solicitor.' It was the first time he'd laughed in days.

'What's with the get-up? Is he kidding on?'

'It's his idea of being a rebel. His family are loaded, but he's no' got the balls to give it all up and become an urban poet. Quite sad really. Dresses in that flamboyant way to make up for his rather dull personality. Thinks if he acts like a mad old eccentric it'll make up for his lack of character, which is hilarious considering most of his peers are just recovering from the rave scene. Don't let him fool you though. He's shit hot at what he does. Come on, hurry up, he'll be giving the desk sergeant laldy.'

Inside, the tartan-clad solicitor tapped his cane on the ground until he got the attention of the policeman behind the desk. His behaviour did not go down well.

'Whit?'

'I believe you're holding my client.' He took a pinch of snuff from a lacquered box.

Davies intervened before the policeman charged him with being an arsehole. 'Mr Henderson, I'm afraid you can't speak to your client at the moment. We really are in the middle of a very delicate situation.'

Henderson started his tried and tested speech about the outrageous fascist regime of Strathclyde Police. He was small – five foot four – and slightly built. Davies placed both hands on his shoulders to calm him down. It made him look all the more ridiculous, like a demented pixie.

'Now, you're welcome to wait.' Davies held up his hands, ignoring Henderson's protests, and walked straight to his office, closing the door behind him. He pulled down the blind on his window just in time to see Henderson flap his handkerchief onto the wooden bench before sitting down. If there was ever a man who'd missed his thespian calling...

Davies collected his thought for a few moments.

Finding the cash in St Patrick's gave them enough to link Cranworth to Oonagh's attack, even if it didn't put him at the scene of the crime. Still, they had little else to go on – Antonio's wife hadn't come up with much; but then she was undoubtedly still in shock after having to identify the body. No, he'd have to stick with it for now, despite his nagging doubts.

McVeigh knocked and entered, clutching a paper bag, their colleague Amy Law at his back.

'Before we go any further,' said Davies, 'get someone to keep an eye on Cranworth's wife. And for God's sake be discreet, I don't want us hit with a harassment suit.'

Amy passed the order onto the uniformed man in the hallway, before following McVeigh into the room.

'Right, what have you got?' McVeigh passed him the bag that contained the discarded pregnancy kit. 'It's got Oonagh's fingerprints. We found it in Charlie's bin.'

Davies rubbed his face. 'Find out when the bins get emptied in Hyndland.'

'Tuesday,' McVeigh told him, looking a little smug at having already checked. 'And Oonagh said she did the test on Tuesday morning. Which means…'

Davies finished his sentence, '…that Charlie must have taken it from the bin *inside* Oonagh's house. So it *was* him who staged the wee break-in the night before. Good. We need some definites.' He put his hand on the phone, preparing to dial, but looked at McVeigh first. 'Well, what do you think?'

'Me?'

'Aye, you.' Davies shook his head. 'What the hell was Antonio doing at Oonagh's? She couldn't stand the little prick. Do you think maybe it was Cranworth's wife who got Charlie to pay Oonagh a wee visit?'

'Maybe. But that doesn't explain what Cranworth was doing with the cash at the chapel.'

'No, it doesn't. But I don't believe Cranworth and his wife would both hire the *same* man to do a break-in and a murder in the *same* house within the *same* twenty-four hours, do you?'

'Seems unlikely. D'you think the money was a set-up? D'ye think he was round there and something happened, maybe it all just got a bit out of hand?'

Davies had been in this job long enough to know it didn't take much for things to get so out of hand that a woman could end up with her throat slit. 'Don't know, but five grand's not a lot to kill someone, not nowadays.' Davies had his own theory spinning inside his head. He looked at Amy. 'What about you, what've you got?'

'Well, sir' – she unclipped the pink carbon paper from her clipboard and put it down on his desk – 'we found this.'

Davies felt the colour rise in his cheeks as his eyes scanned the details of the six-month-old arrest form. He slammed his hands down on the desk. 'Get me that wee shite Findlay on the phone.' Davies watched McVeigh crease his eyebrows together. 'No, on second thoughts don't bother. We'll pay him a visit.'

CHAPTER 39

Glasgow, 2000

'How much did you listen to?' Her voice was so quiet that Tom struggled to hear.

'Not much really. Just enough to twig it was you.'

Anna Brady picked up a few fragments of the destroyed tape, which lay dotted around the lino. She gathered them into the palm of her hand then dropped them in the bin.

'Mrs Brady, why didn't you let on that you were with Oonagh the day she was attacked?'

The housekeeper slumped onto the chair and wiped her tears away with the heel of her hand. 'You don't understand. This never goes away.' She banged her chest with her fist.

He looked at Anna Brady, perhaps for the first time. Her grey hair gathered in wisps around her forehead. Creases formed round her eyes, but he noticed there were no laughter lines. None of the characteristic features of a woman her age.

'Mrs Brady, were you there when Charlie Antonio attacked Oonagh? Did you see anything? Did he threaten you?' Tom remembered seeing Charlie Antonio leave the chapel house on the day Oonagh was attacked. He'd assumed at the time that it was *him* he'd come round to see. He wondered now if Mrs Brady had been his target.

She didn't answer him. Just stared blankly ahead. Her fingers traced lines on the table and her lips continued to tremble. Oonagh had refused to admit Mrs Brady had seen anything. Claimed it was why she hadn't mentioned it to the police. But was it just Mrs Brady she was trying to protect?

'Mrs Brady, did you see anyone else at Oonagh's that day?' She looked at him for a moment. 'Was there another man? A tall man, maybe, with grey hair?' He described Jack Cranworth, from what he remembered from their single meeting in Saint Patrick's. 'Mrs Brady, please try and think.' Tom clasped his hands tightly together. He was pleading with her.

'I don't want to have to speak to the police. I don't want everything getting dragged up.' She spoke in little more than a whisper.

Tom grasped at this fragile link and stood over her. 'No, no Mrs Brady.' He tried to restrain his excitement. 'I promise. The police have their man. They don't care about anything else now.'

She looked unconvinced.

'Why did you go to Oonagh's house that day?'

'She called me, asked me to come over. At first I thought it was you she wanted. I know you two were, well, y'know, friends like.'

Tom jumped in, eager to put the record straight. 'It wasn't anything like that. There was nothing in it.'

She gave him a *who cares* look. 'Hardly likely with you being gay.' She wiped her nose, and folded her tissue before tucking it back inside her sleeve.

The colour rose in Tom's face. 'How the hell did you know? I mean who told you that?'

She tutted. 'It's easy to recognise troubled souls. We stick out like sore thumbs.' She gave another blow into her hankie.

Tom felt like a complete shit for not recognising the troubled soul trapped inside Anna Brady.

'Anyway, I went round to see her. Turned out she recognised me from the picture.'

'The picture?'

'Yes, the one with the Glasgow Magdalene girls. She showed it to you once, remember?' She looked so scared that Tom didn't have the heart to tell her he had no more than a vague recollection of the picture. 'She's a smart girl, Oonagh O'Neil,' she continued. 'I knew she'd work it out eventually'

'So what happened? Was Charlie Antonio in her house when you got there? Did she call him?'

'You're sure the police won't come round asking questions. I couldn't bear that.'

'No, Mrs Sweeny. The police won't come anywhere near…' A bang at the door shook the entire house. '…here.' He peered out of the window towards the door. 'Shit.'

★

Tom saw the rage in Davies' eyes.

'I want a wee word with you,' the detective said. He prodded Tom hard in the shoulder, almost pushing him over as he stepped in out of the rain.

'Eh? Yeah, of course.' Tom glanced back at the kitchen door, to where Mrs Brady was sitting. 'We'll go into the living room. Just let me organise some tea.' He wanted to warn Mrs Brady to stay out of the way, but Davies blocked his path.

'Fuck the tea, sunshine, we need to talk.'

Tom winced as he was frog-marched him into the room. McVeigh just shrugged his shoulders as though to say, 'what did you expect?'

Davies paced the floor like a caged animal. 'Why didn't you tell me you were at it with Charlie Antonio?'

'At it?'

'Aye – canoodling like a pair of loved-up teenagers in Kelvingrove Park.'

'You didn't ask.'

Davies let out an exaggerated sigh, and pushed his hands through his hair. He breathed in deeply through flared nostrils, the corners of his mouth turned downwards. His voice was slow and deliberate.

'I didn't ask? *I didn't ask?* So it's *my* fault?' He turned to McVeigh, pointing his finger. 'Take this as a valuable lesson in police work, son. The next time you uncover a dead body in a church, don't forget to ask the priest if he's shagged the corpse. Sweet Jesus, give me strength.'

'I didn't *shag* him. I just... Anyway I thought you knew. You knew that *I'd* been picked up in Kelvin Way. I naturally assumed you knew who I'd been with at the time.'

Davies calmed somewhat and sat down on a foot stool near the window. Tom took this as a sign that he was being believed.

'And what happened after that? After the pair of you were picked up?'

'Nothing. I never...'

Davies stood up again. 'Right, up you get. I've had enough farting about. I cannae be arsed any longer. I'm arresting you for withholding information and taking the bloody piss.'

Tom realised his only option was to play ball. 'Okay, okay,' he took a deep breath, wringing his hands together. 'He was blackmailing me.'

Davies sat back down. 'Go on.'

And the events of the past four months tumbled out like so many confessions he'd heard over the years. Every sorry, grubby, wee humiliating detail.

'Why didn't you come to us?' Davies eventually asked.

'Are you kidding? The papers get one whiff about a priest being gay and right away he's a pervert, a paedophile, touching-up young boys. You know that's how it is. I was terrified.'

'What about Oonagh? Does she know about this?'

'Yes, I told her. Just last week actually. We had a bit of a heart to heart.'

'D'you think that's why Antonio was round at her place. Think she maybe tried to get him to back off?'

Tom slumped back in his chair and stared at the window. The rain wasn't letting up. Little puddles were gathering at the bottom of the frames, on the inside.

'No, no I don't,' he said. And for the first time he considered the possibility that he might have been an unwitting accomplice in what had happened. He pictured the scenario, Oonagh inviting Charlie round to discuss the situation. It all going wrong. He felt the lump rising in his throat, clenched his teeth and bit his lip; he didn't want to cry in front of Davies, not again. He stood up, stuffing his knuckle in his mouth, biting down to stem the tears. 'Dear God!' he screamed, 'don't tell me I've caused all this. Shite, I could have had her killed.'

Davies and McVeigh were visibly taken aback.

'Ach, sit down and don't be so bloody hysterical,' Davies said. 'She's not dead, and nobody's saying it's your fault. But if *she* can't remember, then *I* need to try and piece together exactly what happened.'

Despite all his efforts, Tom blubbed into his sleeve. He was aware that Davies had at least turned his back and was staring out of the window, arms folded tightly across his chest.

McVeigh was left to do the reassuring, mouthing platitudes about things sometimes just happening and it being unlikely to have been because of anything *he'd* done or said.

Davies turned again, looking at his watch. He seemed anxious to leave.

'Right, Father, you think of anything else we should know and you're on the blower to us straight away. Right?'

'Anything else?' said Tom. 'Like what? You know who did it, what else do you need to know?'

But both Davies and McVeigh were already walking out the door.

★

CHAPTER 40

Glasgow, 2000

It was soft underfoot and her feet sank into the wet sand, making every step an effort. Her dad held the baby in his arms, just out of reach, and beckoned her to join. The sun was blinding and her legs didn't have the strength to pull her feet up through the wet ground. The tide was coming in and the sea lapped up against her ankles, then her thighs, until she was pulled under. Her dad seemed to drift further away until he and the baby were just a dot in the distance. Her own arms ached with loneliness and she allowed the water to come up over her head.

When she awoke the water was stone cold and her mum was frantically banging on the bathroom door. 'Oonagh! Oonagh! Are you all right? Can you hear me?'

She sat up, dazed and confused. Then all hell seemed to break loose.

Davies came crashing through the door, shoulder first, sending splinters of wood flying in all directions. Her mum quickly followed and rear-ended him. McVeigh wasn't far behind, and rushed in like the last of the Mohicans.

'God Almighty!' was all he said at the sight of Oonagh in the cold bath, struggling to cover her naked body with a face cloth.

'I'm fine,' she screamed.

Her mum immediately shoved both men out of the broken door – 'Ok boys, show's over' – and held up a towel for Oonagh as she climbed out of the bath. 'You ok?'

Oonagh nodded. 'I'm fine, Mum. I…maybe dozed off.'

'Thank goodness. I got quite a fright when you didn't respond. Sorry about the…' She nodded at the damaged door. 'Right, I'll go down and finish lunch, make sure those two aren't scarred for life!'

Oonagh pulled on a robe and staggered downstairs. Her legs were wobbly and she clung to the banister to steady herself.

She joined the other three in the kitchen, scraping her wet hair behind her ears. She shot McVeigh a look that warned him never to conjure up the sight of her naked again. Davies at least had the decency to look mortified as he was poured a cup of tea and quizzed about the goings-on at Saint Patrick's.

'You might have at least let me know, Alec,' she said, pulling up a seat at the table. 'Mum, can you give us a few minutes here?'

She waited until her mum had left the room before she spoke again, though it was hard to restrain herself even that long.

'What the flaming hell's going on?' she finally burst out. 'Is it true? Was it Charlie Antonio who attacked me?' She didn't give him time to answer. 'And what've you taken in Jack Cranworth for? He's got nothing to do with this. I've told you already, Alec; if you go down this path I'll drop any charges. You can't force this without my cooperation.'

Alec blew on his tea before taking a sip. 'Oonagh, can you come down off your high horse for just a few minutes? I did call. I left a message, for God's sake. Two actually.'

She nodded. He was right, she was just pissed off.

'And before you start blowing on about Cranworth,' Davies continued, 'it's not quite as simple as that.' He told her about Jack being in Saint Patrick's when Antonio took his tumble. And about finding the cash. Oonagh was miffed at the thought of her life only being worth a measly five grand. 'Cranworth might have paid him to attack you. We just don't know yet. Nonetheless, we're still questioning him over Antonio's death.' Alec held up his hand to stop her interrupting.. 'Yeah, I know it was probably an accident, but until that's proved, like any sudden death it's being treated as suspicious.'

Alec had his copper's hat on and wouldn't let up. He dropped his voice, so her mum wouldn't hear, and told Oonagh about her pregnancy kit turning up at Antonio's house. 'It looks like it was Antonio who pulled the break-in stunt and staged that bleeding phone call the night before you were attacked. But, whatever happened, he obviously thought it worth his while to go back the next day. My bet is someone put him up to it.'

Oonagh's flesh crawled at the idea of him going through her house. Touching her things. She instinctively wiped her hands on her dressing gown.

'And that someone is Jack, eh?' She got no answer. 'Alec, apart from anything else, I just don't think Jack would risk it. It's not his style.' No it wasn't his style. But no matter how much she struggled, she couldn't come up with a single plausible explanation as to why Jack would be in a Catholic church with a fist full of dollars, waiting for that shit Antonio. Well, there *was* a single plausible explanation, but she refused to even countenance it, afraid that if the seed was sown it would take root and never leave. She had to speak to Jack herself.

Davies reached across the table to touch her hand. 'You've had a rough time of it, haven't you? You looked pretty battered up there.'

Never one to mince his words. And he was right. The bruise from Charlie Antonio's heel might have faded to a yellow and red sunburst across her shoulder, but the stitches holding together the wound on her neck were black and crusty, and her arms and legs still bore the scratches and bruises from when she'd run barefoot and screaming from her house the night Charlie Antonio had broken in. Free of make-up, she knew her face was pale and drawn. She could almost forgive Alec for patronising her; she knew she looked small and vulnerable.

'Can't you remember *anything* about the attack, Oonagh?'

She shook her head.

'Are you sure?' He squeezed her hand. 'Is there something

you're not telling me?'

Oonagh had known Alec for long enough. He'd get to the bottom of this sooner or later. She could tell by the look in his eyes that he didn't quite believe her. She rubbed at her forehead, and tried not to ham it up too much.

'Now that you mention it…I do remember something about Charlie Antonio. I *think* I remember seeing him. But it all happened so fast. Honestly, Alec, it was over in a flash. And if you hadn't mentioned him…I don't know if I would ever have remembered it was him.' That bit of it was true. Every time she thought about it the back of her head throbbed and her wound stung.

'What about that clown Watson? Have you thought to question him at all? I bet it was him. Tried to shut me up to stop me blabbing about that flaming baby racket. Instead of wasting time keeping Jack under lock and key you should be after him.'

She was aware that she was trembling now, her voice croaking.

'Oonagh, you give me proof that Father Watson has a letter Father Kennedy intended for you and I'll investigate, but until then…' He shrugged his shoulders. 'You say Watson was gobsmacked when you told him you had a copy of the letter.'

'Yeah. So?'

She resented that he looked embarrassed for her.

'You know I'm on your side,' he said.

'But…?' There was always a but.

'But – don't you see? If what you're saying is true, then he didn't know you even had an inkling about the letter until *after* you were attacked. It just doesn't tie in, Oon. Sorry. Anyway, my hands are tied here. I can't just start accusing him of things with no evidence. But I promise I will look into it.'

'Listen, Alec, I need a favour.'

'Just the one?' He raised his eyebrows and smiled.

She gave it her best shot. 'I really need to speak to Jack. Alone. Can I visit him at the station?' He shot her a look that said *no way* as he pulled his jacket on. She reasoned with him. 'Let's face it, without me you'll have a job on your hands getting a conviction, so you'll need to let him go, and then I'll be able to speak to him anyway.' Alec said nothing, but the muscle twitching in his jaw told her she was making headway. 'If it was him who put Antonio up to this then I'll know immediately. And if that's the case we can press charges. Deal?' She held out her hand. He took it in both of his.

'I'll see what I can do,' he said. 'If you come down to the station in a couple of hours – then maybe. Do you want McVeigh to come back and drive you?'

Oonagh looked at McVeigh, who'd been watching her like an excited puppy since seeing her in the bath. 'No, I'm all right,' she said.

★

Oonagh was dead beat and bleeding heavily as phantom contractions squeezed her empty womb. The lump on her head pounded, and her aching limbs begged her to take them to bed. She wanted to crawl under the covers and stay there for a month. Instead she took two Ibuprofen with her coffee and lit a cigarette, but immediately felt queasy and stubbed it out.

Upstairs she set about getting ready.

Despite Alec's theory, she needed to prove that Father Kennedy had written her that letter. And, according to Anna Brady, he'd written a full confession too, only to be opened on the event of his death. The old man had known he was dying. He must have wanted to make his peace before the end. No wonder Father Watson had insisted on clearing out the old man's personal belongings himself.

She put on the back-up tape she'd made of her interview with Anna and took some notes. The housekeeper explained that

Father Kennedy's letter to Oonagh claimed healthy babies had been sold regularly to places all over the world; that those who were sick, or needed specialist care, were often left to die; and that the adoption racket had continued long after the Glasgow Magdalene had closed its doors.

Oonagh almost wept as she tried to piece the information together from what Anna Brady could remember. By all accounts the birth certificates had been doctored from the start, with the adoptive parents registered as the birth mother and father. And it had been easy enough. Lochbridge House had kept its status as a private nursing home; all that was needed was for the resident doctor to sign the document and the birth could be registered with the names of the new parents. The poor girls had probably been so browbeaten and institutionalised that they had never even knew that what was happening was illegal.

But how to prove it? Without the letter there was only anecdotal evidence and that would never be enough to take the case to trial. Even *with* the letter she would be on shaky ground. Oonagh didn't care. But she at least had to try. She picked up the phone and called Tom.

'Hi, it's me. Eh, how's the face?' She thought she'd better ask. If the pain in her knuckles was anything to go by he'd be pretty sore.

'Oh I'll live. Tougher than I look. It's the scars you can't see that hurt the most.'

She guessed he was making a sarcastic reference to her not telling him about Mrs Brady sooner. 'Tom don't be petty about this. It would have been completely unprofessional of me to tell you Anna Brady's story. I promised her full confidentiality.'

'I suppose.'

'She's had a rotten bloody life, Tom. She deserves a bit of peace.' Oonagh felt a wave of guilt at having exposed Anna to such scrutiny in the first place. 'If you want to be more involved,

Tom, then this is your chance.'

'*My* chance? Eh, leave me out of it.'

It wasn't quite the response she'd been hoping for.

'Tom, I can't ask Mrs Brady to go to the police. She's not a reliable witness.'

'Meaning?'

'Well, she's been through a lot.' She paused before she continued, already feeling like a traitor. 'Anna Brady had a breakdown not that long ago. She'd go to pieces if she were quizzed. You're the only one who can really do this.'

He sounded shocked. 'A breakdown? Well, is she all right? I mean, is she fit to…'

'Don't worry, she's not mental, she won't come at you with an axe in the middle of the night if that's what you're worried about.'

He tutted. 'I didn't mean that. I just meant… Och, right,' he said. 'Tell me what I've to do.'

She knew he was only agreeing to get her off his back, but she didn't care. 'Oh Tom, you're a star.'

'It said on my school report card I was easily led.'

'That's a good thing,' she reasoned. 'There's always a chance you'll be led somewhere nice.'

'Aye, knowing my luck it'd be Saltcoats rather than Sicily!'

CHAPTER 41

Glasgow, 2000

He ignored the No Entry sign and cut off Nithsdale Road into Kenmure Street. It was late afternoon and already dark, with thick angry clouds overhead. Still, a few mothers with prams were risking the rain. The only space outside the cafe was on a double yellow; Davies reversed in easily, and winced as he locked the car, rubbing the space between his ribs.

The cafe buzzed with life. Steam hissed from a stainless-steel coffee machine at the counter. Davies squeezed past a table with two elderly women arguing over the bill and took a seat by the window, opposite McVeigh. The pane was thick with condensation and blocked the dismal street outside. The white Formica table shoogled between them. A row of workmen laughed and joked as they stood in a line waiting for a carry-out in their dirty white T-shirts and ripped jeans. No jackets, of course. Puddles gathered at their feet as the rain dripped from their boots. The radio crackled in the background, barely audible above the din. Two men served at the counter, using tried and tested banter as they stuffed hot food into paper bags and twirled each one around to close it, before passing it to the customer.

'All right, Alec.' One of them waved over to Davies. 'Usual?' he yelled above the noise.

Davies shook the excess water from his anorak before putting it on the back of his seat. 'Aye, please.'

'And what about your pal?'

'He'll have the same,' Davies answered for McVeigh. 'And a couple of coffees. Large ones.'

McVeigh looked relieved when 'the usual' turned out to be two full Scottish breakfasts. The waiter plonked them down on the table. 'Mind those plates, they're pure roasting,' he said, twisting his head to eye up the rear view of the damp workmen. He worked the room like a pro. Moving onto another table, mothering an old woman with twisted arthritic hands, cutting up the food on her plate. 'You're a wee darlin', Jez.' She beamed up at him. He winked at her – 'Anything for you doll' – and she giggled as she pulled at her wig, which had slipped down her head to come to rest at a jaunty angle over one eyebrow. Two albinos sat at a table near the counter, black Ray Ban sunglasses protecting their pink eyes from the artificial light, their platinum-white hair cropped into identical crew cuts.

'Y'all right, Mohamed?'

'Nae problem, Jez,' replied the older of the two.

McVeigh smirked at what he thought was Jez's sarcastic humour. It was only when the two men started talking Urdu to each other that he realised they were in fact Asian.

'Thanks, Jez,' yelled Davies. Two fried eggs, square sliced sausage, three rashers of bacon, two potato scones, black pudding, a portion of mushrooms and a slice of fried bread. The pain in his gut eased after just the first mouthful. He savoured the second, holding it in his mouth to enjoy the taste. Soon he no longer felt such a grumpy old bastard.

'You really should get that seen to,' said McVeigh mopping up his egg yolk with his bacon and sausage. Davies ignored him, concentrating on the job in hand, but McVeigh persisted. 'It could be an ulcer. Sounds like an ulcer to me.' He crammed a ridiculously large forkful of food into his mouth. Again, Davies ignored him, and changed the subject to what was on his mind.

'I'm letting him go.'

'Who?' McVeigh washed down the food with the steaming coffee.

'Cranworth, I'm letting him go.'

McVeigh stopped, mid chew. A piece of bacon dropped back

onto his plate as his mouth gaped open.

'Awe, come on, boss. Letting him go? But…'

'Look, we've not enough to charge him just yet. I need more time. I'm no' going into this half arsed. You could run a team of horses through the case we've got just now.'

'But the money? For God's sake, it had his prints on it. Proves he was involved.'

'Ach,' Davies shook his head, 'his solicitor'll tear that to shreds. We've already got Findlay admitting Antonio was a blackmailer, Cranworth could easily say the same. It's just not right. There's something we've missed. An' his wife knows more than she's letting on.'

'Think she set him up?'

'Dunno. But I think we'll get more from him if we let him go.'

'You know best,' said McVeigh.

'You're learning fast. Right, finish up now,' Davies was already pushing the grease smeared plate away from him. McVeigh was only halfway through his.

'Ouch!' A high-pitched scream came from behind the counter, then laughter. Jez was flicking a tea towel off his partner's bum, encouraged by the workies' laughter.

'Eh, do you come here a lot?' McVeigh asked, looking like someone who had just happened on the yellow brick road and realised he wasn't in Kansas anymore.

'Aye, food's great,' said Davies, a burp escaping, choosing to ignore any other reference. He banged his chest with his fist, encouraging just a bit more wind. They got up to leave. The two old dears at the next table were still fighting, sliding two one pound coins back and forth between them.

There was no let-up in the rain. Davies held his anorak above his head, as he ran to open the car door, taking a leap to avoid a puddle. McVeigh pulled the lapels of his suit jacket together, and was soaked by the time he sat in the passenger seat.

'Can you no' get yourself some decent clothes? Jesus Christ, you're always ringing wet.' Davies tutted as he shook his head, and flicked the heater onto full blast.

'Thanks,' said McVeigh, as he rubbed his hands together, and held his damp trousers away from his leg, towards the hot air.

'It's to clear the window,' Davies said drily, before putting his foot down.

★

They got back to the station and marched straight through to the interview room. Cranworth was resting his head on his folded arms, which were on the table. A uniformed officer was swinging back on his chair until it touched the wall behind him. They both jumped up when Davies and McVeigh entered.

'Right, let's talk about this five grand shall we?' Davies pulled out a chair, twisting it round to sit on it backwards. He leaned over the wooden slats and switched on the tape machine. McVeigh nodded for the attending policeman to leave, and took his seat.

'What five grand?'

Davies threw a clear plastic bag down on the table. 'That five grand,' he yelled. 'The five thousand pounds we found in Saint Patrick's.' Cranworth didn't respond. 'It has your prints all over it. Was he blackmailing you?'

'Who?'

Davies lost the rag. 'You're at it, sonny.' He pointed his finger into Cranworth's face. 'Charles Antonio. The guy who dived off the balcony, straight into your arms, remember?'

Again, Cranworth said nothing. Just sat back in his chair and let out a low moan. 'How many times do I have to tell you? I didn't know the man. Never saw him before in my entire life. You'll really have a lot to...'

Davies cut him off, waving his hand across his face. 'Aye, aye I know. You'll have my job for this. Well you'll have to join the queue.' He took a packet of cigarettes out from the breast pocket of his shirt and lit one with a green clipper lighter. He blew the smoke sideways, out of the corner of his mouth, away from his face, and held the cigarette under the table, flicking the ash on the floor.

'We've spoken to your wife.'

Cranworth sat up and his eyes widened. 'What did…? I mean was she…?'

'Doesn't seem too bothered you're in here. You two not get on too well, then?'

Cranworth shrugged his shoulders. 'As well as any other married couple.'

Davies rolled his eyes. 'As good as that, eh?' For the first time he felt some sympathy for Oonagh's lover. 'Did your wife know Antonio?'

Cranworth looked genuinely shocked. 'Don't be ridiculous. You've met her. Does she look as though she'd know someone like him?'

Davies took a long final drag on his cigarette before stubbing it out on the floor. 'If he was blackmailing you, then you might as well tell us. Save us all a lot of time. Do yourself a favour.'

Cranworth stopped twirling his eyebrows between his fingers and sat forward in his seat. 'Listen. I didn't know Antonio. I'd never seen him before. I don't know anything about that fucking money.'

There was a timid knock on the door. Davies opened it and the uniformed officer who had been in earlier mumbled in his ear. He closed the door and leaned towards the tape machine. 'Interview terminating at…' – he looked at his watch – '…four thirty-nine p.m.' He turned to Cranworth. 'Right,' he said, 'off you go.'

Cranworth stopped drumming his fingers on the table. 'Me?'

'Aye. Just go. You've got a visitor.'

He opened the door and instructed the policeman in the corridor. 'Usual rules apply,' he told Cranworth. 'Don't go too far away, and keep in touch.' He watched him walk down the corridor, his massive frame dwarfing the young policeman at his side.

Davies watched through the glass doors and saw Oonagh at the front desk. Cranworth hesitated slightly when he saw her, then bent to kiss her. She pulled away and walked out the door. Davies couldn't help noticing that she barely reached his chest.

'Was that wise, boss? Letting him go like that, I mean?' said McVeigh.

The relief of the full Scottish breakfast was proving to be short-lived. The burning sensation had reappeared in his gut again, and was clawing its way towards his chest. He sensed the return of the grumpy old bastard.

'*Wise?* If it's wise you're looking for, I suggest you go and buy yourself a fucking anorak and get off my back.'

CHAPTER 42

Glasgow, 2000

The air outside Govan Police station was rank. The building itself was new, but there was the distinct smell of pee at the entrance. Oonagh walked to her car and unlocked the doors with the remote. Jack was at her back. They hadn't spoken yet. As they reached the car she spun round and winded him with a sharp blow between the ribs.

'What the fuck did you do that for?' He crouched, clutching his stomach, trying to catch his breath.

'Because I can't reach your pigging face,' she yelled. 'Now get in.' She tipped her head towards the car, opened the driver's door and slipped behind the wheel. Her propensity for violence was on the up. She reasoned that all the wishy-washy liberals were indeed correct in their hypothesis that violence really does breed violence. Since the break-in and subsequent attack she felt like kicking the shit out of everyone who crossed her path. And Jack was the third man in the last twenty-four hours to have felt the back of her hand.

'Right, do you want to tell me what the hell is going on?' She started the engine and screeched out of the car park, refusing to swerve for the two beat coppers crossing the tarmac. She took a sharp left at the exit, almost clipping a single-decked bus on Paisley Road West. Her blood was growing hot and she chewed on her bottom lip to stop the swell of anger. She signalled right at the lights, heading for Pollokshields. 'You can speak to me here or at home with your wife. I don't care which.' Her foot almost touched the floor as she raced along Dumbreck Road.

Jack gripped the dashboard to steady himself. 'All right. All right. Slow down for God's sake, before you get us both killed.'

'Oh, as opposed to just *me* getting killed.' She turned into a side street.

Jack exhaled a sigh of relief when she pulled over and stopped the car. As soon as she switched off the engine he reached across and grabbed her, burying his face in her neck.

'Oonagh, thank God you're all right. Oh, I've missed you.' He held her too tight and she winced as her bruises ached under his embrace. She pushed him away.

'Just one question. Did you…?' She hesitated. Jack was a mind-games freak. Every question had to be planned and executed with military precision. She chose her words carefully. 'Were you behind Charlie Antonio attacking me?'

He looked her straight in the eye. 'No,' he said. 'I wasn't.'

She didn't have a clue whether he was telling the truth or not and it scared the shit out of her.

'Well, what on earth were you doing meeting him at Saint Patrick's?' She choked back the tears. They were entirely justified, she felt. The worst thing most women would have to do was ask if a partner had cheated on them. Few would need to ask if they'd planned to have them killed. 'You need to tell me what's going on.'

Jack banged the dashboard with his fist. 'I wasn't meeting him, Oonagh. I swear it.' He pointed his finger into her face. 'And if you can't fucking believe me then that's *your* problem.'

She gave him a couple of seconds to calm down, then spoke very softly, belying her rage. 'Jack, I was attacked and left for dead. I've lost my baby. I'm scared shitless to sit in my home alone, and *you*'re the one who's angry. You don't even care that I had a miscarriage, do you?' She was getting nowhere. Jack was looking right through her. 'You're glad the baby's dead, aren't you?' He continued to look straight ahead. 'Aren't you!' she demanded.

He nodded his head. 'Yes, I am. I won't lie to you, Oonagh.'

Her softly-softly approach must have caught him off guard.

He didn't even duck when she drew her hand up and smacked him hard across the face.

He grabbed her wrist. 'Hit me again, Oonagh, and I swear, I'll hit you back.' The words were spat out.

A sob hiccupped in the back of her throat and she rubbed her tummy. 'How can you be glad the baby's dead? What a thing to say! You're evil.' Her throat convulsed and her tears cut a ribbon through the make-up on her cheeks.

'Oonagh.' Jack let her go and pushed his fingers up through his hair. 'I can't have children, Oonagh, not now, not ever.'

Her grief turned into anger once more, and her voice became a scream. 'Are you saying it wasn't yours?'

He shook his head. 'Just listen, eh?'

Oonagh felt a chill go through her stomach. She wasn't sure that she wanted to hear what he had to say.

He laced his fingers together and stared at the window, despite it having misted over. 'You know I was brought up by my aunt.'

Jack had told Oonagh early on about his childhood. They'd lain in bed one afternoon, swapping memories. He hadn't been emotional as he'd unravelled his past. His parents had died in a car crash, and his aunt and uncle had reared him. He'd been lucky really. They were enormously wealthy. No children of their own. He'd just told her as a matter of fact.

'Oh Christ, what a bloody mess.' He rubbed at his chin and swallowed hard.

Oonagh didn't speak. The cool, controlled Jack was breaking down in front of her and she was terrified. She touched his arm. He glanced as if he'd forgotten she was there. It prompted him to continue. 'Well, I've found out the truth. My Mum's not dead. She didn't die in a car crash.' He was crying now, and Oonagh was scared for him. For both of them. She stroked his hair and his mouth crumpled as he carried on.

'Ooh Oonagh, my real mum was insane, mental, retarded, simple, whatever the fuck you want to call it. And do you know what? She was raped. Pinned down and raped, and I'm the happy product.'

Oonagh reached across and held him, tried to calm his sobs. 'There, Jack. Ssh now.' There was nothing she could do to make it all better.

'I can't risk having kids. I'm a doctor for fuck's sake.' He wiped the back of his hand off his nose. 'I know only too well how genetics work. Do you think I want to be responsible for bringing some poor bastard into the world with that sort of gene pool?'

'Don't torture yourself like this, Jack. There's every chance any children you had would be fine. There's nothing to say this…this mental illness your mum had will be passed down.' She was trying to make him feel better, but realised she was coming across as trying to fight for them to have kids together.

He squeezed the top of her arm. He was hurting her but she said nothing.

'Will you just listen? Please!' He was yelling into her face, slightly hysterical. 'She wasn't just raped, my mother. No, she was raped by her own father.'

Oonagh's insides turned to water and she slumped back in her seat.

He held her hands in his, too weak, too shocked to respond. Her hands became limp. The shouting had stopped.

His crying subsided, and he affected a smile as he wiped away the tears with a tissue. 'There's a reason why relatives can't marry and have children, Oonagh – why incest is illegal. We'd all be psychotic maniacs with two heads.'

He was exaggerating, but she got the drift.

'Fuck,' he said, 'it would've been better if I'd never found out. Better if I'd never been born.'

The penny suddenly dropped and nearly deafened Oonagh. 'Is that what's been wrong these past few weeks? Is that why you were avoiding me?'

He nodded. 'As soon as I found out I...went to pieces. No, that's not strictly true. I got a vasectomy, *then* went to pieces.'

Despite her pity she was angry at being shut out. 'You should have told me, Jack. Does Jean know?' As soon as she said it she could have bitten off her tongue. She didn't want to turn this into an emotional intimacy contest with his wife. 'Sorry,' she blurted before he could reply.

He shivered and she switched on the engine, letting the hot air blast through the vents to warm their feet.

'I feel like a fucking time bomb,' he said. 'There could be a million things wrong with me that just haven't manifested themselves yet.'

She rubbed his thigh in pity as she pulled back out into the street. She wanted to be away from it all. Her nerves were shattered. It was too much to cope with. 'I'll take you home, eh?'

Within moments the old Jack was back. Controlled, assured, smiling. 'Yes. I suppose I have to face the music.'

It had always worried Oonagh that he could so easily switch on and off. She wondered if his revelation went some way to explaining his mood swings.

They were nearly at his house when it suddenly hit her that he still hadn't answered her original question. 'Jack, what were you doing in Saint Patrick's with Antonio?'

'I wasn't. I mean I was there, but that was just a coincidence. I didn't know who he was.'

'Yes,' she said, unable to let it go, 'but why go there in the first place?' 'Please don't say you've found Jesus and forgotten to tell me that wee snippet too? She pulled the car into the kerb outside his neighbour's house.

'Oonagh, it was nothing, honest.' He leaned across and

kissed her cheek. 'Don't worry about it. I was meeting someone close by and I had a few minutes to spare, so I just went in.' He opened the door. 'I really need to go in now. I'll call you?'

She raised her eyebrows. Not quite a nod.

Oonagh watched him walk away, her heart a lead weight. Her Dad's warning rang loud in her ears. *'You'll know the devil when you see him.'*

CHAPTER 43

Glasgow, 2000

Davies was standing outside the door of the station. He lit a fresh
cigarette with the butt of his last one and watched a uniformed
WPC help a woman out of the back seat of a police car. He stood
aside to let them pass, then tapped the officer on the shoulder
and beckoned her over.

'Is that Antonio's wife?' he whispered, inhaling a mouth full
of smoke.

'Widow,' she mouthed. 'She's in to collect his stuff''

'She up to having a wee chat?'

The officer shrugged her shoulders and pressed her lips
tight together, sucking in breath between her teeth. 'Dunno, it's
a heavy one. But to be honest, now's about as good a time as any
I suppose… I really don't think she knew too much about what
he got up to, y'know. So go easy on her, eh?'

'Okay, give us a couple of minutes then bring her through
to my office.' He held open one half of the double doors and
took three more long draws before throwing the half-finished
fag outside.

*

The few meagre belongings looked pathetic. They were laid out
on top of a large manila envelope the table. A mobile phone,
gent's watch – the face cracked in the fall – a brown leather
wallet and a gold wedding ring. Davies stood up as the two
women entered the room. He offered them a seat, pointing to
the two chairs in front of his desk.

Mrs Antonio sat down first. He noticed a ladder in her tights,
running from her ankle and up her calf. She caught Davies'
line of sight and stretched her hand down to cover the tear. As
though it mattered.

'Do I have to sign for them?' She leaned over and touched the items on the table.

'Mrs Antonio, I'd like to ask you a few questions.'

She held up the small gold wedding ring. 'This wasn't his you know.'

'Eh?'

'I mean I didn't give it to him. It was his mother's. He wore it on his pinkie.'

'Mrs Antonio, please, if you could just...' Davies was interrupted by an electronic twang of *The Sash*. It took him a few seconds to register that it was coming from Antonio's mobile. He gestured to the widow. 'Would you...?'

She waved her hands in front of her face, and asked him to take the thing away.

Davies looked at the number withheld display and clicked the answer button. 'Hello...?'

'*What the fuck's going on?*' The woman's voice was urgent and high-pitched. Loud enough for Antonio's widow to hear.

'Who is this?' asked Davies. The tell-tale breaths of a woman exhaling a cigarette lasted just a few seconds before the line went dead. Davies picked up the internal phone.

'Get McVeigh in here.'

His sidekick appeared within seconds and Davies handed him the mobile phone. 'Find out from the network if they can trace any incoming calls to this phone.'

'What's the number?' McVeigh asked.

'Mrs Antonio?'

'What? Oh right...' She rhymed it off and McVeigh wrote it down on a sticky note.

'Actually, get someone else to take care of it,' said Davies, standing up. 'I need you with me.' He had one arm stuck in the sleeve of his jacket by the time he stopped at the door. 'Can you take care of things here for the minute?' he asked his female colleague before nodding towards Charlie Antonio's widow. He didn't wait for a reply from either of them.

★

Rush hour traffic was building as they raced back towards Pollokshields.

McVeigh clung to the passenger seat as Davies weaved in and out of the traffic.

'I take it we're paying Dr Cranworth another wee visit? Told you we shouldn't have let him go so soon.'

'Wrong Dr Cranworth, sunshine.'

Hamilton Avenue was as quiet as ever. Huge oak trees lined the pavement, their branches bent towards the road and their autumn leaves gathered in the kerb. Davies didn't slow as he swung the car into the driveway. He heard McVeigh take a deeper breath than usual as they narrowly missed the stone towers that supported the wrought iron gate. He brought the car to a dead stop outside the front door.

He ignored the bell and pounded on the door. It was the knock he usually reserved for the rundown council flats on the sprawling housing schemes that littered the outskirts of the city.

Jack Cranworth answered the door after just a few seconds. He was out of breath and blood was trickling from three deep scratches gouged into his left cheek.

'Your wife in?' Davies asked, his foot already in the front hallway.

'What do you think?' He dabbed at the wound with a handkerchief.

Davies barged past him into the main living room. Jean Cranworth paced the floor at the huge fireplace. Davies noticed two brightly-painted fingernails on her right hand were broken down to the quick. A lamp lay on its side on the floor.

'Trouble in Paradise?'

'Piss off,' she said, turning her back on the two policemen

and folding one arm defensively across her chest.

'Dr Cranworth, you told me you didn't know Charlie Antonio.'

'So? I don't.' She didn't turn round.

'Well, why did you call him on his cell phone just a few minutes ago?'

'I think you're mistaken, *constable*.' She breathed deeply.

'I know you phoned him. I took the bloody call.'

He was well and truly pissed off with being mucked about. He picked up the receiver of the telephone that lay on the glass coffee table and pressed the redial button. It was answered after just two rings. *'Glasgow cabs?'* a voice asked. Davies slammed it down without a word. He glanced round the room, spotted her handbag and picked it up with both hands, turning it upside down and scattering the contents onto the leather settee.

'What the fuck do you think you're doing?'

Her attempt to push him out of the way was useless. He picked up her mobile and again pressed the redial button.

'You need a fucking warrant to do that,' she spat, as her fist flew in front of his face. He held onto both of her emaciated wrists with just one hand.

He kept her at arm's length, as she struggled to grab the phone.

'I suggest you shut your mouth,' he said. 'You're in enough trouble. You don't want an assault charge on top of everything else.'

It rang once, twice, three times before an answering machine kicked in.

'Charlie Antonio here. I can't speak at the moment. Leave a message and I'll get back to you, or try me at home on…'

Davies had heard enough. He squeezed hard on her wrists, watching the skin turn white beneath his fingers. 'Listen, lady, I ain't kidding on here. You start telling me the truth. Now.

Okay?' He deliberately twisted her skin, pinching her hard before releasing his grip and throwing her onto the settee.

'Bloody animal,' she yelled, and rubbed both her wrists. She looked to her husband, who was standing in the doorway, apparently dumbfounded. 'Can't you do something here, you useless bastard?' she screamed.

Jack Cranworth shook his head. 'You disgust me,' he said under his breath as he turned and closed the door.

'Well don't expect me to lose any sleep over that little bitch! I hope she dies then rots in hell!'

Davies perched himself on the glass coffee table in front of her. He tried not to look at the marks forming around her wrists and convinced himself he'd acted in self-defence. He fought to catch his breath. The struggle had taken more out of him than he'd realised.

Jean Cranworth's hands shook as she lit one of her long, pink cigarettes. Instinctively she picked off a piece of filter tip from her tongue with her thumb and ring finger.

'Right, let's get down to business.' Davies craned his neck round towards McVeigh. 'You stay outside, check he's all right. I don't want him going walkabout.' Then, turning back to Jean Cranworth, he said, 'Charlie Antonio. I want the hows, the whys, the wherefores…the lot.'

She let out a snort, and tossed her head back, refusing to answer.

'You're on a conspiracy to murder charge *at least*. So a wee bit of co-operation is as much for your benefit as mine.'

She pushed her candyfloss hair behind both ears, still holding the cigarette between her fingers. The contents of her bag were scattered on the seat next to her.

She rattled her tongue around in her mouth before she spoke. It irritated the hell out of Davies. His ex-wife had done the very same thing when explaining why he wasn't good enough for her. Without leaning forward, Jean Cranworth pointed to the ashtray next to Davies with a bony index finger. He held it out for her and she tapped the inch-long ash into it.

'How did you come to know Antonio?'

'I'd hardly say I *know* him. He did a job for me, that's all.'

'Go on.'

'Look I don't know what that little shit has told you.' She stood up and walked over to a lacquered table by the window and poured herself a Scotch. She didn't offer Davies one. She swirled the amber coloured liquid around the glass as she sat back down.

'Antonio came to me a couple of days ago. Tried to sell me some…information.'

'What sort of *information*?'

'The kind that lets you know your husband's screwing another woman.' She made no attempt to keep the sarcasm out of her voice.

'I thought you didn't care about your man's extracurricular activities.'

She stubbed the cigarette out. 'He told me that Oonagh O'Neil was pregnant, and that by all accounts Jack was the father. Said he could sell that one on to the tabloids. Wanted a couple of grand for it.'

'And you paid him?'

'Of course.'

'You know he sold it to the papers anyway?'

The colour rose in her already tanned cheeks. 'Bastard, wait until I get my hands on him.'

Davies ploughed on. He had no intention of interrupting his flow to bring her the breaking news.

'Did you pay Antonio to go back the next day?'

'No.' She finished off the whisky, throwing her head back as it slid down her throat.

Davies leaned his elbows on his knees, and clasped his hands. 'To kill her?'

'What? No!' She put the whisky glass down on the table and mimicked his pose. 'I don't know what this Antonio fellow has told you, but that's the extent of my involvement.'

'Dr Cranworth, Charles Antonio is dead.' He noticed a flicker of a smile cross her lips.

'How?'

'That doesn't matter. What does matter is that he stabbed Oonagh O'Neil, and I think you paid him to do it.'

Her smile was extinguished, and with it any hopes of an alibi. Her face turned pale and ashen beneath the leathery suntan. She shook her head quickly from side to side, wringing her hands together. 'No. No. No.'

'I think you wanted her out of the way once and for all.'

'That's not true…' – her voice cracked – '…just ask…'

'Ask who? Antonio? Can't, I'm afraid, he's dead.'

He couldn't muster any sympathy as he watched her cry. He yelled out of the door for McVeigh to bring Jack Cranworth back into the room.

He'd cleaned the blood off his face, leaving just the raw scratch marks.

His wife stared at him for just a few seconds, then picked up the heavy whiskey glass and threw it straight at his head. It skimmed past his ear and smashed against the wall behind him.

'You psychotic bitch,' he yelled. 'That could have killed me.'

'It's all your bloody fault. If you hadn't been screwing the little bitch none of this would be happening.'

'Sit down,' Davies told Jack Cranworth. Then, turning to Jean Cranworth, he said, 'And we can do without the hysterics, okay?'

Jack did not sit beside his wife. He pulled up a hard-backed regency chair beside the fireplace. McVeigh sat on the settee beside the upturned contents of Jean's handbag, keeping a safe distance between the couple.

Jean Cranworth pulled a tissue, then a vanity mirror from her make-up bag and wiped her eyes clean. She was beginning to reapply her make up when Davies coughed loudly.

'If you don't mind?'

She let out an exaggerated sigh and put the mirror and eye shadow back down, but kept hold of the tissue.

Davies turned to Jack. 'Did you know your wife knew Charlie Antonio?'

'Not until you found his number on her mobile.'

'What were you two fighting about when we arrived?'

Jean Cranworth started to speak, but Davies interrupted her. 'I was asking your husband.'

'Three guesses.'

Davies was in no mood for guessing games. 'Just tell me.'

'She was in a blind rage about Oonagh.'

'Was this the first time she brought the subject up?'

'Well, yes.'

He turned to Jean Cranworth. 'Why didn't you speak to your husband about it before now? After all, you'd know about it for days.'

She was up again, pouring herself another drink. Again she didn't offer one to anyone else. 'I was choosing my moment.'

'Setting *me* up, more like it.' Jack turned his back to them. His arms were folded tight across his chest, and from his reflection in the window, Davies could see a muscle twitching on the side of his jaw.

'Don't be so bloody stupid. I had no idea that little bitch had been attacked when they took you away for questioning. I only heard it on the news later that night – much later.' She drained what was left in her glass, and wiped the lipstick from the rim with her thumb.

Jack Cranworth shot Davies a look that told him he wasn't unconvinced.

'What about the money?' Davies asked.

'What money?'

'We found a bundle of notes in the church after Charlie Antonio took his tumble.'

Jean Cranworth shrugged her shoulders as if she couldn't care less.

Jack Cranworth pressed the heels of his hands hard against his eyes. It seemed that he could no longer bear to look at his wife.

CHAPTER 44

Glasgow, 2000

Oonagh was left reeling from her encounter with Jack. Slap bang in the middle of her Magdalene research here he was suddenly revealing that he'd been the innocent by-product of an incestuous rape. Was she being too cynical or was it all too convenient?

They were in a wine bar because she didn't want to be at home. She looked across at Tom, who was warming a glass of blood-red cabernet sauvignon between both hands. He'd told Oonagh he was glad Antonio was dead. He'd been glad even before he'd realised it was him who'd stabbed Oonagh. His face flushed pink with shame as he'd recalled the pleasure he'd felt from his tormentor's painful, horrific demise. The picture in his mind of Antonio's body broken over the back of the pew didn't so much haunt him as fill him with relief.

'Ten Hail Mary's for you, Father.' Morbid curiosity got the better of her. 'His body…what was it like? Was it just…?' Oonagh pulled a face.

'Why d'you always need to know the gory details about everything?' Tom grimaced at the memory. 'Oh, it was really smelly. That was the worst part. It was just…yeuk.' He pushed his hand away from him and a shiver ran violently down his back as he tried to shake off the stench.

'Has, eh, Mrs Brady said anything?' Oonagh still couldn't shake off the sickening guilt at having dragged her into everything. 'I'd no idea this was going to grow arms and legs, Tom. But when she told me about seeing those letters. Well…'

'You flipped?'

She nodded her head, wondering how long she could protect Anna Brady and her rotten wee life that hadn't had a moment's happiness.

The place was filling up. It was attached to a Greek restaurant and the smell wafting through from the dining area reminded Oonagh that she hadn't eaten properly in days. 'Fancy a bite to eat?' she asked, already giving the menu the once over.

'Oh God, Oonagh, how can you eat at a time like this?'

'You know what they say: starve a cold, feed anxiety.'

The waiter sashayed past, balancing three plates on one arm. He gave Oonagh a wink, then pouted his lips and blew a kiss at Tom before she had a chance to feel flattered.

They ordered and allowed the atmosphere and chatter from the neighbouring tables to wash over them as they waited for the food to arrive. Neither spoke much.

Eventually Tom told her about his meeting with Davies. But she was only half listening. Too many other things were rattling around her mind.

'Don't let him bully you, Tom. He's actually really nice. I get on dead well with him.' She crammed a meatball into her mouth.

They judged the passing of time by the amount left in the bottle.

'So,' Oonagh said as she lay her knife and fork on her plate, 'you haven't answered my question. What did Mrs Brady say? How much did she tell you?'

Tom told her that Mrs Brady had scarpered upstairs when Davies had arrived. And as far as he knew she was still there. He'd speak to her soon. Soon, but not yet. This whole business had scared the shit out of her. Dead or not, Charles Antonio still petrified her.

'Why?' asked Tom, 'how much did she tell you?'

'To be honest, she really just glossed over the facts. Told me she was sent away 'cause she was pregnant. Must have been years ago. But we got onto other things, then...well, you know what I'm like, once she mentioned seeing those letters, then the fact that they were gone after Father Watson came… Anyway, she was only with me for a wee while. We planned to meet again, to chat more.' She looked into her glass. 'I'm going to write a book,' she said. 'On the Magdalenes.' She avoided his eye. Anyway, the last thing I remember about that day was Mrs Brady leaving. You know, it's funny, I gave her a hug, and she just felt limp in my arms. No, not limp…empty'. A big lump had been swelling in Oonagh's throat and she swallowed hard. 'Life's shite sometimes, eh?' She pressed her thumbs into the corners of her eyes. 'Anyway, I never really got the chance to get her story, but she needs to talk to someone, Tom. So I've asked her to come round again. Even if I never use it, she needs to talk. She's so fucking lonely, Tom.'

He nodded his head. 'Yeah, I know. She had a baby girl taken away from her.'

A slight shiver ran down Oonagh's spine. 'No,' she said, squinting her eyes at Tom, 'she had a son.'

'You sure? I thought… Never mind. I must have got it wrong.' Tom swigged back his drink, draining the glass.

Oonagh gestured to the waiter, who brought another bottle. Tom made a lame attempt at saying he'd had enough, but didn't protest when his glass was filled. Oonagh fished in her bag and put a computer disk on the table between them. She pushed it towards Tom with her index finger.

His face fell. 'Is that it?'

She nodded, and told him she'd put two letters on it. Letters supposedly written by Father Kennedy. It didn't matter that they weren't word for word accurate – it was enough that the main gist was there. The only person who could possibly know they were fakes would be Father Watson, and he could hardly come forward and say he'd seen the originals. 'Look, upload this onto your PC at home, then all you have to do is say you've just found it and pass it onto Alec.'

He didn't look convinced by her Nancy Drew, home-spun detective idea, and sat biting his cheek. He was going to wimp out. She just knew it. He'd find some excuse why it couldn't work, and another excuse as to why he should have nothing to do with it. Disappointment edged its way into her chest and she was about to put the disk into her bag when Tom snatched it from her hand.

'You know they'll never be able to prove any of this.' He waved the disk under her nose, 'but if it gets the wind up that bastard Watson, even for just a minute, it'll be worth it. He can stuff it. Fucking stuff it, that's what.' His courage had obviously been buoyed by alcohol and he was attracting too much attention from the other diners.

Oonagh stifled a giggle as she shooshed him. 'Bloody hell,' she said, feeling happy for the first time since her attack, 'this is great, Tom.' And at last she felt a bit of relief that Mrs Brady could just be left out of the whole sorry mess.

Outside, there was a steady stream of traffic towards Shawlands. Oonagh stuffed her hand into Tom's pocket and they linked arms as they walked back to the chapel house. In the distance a row of shops lit up the night. Mostly takeaways: a kebab shop, Kentucky Fried Chicken, a drive-through MacDonalds. All offered the finest cuisine. The chippie had closed down years ago.

They passed a late-night newsagents, picking up a first edition of the morning's paper and reading the headline: *Little Angels in Church of Death*. A grainy picture of Charlie Antonio was splashed across the front-page. She groaned as she read the story, which focused on the children who had witnessed his horrific fall.

'Typical bloody tabloids,' Oonagh said, and then reminded herself that she was part of the same food chain.

Church of Sorrow sang the sub-headline as the story continued on page five.

Oonagh flicked back to see if there was anything else. Nothing. Page three was dominated by Ranger's latest signing, who had apparently had a Catholic grandmother, and who claimed not to give a toss about religion. And who could blame him at twenty grand a game?

She was relieved that there was no mention of herself in the story about Charlie. It had all been a tragic accident. A loving husband. A hard working journalist who'd been in St Patrick's to watch the children rehearse their hymns for Father Kennedy's funeral, and do a wee write up. The link obviously hadn't been established yet. That would all change with tomorrow's editions. By then the police would have made an official statement. By then Antonio would be an evil bastard who had plunged a six-inch blade into an innocent woman. Oonagh guessed the official statement would say Charlie Antonio had been wanted for questioning by the detectives investigating her attempted murder. That the case was now closed, that they weren't looking for anyone else in connection with the attack. End of story.

CHAPTER 45

Glasgow, 1958

When Lochbridge House closed down Irene Connolly had nowhere to go, so she teamed up with Sally and Bridie Flanagan. Her new best friends. All three stayed in a single end in the Gorbals; with Bridie's granny, who was glad of the company. There was only one room, with a wee scullery off. And only one bed. The old woman slept in that. The other three lay on layers of newspaper on the floor, with old coats on top of them. Bridie's granny had a clothes stall at Paddy's Market, so there was always a selection of thick crusty, hairy old coats to keep them warm at night.

By day, Irene, Bridie and Sally would sell the flea-ridden rags, which allowed the granny to stay in bed, keeping warm and reading week-old newspapers. For it could be bitter outside. She told the girls she remembered the days when the Irish actually sold the clothes off their backs as soon as they got off the boat. Hence the name of the market near the docks. But Irene never knew whether to believe her or not.

The three promised to stay friends forever. Sally, Bridie and Irene. But three months after they moved in, Sally died. They found her dead on the floor one morning. Stone cold and stiff she was, lying between them. Probably pneumonia, the doctor said, but he wasn't entirely sure. It didn't seem to matter much to anyone but them. Bridie's granny went three months after that. Probably pneumonia, the doctor said...

So it was just Irene and Bridie. And they promised to stay friends forever.

During the day they'd be down at Paddy's with the rest of the gang. You could buy and sell just about anything there. Second hand clothes, old sinks, bits of bicycles, shoes – not pairs of shoes though, just shoes – fruit, vegetables, the lot. The food stalls were a godsend to most folk living close by.

She'd share the craic. 'Aye these clothes are just in, fresh this morning off the Paris catwalks,' she'd say. 'Aye, yer arse,' customers would laugh back. And, as she laughed with the others, she'd stab at her thigh with her keys, or anything else sharp that came to hand.

The physical pain gave her some relief from the mental torment that made her feel as though she would burst. Irene was haunted by the past. The euphoria at being free from the Magdalene institute wasn't enough to shake off the gnawing feeling that ate away at her insides. The guilt, the shame, call it whatever, it was a physical pain that settled in her gut and never went away. At night, when she slept, her dreams would be filled with her father, an enormous giant, towering over her; Little Isaac, a tiny scrap of a thing, before they carried him away; and baby Patricia dying in her arms. Wee Patricia, doomed forever to suffer in limbo because she wasn't baptised.

Like most of the flats along Cumberland Street, they had an outside lavvy, where Irene had an occasional wee fly fag and a few moments with her own thoughts.

It was only when Bridie walked in on her one night that the truth was outed. She found Irene sitting on the grubby toilet pan, eyes tightly closed and face distorted in pain, a glowing cigarette end pressed into her flesh as she offered up her suffering to God, begging and pleading with him to stop baby Patricia's suffering – to take her out of limbo and let her into Heaven.

'Fuck's sakes, Irene. What're you doing?'

Bridie slapped the cigarette out of Irene's hand and stamped on it. She said nothing as she led her friend upstairs. All she had to ease the wounds was bicarbonate of soda. She dipped the clean rag into the watered-down mixture and gently dabbed the burns across Irene's breasts and shoulders.

'Why didn't you tell me, love?'

Her whole body shook as she told Bridie about Patricia and Heaven. 'Don't tell anyone, eh? They'll think I'm a nutter for sure and put me away again.'

Bridie held her close, rocking her. 'Shh shh, there, there,' she said, patting her back and cursing Sister Agatha, God...anyone and everyone she held in any way responsible. It was all a bag of shite, Bridie told her. God wouldn't make a wee baby suffer, make it linger in limbo. Why would God make up a stupid rule like that? Irene wanted to believe her. But just to make sure, just in case...

The next day they were back down at the stall, making sure they had food on the table. Three evenings a week Bridie did a few hours at a pub in the East End. Irene was barely nineteen, and had never even heard of women going into a bar, let alone working in them. She'd roar with laughter at some of the tales Bridie told her. Bridie could tell a good story, had good craic. Thursday nights she'd bring home fish and chips wrapped in newspaper, and a bottle of cider, Bridie's treat. And the two friends would gorge themselves on the hot greasy food.

One night when she was picking the last pieces of crispy batter off the paper when she realised she was looking at a copy of the *Irish Times*. What the hell was a Glasgow chippie doing with a copy of an Irish newspaper? And then she saw it. A picture of her dad. She struggled to read the words through the grease. '...*died peacefully at home...*' She showed it to Bridie, who didn't know what an obituary column was and couldn't read, period. So Irene had to read it out to her.

'Bloody hell, hen, you were dead posh.'

That was all that was said on the matter.

One Thursday night she waited for Bridie, but she didn't come. She fell asleep, alone in the granny's bed. When, come the morning, there was still no sign of Bridie she went out to look for her.

No one had heard of a pub called the Sorry Head. Eventually a guy twigged. He was unloading fish – packed in huge blocks of ice – from the back of a truck. 'Oh, the Sarry Heid?' Even with his directions it took her another twenty minutes to find it. And only when she read the sign above the door did she realise it was actually called *The Saracen's Head*. But the doors were locked tight. It was still early.

No one paid her the slightest bit of notice as she asked if anyone had seen her friend. People ignored her pleas as they rushed past to join a small crowd that had gathered further up the street. She could see the tops of policemen's hats above the sea of heads. Women huddled together, pulling their shawls tight around them, arms folded. Some blessed themselves. Grown men took off their caps and shook their heads. Irene squeezed her way through just in time to see them lift Bridie Flannigan's body into an ambulance. It didn't bother sounding its bell.

She'd been strangled with her own knickers, the policeman said. One of the hazards of being on the game.

There had to be some mistake, Irene told them. Bridie had been a bar-maid, she'd worked in the Sarry Heid, they could ask anyone.

The bar's owner eventually admitted that she had worked there a few times a week. But it hadn't been behind the bar.

They never did find out who did it.

Once again, Irene was alone.

Then and only then did she contact her mum. A letter. A few lines. She didn't say she was sorry her father had died. Didn't mention him at all.

Her Mum wrote back. Did she need anything? Money?

Irene was freezing to death in a damp flat in the Gorbals. Her only two friends in the world were dead. Of course there were things she needed. She didn't say that though. Said she

259

was fine. And she was. Eventually.

And that was how it was. The odd letter, sometimes a Christmas card with a few pounds inside. No mention of little Isaac, no questions about baby Patricia. Nothing. It was as though they'd never even existed. And Irene was never invited back home.

Some days she would walk up Maryhill Road and stop at Lochbridge House, which by then was empty and abandoned. She'd say a prayer over wee Patricia's grave, unmarked and long since overgrown with weeds. Even when the building itself was razed – even when the land was sold on and bright new flats were built and the memory of Lochbridge House was forgotten – she still took a walk past and said a silent prayer for her baby daughter who had lived and died that night so long ago.

And the years past. It was an ordinary enough life. No one paid her too much attention. Only one time was she bothered. Three boys they were. Outside St George's Cross underground. Thought they were men. One held a knife. 'Gees yer bag. Haun it over ya old bitch.' Spitting out the words in his nasal whine. Irene looked around. The place was deserted. She rolled the sleeve up slightly on her raincoat, and stubbed her cigarette into the flesh on her forearm. She closed her eyes tight, and offered them a wide smile, with her teeth tightly clenched. When she opened her eyes the boys were running up Great Western Road. The knife was at her feet, dropped in the panic. 'Fucking psycho,' they shouted after her. 'Mad fucking bitch.' Whatever else they yelled was drowned out by the noise of the underground train thundering into the station. She kicked the knife into the kerb before walking down the stairs to get the subway home.

On what would have been baby Patricia's thirty-sixth birthday a telegram arrived. Irene's mum was dead. She decided to go to the funeral.

It was the first time she'd been in Ireland since the age

of fifteen. No one gave her a second glance as she stood and watched the coffin as it was lowered into the grave. No one recognised her as she mingled with the other mourners. No one saw her spit on her Father's name engraved on the head stone.

She felt like a stranger going through her mum's things. The housekeeper helped. All the important documents were in one box. Her will, title deeds for the house, insurance policies. And a letter for Irene. It had been written six months previously. Her mum must have known the end was near. But she'd had a good innings. Better than most.

Her mum's spidery scrawl filled four pages. Four pages of sorrow, begging for forgiveness, pleading for her to understand. Irene didn't. She scanned her eyes along the words. All pretty predictable stuff really. But what was on the fourth page made Irene's legs buckle from under her, and turned her bowels to water. Her hand shook uncontrollably as she sat on the bed. The words swam in front of her. Baby Isaac had not been sent to America as she'd been told. Her son had been adopted by her mother's cousin and his wife, in Edinburgh. Names, dates, addresses, all were there in black and white. *The past belongs in the past Irene,* was how her mother finished before signing off.

Irene pulled the rest of the papers out of the box. Tore at them, scattering them over the floor. The photographs were at the bottom. She knew they would be. Hundreds of them. The baby picture was the easiest to recognise. His tiny little face. Just as she'd remembered him from almost forty years earlier. As she laid the photographs out on the floor, her son's life unfolded before her. A gorgeous wee babby, a fine looking boy, growing into a handsome man. And the cruellest picture of all: her own mother holding Isaac's hand as he stood proud in his school uniform. All this time they'd kept in touch while Irene had rotted her life away. Only the first few letters had an Edinburgh address on the top. The family had moved to Glasgow in the early Sixties.

There were no tears in Irene's eyes when she called and ordered that the headstone be removed from her parents' grave. 'No,' she insisted when the man on the other end of the phone tried to reason with her. 'The grave is to be left unmarked. From first thing tomorrow.' Her mind was made up.

The will held little surprises. What little money there was had been left to the Church. The house was Irene's but she didn't want it. Instead she gave it to the housekeeper. At first the woman refused. 'Dear God,' she said blessing herself over and over again. 'I couldn't own such a grand house as this.' Her rosary beads clacked together in her apron pocket.

'Please,' Irene said, 'you'd be doing me a great favour. It would break my heart to think of strangers living here,' she lied. 'I have my own house in Glasgow.' She thought back to the grubby bed and breakfast off Hillhead, paid for by the DHSS. 'Please, as a favour to me?' That seemed to sway her.

'But your dear mother, God rest her soul' – again more blessing herself, this time her rosary beads in full view – 'your poor mother's left me very well provided for.'

It turned out that "very well provided for" meant another job as a housekeeper. It had all been arranged. There was a position waiting for her in Glasgow. Housekeeper to a priest no less. Again the woman blessed herself. 'A very good friend of your mother's.'

'Good friend of my mother's?' said Irene. 'In Glasgow? Are you sure?' This time Irene did weep. Hot wet tears stung her face as she listened to her mother's housekeeper tell how Father Kennedy really was a Saint among men – of how he did such good works in the parish. And he never forgot Dr and Mrs Connolly. Always visiting when he was back in Galway. And indeed they were always very generous and made sure they spent time with him when they visited relatives over in Scotland.

Irene was sick to her stomach. The housekeeper's voice droned in the background as she waxed lyrical about the fine work Father Kennedy did for those less fortunate than himself. Irene guessed that covered just about everybody. When she went on to talk about how he gave food and shelter to the fallen women of the Magdalene, all with the help of her mother's money, Irene excused herself and threw up.

Irene arrived back in Glasgow the same way she'd left it: penniless, without a friend in the world. The only thing she took from her mother's house was the letter she'd found in the box. She didn't even take all of it. Just the last page, which told her where Baby Isaac was. And the photographs of course. All of them, chronicling her little boy's life.

★

She had no plan of action as she walked up the path. Had no idea what she was going to say. She held her finger on the bell until he opened the door. The sickness rose in her stomach.

She recognised him immediately. Forty years had done nothing to wipe his face from her memory. He looked right through her, didn't know her from Eve. He was wiping his mouth with a linen napkin.

'Yes?'

She waited just a few seconds. Gave him the chance to place her. Nothing. She held out her hand, carefully pulling the worn cuff of her raincoat down over her wrist to conceal the cigarette burns on her arms.

'Father Kennedy, I'm…I'm Mrs Brady. Mrs Connolly made arrangements for me to come?'

And that was how it had come to be.

Day after day she'd sit on the same park bench. Stealing at least a couple of hours in the hope she'd see her baby as he drove past. And occasionally she did. Her legs would ache from the cold sometimes. Purple hexagons formed on her shins. Her hands were often blue. Nothing she wasn't used to. She got to know the regulars by sight. Joggers, walkers. Some with dogs. No one paid her much attention. Just the odd nod, a raised eyebrow. On the whole people were creatures of habit, and that's what she banked on. He wasn't such a creature though. Sometimes months would go by with nothing, not even a glimpse. Then she'd see him two, maybe three times in one week. Wednesdays were her best bet. She had Wednesday afternoons off, so could sit for hours on end, not having to worry about rushing back. She'd make a day of it, taking a flask of hot sweet tea and a few sandwiches wrapped in paper. She fed her crusts to the ducks. Hated crusts. Ever since she'd been a child. 'They'll give you curly hair,' her mum had always said. 'Eat up.' Despite leaving them on her plate, her hair had still grown in masses of thick coarse curls that clung tightly to her head. Like the children of Africa, the nuns had said. Said she looked like a heathen. A curse, she thought. Wishing for soft waves like her sister.

CHAPTER 46

Glasgow, 2000

Davies waited in the Cranworth's house. He'd called for another officer to come, so that he wouldn't have to join McVeigh in accompanying Jean Cranworth to the station. Now he had a chance to talk to Jack Cranworth. Off the record, of course.

Davies saw Cranworth wipe a tear from his eye and heard him sniff as the patrol car eased out of the driveway, the gravel crunching beneath its wheels. Cranworth watched from the window until his wife was out of sight.

'Sit down,' said Davies. He pointed to the settee opposite. Cranworth ignored the invitation and poured himself a large one. 'Would you…?' He held the decanter of whisky up. Davies shook his head. 'Na. I'm fine just now.'

Jack stood in front of the fire. The scratches on his face were red and angry. A few drops of blood had stained the collar of his shirt.

'Your wife work with you?'

'Hardly!'

'She doesn't really seem like…' Davies tried to choose his words carefully, '…a…a doctor'

'Doctor! Don't make me laugh. She carries out minor cosmetic procedures at a private clinic.' Cranworth sat down. 'The closest she'll ever get to being a doctor is wearing a white coat!'

'Does she get violent often?'

He touched his cheek. 'No. No, it's not like that. She's not usually so…so passionate.' He smiled a sarcastic smile and changed the subject. 'Do you really believe she set me up?'

'What, with the money and stuff? Well, I don't know. That would mean she knew you were going to be at the church at that particular time.' Davies tried to find a sign in Cranworth's eyes. 'Did she have any way of knowing you'd be there?'

The burning pain returned to Davies' gut with a vengeance. He squeezed his eyes tight shut until the wave of agony subsided into a nagging heat.

'I can get you something for that.' Jack left the room and returned a few moments later with a glass full of milky liquid. Davies eyed it with suspicion.

'Here.' He pushed it towards him, 'I'm not about to poison you. I know better than to bump off a police man.' His Kelvinside accent separated the words police and man.

Davies took the glass from him. 'You wouldn't be the first, you know.' He downed the drink in one. The chalky draught immediately soothed his insides, creating comfort from chaos. He breathed in deeply through his nostrils, enjoying the freedom from pain. 'My God, what was that? It's bloody terrific.'

'Nothing special,' said Cranworth. 'Available from all good doctors.' Then he added, 'Look, I know it's none of my business, but you really do need to get that seen to. Before it turns sinister.'

Davies nodded. He was beginning to warm to Jack Cranworth. Maybe he wasn't such a prick after all. But it didn't change the need for his question. 'Well, did she?'

'What? Oh, know that I was going to be in St Patrick's? I've no idea. I don't think so.'

'You never did explain why you were there.' Davies sat forward, hunching over his legs, his elbows resting on his knees. 'Look, these things have a habit of coming out in the wash. I know Antonio was a nasty wee shite. If he was blackmailing you, or your wife, then best to tell us about it now.' He was out of practice with the softly-softly approach and hoped it didn't sound too stage-managed.

Cranworth ran his hands through his hair, and held his head. Davies said nothing. Just waited. As long as it took.

'I got a cryptic phone call. I don't know from whom. Just telling me to go to St Patrick's. Told me to bring cash. Warned that Charlie Antonio could make life difficult if I didn't pay up. *That* was the first time I'd heard of him. Had no idea who he was. Or that he'd….' His eyes filled up.

'So who made the call? Antonio?'

Cranworth shrugged his shoulders.

'And you went along with this?'

He nodded as he upended his glass and finished his whisky.

The room was stifling. A thin trickle of sweat made its way down Davies' back. 'Listen,' he said, unzipping his jacket, 'I'm just not quite getting all this. What exactly were you paying the money for? Having an affair isn't enough to be blackmailed over.'

Cranworth wiped his hand over his mouth and refilled his glass. 'Maybe not for you,' he said. He held the glass to his lips and said nothing for a few moments. He took a deep breath and sighed, putting the glass down hard on the table. 'Listen,' he said, 'I knew Jean had paid him. I wasn't prepared to take any risks and have my wife's name dragged into this. Anyway, I was told where to leave the money, and told that after that I could just leave. I didn't know he was waiting in the gods, did I?'

'Why didn't you tell me this earlier?' Davies' patience was wearing thin again. 'Jee-sus, you could have saved us all a lot of hassle.'

Jack was looking deep into his glass. 'As you said yourself, these things have a habit of coming out in the wash. And I didn't think you'd believe me. Anyway,' he added, 'I didn't want to get anyone into trouble. Believe it or not, Inspector Davies, I do try to do the right thing when I can.'

'So. Did your wife pay Antonio to attack Oonagh?'

Jack shook his head. 'Oh no. At least, I don't think so.' He didn't look too sure. 'Just wanted him to break in and get a bit of evidence. Something to tie Oonagh and me together.'

'Your wife's version's a bit different. Claims Antonio brought her the evidence off his own back. Says she never asked him to break in.'

'Believe what you like. All I know is that I wanted kept out of the whole mess. And if that meant paying off some sleazeball to keep his mouth shut then so be it. *My* conscience is clear. *I* didn't stab her.' He seemed to perceive a look Davies wasn't aware he'd given him. 'And neither did my wife,' he added without much conviction.

Davies stood up to leave. 'Take my advice. You know, you don't do yourself or your wife any favours by playing detective, keeping things from us.' He zipped up his padded jacket, which he'd left on during the whole of his time in the house.

They walked through to the hall, and stopped by the front door. Cranworth picked up a small brown bottle sitting on a table. He handed it to Davies. 'And you don't do yourself any favours playing doctor. This is only a temporary measure. You really have to go and see someone about that.' He nodded to Davies' gut, 'it's quite urgent.'

Davies put the bottle in his pocket. 'Thanks, I will,' he promised.

'What about my wife?'

'Look, I know you're just being loyal, but…well I wouldn't wait up for her if I were you.'

★

As Davies arrived back at the station, McVeigh was running down the steps towards his own car, keys in his hand. 'Hey,' Davies called, struggling to make his voice heard over the night rain. 'Where are you going?'

McVeigh looked up. 'Mrs – I mean *Doctor* – Cranworth disnae like the tea out of the machine,' he yelled, as though that explained things. 'I'm going to Asda, to get her some Twinings.'

Davies' mouth hung open in disbelief. '*Asda?* Are you fucking kidding me on?'

'Aye, I know. Pure mental, isn't it. But don't worry,' he shouted, missing the point entirely, 'the one along the road's open all night. I'll be back in five minutes tops.' And with that he started up the engine of the car and was gone.

Davies needed no more convincing that the world truly was a madhouse.

He braced himself before going into the interview room. He was in no mood for Jean Cranworth. Even if her husband had worked miracles with his gut.

Inside she sat cross-legged on a padded, swivel office chair that normally sat out at the front desk. Her left shoe dangled on the end of her toes, swinging a few inches from the floor. She was filing her two broken nails with an oversized emery board.

'Quite comfy are we?' asked Davies.

'Hardly,' she snorted back, then looked over his shoulder as the door opened.

McVeigh rushed in, shaking the rain from his frizzy hair, rustling an Asda carrier bag.

'Kettle's on,' he assured her, then fished out a packet of cotton wool pads and a bottle of Evian water. She took them from him and began dabbing her face with the pads, which she soaked with the bottled water. McVeigh's smile beamed across his face. 'You want a wee coffee, sir?' he asked, heading back out the door.

'Aye, son. Got any decaffeinated double mocha delight with extra shite?'

'Eh?'

'Jesus Christ, what is this, Mrs Cranston's Bloody Tea Room? Get someone else to get the bloody drinks and get yer arse back in here.' His voice bellowed through the room. He could feel the colour rising in his face. When Jean Cranworth rolled her eyes he looked at her directly and said, 'Right you. Cut the crap. Were you in Oonagh O'Neil's house the day she was attacked? We know she had a visitor. I think it was you.' He didn't wait to hear her protests. 'That means either you stabbed her, or you watched while Antonio did it. Fancy sharing that wee precious moment with me?'

'You're out of your mind.'

Davies dragged a chair out from under the table and sat down. 'Did you go round there to confront her about the affair?' He took the bottle of medicine from his jacket pocket and took a quick swig. 'Well your husband was prepared to pay Antonio to keep his mouth shut about you.' He was trying to gauge her reaction when the door knocked and what looked to Davies like a twelve-year-old uniformed officer came in with two machine coffees and an Earl Gray in a china mug, all on a tray. Davies noticed it was *his* china mug, but decided to say nothing. He couldn't be bothered. Jean Cranworth blew on the steaming tea before taking a sip. He pictured her sitting at Oonagh's table, drinking her tea, planning her death. The thought made him feel sick.

Jean Cranworth wiped the lipstick from the rim of the mug with her thumb each time she drank from it. Shite, he could imagine her doing the very same thing with Oonagh's cups.

'Well, were you there? Were you there when Antonio stabbed Oonagh? Or had you left by that time?'

'Honestly. Don't you ever give up? You've got your man. Leave it at that.'

Davies had seen some cool customers in his time but she took the biscuit. 'Look, it's only a bloody miracle that Oonagh O'Neil wasn't killed.'

'Oh fucking hell. *I* don't know why the little bitch got done in!'

'Why was your husband paying Antonio five grand?'

She shrugged her shoulders, examining her newly filed nails. 'Ask him.'

'Told me it was to keep your name out of things.'

'Then he's a lying bastard, isn't he?' Jean Cranworth folded her arms across her non-existent breasts. 'You don't look like a stupid man.'

Davies sat back, waited for her to continue. He knew a statement like that always carried a punch line. A 'you're not a stupid man *but*' type of a punch line.

'My husband can be a very charming man. He's obviously convinced you that I'm the guilty party.'

'No, actually he tried to convince me otherwise.'

'Really?' A mocking smile played on her lips. 'Yes, he's very clever with words, isn't he? Listen sergeant, detective, whatever they bloody call you. I'm not exactly weeping buckets over this Molly Malone character.'

'Oonagh O'Neil,' Davies corrected.

'Yes, right. Nevertheless, I didn't pay to have her killed. If I had she'd be dead by now. Anyway, do you think if I had I'd have trusted a loser like Charlie Antonio? And for what? Five thousand pounds. Hah!' She let out a laugh. 'For God's sake. I spend more than that a year on tights.'

Davies didn't doubt that she was right about the tights.

'Can I have a cigarette?' She fished into her handbag before he had a chance to answer. She lit the by now familiar pink stick with a slim silver lighter. She sucked in hard then licked her lips. 'Listen,' she said after her first draw, blowing the smoke high up into the air. 'I called Antonio *after* you guys left because I wanted to know how the hell you connected him to me.'

Davies let her speak.

'I didn't know he'd stabbed her. I just thought he'd broken into her house. And I was happy to pay him for what he told me. End of story. So obviously when the police turn up asking questions, well, I want to know the reason why.' Before Davies could respond she said, 'That's the extent of my involvement.' She sat back, and exhaled.

'Sorry, love. Not good enough. You paid him to go back the next day, didn't you? You wanted *proof* that that Oonagh O'Neil and you husband were having an affair.'

'Prove it.' She tipped her chin upwards, daring him to take her on.

'What about the money?'

It was her turn to lose patience. She leaned her skinny arms across the desk. 'I'll say this for the last time. I'd already paid Antonio two thousand pounds. I don't know why Jack was giving him any more. All I do know is that if someone was being blackmailed, it wasn't me. I've done nothing that would interest a blackmailer.'

She leaned forward, cigarette between her fingers McVeigh almost fell off his seat as he quickly shoved a tobacco-stained ashtray under her hand, just in case any of her precious ash got ruined among the filthy fag ends on the floor. Davies feared that if there hadn't been an ashtray nearby the idiot would have held out his bare hand. Some men were more easily impressed than others. She flicked the ash in without giving him a single glance.

CHAPTER 47

Glasgow, 2000

The chapel house was in darkness by the time they got back. The glow from the streetlight guided Tom as he struggled to fit his key in the flimsy lock. The now soggy newspaper was wedged under his arm. At the crack in his elbow Charlie Antonio gazed up at Oonagh from a black and white front-page photo.

Tom felt the lock give and pushed the door open. A good hard nudge from a strong shoulder would probably have done the job equally as well.

They left the lights off as they made their way into the kitchen. It seemed that Mrs Brady had gone to bed and Oonagh wasn't entirely surprised when Tom told her Father Cameron had given up the ghost and had gone on retreat. His nerves were in tatters after witnessing Charlie Antonio's body.

Oonagh adjusted her eyes to the gloom. And it really was gloomy. No place to call home. There was a brief moment of illumination as Tom opened the fridge and took out the milk for the coffee. He left it open as he put the kettle on. 'You should shut that,' Oonagh told him. 'You'll send the motor into overdrive.' Tom rearranged the food inside before he did so. He stepped back to make sure things were evenly placed.

'How the hell did you manage to survive in Milton for so long?' Oonagh imagined Tom roughing it out during his teenage years in the grim mining village, and realised why he'd have been so keen to join the priesthood. In another life he might have taken an altogether different path.

'Mm, too anal, eh?'

She nodded and smiled as they walked through to the living room. They were just at the bottom of the staircase when they felt the carpet soft and soggy underfoot. Their shoes squelched in a shallow puddle on the floor.

'Oh not a burst pipe!' said Tom. 'This is all I bloody need.'

Oonagh felt a flush of panic in her throat as her eyes drifted up the staircase and she realised the water was pouring down from the first floor landing. Her cup crashed to the floor as she took the stairs two at a time.

'Mrs Brady! Mrs Brady!' she screamed.

Tom overtook her before she was halfway up. He too yelled at the top of his voice. 'Mrs Brady, are you all right? Mrs Brady!' He tried the bathroom door. Locked. He banged on the old wooden panels with his fist. Nothing. Silence. He grabbed the handle and shook it violently. The water flooded out beneath the door, soaking his feet. He slammed both hands onto the door. 'Mrs Brady! Can you hear me? Are you in there?'

Oonagh was at his back. 'Tom,' she gasped, trying to get her breath, 'just kick it in.'

He stepped back and raised his foot, kicking with his heel until the door gave way. It burst open, quicker than he'd expected and he staggered forward, landing on his hands and knees in the pool of water on the tiled floor.

Oonagh saw her first. Anna Brady's grey, naked body in the bath of overflowing water. Both wrists expertly opened with single vertical slices. The pure white tiled walls stained red with her blood. The mirror above the sink was smashed, one long shard still clutched in her hand.

Shaking, trembling, Oonagh reached into the deep pink water, pulled out the plug and turned off the tap. Tom grabbed Mrs Brady under both arms and dragged her out, her legs banging hard against the edge of the cast iron bath. She slipped from his grip. Her head cracked off the floor. Oonagh pressed her fingers against her neck. A faint pulse. Very faint. 'Where's your phone?' Tom nodded towards the hall.

Oonagh grabbed the phone and dialled for an ambulance as

she charged back up the stairs, handset to her ear.

She watched as Tom tried to stem the life flowing from Anna Brady's body. He dragged her across the floor, nearer to the door. Oonagh helped him keep her arms above her head as they wrapped her wrists in a towel. He bound her wounds as tightly as he could, then reached towards the door and grabbed her housecoat from the hook. With the cord, Tom attempted a makeshift tourniquet round both arms to stop any more blood escaping, whilst Oonagh laid the dressing gown over Anna's body.

Oonagh told Anna Brady she'd be all right. Let her know she wasn't alone, that help was on the way. But Anna just lay there. Pathetic and helpless.

The paramedics didn't wait for an answer. One good hard shove was indeed all it took to open the door of the chapel house. They were at Anna's side in seconds. One gently ushered them out of the way as the other got to work.

Oonagh gripped Tom's arm tighter than she intended. Her legs momentarily buckled underneath her. Tom held on, trying to steady her. 'You okay?'

She nodded, pretending she was fine when she wasn't. 'You were great there, Tom.' She gestured at Anna, the bathroom, the blood. 'Just brilliant.'

Concentrating on the paramedics took her mind off the pictures that were unfolding in her head.

Within a few minutes Anna Brady was hooked up to a saline drip, lifted onto a stretcher and carried down to the ambulance. Tom and Oonagh stayed with her the whole time until the sirens blared down the road.

★

It took less than six minutes to reach the Victoria Infirmary, one of two hospitals on Glasgow's South Side. Oonagh took Tom's arm and guided him over to the orange plastic chairs; they were even less comfortable than they looked.

A dozen or so other people were dotted round the waiting room, looking bored. A blast of cold air shot through every time the automatic double doors opened. The flashing light overhead told them there was a waiting time of seventeen minutes.

Oonagh held Tom's hand as he kicked around the flattened fag ends that lay under his seat. Some of Anna Brady's blood was still on his hands. His face was in a bit of a mess too.

'Christ, this is all my fault.' Tom broke his hand free from Oonagh's and drummed his fingers together.

'Don't be silly, Tom. You may have saved her life. None of this is your fault.' Oonagh spoke with conviction, safe in the knowledge that it couldn't be Tom's fault, because it was her bloody fault. They wallowed in collective guilt.

'Father? Father?' Only when a hand was laid on Tom's shoulder did either of them realise the woman was talking to Tom. She stood in front of them, dressed in a navy-blue trouser suit under a white lab coat.

'I'm Doctor Simmons. You brought in Anna Brady?'

Oonagh's heart thumped in her throat. Tom stood up. 'Yes?'

'Would you? She held out one arm, gesturing for them to come with her.

'Is she…?' Oonagh wasn't sure what to ask. 'Is she all right?'

'Well, she's alive,' was all the doctor gave away as they walked down the corridor.

Both Oonagh and Tom expected to be taken straight to her, and were surprised when she led them into a small room with vertical blinds blocking out the view to the corridor.

'Mrs Brady? Can I see her?' Tom sounded anxious.

'Sit down please…'

'Father Thomas,' said Tom, holding out his bloody hand by way of introduction. She didn't shake it, and instead gestured for him to sit down. 'And this is Oonagh O'Neil, my…' – he hesitated – '...a friend of Mrs Brady's.' Oonagh was too tired to smile and slumped into the chair. Dr Simmons looked straight at Tom.

'How long have you known Anna Brady?'

'Four years. Why?'

'In that time has she tried anything like this before?'

Oonagh knew where this was leading.

Tom shook his head, apparently shocked at the question. 'Good God no!'

'We're worried she may try to kill herself again.'

'Look, you don't understand,' Tom said. 'She's been under a tremendous amount of pressure. Our parish priest died last week, and, well...' He wasn't sure how to tell her the rest. '...she took it quite badly, that's all. I'm sure if I speak to her...'

She raised one eyebrow.

'Father Thomas, Anna's body has evidence of self-abuse going back years. Old scar tissue that would indicate this isn't the first time she's tried to kill herself. We'd like to transfer her to a psychiatric unit as soon as she's fit.'

Tom nodded, but Oonagh jumped out of her chair as though it was on fire. 'NO!' She slammed her hand on the desk in front of her. 'There is no way you're sticking her in a mental ward. Is that clear?'

Tom looked slightly embarrassed at her outburst but Oonagh didn't care.

Dr Simmons was on a roll. 'Self-harm is actually very common in people who themselves have been victims of abuse. With the right treatment and the correct medication she could actually be...'

But Oonagh cut her off. 'Doctor.' She took a breath and tried to remain calm. 'It's because of the so-called *correct treatment* that she's ended up in this state. Anna Brady's been abused by the system her whole life and I don't care what it takes, I don't care what it costs, she's not going back into an asylum.' Oonagh was aware her voice was getting louder, but didn't care. 'Now, please just treat Anna Brady with the dignity she deserves and not as some problem to be shunned away in a loony-bin.'

Doctor Simmons looked somewhat shocked at this last remark. 'Remarks like that can be very damaging to those suffering from mental illness…'

'Save it,' replied Oonagh, who had no time for niceties.' She could feel herself shaking. She walked out of the office before Doctor Simmons had a chance to find her a bed in the ward next to Anna Brady.

★

Anna Brady was in a small single room off the main surgical ward. Blood was being slowly fed into her veins through a tube connected to a needle in her left arm. Her right hand was still hooked up to the saline drip, which hung on a rail. Her wounds had been expertly bandaged. A single sheet covered her body, with four heart monitors stuck to her chest. Her eyes were closed, but Oonagh could tell by her shallow breathing that she wasn't asleep.

A nurse was sitting by Anna's side. Oonagh pulled up a chair and sat down. She'd calmed – Dr Simmons had insisted that she do so before being allowed onto the ward – and Tom was behind her. The nurse seemed grateful for the break, rose and left.

As she stroked Anna's hand, Oonagh saw for the first time the silvery purple scars gouged deep into her forearms. The small, round, shiny red marks on her shoulders that Oonagh hoped to God weren't cigarette burns even though she knew that they were. On both wrists, just above the bandages, were the scars from years gone by that Dr Simmons had spoken about. Horizontal scars, presumably from before she'd perfected the art of opening up her veins properly.

'It's easy to recognise another damaged soul,' Tom said.

'Eh?' Oonagh turned round, but Tom shook his head.

'Nothing,' he said, 'just thinking out loud.' He reached across and touched her hand. 'You know I've never noticed her pain before. It was there staring me in the face. And I never even saw the damage in her eyes.' His eyes filled with tears as he held Anna Brady's fingers. He whispered her name.

Oonagh shifted in her seat to let him pull a chair up beside her.

Anna Brady's eyelids flickered for a few seconds before opening. She knitted her brows together and let out a low moan, turning her head away when she saw them at the side of her bed.

'Hi there.' Oonagh pulled the sheet up to cover the scars on her chest. 'I'm...here if you need to talk.' It was all she ever seemed to say to her. It sounded pathetic and impotent.

'Mrs Brady, please. Let us help.' Tom's voice was very calm. 'They want to put you in a psychiatric unit. Please, just...'

Oonagh jabbed her elbow into his ribs. He gasped in pain.

Anna gripped Oonagh's hand, her eyes wide, fearful. 'Can't go back there.' She took another breath. 'Not going back.'

'Shh shh.' Oonagh stroked her forehead, and gestured for Tom to get out. 'It's going to be okay, just try and get some rest. I promise you, everything will be okay.'

The tears fell from the corners of Anna's eyes and dropped onto the pillow, wetting her hairline. Oonagh dabbed them with a tissue and held Anna's hand until her quiet sobs subsided and she drifted off to sleep.

The door opened and the nurse entered, wiping a crumb from the corner of her mouth with her pinkie. She swallowed a last mouthful before she spoke. 'She needs her rest, better go now.' It was more of an order than a piece of advice. She straightened the covers on the bed and busied herself with nursing duties. As Oonagh watched, she tried not to think of the horrors that would no doubt haunt Anna's dreams during the night.

Outside in the corridor, Tom grabbed her arm. 'What the hell's going on?' His voice was a high-pitched whisper.

'I don't know. What do you mean?' Oonagh twisted her arm free and quickened her pace towards the stairs.

But Tom caught up with her. 'Stop.' And when she tried to carry on he forced her shoulders back against the wall. 'Listen, Oonagh, what the hell's making Anna Brady so fucking scared?'

It was as if her attack was happening all over again. She broke free and pushed him away, descending the stairs as fast as she could. But her legs had turned to jelly and buckled on every step. The stairs stretched before her like an eternity.

'For God's sake speak to me, Oonagh.' Tom grabbed. 'I'm not stupid. The pair of you know more than you're letting on. If she was there that day, why won't you let her speak to the police?'

'What difference does it make now?' Oonagh sobbed. 'Charlie Antonio's dead.' Even on a good day Tom could get on her nerves, but now his questions were like a vice round her throat. Her breath grew shallow and her chest tightened. She clung onto the banister and let her arms slide her down as her legs eventually gave way completely. She pulled her inhaler from her bag and sucked hard, allowing the steroids to flood through her and open her airways. She gasped and a breath of stale air filled her lungs.

Tom sat down beside her. He looked scared. 'God, Oonagh, I'm sorry. Are you all right? Just try and breathe deeply, come on. Want me to get someone?'

She shook her head and wiped her nose with the edge of her sleeve. She took comfort from the noise leaking through from accident and emergency.

Tom had his arm round her. His voice was calm. 'Oonagh, did Anna Brady see Antonio in your house? Did she see him attack you?'

Oonagh looked down at a stain on the bottom stair. 'You need to just stop it now,' she said in a small voice. 'Please stop asking questions. She pinched her nose with her fingers to stop it dripping onto her jacket. 'You got a hankie?'

'Oh, right. Here.'

Tom stuffed a crumpled tissue into her hand. It looked as though it had been used but she didn't care.

Tom seemed to think his hankie had bought him some favour. 'This doesn't make any sense, does it? I mean, I know she's vulnerable and that, and if Antonio was threatening her, to keep her mouth shut, she'd have been terrified, but...'

'But what?'

'Well, why is she *still* scared? Scared enough to try and kill herself? You said it yourself, Antonio's dead. What difference does it make now?' Tom stood up and raised his arms as though he'd just had an epiphany. 'Oh bloody hell, what if someone else was there? What if the police were right and he wasn't working alone? You said it yourself, he had no real motive. What if...?'

Oonagh's scream pierced the stairwell. It carried on until it drowned out his words and her throat was raw. She saw two nurses throw open the fire escape door and look up as if someone was being murdered.

'She's alright,' Tom called, covering for her, 'she's just had some bad news.'

The nurses gave Oonagh a pitiful look, waited for her slight nod, and shuffled back out into the corridor.

Tom resumed his seat beside her on the stair and put his arm round her shoulder. 'You look dreadful.'

She shrugged off his arm and took in large gulps of air to calm herself. She didn't like the shift in the balance of power – didn't much care for Tom being the strong capable one while she struggled to come out of the other end of a panic attack.

It was a few minutes before she trusted herself to speak. 'Never join the Samaritans…' she whispered.

Tom finished the sentence for her. '…they'd need to employ a locum to cope with the increase in the suicide rate.' He nodded his head. 'I know. But Oonagh' – he clutched at her wrist – 'you do remember more about the attack than you're letting on, don't you?'

The strength was coming back to her legs, and the fear in her chest was subsiding. Her heart was returning to a more stable rhythm. She hadn't ever understood what a panic attack really was, not until now.

'Tom, please, just give me a break here. I'm not sure what I remember. It's still all muddled up. Things just flash up in my head and it's…I can't explain it. It's like I remember, then when I *try* to remember, it's gone. Just leave it for now, Tom, eh?'

★

They dragged themselves back to the chapel house, exhausted, and set about trying to secure the front door. Oonagh wedged an upside-down broom under the Yale lock. 'That's about the best we'll manage tonight.' She looked at Tom. His suit still showed traces of blood. 'Best get them off, Tom.'

He stared down at the soiled trousers and shoes. 'I, ehm, what'll I do with them…?'

'Och, have you never dealt with your own laundry…? Actually, don't answer that. Just stick them in a bin liner, Tom. We'll sort them out later.' Oonagh didn't know what to do with them either and made her way up the stairs while Tom took a shower. At least he had his own bathroom and wouldn't have to use the main one with its wrecked door. Destroyed bathroom doors seemed to be becoming a feature of her life.

For all that the house was old and full of character, it reeked of decades of loneliness. 'Why don't you stay at mine tonight?' Oonagh shouted through the bathroom door once the shower had been turned off. She didn't really fancy being alone.

'Are you sure?' he said quickly, seemingly welcoming the suggestion.

Out on the landing, Oonagh realised the door to Mrs Brady's room was open, as if reminding her why they were there. She poked her head in.

The room was sparse, bare. Desolate. Nothing gave any hint to the occupant's identity. A faint smell of damp hung in the air. Under the bed lay a wooden crucifix and a picture of the Sacred Heart of Jesus, both stuffed into a single see-through carrier bag. A cheap plywood bookcase crammed with books was the only piece of furniture that looked as though it was in use. But there was none of the usual romantic fiction they'd expected. Instead Hobbes, Dante and Sartre stared back. A copy of Nietzsche lay on the bed, an Underground ticket serving as a bookmark. Oonagh opened it at the page, and read the words underlined heavily in pencil.

'The thought of suicide is a great source of comfort: with it a calm passage is to be made across many a night.'

Oonagh hurried back to the landing and rapped on Tom's bedroom door.

'We've got to go back to the hospital,' she called. 'We can't leave her on her own tonight.'

CHAPTER 48

Glasgow, 2000

Oonagh stood behind Tom as he popped his head round the nurses' station. He had a fresh suit on. She'd insisted he wear his collar; always easier to curry favour.

Giving his perfected concerned look, he asked to see Mrs Brady. 'I know it's really late. But…well, I'm really worried about her. To be honest…' He didn't have to finish. The same nurse they'd seen earlier was watching a repeat of ER on a small portable. The sound was turned right down, and she craned her neck forward to hear.

She dismissed him with a wave. 'Aye, no problem. On you go.'

It was late. They were both dead beat, but they'd be as well sitting awake all night at the bedside as anywhere else.

'I'm just going to take a leak,' Tom told Oonagh. 'I'll be there in a minute.' He doubled back to the toilets.

She watched him tiptoe away, trying to stop his leather-soled shoes squeaking on the floor.

★

Jack had his hand over Anna Brady's mouth when Oonagh opened the door. He didn't hear her come in.

'I'm warning you,' she heard him say, 'don't even think about going to the police.'

'Jack! What the hell…?' Oonagh flew at him, clawing at his arm, trying to pull his hand from Anna's face. But as he swung round his elbow caught the side of her jaw and sent her crashing to the floor. She was on her feet again in seconds. But this time Tom pushed her back as he went for Jack Cranworth himself.

'You fucking bastard!' she yelled. 'It was *you* all along! I knew it!'

Oonagh ran to Anna Brady's side as the nurse ran in from her station. As soon as she saw the fight she rang the security bell, then pushed herself headfirst between the two men. Her thick, solid legs held her steady.

It was only moments before a security guard appeared at the door, looking ready for a bit of action. He grabbed Jack's arms and tried to pin them behind his back.

It gave Tom the break he needed. He brought his knee straight up. 'Fuck you,' he hissed and kicked his heel into Jack's balls. The big man doubled up in agony. Cupping his hands round his groin, gasping for breath, he writhed around on the floor.

For Oonagh, time stood still. She couldn't believe what she'd just seen. Or heard. Sweat was lashing off Tom's forehead. He crouched forward, resting his hands on his thighs.

Anna Brady let out a snigger, then slapped her hand across her mouth when she realised no-one else was joining in.

Oonagh stood beside the bed and Anna flung her arms around her waist, clinging on tight. Oonagh held Anna Brady in her arms and rocked her back and forth. The taste of blood was in her mouth from the blow to her face and she glared at Jack, glad he was still writhing in pain.

He was still on the floor when the police arrived. They'd been down in A&E. They helped Jack to his feet, sat him on a chair, then cuffed him. His face, chalk white from the kick, slowly regained its colour.

Tom leaned against the wall and struggled to catch his breath.

'He was trying to kill her,' Oonagh told the policemen, pointing at Jack without looking at him, 'I caught him with his hand over her mouth.' Her voice was no more than a whisper.

'No, that's not true,' Anna protested.

'It's alright,' said Oonagh, 'no one'll hurt you now.' She

looked towards the police. 'He also assaulted me.' She stroked her hand over her cheekbone and looked directly at him. *Get out of that you pig*, she thought.

'No. Please.' Anna tugged at Oonagh's sleeve like a child. 'I got a bit of a fright when I woke and saw him in the room, that's all. He was trying to stop me screaming. I'd had a nightmare. He's a...he's a friend. Please let him go. I'm sorry, it's just a mistake.'

The skin tightened round Oonagh's scalp as she recognised the likeness between Jack and Anna, and once more her heart ached for all the lost years and emptiness that had filled Anna Brady's miserable wee life.

Jack stood and stretched out his hands for the cuffs to be unlocked and removed. The two policemen ignored the gesture and each took an arm as they pulled him towards the door.

'No!' pleaded Anna, 'Please, don't.'

Jack stared back at both women for a few seconds before being led away.

'Is someone going to tell me what the hell's going on?' said Tom as the doors closed. 'Mrs Brady?'

'Her name's Irene,' said Oonagh, taking a damp flannel from the bedside locker and wiping Irene's forehead. 'Irene Connolly.'

Tom opened his mouth to speak, then seemed to think better of it.

Oonagh combed her fingers through Irene's wiry hair, smoothing it back onto the pillow behind her. 'Irene,' she said, 'was it...was it *you* Jack was meeting in St Patrick's?'

Irene Connolly tipped her chin and blinked hard.

But Oonagh already knew the answer.

★

When she'd first turned up after all those years he had offered to pay her off. To write her a cheque. Said she could name her price, he just wanted her the hell out of his life. But Irene didn't have a price. She already had a place to sleep and food in her belly. She hadn't needed money until Charlie Antonio had called, barking his demands.

She'd asked Jack to bring five thousand pounds in an envelope, and leave it behind the back pew at St Patrick's. From his reaction, Jack had obviously thought *that* was her price. Five thousand pounds for her to leave and never contact him again. But it hadn't been *her* price, it had been Antonio's, though she'd realised Antonio wouldn't stop at that. Blackmailers never stopped, not unless someone put a stop to them.

Irene had forgotten that all the kids would be in the Church that day. They sounded so innocent as they sang: *'All things bright and beautiful, All creatures great and small…'* She heard their voices as she climbed the stairs, stopping every so often because her swollen veins throbbed, causing her legs to ache with each step. She gripped the banister for support. *'…All things wise and wonderful…'* Years of living in cold, damp bedsits and smoking roll-ups had left her with a bronchial wheeze. She caught her breath, and wiped the sweat of her face with her hand. *'The Lord God made them all…'*

Aye, she thought, *they don't sing about all the other things God makes.*

She didn't see him until she reached the top. He was straining over the balcony, his fat body resting on the banister, his gut spilling over the edge. One leg was hoisted as he hung over to get a better look.

She hadn't expected him until later. And he couldn't hear her above the noise of the singing.

She was surprised at how easy it was. One shove was all it took. One shove. She didn't even need both hands to make him tumble over the top and crash onto the pews below.

The screams of the children and teachers blocked out any noise she made on her way out. By the time she walked the four blocks to the mini-market, she could hear the sirens wailing in the distance.

The muzak hummed softly in the background as she filled her trolley with all sorts of things she didn't need. Tampons, baby milk, Sellotape. By the time she was finished she had four bags full, and began the long walk home.

She was mortified when Oonagh O'Neil stopped the car and made her get in. She was grateful the tampons and baby milk were at the bottom of the bags as she put them in the boot.

CHAPTER 49

Glasgow, 2000

'They wouldn't even let him keep the name I'd given him.'

'Oh Irene, I'm so so sorry.' Oonagh held Irene close and felt her ribs jutting out. 'Tom,' she said, without turning round, 'see if the nurse can't get Irene a proper robe or something to put on.' Then, shaking her head, she added, 'We should have brought up her stuff. Why didn't we bring up her stuff?'

'Oonagh. Forget her stuff. You need to call Davies and tell him.' Tom was strutting around the room, his spirits obviously galvanized by his display of macho violence minutes before.

'Oh just shut up, Tom.' Oonagh kept her voice low and laid Irene Connolly back down onto her pillow.

'Look, I know I don't know the full ins and outs of it, but I'm not daft. Cranworth was trying to kill her and he walloped you.' Tom stared straight at her as though expecting her to reveal all. 'Are you trying to tell me he's got nothing to do with your attack?'

Oonagh slid out from Irene's grip, grabbed Tom by the elbow and ushered him over to the window. She squeezed hard into his flesh. 'Can you just shut it for now, Tom? We'll talk about it later.' She glanced back at Irene, whose eyelids were flickering in and out of sleep.

'Later? The guy's a maniac! Just tell me one thing.'

'What?'

He took a deep breath. 'Was it him who stabbed you? Did…' he hesitated before he said her name, '…did Irene see him do it? She's trying to protect him isn't she?'

Oonagh rested her head on the glass and looked out to the street below. 'No,' she said. 'No.' She'd had enough. She was tired.

Tom twisted her round to face him. 'I need more than you're telling me, Oonagh. I didn't ask to be dragged into all of this.' He looked hurt and disappointed.

The room was hot and claustrophobic, and Oonagh didn't feel like explaining anything. The last thing she wanted right now was to talk.

Low moans from Irene bed gave her an excuse to tend to her. 'Come on now you, try and get some sleep.' Her pillows were plumped and the sheets were tucked in as tight as they were going to go. There was nothing left for Oonagh to do.

Irene reached for her hand. 'You're a good girl,' she said. Her voice was weak.

Oonagh wiped her eyes and felt Tom's hand on her shoulders. Suddenly she was glad he was there. 'This is a mess, Tom. A bloody mess.'

He pulled up a chair, patted Irene's legs through the sheet and sat by the bed. 'I'm here,' he said. 'If you need to talk.'

'She's exhausted, Tom. She'd be better going to sleep.'

Irene's small voice cut in. 'No, love,' she said, tapping Oonagh's hand, 'I want to talk.'

Oonagh felt her adrenaline drain away, taking with it every last ounce of emotion. She didn't want this. Didn't want Tom to hear Irene's outpourings. She couldn't bear it. 'Please, Irene. Don't.'

But Irene insisted, and told him. Told him all about her dad. The rape. Baby Isaac. How her flesh had burned when they'd stuck the electrodes to her head in the asylum. She could never go back there. She'd rather die.

Oonagh watched the expression on Tom's face turn to horror as Irene calmly relayed how she'd watched from the icy window as they'd buried the poor dead infants in the back yard of Lochbridge House. Baby Patricia first, then three more the following night. How she'd held her daughter's twisted, broken body in her arms until the girl had died.

They both smiled at the story of Bridie Flanagan, her Granny and the big hairy coats and were gutted at how Sally had just faded away one night. Irene even told him about spitting on her parent's grave. Didn't flinch from any of it.

Tom hung his head and held her hand when she told him about her efforts to get Patricia into Heaven. Blessed himself at her campaign of self-abuse lasting more than forty years.

Oonagh watched Tom pick at his dog collar like a wound.

'Irene,' he said, 'we don't believe in limbo anymore.'

Oonagh flinched slightly but said nothing. Just sank further back into the chair. Tom obviously thought this would give Irene Connolly some comfort. Poor Irene Connolly who'd burned and scratched and cut herself for forty years for nothing.

'Babies who die without being baptised,' he explained, 'well, they go straight to Heaven.'

Irene Connolly looked neither pleased nor relieved. Her dead eyes sank further back into her head. 'Oh.' She struggled to prop herself up on the bed. 'And when did you decide on this?'

'It wasn't me. It was the Vatican Council…'

But she cut him dead. 'The Vatican Council! So the babies who died before then, are they still in limbo? And the ones who died afterwards…are they in Heaven? Where's my Patricia?' Her voice shook with emotion.

Oonagh stroked Irene's arm in an impotent gesture of comfort. Inside she screamed at the injustice this poor woman had endured. But she said nothing. This was Irene's moment.

'Where's my Patricia? Irene repeated. 'Where's my baby girl?' She tugged at Oonagh's arm, then stared at Tom. 'Who decides who can and who can't get into Heaven?'

Tom didn't have the answers she was looking for, and Oonagh couldn't – wouldn't – help him.

'You bunch of horrible, evil bastards.' Irene pulled her hand away from Tom's and reached again for Oonagh.

Tom was visibly shocked. 'What?'

'What gives you the right? Just what gives you the right to play with people's lives?' Irene was sobbing now. 'Do you honestly think God is sitting in his Heaven, looking down on all those poor innocent wee babies in purgatory waiting until *your* lot make a decision?' She looked straight at him. 'It's not your decision to make!' Her voice was weak even though she was screaming. 'It's not your decision to make!' She scratched at her arm and tried to gouge the flesh with her bitten nails. 'Jesus Christ, what makes you think you're all so important?'

'We don't,' Tom said, unconvincingly.

'Oh just give up, Tom,' Oonagh told him, holding out both her hands to stop Irene hurting herself any more. 'Break rank and tell her she's right and you're wrong.' Oonagh felt the pity burn the back of her throat. 'Tell her the Church made a mistake.' She held Irene Connolly's sobbing body close to her chest and felt the hot tears seep into her blouse. 'Just tell her you're sorry.'

Tom had no answers. 'We're all a product of our time,' he mumbled feebly.

'Dear God,' said Irene, her voice muffled by Oonagh's embrace, 'do you know what you've done?'

The nurse from the ward station pushed open the door.

'She's just a bit upset,' Tom tried to explain.

Oonagh drew him a dagger.

'Want a sedative?' the nurse asked. Irene shook her head and the nurse seemed relieved to be able to leave.

It took a few moments for Irene to pull herself together. Then, unprompted by either Oonagh or Tom, she continued her story.

She'd had no great master plan the day she'd arrived at Father Kennedy's – hadn't known what she'd say to him. Oh she'd known in her head for years – had gone over the conversation countless times, changing wee bits here and there depending on how vicious or magnanimous she was feeling – but when she'd seen him – a pathetic, sad old man – he'd meant nothing to her. She hadn't even been able to drum up enough feeling to spit in his face as she'd planned.

She should have left there and then, but she didn't. Introduced herself as Anna Brady and stayed. Never went back to her bed and breakfast. Left her meagre belongings to be dumped by the next tenant.

'So did you only arrive at St Patrick's a few months before me then?' asked Tom. 'I thought you'd been there…well, years.'

Oonagh looked at the grey, faceless woman with no life and wondered what might have been. She thought Tom looked as though he could have kicked himself. She urged her back to her story.

It had taken Irene three years to gather the courage to speak to Isaac, her son. She'd gone over the scenario in her head time and time again. Holding him, kissing his face, smelling the back of his neck the way she should have done when he was a baby.

'I should have written him a letter first.' she said. It had been her own fault; he was bound to have been shocked. Her turning up at his door like that, out of the blue. Really, what was he supposed to do? He'd hardly be pleased. A man in his position finding out that his real mother was 'a fucking retard'. She flinched as she recalled his words.

CHAPTER 50

Glasgow, 2000

Davies had managed to shower and change. Spending three, maybe four days on the trot at the station was nothing new. At least Govan was fairly state of the art as far as staff facilities went. Back when he'd been at Craigie Street he'd resorted to nipping round the corner to the public swimming baths in Calder Street to get a shower.

He stood in front of the mirror, shaving. Holding up his nose with one finger as he carefully pulled the razor down over his top lip.

McVeigh was four sinks along. It had taken a while, but eventually he'd got the message that Davies didn't care for anyone standing too close. McVeigh rinsed his face with cold water, then dried it with a hand towel and wiped off the stray blobs of foam round his ears.

Davies squinted. 'Hey,' he said, tapping his own lip, 'you've no finished yet.'

'Thought I'd grow a moustache. Looks kind of…well, distinguished, don't you think?' He looked in the mirror, twisting his head from side to side.

'Get rid of it.' Davies didn't look at him.

'Why?'

'That fucking hair of yours is bad enough. If you think I'm parading round with you sporting a bloody ginger moustache, you've got another think coming.

McVeigh refilled the sink with hot water and finished shaving. Davies left him to it.

His heart sank moments later when he saw Cranworth at the front desk, in hand-cuffs. 'What the bloody hell's going on here?'

'Attacked an auld woman at the hospital,' volunteered one of his uniformed colleagues, who didn't look up, keen to finish filling in the charge sheet.

Cranworth sighed. 'Don't be so bloody ridiculous, man.' Then, looking at Davies, he said, 'Is there somewhere we can talk?'

He nodded. 'Aye, aye, of course.'

Davies led him through the double swing doors once the cuffs were removed. Cranworth looked relieved to see they were heading for the office, not the interview room.

★

For all Irene had been through, the last few weeks had been the most painful, she said. She'd never meant to ruin Jack's life. She'd rather take her own than ruin his.

'He came round to the house to see me tonight, you know. Before…before all this.' She raised her wrists slightly.

Oonagh was too terrified to speak. Jack was a bastard, but surely he couldn't have hurt his own mother. She wanted to know just what had gone on.

'I wanted to go to the police.' Her eyes pleaded with Oonagh. 'Honest I did. But he begged me not to. Said I owed him that much at least. And I do. He's my baby boy.'

Tom butted in. 'Irene, if he tried to kill Oonagh, then it's wrong to protect him.'

It seemed to Oonagh that Tom was determined to pick at the scab until he made it bleed.

Irene's grip tightened around Oonagh's hand. 'Don't you tell me what's right and wrong.'

The beep from the heart monitor quickened. Oonagh tried to calm her. 'Shh. There, Irene. C'mon'

Oonagh looked out of the window. The vertical blinds were only half drawn. She could see the taxi rank across the road on the street below. The cabs' yellow lights shone in the darkness.

Could just about make out a few people walking home after a night out. The glow of a high-rise in Toryglen in the distance. Life did indeed go on.

'Father Thomas,' Irene said, 'do you believe in the sanctity of the confessional?'

'Well,' said Tom, 'I'm a priest. Yes, yes of course.'

'Then, will you hear my confession?'

Oonagh's heart quickened. 'No, Irene.' Her voice was louder than she'd intended. She looked at Tom. 'She's tired, she needs to get her head down.' She could see he didn't believe her.

But Irene Connolly was remarkably calm.

'You can stay or go as you like, pet,' she said to Oonagh.

Oonagh stayed put and held her hand. Tom sat by her side, waiting.

'Father, does God forgive? Truly forgive.'

'Well, if you're truly sorry he does,' said Tom. Oonagh kicked him on the leg. 'Yes, Irene,' he added, rubbing his shin, 'God truly does forgive.'

'Irene,' said Oonagh, trying to soothe her, 'you don't always have to say it out loud though. God forgives you anyway.' She was trying to shut her up. Once out, it would be impossible to force the genie back into the bottle.

'I don't want to feel like this anymore,' she said. 'Jack told me his wife was being questioned about you, Oonagh.' She lifted her head off the pillow. Her breathing was shallow, talking was an effort. 'She never paid anyone to try and kill you, pet. Honest. I told Jack I couldn't let her take the blame for this. But he told me to keep my mouth shut.' Irene started to sob and wiped her eyes with the sheet. Oonagh handed her a hankie from a box by the side of the bed. She remained silent, terrified of what was coming next.

'He made me promise not to tell. Said if I couldn't live with myself, then that was up to me.' She broke down.

Fury, anger, disbelief rose in Oonagh. 'Is that why you tried to kill yourself, Irene?'

She tried to keep calm as Irene nodded. 'I had no choice. I couldn't live with myself.'

'Irene,' interrupted Tom, 'you *have* to tell the police.'

'I wanted to. But he said no.' Spasms contracted her throat. Her cries came out in convulsions. She gulped back her tears as they spilled onto her cheeks.

Tom leaned over the bed. 'Irene, I know Jack's your son. But if he tried to kill Oonagh, he could kill again. He needs help. You can't really protect him any longer.'

Her sobs stopped momentarily. 'I'm not protecting Jack. *He's* protecting *me.*'

'You?'

She looked at Oonagh, and very calmly said. 'Jack didn't stab you, Oonagh, neither did that fat man. I did it.'

Oonagh's head swam as the final piece of the jigsaw slotted into place. She saw the silver blade once more plunge into her throat. She tugged at her collar, gasping for air as the room closed in on her. Dryness closed her throat, fear caught her breath. She felt sickness rise in her gut and the room started to spin. And then arms were grabbing her as she fell onto the floor.

She was thankful for Tom helping her back onto the chair. He held a glass of water to her lips. But it tasted stale and did nothing to make her feel better.

'She didn't like crusts either.' Irene Connolly's voice was so small that she was barely audible.

'Pardon?' Tom said.

'Oonagh,' said Irene. 'She doesn't like crusts on her bread, and neither do I. They're meant to give you curly hair. That's what my mum said.'

Fear and panic merged into pity as Oonagh watched Irene Connolly's sanity unravel before their eyes.

'She was nice. She made me tea and toast. I like tea and toast. I like Oonagh. She's pretty.'

Oonagh started to cry. Irene was looking right through her.

'Why did you attack Oonagh, Irene? Why?' Tom's voice had no emotion.

Irene swayed back and forth on the bed. Her nails left deep red marks on the backs of her hands. Her eyes widened as she spoke.

'I think Patricia would have turned out like Oonagh. Do you think Patricia would have turned out like Oonagh?' Her question was aimed at Oonagh, as though she was someone else entirely.

The tip of Oonagh's nose stung red with sadness and her throat swelled.

'Yes, Irene, perhaps she might have.'

They were losing her and had no idea how to get back inside her head. Irene's lips trembled and her face crumpled, pain in her eyes. 'Do you think she'll be all right? Will Oonagh die?'

'Irene.' Oonagh took the woman's hand. 'I'm here, look, I'm fine. It was just a scratch. You didn't hurt me, honestly.' The pain of her attack throbbed through her entire body but she was determined not to let it show.

The bloody scratches darkened the backs of Irene's hands as her nails dug deeper. Oonagh prised the housekeeper's fingers apart and rested her arms by her sides.

Tom looked to Oonagh for an explanation. 'Is this true? Did *she* stab you?'

Oonagh nodded. 'It was an accident. A stupid bloody accident.' And this time she was telling the truth. She tried to smile at the bitter irony, and ran her fingers through her hair. The memory unfolded like a film. 'I'd been interviewing her and suddenly Antonio was at the kitchen door.' A shudder ran through her as she remembered him standing in the hall, laughing at her. 'He seemed to appear from nowhere. I don't know how he got in. And he threatened to spill the beans about Irene. Said he'd sell her story to the papers and...' Oonagh eased the crick out of the back of her neck. 'He was going to blackmail her. Everything happened so fast. I remember him standing at the hall door ready to leave when...' She faltered, trying the patch the detail together. '"I'll be in touch." That was the last thing he said. Then I think you' – she looked at Irene – 'you grabbed the letter-opener and went for him, and after that...' She remembered Antonio's scream. High-pitched, like a woman's. 'I just sort of got caught in the crossfire.'

Irene's head was back against the pillow. 'You tried to save him.' Her eyes were closed. Apparently she was seeing the same picture as Oonagh. 'You tried to shove my hand away but you were too small, so you stood in front of him and...' Her voice choked in the back of her throat.

Oonagh remembered the blade plunging into her neck. Remembered everything going red, then black. Then nothing. Thank God she couldn't remember Charlie Antonio standing on her shoulder to work the blade free from her neck.

'I'm sorry. I ran away. I was scared. I just ran.' Irene sniffed, and Oonagh stuffed more paper hankies into her hand.

'I'm fine now, Irene, and that's what counts.'

Tom seemed to forget about the sanctity of the confessional. 'What a bastard. He must have known you were alive when he left you.' He hung one arm loosely round Oonagh's shoulder and tried to comfort Irene with the other.

Oonagh shrugged him off and stood up. 'Will we get going and let you get some shut-eye, Irene?' She waited for Tom to follow. But his face was fixed on Irene.

★

'Surely her being Jack's mother would be a nine-day-wonder for the media.' Tom was speaking to Oonagh, but his eyes never left Irene.

Irene looked puzzled. Shook her head. 'He wasn't threatening to blackmail me for that.'

Oonagh held Irene by the shoulders. She didn't want Tom to hear any more.

'No, Irene. Stop this. You don't know what you're saying.'

Irene Connolly wriggled free, and Oonagh was terrified for her.

'No,' – Irene's voice was coming out in short sharp breaths – 'he heard me telling Oonagh that it was me who killed Father Kennedy.' There was no remorse in her voice. 'I poisoned him.'

Oonagh could've wept. Instead she checked the bed for hospital corners and tucked the sheet flat under the mattress. 'Oh Irene. You're just all confused.' She turned to Tom, 'It's called transference,' she whispered. 'She's probably dreamt about bumping off Father Kennedy so many times that now she's convinced herself she did it.'

But Tom was having none of it. He rubbed his eyes and slumped back in his chair. 'Why did you kill Father Kennedy, Irene? Why now?' He was as calm as Oonagh had ever seen him. He wasn't letting go.

'This doesn't leave this room, Tom.' Short of putting her hand over the woman's mouth, Oonagh was powerless to stop Irene Connolly's confession.

Irene let out a breathless laugh. '*Why?* Why *not?* I read those letters he'd written. Making peace with God and the world before he died. Well, no. I couldn't allow that.' She looked at Oonagh, as if to find reassurance. 'Why should he have had the chance to make peace? Why should he have been allowed to die happy? I wanted him to rot in purgatory.'

'But you'd found Isaac,' Tom said. 'Surely *you*'d found peace.'

Oonagh despaired. Tom just wasn't grasping this at all.

Irene shook her head. 'Peace? I've never had a day's peace in my life. I killed him because I felt like it, I killed him because it was Patricia's birthday and it was the best present I could think to give her. I killed him so his suffering might let a few more babies into Heaven.'

'You knew all this?' Tom turned to Oonagh, 'Is that what was on that bloody tape?'

Oonagh shrugged her shoulders and said nothing.

Irene's wee voice was tearful. 'I'm so, so sorry, pet.' She struggled to reach the wound on Oonagh's neck.

'Irene, it was an accident. And I'm fine. Stop torturing yourself like this.' But Oonagh knew why Irene was still so tortured.

'I'd no idea you were pregnant. Oh God, please forgive me.'

Oonagh took what felt like the biggest breath of her life. 'Irene, it just wasn't the right time.' She struggled not to cry. 'Some babies aren't meant to survive.'

Oonagh thought of the deck stacked against the wee mite from the start. 'And Tom gave me the Last Rites, so...'

Irene cut in. 'That means your wee baby will go straight to Heaven, doesn't it?' she said in a child's voice. Oonagh smiled and nodded. Some things were so black and white for Irene Connolly.

Oonagh felt a familiar chill run down her spine. 'Irene, did you tell Jack all this when he came to see you earlier.

★

The tea had been made and the pot sat in the middle of the table. She took the cosy off and pressed her hands against it until the metal burned her skin.

She jumped when he rattled his hand off the back door. She hadn't been sure if he'd come.

She led him into the kitchen and pointed her hand towards a chair, then waited until he'd sat down before pouring his tea. He didn't drink it.

He was the first to speak. 'You know the police have the money.' She looked confused. 'The five thousand pounds,' he explained, 'the police took it.'

'Oh.' She'd forgotten about the money.

'But I can give you more. Money's *not* the problem here, Irene.' He reached into his inside pocket, but she stopped him. She hadn't expected him to call her mum, but she'd hoped he might. But at least he was making an attempt to be civil, and she thought that was nice. 'No, son.' She reached across to touch his knee but he pulled back. 'I don't need any money. I just wanted to talk, that's all.'

He looked at his watch.

'It won't take long.' She patted her frizzy hair away from her face and smiled as she looked at him. She felt a swell in her chest. His eyes hadn't changed in all those years. 'Jack, that money wasn't for me. It was for that man Antonio.'

She slid a plate of cheap digestive biscuits towards him. He pushed it to the other end of the table.

He stopped drumming his fingers on the table. 'The one who fell? How did you know him?' He rubbed his hand along his face. 'Please don't tell me he was another of your long-lost babies?'

'No. No, nothing like that, son. It wasn't that.' Her short stubby nails were already bitten to the quick and she chewed the skin round her fingertips.

Jack sat back, crossed his legs.

'I've done something, son. I've done a bad thing.' She looked down and picked at a loose thread on her overall. Outside, the rain from the gutter bounced off the wheelie bin in the back garden. She scraped the edge of her finger along the seam of her nylon overall, gathering enough fluff to roll into a ball.

'How bad?' he said. She thought his eyes looked scared. 'You better not have told anyone that you're my...' He stopped. '...

About us.'

She managed a half-smile and shook her head as she pulled a roll-up from her pocket. 'I'd never tell, son. Never.'

He sighed as he let himself fall back into his chair and sat stony-faced for a few seconds. 'Good,' he said. Then got up to leave.

She flicked her thumb against her disposable lighter, but the gas was running out and she struggled to light the two-inch stub. 'I've killed someone,' she whispered, taking a deep draw.

He quickly swung round, grabbing her by the shoulders. 'What?' He shook her until her head snapped back against her neck. She dropped her cigarette, breathing in the pain of his fingers digging into her flesh. Irene wasn't used to answering questions. She wasn't sure which bit to tell him first. She cupped her hands over her face and wiped away a tear before telling him about Father Kennedy…and Oonagh O'Neil.

She looked up at his face and reached towards him.

He recoiled. 'Don't come near me.' He retreated to the other side of the room.

A flutter of panic stirred in her chest. 'Isaac, please…'

He was leaning with both hands against the wall. She tugged at his jacket.

'Don't fucking come near me. You're psychotic.' He spat the words into her face 'And don't call me that. My name's Jack. Jack Cranworth.' He slumped down onto a chair and dropped his head into his hands. 'Do you know what you've done? Have you any idea what you've done?'

She hesitated before resting her hand on his shoulder. He pushed her off. She fell against the wall. Her bony shoulders smashed against the tiles. Irene didn't scream. She didn't like noise.

'Oonagh was pregnant.'

Irene struggled to hear Jack's low voice.

'Oonagh,' he said, 'was pregnant with *my* child, and *you*'ve killed it. You've killed your own grandchild, you mad fucking, stupid bitch.' He raised his hand above his head and slapped her full force in the face.

Irene knew she'd done wrong. A pain hit her gut and spread throughout her body as she took in the horror of what he'd said.

He grabbed her by the throat and she struggled for breath as he squeezed. She felt her legs go limp and when he let go she fell in a crumpled heap on the floor.

She pleaded with him. 'Oh Dear God, say it's not true.'

'You've *ruined* my fucking life,' was all he said as she begged for forgiveness.

She got onto her knees, hugging her arms round his legs. 'I'll go to the police. Tell them everything. Oh God, I'm so sorry. So, so sorry, son,' she sobbed.

'Don't you *dare* go to the police. It's already bad enough without you making things even worse.' He pointed into her face. 'Listen to me, just keep your mouth shut. Tell no one what happened with Oonagh. The police are already on top of things, okay?'

She nodded eagerly and drew her finger across her chest. 'Cross my heart,' she said. 'I'll tell no one.' She curled up in a ball on the floor at his feet. She hugged his legs and dragged herself closer. 'Cross my heart and hope to die, Jack.' She sobbed into his trousers and clung on as he tried to leave. Dragged herself along the floor – let herself be dragged. She kissed the hem of his trousers, kissed his shoes. Telling him over and over again how sorry she was. Sobbing. Crying. Screaming. Pleading. He prised her hands from his legs as he struggled for the door.

'Jack, I didn't *know* she was pregnant. I didn't know!' She scrambled across the floor after him. Clawing, pulling him back as he was leaving. 'I wish I was dead,' she screamed after him. 'I wish I was dead.'

He gave her one last look. 'Well that makes two of us.'
The door slammed hard behind him.

CHAPTER 51

Glasgow, 2000

The rain had stopped. The dawn struggled through with some watery sunshine.

Oonagh opened her eyes. Her mouth was thick and sticky, her neck stiff from sleeping on the chair all night. She rubbed it with the palm of her hand, standing, stretching her back and listening for cracks and groans as her spine slipped back into place.

Irene Connolly lay on the hospital bed, eyes closed, breathing slow and rhythmic.

Tom opened the door gingerly, and entered carrying a tray with three steaming cups of what Oonagh hoped was coffee. It was, and it was awful. She blew on hers; it made no difference to the taste.

'Christ, Tom, it's a mess,' she whispered. She couldn't bear to think of Jack attacking Irene, slapping her, goading her into taking her own life. By rights she should afford him at least a scrap of sympathy. If ever there was a case of the sins of the fathers.

Tom read her mind. 'Jack maybe needs help, Oonagh.'

Oonagh sipped on her coffee and tipped her chin at him. She couldn't answer. What could she say?

'I mean,' Tom continued, 'he's maybe not right. Doesn't think straight...you know?'

'You mean he's an inbred? God, he'll be skinning rabbits and claiming he's seen UFOs next.' She tried to inflect a bit of humour into her voice, but it was dull and flat. Tom gave a wry smile – out of politeness, she imagined.

Oonagh made her way to the bathroom down the hall, where she caught her reflection in the mirror. She looked like shit.

She put the lid down on the pan, then sat and wept. Wept for Irene Connolly's miserable life, for her dead baby, for Jack's twisted logic…and at the cruel fate that had conspired to collide such disparate elements.

Eventually she dried her tears and walked reluctantly back down the corridor. The door of Irene's room was open. Strange voices carried above the clatter of the breakfast trolley being wheeled into the main ward. Her heart raced. Something was wrong. Oonagh ran.

A doctor was leaning over Irene, pumping his hands up and down on her chest. A nurse stood by, anxious. Tom was at the side of her bed giving her the final Sacrament. The Last Rites. Anointing her forehead.

No one tried to stop Oonagh as she raced to Irene's side and held her hand. She prayed to God to take her quickly before they managed to revive her.

For once God was generous and looked down with pity on poor Irene Connolly.

Oonagh squeezed Irene's hand. It was still warm. She was sure Irene's mouth had formed into a faint smile, her lips slightly parted.

Tom leaned across the bed and kissed Irene's forehead. Oonagh guessed he was the only man, other than her own father, who had ever kissed her.

★

They walked to where Oonagh had left her car the night before. A parking ticket flapped under the windscreen wiper. 'Bastard,' muttered Oonagh as she ripped it off and opened the passenger door for Tom.

She drove towards Govan. It wasn't yet six in the morning so the roads were empty. She flicked on the stereo. Billy Holiday's sad lament came out the speakers, telling them to *Weep No More*.

Alec Davies was standing outside at the door of the police

station. Oonagh turned the car left off Helen Street through the entrance of the car park. She stopped under the No Parking sign and waited for a few moments, letting Lady Day finish her song before switching off the engine and getting out. Neither she nor Tom had uttered a word since leaving the hospital.

Davies drew on a cigarette and descended the stairs to meet them. He didn't look surprised to see them.

'She's dead,' said Oonagh. 'Mrs Brady. She took a heart attack.'

Davies tutted, looked down at his feet and shook his head. 'Ach. I was on my way to see her. I've got Jack Cranworth in here – after last night.'

'I know,' said Oonagh.

'Claimed Anna Brady was his mother. Said Charlie Antonio was threatening her because she saw him stab you. Is that right, Oonagh?' He didn't wait for her to answer. 'Said the money was for her to clear off back to Ireland.'

Oonagh looked at Tom. He said nothing, just drew circles on the ground with his toe. Oonagh nodded. 'Kind of, Alec. She spoke to Tom and me before she died. Told us everything.'

'And?'

'Antonio didn't mean to stab me. It was an accident, Alec.' Davies took her by the elbow and led her back up the stairs. She continued, 'To be honest, it was starting to come back to me, anyway. Antonio was in my house and I started waving a weapon around to get him out. Backfired I'm afraid.'

Davies threw his cigarette on the ground and stubbed it out with his foot. 'I wish she'd come to me.' He pushed his arms through the sleeve of his jacket and pulled it up over his shoulders. 'You'll need to make a statement.' Then, looking at Tom, he added, 'Both of you. And Oonagh, I want you to take a look over Cranworth's statement. Make sure what he's told me is true.'

'Yeah. No problem.' Oonagh followed Alec up the steps.

She paused at the door and said a silent prayer for all the Irene Connolly's of the world. 'I'll be right there, Alec.'

She turned to make sure Tom was coming too. And he was. Right behind her.

'Just one thing,' Tom said, and her heart sank. Lately she'd become used to preparing for disappointments. 'Have you got the disk?' he asked.

She'd almost forgotten about it. She'd taken it from him the previous evening before he'd thrown his blood-soaked clothes into a bin liner. 'Yeah, right here.' She patted the side of her handbag.

'Good,' said Tom. 'Then let's go.'

She waited for Tom to catch up and watched as he took a deep breath on the third step before pulling off his dog collar and throwing it onto the ground.

EPILOGUE

Glasgow, 2000

She dried her eyes. There would be plenty of time to cry later. Oonagh drove through the city centre and everything reminded her of Irene Connolly. Every turn, every street corner, there she was. She'd left Tom back at the chapel house. He'd been packing his bags as she'd said goodbye.

She didn't wait for the lift and took the stairs, dragging the black plastic bag up the three storeys. This time the grey nun spotted her as she reached the edge of the corridor. *You dare*, thought Oonagh. *You fucking dare.*

The nun didn't dare, instead staying in her seat, typing like mad, knocking lumps out of the keyboard.

The door was already open. Father Watson was standing at the window. The room reeked of garlic.

'Early lunch?'

He turned and looked her up and down. His face fell. 'Oh not again. Dear God, woman, will you just go away.'

Oonagh lugged the black bin-liner across the carpet. She was wheezing and her arms ached. It was heavier than she'd imagined. 'Irene Connolly died this morning,' she said, settling in the centre of the room.

A slight flicker of something passed across Father Watson's face. 'Oh. I'm sorry. Was she a...'

Oonagh reached into the bag and took out a photograph. 'She had forty-two separate injuries on her body. Cigarette burns, cuts, scars.' She placed the picture on the desk in front of him. It was an old photograph of three teenage girls. 'Recognise them?'

'Eh?'

'That girl there is Irene Connolly. The one at the front is Bridie Flannigan. The other one's called Sally. Don't know her second name.'

'Listen, Miss O'Neil. I'm sorry for your loss and all, but really. Take your crusade elsewhere, eh? This is getting bloody tedious and quite frankly I'm bored with it all. It's got nothing to do with me.' Father Watson sat down and flicked the grainy picture off his desk with the back of his hand.

Oonagh bent to pick it up. 'Irene Connolly. She's dead. As are the other two. I didn't know them, but I knew Irene.'

'Oh I see. Is this your merry band of harpies who were supposedly used and abused by the big bad Church? Well, you have my sympathy... Now close the door on the way out, won't you?'

But Oonagh wasn't listening. She reached into the black bag and took out more copies of the photograph – dozens of them – and tossed them into his face. He flinched and tightened his lips, but said nothing. Just stared at her. Then she took out the rest. Hundreds. Photographs she'd downloaded from the internet. The faces of all the men and women who'd searched for years for their mammies. She plastered some of the pictures onto the window. The condensation made them stick. Then she turned the bag upside down and scattered the rest across the room.

'Look at them. Go on,' she screamed. 'Take a fucking look! I want you to see every single one of their faces and then tell me you've done nothing wrong, you big bastard.'

Father Watson stubbed out his cigarette, stood up and picked up the phone. 'Right. That's enough. I'm calling the police. You're a bloody lunatic.'

Oonagh grabbed it from his hand. 'I wouldn't bother if I were you. They'll be here soon enough. Why not catch up on a bit of television while you wait.'

He glanced over to the set nestling in a cabinet in the corner. Oonagh picked up the remote control and flicked it on. The lunchtime news was just starting.

For the first time she saw a glimmer of panic in the man's face. She turned up the volume as the opening credits rolled. The signature tune blared through the office and the newsreader came in on cue.

'In today's lunchtime news…in an exclusive report…the Catholic Church apologises for the misery of the Magdalenes…'

'What the fu…?' Father Watson leaned forward in his chair. His hand trembled as he lit another cigarette while the rest of the headlines were read.

Oonagh perched on the table next to him, swinging her leg, kicking the back of his chair with the toe of her shoe. And then the lead story commenced. Tom filled the screen. He looked better on camera than she'd expected, but that was often the way with small guys. The caption read *Father Tom Findlay – St Patrick's Parish Church, Glasgow.*

'What the hell is this all about?'

'Call it parallel justice! Now shush.' She wafted her hand across Father Watson's face to shut him up. Her eyes were glued to the screen. She couldn't believe her luck. The duty editor was new, and had clearly believed Oonagh when she'd told her the whole interview had been passed by the station's legal team.

Tom didn't look at all nervous. The light-blue shirt with the black suit and white dog collar was a good choice. *'Firstly,'* – his voice was calm and steady as he recited the lines Oonagh had prepared for him – *'can I make a public apology on behalf of the Catholic Church for the misery endured by these poor women over the years.'* Tom waved the document Oonagh had printed off for him, and licked his lips. He was really camping it up as he got into his stride. *'And it is with deep regret that this latest allegation – of an illegal baby trade at Lochbridge Magdalene Asylum in Glasgow – has come to our attention. Obviously I can assure not only Scotland's Catholics, but the public in general, that each and every allegation, no matter how many years it goes back, will be fully investigated.'*

There was a brief pause and her heart sank as she thought for a moment the end had been edited out. Then came the payoff she was waiting for.

'There is no room for this sort of contamination in the Catholic Church. But, I would like to say at this point that there is no proof – no proof whatsoever – that Father Patrick Joseph Kennedy took his own life because of these allegations. And furthermore, it would be unfair to implicate Father Michael Watson of the Catholic Press Office at this stage. It is now up to Strathclyde Police to fully investigate the matter.'

The camera switched to the pre-recorded section with Oonagh. *'This is the latest in a long line of damaging allegations to hit the Catholic Church in recent years. Strathclyde Police have confirmed that a full investigation will be launched but refuse to say whether a report will sent to the Procurator Fiscal, or indeed if any charges will be brought.'* The screen switched back to the newsreader.

Father Watson's cigarette had burned all the way up to his fingers as he dissolved into his chair. 'You bitch. You fucking stupid bitch. Have you any idea what you've done?'

'Probably lost my job?'

'I'll drag you through the courts for this.' He was jabbing his finger in the air next to her chest, pointing towards the television. 'That is fucking illegal and you know it.'

Oonagh was picking her nails. 'Mm, you're right. But you know, sometimes shit happens. So deal with it.'

'I'll sue you. I'll fucking ruin you.'

His words were music to Oonagh's ears. 'Have you ever been to a libel case, Father Watson?' He said nothing. Oonagh sucked the air in through her teeth and tutted while shaking her head. 'Nasty businesses. They drag on for months. All sorts of dirt comes out.' For the first time in a long time Oonagh laughed out loud. Really laughed. She slapped her hand off his chest. 'Do yourself a favour, stupid! Quit while you're ahead. D'you think I don't know how to wangle my way round Scotland's libel laws? Take this to court and you'll come out looking like a bigger prick than you are already.'

She strode to the window. Most of Glasgow's news agencies were within spitting distance. She spotted a white van with a satellite dish pulling into the kerb. A camera crew jumped out and ran along the pavement.

Father Watson attempted to rationalise what had just happened. 'But Thomas Findlay is not a spokesperson for the Catholic Church!' The veins on his neck bulged as he gripped the side of the desk. 'He has no right. No fucking right to stand there apologising for the Church.'

Oonagh noticed even his nicotine-stained fingers had turned white. She found it hard not to spit in his face. 'Oh, really? Thanks for the tip. I'll make sure we don't use him as a contributor again.'

Raised voices carried from the corridor.

'Now's your big chance to explain yourself,' Oonagh said as she opened the door. The grey nun was trying to hold back a big bearded highlander, who was stuffing a microphone into her face. A girl with a camera perched on her shoulder stood behind him. The rest would soon follow.

'He's all yours, mate,' Oonagh said, leaving Father Watson scrambling on his hands and knees as he tried to scrape up the pictures strewn across his floor.

*

Oonagh saw Alec Davies leaning against his car as she exited the building. He was parked on a double yellow and shaking his head. Her bravado of moments earlier evaporated and she felt her legs tremble.

'What the hell am I going to do with you, Oonagh O'Neil?'

'Buy me a large gin?'

He held out his arms and she collapsed into them. He hugged her and she breathed a long sigh into his shoulder.

'You do realise that by getting Tom to name him you've now prejudiced any possible court case against him.'

'Oh come on, Alec, both of us know there's not a hope in hell's chance of that case getting anywhere near a court. We've got no reliable witnesses, no real proof. But I couldn't just sit back and do nothing. At least...' She thought for a moment. 'Well, at least this way it's something.'

It wasn't much though. It wasn't much for all Irene Connolly's pain and suffering.

'I'll never forget her, Alec.'

'I know.' He squeezed her hand and opened the car door.

Oonagh belted up. 'So, where are we going?'

Alec Davies stared straight ahead for a moment, then said, 'As far away from here as possible.'

Huge thanks to:

My long suffering publisher, editor and friend Keith Charters. His hard work, calm nature and custard creams have been the making of me.

Mum and Dad, who although no longer here in person are never far away; their imaginative ghost stories at bedtime not only gave me childhood insomnia, but filled me with enough material for many more books to come!

My beautiful sister Tricia Law for looking out for me, my brother Martin for not putting pen to paper first and my brother Stephen for teaching me about opportunity cost at an early age, thus giving me the courage to enter the scary world of the freelancer writer!

William George, my early reader, who laughed and cried in all the right places. And of course a special mention to The Burst Oot Greetin' Club – especially founding member and El Presidente Paul Kerr and fellow comrade Gillian Weinman – they picked me up when I fell at the final hurdle stayed with me to the finishing line. Thanks guys!

And special thanks to:

Stewart Carle and Stuart Brennan – part of Strathclyde's finest - for their help with police procedures. Also Ida Henrich who created the wonderful, evocative front cover and went above and beyond the call of duty!

But of course my biggest debt goes to all the women who were incarcerated, without a voice, in institutions like the fictional one that features in this book. We may never know their names and we may never see their faces, but as long as we spare a thought for them, they'll never be forgotten.